DREAMER

Phillip L. Davidson

iUniverse, Inc.
Bloomington

Dreamer

Copyright © 2009 Phillip L. Davidson

All rights reserved. No part of this book may be used or reproduced by any means, graphic, electronic, or mechanical, including photocopying, recording, taping or by any information storage retrieval system without the written permission of the publisher except in the case of brief quotations embodied in critical articles and reviews.

This is a work of fiction. All of the characters, names, incidents, organizations, and dialogue in this novel are either the products of the author's imagination or are used fictitiously.

iUniverse books may be ordered through booksellers or by contacting:

iUniverse
1663 Liberty Drive
Bloomington, IN 47403
www.iuniverse.com
1-800-Authors (1-800-288-4677)

Because of the dynamic nature of the Internet, any Web addresses or links contained in this book may have changed since publication and may no longer be valid. The views expressed in this work are solely those of the author and do not necessarily reflect the views of the publisher, and the publisher hereby disclaims any responsibility for them.

ISBN: 978-1-4401-4928-3 (pbk)
ISBN: 978-1-4401-4926-9 (cloth)
ISBN: 978-1-4401-4927-6 (ebook)

Library of Congress Control Number: 2009930715

Printed in the United States of America

iUniverse rev. date: 1/12/11

For my wife Karen.
I thank her for her unfailing faith and support.
I also want to thank Dian Gainer for her invaluable work in the editing of this work.

PART ONE

The Messenger

Behold, I will send a messenger,
and he will prepare the way before me.

Malachi 3:1

Chapter 1

Alexandria, Virginia - March 1, 1982

In the cold darkness of his mind, David could see them again.

Like hunted animals, they scurried through the knee-deep rice paddy water, slipping and falling, cursing, and gasping for breath. Above, unseen in the blackness of night, fast-moving clouds unleashed a torrent of monsoon rain that fell across them in rippling waves.

Suddenly, they froze. Overhead, sizzling noises broke the dull drone of the rain as the sky became filled with flickering candle flares.

He dove into the filthy water and fitfully pawed his way along the muddy bottom of the paddy until he reached an earthen dike. Lying with his face against the muddy slope, he could only sense the desperate gathering of the gray silhouettes of his men as they one by one pressed up against the dike, like boats seeking the protection of moorings in a storm.

He looked down at the luminous dial of his Rolex. They were fast running out of night. Before the sun came up, he had to lead his men across the vast expanse of flat rice plain to an obscure island of jungle where they could hide during the day and wait to escape the next night under cover of darkness.

One by one, the flares burned out and the sky became dark once more. Cautiously, he raised his head. Had they been quick enough? Or had they been seen, caught in the open like deer stunned by the headlights of a car?

He turned to his men. He knew they were exhausted. For the better part of an hour they had been moving at a dead run. In the distance behind them, the fires from the burning village gave off a faint shimmering glow.

But it was not how tired they all were, or the downpour of rain, or Keaton's heavy breathing that most troubled him. It was Jude's haunting face. Even in the darkness, he could see it, could feel Jude watching his every move, waiting for what he knew was coming, for what he knew David would soon have to do.

"Where am I?" he asked the darkness.
"*On course*," answered a voice, powerful and alluring.
He reached out to touch the voice, but found nothing there.

"*Dai Uy*, did you have to bring him with us?" Force asked as he crouched next to him in the water.

He grabbed Force's shoulder strap and pulled him close to his face. "Get the hell back, Sergeant. We couldn't just leave him there," he hissed.

"I was afraid we were lost," he said to the darkness.

He lifted the lensatic compass that was securely tied around his neck and flicked its cover open. The rain was coming down so hard it was impossible to read its dial, so he took off his beret, held it against his forehead, and brought the compass up close to his face. He smiled. The two illuminated dots had nestled correctly between them the compass's arrowhead indicating that he was guiding the team in the right direction. He closed the compass, let it fall, and climbed to the top of the dike. In the darkness, he could hardly make out the huddled figures of his men who had spread themselves along the dike in various dark contortions.

"It felt good," he explained to the darkness.

It *did* feel good. He could feel the ooziness of the rice water inside his jungle boots and the trickling rain water flowing inside his tiger fatigues, uninhibited by useless underwear.

His web gear was hooked securely across his back and chest and carried everything he needed to survive in the jungle: knife, first aid pouch, flashlight, and grenades. His canteen was half full and his Webley was resting securely in its holster. Across his chest was strung his faithful Car-15 still awaiting his command. He had forgotten how good it felt to be on a battlefield.

"Keaton?"

He quickly turned over. Keaton was too old for his now. Why was he here?

"Keaton?"

Even above the incessant drone of the rain, he could hear Keaton's labored breathing. He sloshed his way heavily to the end of the formation where Keaton was guarding their rear. As he squatted down breathlessly beside him, Keaton's rock face turned and he spoke.

"*Dai Uy*." Keaton's voice was deep and gravelly. After he spoke, he coughed and spit.

"How you holding up, Sergeant?" he asked, getting his wind.

"My Ranger tabs keepin' me warm," Keaton said under his breath.

"Yeah. Can you see anything out there?" he asked, squinting into the rain.

"They can't be too far behind. My guess is they're fanning out, hoping to get a scent or to hear something."

"Jude's been talking to himself," he said, dropping his head.

"*Dai Uy*, I didn't know," Keaton said as if trying to explain, but he stopped him.

"It's not your fault. It's nobody's fault," he said evenly, trying not to meet Keaton's eyes. *No. It's my fault*, he thought. *I'm their leader. I'm responsible for everything*. Then he returned his attention to the moment. "How far away you guess the jungle is?" he asked.

"Not far . . ."

Suddenly, red tracer rounds flew over their heads like a swarm of mad hornets. Then followed the sound of random drum-roll bursts. He chuckled, and Keaton coughed again.

"They're recon'n by fire. They don't know where we are," Keaton said with a raspy laugh, hope evident in his voice.

"Let's don't let them get lucky," he quipped. "I'll get us moving."

He made his way back to the head of the formation, and grabbing Force by his arm said, "Help Jake carry him." Force and Jake lifted Jude by the shoulders and with the rest of the men followed him into the gray mist that had begun to rise off the paddy water.

Behind them, not far, fierce warriors pursued. Men with different moralities, different truths, different needs. Men who had forsaken emotion and inhibition. Men who understood the meaning of sacrifice. Men who would stop at nothing until they had killed them all.

Another swirl of brilliant tracer rounds licked across the sky.

Faster, he thought frantically. *I must go faster*. He quickened the pace. But when he looked back over his shoulder, he couldn't see his men. Their lives depended on his ability to read a compass and their ability to keep up with him. It was easy to become lost, even this close. *Where were they?* Two flares lit up a patch of rice paddy to his left about a mile away. *Got to go faster. No.* He stopped. *Jake? Force?* Then he heard sloshing and breathing. *There.* Yes, they were there. "Over here," he said plaintively. The sloshing stopped. Two more flares lit up the horizon to his right.

"*It's all right*," the voice said softly in the darkness.

He hurt. He no longer had any feeling in his feet and legs, and his back throbbed with a deep pain. *I've got to get in control of it, the hurt, the pain, the exhaustion. I'm their officer*, he thought resolutely. *No matter how bad it gets, I'm their officer.*

"It's so hard to go on. Help me," he cried in desperation.

Wearily, he rose up from where he lay and reached out again for the voice, but again the darkness around him was empty and cold.

"Look, *Dai Uy!*"

Startled, he turned to see Jake standing next to him. He cupped his hand over his eyes. Not far ahead of them, the horizon became darker than the paddies. He smiled. Jake's eyes were the best at night. The jungle was just ahead of them. They were going to make it.

"Let's go, men," he ordered confidently.

He left Pratt, Chip, and Julio at the jungle's entrance as lookouts while the rest of the team moved further inward.

"Put him against that tree," Keaton ordered.

Force and Jake let Jude drop to the ground. He had passed out from the pain of his wounds.

"Bring him to, Doc," he ordered, his commanding voice beginning to fade.

Doc bent down and broke open a vial of ammonia under Jude's nose and he began to shake his head from side to side. "Wake up, you motherfucker!" Doc said, slapping Jude's face.

He grabbed Doc's arm. "Don't do that," was all he could say.

The rain had suddenly stopped, and in its place an eerie pall had spread over the jungle.

He and Keaton stood side by side looking down on Jude. Keaton turned to him with a demanding look on his face. "Does this have to be done?" he asked breathlessly.

"*Dai Uy*," was all Keaton said, as he handed David the Walther with a silencer attached to its barrel. The little pistol felt hard and cold as it lay in his open palm, its blue steel frame well oiled and covered with little drops of water. He curled his fingers around the grip and the trigger. It was like holding death itself.

The rest of the team backed away from him and Keaton. It was still strangely quiet. The rain had left a vacuum that the coming dawn could not fill. Each man's different breathing could clearly be heard.

"Why?" he said, feeling sick as the rice he had eaten wanted to come up. He wanted to run, to escape from it. The responsibility. It was never supposed to have come to this.

"Have I not commanded you? Be strong and of good courage," the voice from the darkness said.

He tried to take a step back, but Keaton's huge shape stopped him.

"It's got to be done, sir. You know what will happen if they find us out here in the open. Besides, he's not one of us anymore," Keaton said as he took hold of his arm.

"I've got to know why," he said, wrestling his arm free from Keaton's grip. He squatted down in front of Jude. "Why, you bastard? Why?"

"Why? You want to know why? You think knowing will make it easier for you? It won't. Besides, what does it matter? I did what I had to do. What I was led to do."

"Tell me, you damn traitor."

"I'm no traitor, Captain. You're the traitors. All of you," Jude said loudly, waving his arm at them. "But . . . I . . . didn't think any of us would get hurt. Only the scouts. Only the scouts. But you know John. He was always the hero."

Jude began laughing to himself.

"Kill him!" Force hissed.

"God, just shoot him and let's get out of here!" Jake said flatly, turning his head.

"No. Let him finish!" he snapped.

Jude looked up impassively at him. "Thanks," he said quietly. Then he turned to the others. "I could see it, even if no one else could. What we were becoming. Don't any of you understand where we were heading? Whom we were serving?"

"The Buddha," Jake chuckled.

"Kill him!" It was Force again.

"Who? Who were we serving?" he screamed, so close to Jude's face he could feel his breath.

"*Dai Uy*, this is a waste of time. Shoot the bastard so we can get the hell out of here before they find us. Shit," Keaton implored with a worried look on his face.

"He's talking bullshit, *Dai Uy*. He led those bastards to us and now he's just trying to talk his way out of it," Force said.

"Everybody just shut up!" he shouted. "Now, what are you talking about? Who were we serving? Fuck. Who were *you* serving?"

"*He was serving me, David*," the voice from the darkness said evenly.

"The rest of you get the hell out of here," he ordered. "Keaton, set up an RP at the other side. We'll push out of here at nightfall and try to make Ba Chuc." Keaton did as he was told. The team quickly gathered themselves and their gear together. Each knew he had to do it. And the sooner they left the better. As they filed past Jude, each man took one last look. Some even shook their heads. He watched anxiously as the last man disappeared into the mist.

"Before I do this, I need to know the reason why," he said flatly.

"I always thought you were smart," Jude said, not looking up.

"Tell me!" he yelled impatiently, but Jude just hung his head and seemed to sway back and forth as if praying.

He pulled the hammer back on the pistol.

Hearing the click, Jude looked up with a jerk. "Phoenix," he said quickly.

"Why Phoenix? Just tell me that. The things we were doing, the people we were killing, women, old people. God, Captain."

"You turned Judas. You got John killed. Why didn't you just get the hell out if things bothered you so bad? Why didn't you just cross the canal and go to Cambot?"

"I didn't mean for John to get killed. What he did was foolish. You know he'd been reckless ever since he got word that his wife had left him."

"You still haven't told me why."

"I've been telling you. You just haven't been listening. I did it for you and the others. If we got hit really badly and we lost our scouts, SOG would have to pull us out."

He raised the gun.

"Do it," Jude said breathlessly.

He stared into Jude's eyes, looking down the sight of the pistol.

"You were losing your soul, Captain. I couldn't let that happen to you. What would I have said to *Him* when he asked me why I, knowing the truth, did nothing to save you?"

As his finger tightened against the gun's trigger, he began to feel lightheaded and dizzy. Was it the fever again? No. Something else. Something was there, an unseen presence. He could feel its warmth and sense its power. The pistol became suddenly very heavy, so heavy that he struggled to hold it in his hand. "What's happening?" he cried out.

The pistol fell from his hand to the soft jungle floor. For a moment, neither he nor Jude spoke, as if each was pondering the consequences of what had taken place between them.

"Why didn't I have the strength?" he asked out loud.

"*Because I was with him,*" the voice answered.

After an eternity, he asked, "Will you go to Cambodia?" His mind raced for an answer.

"I don't know," Jude replied quietly.

"Will I see you again?"

"Yes. You will see me again."

"The others won't understand."

"They will in time."

"I don't understand."

"You will, in time."

"I'm cold."

"I know," she said, holding his head against her warm breasts. She wiped the sweat from his forehead and kissed him. "I'll close the window, okay?"

David nodded, embarrassed. Sunny got up from the bed and went to the window. A cold breeze was blowing across the city. Far out in the distance were the Capitol and the Washington Monument, both framed in spears of white mist-laden light. The breeze chilled her naked body. She quickly shut the window and returned to David, who was awake and sitting up. "I'm sorry. It happened again," was all he could say.

Morning had come too quickly. Wearily, David wrapped himself in his bathrobe and leaned against the windowsill. Below, traffic was starting to coagulate as the army of government civil servants made their daily pilgrimage over the Wilson Bridge. In the distance he could see the lights around the monuments and government buildings of the city being turned off as the sun broke the earth's surface. It was going to be a bright, clear day.

Sunny had gone back to sleep. She lay on the bed, her slender legs spread invitingly. A sheet was draped casually across her smooth stomach. Asleep, she looked peaceful, David thought, not seemingly inexhaustible like she did when she was awake. A movement. She turned her face toward David and sighed. A trusting face. Bright and ever smiling. A face that never betrayed the awful truth about her past.

A past filled with fear and terror and personal courage. Her large brown eyes were closed. Eyes that had given him solace. Eyes that hungered for truth, eternally hopeful of finding in others substance, not form. Someone she could trust. Someone like her.

David stood next to the bed and brushed her long, shimmering black hair away from her cheek. He opened his robe and let it drop to the floor. He pulled the sheet from her stomach and gently moved on top of her. She stirred lazily and opened her eyes. Gently, she guided him inside her. She moaned and kissed him on the cheek and, as he went up into her body, she whispered, "David." And with their fingers clasped, they moved as one as the sun rose and covered them with its warmth.

Later in the morning, Sunny submerged herself in warm bath water. She was in no hurry. Her first class at Georgetown was not until eleven, and David had already left for the War College where he had been assigned as a professor of combined arms tactics. The water calmed her, helped diminish the fear she had felt during the night. She felt threatened and, when she felt threatened, her first instinct was to fight. But how could she fight a memory? How could she fight men long since dead? Men who now lived in her husband's mind and haunted him in nightmares. She hurt for him, but could not help. All she could do was be there when he came back; all she could do was hold his head and cry with him. "Why now?" he would ask. But Sunny had no answer.

She wet her washcloth and placed it over her face. The heat cooled her. Slowly she sank down under the water. She could not bear to hear David's weeping any longer. It reminded her too much of crying she had heard before.

"Why is father crying?" she asked. Her mother took her away from the study.

"Shhh," her mother said. "You must show your father respect."

"Is respect the same thing as love, mother?"

"Yes, my darling."

She had been so young then. The cloth covered her. There had been other crying.

"Sonia!" It was Maria, her blond hair in tangles.

"Maria, why are you crying?"

"They took Paulo!"

"Paulo!"

"They took him right off the street, shoved him into one of their green sedans." No one ever came back from a ride in one of those green sedans.

She had to help him. *David, I will find a way. I will get help. Just have faith, my darling.* But David had no faith.

Sunny sat up in the tub. Still, she could not see, her mind blinded her to the present.

Her father sat impassively at the far end of the room. Her mother stood beside him holding a scarf in her hands. Her mother was crying. Her father's eyes were wet and red. "Sonia, for the sake of our family, you must be careful," her father said.

She felt exposed, naked before them, like she had been caught with her hand in the cookie jar. She had taken chances. She had taken a stand. She had involved them against their will and without their knowledge and consent. She was their daughter. She had become a revolutionary. They were the establishment, the very people who supported the military *junta*. They were guilty by blood, and the *junta* shot the guilty. They had shot Paulo. And yesterday they had thrown Maria against a wall and shot her through her blue eyes.

"How can any person who believes in God stand by and just watch as their friends are dragged off into the night and shot to death?" she asked.

Her father did not answer, just hung his head and sobbed.

"Do you want to die?" her mother asked.

She was unable to answer her mother's question.

The day was bright and brisk, the sky a robin's egg blue. There was a fresh smelling breeze that carried a slight chill along its edge. Sunny strode purposefully across the commons on her way to Dahlgren Chapel and mass. She seemed to blend in with the other students who walked the commons. She wore a gray skirt, an oxford cloth shirt, weeguns, blue knee socks, and a navy blue sweater tied around her neck. As she neared the steps of the chapel, she began to wrap her hair in a maroon scarf.

"*Keaton*," she thought. Who was Keaton? What was he to David and why did David sometimes call out his name during the nightmares? "Keaton," she said softly, faintly letting the name escape her lips.

As she started up the chapel steps, something jerked the scarf from her head. Startled, she turned, but no one was there. A gust of deathly cold wind whirled around her, enveloping her in a tomblike silence. The sounds of the commons became faint and distant, and everything seemed to slow down like a record player turning off. Suddenly she heard it. At first it seemed far off, outside of the wind. Then it came to her. An anguished cry, a high-pitched scream, shrill and then angry. Something thorny touched her back. She twirled around, but again saw nothing. But something was there. It stood close to her. Pulsating, cold, and hateful. She could have touched it if she had dared, but she was mortified, mute and numb. Then, like dust being sucked into a vacuum, it was gone.

The students milling around the commons went about their business as if they knew nothing of what had just taken place. Birds chirped and the bell for mass began to ring. Sunny felt groggy, as if she had just awakened from a deep sleep. She was cold and sweating. She stood, unsteady for a moment. When she realized where she was, she sat down on the steps. In the welcome quiet of the familiar sounds of Georgetown, she began to understand what she had experienced. Having read the scriptures, she knew. It had been a warning, a premonition of something that was to be. She had felt it before. In Buenos Aires. They had come for her in the darkness of night, for that was their time. But she had been warned of their plan, had received a message of her impending death. Now she understood that she had not truly escaped but had been granted only a respite from the terror. When would it happen, she wondered? How much time did she have?

She stood up, her composure regained. Resolutely, she tied the scarf over head once again. *No*, she thought. The drama was not over, and in it she felt she would have a part to play. Only, how soon would it be before the director gave her her cue?

Chapter 2

```
The National Defense University
Carlisle Barracks
Washington, D.C.
```

Major David Elliot, United States Army, stood in front of his office window quietly appreciating the last of the daylight as the winter sun slowly hid itself behind the buildings of the War College as he waited for his friend Andrew to arrive. The long dark days of winter seemed slow to depart, as if the earth was reluctant to wake from its long hibernation. There was a blank, distant look on his face as he gazed absently at the gradually darkening courtyard below.

The monks had been right, he thought morosely. Time is a circle in which all life revolves. Lying dormant on their concrete slabs, they had gazed at him lazily through curtains of incense. Their eyes, catlike and dark, had pierced his very soul. Cautiously, through the flickering candlelight, they had studied his face, oblivious to the stings of the mosquitoes that ruled the night. And after a time, they began to understand his fears, his weaknesses, and his susceptibilities. He had been vulnerable despite his power. He had been ignorant despite his knowledge. And he had been young beyond his belief. They had seen the hunger for meaning in his eyes.

"Ask," they had said. So he had asked, and they had answered. But their answers had led only to further questions. Disturbing questions about meanings and beliefs he had long ago accepted as truths. Begged for, they had taught; needed, he had learned. And after a time, when the bodies began to rot and the blood stained his hands, they had sensed he was ready. Slowly and subtly, they had begun to gather him in, speaking to him softly in the rhymes of the ancient Buddha's past, waking him from a lifelong sleep:

> All life is sorrow
> To die is to live
> To sin is to be haunted
> Haunted until you died
> Until you died, achieved Karma,
> And lived.

But he had not died. He had been sentenced to live. And so now, just as the monks had foretold, his sins had come full circle. The nightmares had come. Were they the harbingers of what would be his recompense on a debt long overdue?

It was dark now. Reluctantly, he returned to his desk. Andrew had not come. He was disappointed because he had decided to talk with Andrew about his nightmares, and making that decision had been a difficult one for him to make. Maybe his friend was out celebrating. Andrew never needed much of an excuse to celebrate, and now he had a good one. He was an expert on naval warfare, which was the reason he had been assigned to the War College for the past two years. But he was a fighter pilot, an *aviator*, he was quick to say. He was at his best at twenty thousand feet and at eight hundred miles an hour.

Unlike David, who had welcomed his assignment to Washington, Andrew had hoped for test pilots school. For the last two years, he had been like a caged tiger. The lack of action in his life had caused him to have constant bouts of depression. But now Andrew Jackson had been granted parole. Only yesterday he had received his orders from Naval Headquarters assigning him to the Pacific Fleet. He would report to Oceana Naval Base the first week of May for flight orientation then fly to the west coast and board the aircraft carrier *Kennedy* for sea duty on the twenty-first. David was happy for Andrew, but also felt a twinge of sadness because Andrew had been with him and Sunny from the first. They would always associate their beginning with him.

Andrew had predilections for Jack Daniels whiskey and Black Jack cigars. He always kept a flask and a holder readily accessible. An ostentatious joker, he glorified in the odd fact that he could perform the trick of drinking and smoking at the same time. He also boasted of having discovered a new species of human being which he had christened the Boomba girl. Boomba girls came in all shapes, sizes, and colors. Their characteristics were: love of drink; uninhibited expression, especially in the field of sexual experimentation and implementation; endurance of effort; and the ability to stay over the target area for an inordinate amount of time. Their habitats were the watering holes of the Delaware-Maryland peninsula, D.C., and the entire State of Virginia. In their mating rituals, Boombas were known to discard all previous ideas of morality. Not everyone could spot a Boomba. In fact, he claimed to have a locked-cog on the ability although, to persons he liked, he had been known to grant special dispensations. Perhaps he had met a girl. He was known to do that in the late afternoons. Practice makes perfect, he would say in his slow Tennessee drawl, a wide grin across his suntanned face.

He slowly folded shut the legal pad that lay on his desk. It was late. If Andrew was coming, he would have been here by now. Better call Sunny, he thought. She'd be worried. He picked up the phone.

Suddenly, he felt a cold draft of wind. It flowed across the room like an unseen whisper. He turned to the window, but it was shut tight. It puzzled him, but the thought vanished with the rapping at the door. He smiled. Andrew had come after all.

For about ten minutes or so, Andrew engulfed himself in a cloud of foul smelling smoke while he reclined lazily on the couch in David's office. He seemed to David to be asleep, his blonde hair falling around his sky blue eyes, his lanky frame folded over the contours of the couch like an accordion

But after staring approvingly at Andrew for a few minutes, David recognized a familiar expression on his face. He had the *look* - that blank, distant stare, where sight, sound, and even feelings were blocked out by the sudden, unexpected resurgence of some long ago repressed memory from the War. It didn't matter where a person was or what he was doing, when he had the *look*, he had gone back. So where was he, David wondered. Sitting in the cockpit of his F4 off Yankee Station? Over Haiphong dodging murderous antiaircraft fire? Or hanging limp and broken in the trees near the Red River waiting for the Spads to save him? It didn't matter. He would come back after a while. And, after a while, he did.

Thoughts of talking with Andrew about the nightmares were difficult and painful. Doing so would be an admission on his part that his character was in some way flawed. And even though he knew Andrew was his friend, he still knew it would be uncomfortable and embarrassing for, in a very real sense, David and Andrew were part of a conservative, closed society: the military, where imperfection was not understood, much less tolerated. Despite the fact of their friendship, David and Andrew were military officers. Their professions required correctness of actions at all times. If Andrew made a mistake flying his aircraft, he crashed and burned. If David made a mistake leading men in combat, some of them died. As David well knew.

"When you came back, did you have any nightmares?" David asked without looking at Andrew.

"Just one," Andrew replied flatly. Yes, it had been only one, but that had been enough. The scene flashed across the heads-up display in his mind.

The SAM hit him high over Hanoi. Within seconds, the cockpit of his Phantom became filled with acrid black smoke.

"Blow the canopy!" someone yelled. It was Mallory, his radar intercept officer.

He hit the canopy explosive bolt handle. Bamm! Swoosh! The Plexiglas canopy lifted straight up then disappeared behind the horizontal stabilizer. The smoke was quickly sucked out of the cockpit. And in its place a loud, fierce wind swirled all around him as the jet traveled through the air at six hundred miles an hour. Andrew tried to turn around, but his leg straps and his parachute prevented him from seeing what Mallory was doing. He tore away his oxygen mask and lifted up his helmet's sun visor. The air was thin at twenty thousand feet, and he began to gasp for breath.

Then he heard it – a blood curdling Banshee scream. He looked straight up into the blue-black sky and there, struggling frantically with the center console headrest that separated them, was Mallory. Mallory had tried to eject himself, but somehow the explosive bolts between his rear compartment and the part of the cockpit that separated him from Andrew had not fired. He reached up and tried to push Mallory free, but he was caught by the tangled straps of his partially opened parachute. Like a sudden chill, a dreaded realization swept over him. If he fired his ejection seat he would cut Mallory in half at the waist, but if he did not eject soon from the burning jet he would be killed in its explosion.

Then, the jet started to yaw to the right. That meant a flat spin was only a breath away, and a flat spin meant a fiery plunge into the South China Sea below. He looked up at Mallory. For a moment the two men stared at each other. Mallory was hanging out of the cockpit and he was still strapped in his seat. Mallory pushed up the sun visor of his helmet and looked down at the tangled parachute and then at him. Instinctively, he knew that Mallory understood their situation. Mallory gave him a forgiving smile.

He screamed, "No!" just as Mallory took his pistol out of its shoulder holster and blew his brains out.

"How long did you have it?" David asked, his voice clearing away the trauma in Andrew's mind.

"It . . . went away after a while."

"Never came back?"

"No. Why do you ask?"

"About a month ago I started having some terrible nightmares."

"They'll go away," Andrew said calmly, waving his hand across the room as if to fluff away the smoke.

"I don't think you understand. I never had any nightmares after Vietnam. None. Now, after all this time, I've begun having these dreams. And it's really like one continuous nightmare, one scene after another. Don't you think that's strange?"

Andrew puffed contemplatively on the Black Jack for a moment. "You know how this place is," he said, giving David a half smile. "These shitheads go nuts at the first sign of something out of place. So if this nightmare is becoming a problem for you, you gotta get it taken care of. *Comprendie?*"

Andrew produced a silver flask from the recesses of his back pocket. David sighed and retrieved two shot glasses with a naval officer's cap badge insignia etched on each and placed them on the desk. Andrew smiled at seeing the glasses and bent down and poured a generous portion in each.

David slumped back in his chair, his feet thrown up on his desk. Andrew had returned to the comfort of the couch. The office was dark except for the light from a green shaded desk lamp, which was diminished by a low hanging cloud of cigar smoke. Black Jacks lasted a long time.

"Tell me about the nightmares," Andrew said matter-of-factly.

God, Andrew, David thought. *I can't expect you to understand. You never received the enlightenment. Why should you have? Your war was so different from mine. You were never down there where I was, in the filth, the waste. You never faced a man you were going to kill. You never smelled his breath. You never tasted his blood. Your war was clean, cold, and fast. For you, it was fresh sheets and a blow job every night.*

"Are you listening to me?" Andrew asked. But seeing David's face, he knew an answer was not coming. He raised his hand up to his face and checked his watch. "Okay, I gotta unass this place. A Boomba's waiting on me over at State." He stood up, stretched, and put out his Black Jack. "You ought to see her tits. Hell, she could put Jersey Farms out of business. Anyway, I'll see you and Sunny tomorrow night at Bayous." Then he left.

Once again, David returned to the window. The office seemed much darker now with Andrew gone. A melancholy, yellowish pallor from the small desk lamp illuminated his reflection against the window. As he stared back at the expressionless face he had seen a thousand times before, he thought darkly of his own mortality. Outside, dim night lights attached to the ivy covered walls of the academic buildings gave off a faint glow, barely revealing the dark courtyard below and giving it a deserted, lonely appearance. The sky, made luminescent from the city lights below, revealed a blanket of dark, puffy clouds rolling in from the cold waters of the Atlantic. *A storm*, he thought, *that's all I need.*

And a storm *was* coming. It was down under. Waiting. A violent storm. Over a dark cold sea, it swirled, gathering strength and intensity. And he was right. It *was* all he needed.

Chapter 3

> When you sit down to eat with a ruler,
> Consider carefully what is before you;
> And put a knife to your throat
> If you are given to appetite.
> Do not desire his delicacies,
> For they are deceptive food.
>
> Proverbs 23: 1-3

The *Club Bayous* was packed with moving bodies. It was cavernous and dimly lit, a place that smelled of perfume, steak, and beer. It was a grotto where contracts for passion were made at arm's length. The singer in the band belted out a syncopated tune as strobe lights flashed on and off with each explosion of sound. The dance floor filled with a melange of civil servants, lawyers, lobbyists, and other nocturnal creatures that pulsated in unison with each beat.

Andrew was beside himself. This was his natural habitat, a jungle in which he was a master predator. He loved the sights of women who knew what they were doing on a dance floor. He loved the smells of hot people, hot women. Women smelled so damn good when they were hot. He was happy. He had eaten a good meal. His two best friends were sitting beside him, and he was almost Boomba drunk. Everything was just right. And he didn't seem to mind that Sunny's friends, Jorge Ortega and his wife Rita, had their teeth in him and would not let go.

"Of course, you must realize that Latin Americans look at your country through jaundiced eyes," Jorge said in heavily accented English, bending low over the table to be heard above the noise. He had a sticky voice. Each word seemed to barely escape his mouth before the next one emerged. "And this is because they lust for what you have. And while that may flatter you, it should also make you afraid."

"Oh, and why is that?" Andrew shouted back.

Jorge's round sweaty face betrayed little emotion as he pondered his next words. He was short and stocky and wore black horn rimmed eyeglasses that kept sliding down his nose. Rita, a slim woman with thin blond hair and thin, razor sharp breasts, peered at the world through round brown eyeglasses, the kind lawyers wore. She was not exactly pretty, but she did have an alluring, large mouth that she kept open and moist with a playfully suggestive tongue. Jorge and Rita were the issue of some of Argentina's wealthiest landowners and had come to America to study international relations at Georgetown. They had been childhood friends of Sunny's, but when the political climate in Argentina turned cold to the freedom of expression and assembly they, like their rich parents, had distanced themselves from everyone the *junta* considered subversive. But the tranquil, liberal campus of Georgetown was a long way from Buenos Aires, and Sunny was an exceptionally forgiving human being.

"Because," Jorge said in a snobbish tone, "history is the story of hungrier, more determined peoples conquering decadent ones."

Andrew let out a condescending laugh.

Military men are all alike, Jorge mused, *they see everything in terms of power, and yet they do not really understand power at all.* "Don't be patronizing, *Commandante*. You are aware, are you not, that there are other hungrier countries nearer America, countries whose people lust for the wealth and power you have, whose people gaze enviously at you across your border?"

"Mexico," Andrew said, holding his glass in a mock salute. "I've heard the theory."

"Very perceptive, *Commandante*. Maybe it will start somewhere else, but for sure it will end by beginning for you in Mexico."

Andrew lit a cigar. "Want one?" Jorge waved him off. "Well, Pancho," he knew Jorge hated to be called Pancho, "the way I see it, you're full of refried beans."

"And what is that supposed to mean?"

"That we have a strong military that just might take exception to any army laying claim to U. S. soil."

"Oh, be sensible. How many Army divisions do you have in America? Nine, maybe ten, totaling only a hundred thousand men? An army coming across the Rio Grande into Texas could overrun that number easily."

"What about air power?" Andrew asked, playfully shaking his finger at Jorge.

"No air force has ever been able to win a war without ground troops. Besides, every time they dropped a bomb they would be taking a chance of killing innocent civilians."

"You're dreaming, Pancho," Andrew said with a look of exasperation. "We have a half million National Guardsman. Don't you think they might have something to say about a Mexican invasion of America?"

"You know as well as I do that they have never fought under one unified command, and that is what it would take to overcome an army of close to a million men."

"You're being ridiculous, Jorge. What in the hell do you know about war? You've never even been in the military. You've never fought in a battle. Hell! The American soldier is the best trained in the world."

"Not since you disbanded selective service and ended the draft," Jorge said, adjusting his glasses. "You have marshaled a volunteer force of undereducated mercenaries who are paid substandard wages. Did you know that American soldiers in Europe live off of food stamps and handouts? Do you really think they would give up their lives for the interests of the rich, the powerful, and the educated, the very groups who have systematically excluded them from the wealth of your country? No, my friend. More than likely they would join the peasant army streaming across the border, an army whose men they have more in common with than their own officers who lead them."

The band stopped for a break, and while in its vacuum there was the sudden sound of talking people, it seemed almost quiet in the club.

Andrew turned to David. "Do you believe this shit?"

David didn't answer. Instead, he turned to Sunny and gave her a chagrined look. Its meaning was unmistakable: *They're your friends. You invited them. Now you do something about them.*

Jorge and Rita's parents were members of the old ruling class in Argentina, the affluent landowners and industrialists who over the decades had exercised substantial control over the ruling military *junta* by supporting them economically and socially. But Sunny knew no one could really control the *junta* that were now in power. Unlike the dictatorships before them, these men had purposefully set about to entrench themselves in power by creating fear in the minds of the Argentinean people. Fear of anarchy and fear of communist subversion. And they had been successful. No, they were not like the dictators of the past. They did not have to depend on the *Families* for power. Their power came from the Argentinean people's fear. As long as that fear existed, so would they. But Jorge and Rita still clung to the illusion that they were still the ultimate power in Argentina, and this false sense of security had manifested itself in arrogance. However, Sunny was not about to let their misassumptions ruin this night.

"Look, let's not talk politics tonight," Sunny said flatly. "This is a time when we should celebrate and be happy for Andrew."

"No, I don't mind at all," Andrew said with his Black Jack crunched between his teeth. He was becoming excited by the sparing.

Jorge took advantage of the opening. "You are, of course, right when you point out that I have never fought in a war. Nevertheless, I still feel I understand the application of military power in ways you do not. For instance, from the moment you greeted us tonight all you have talked about is going to sea and flying your precious airplanes. You seem to take delight in the fact that your ship, the . . . ah . . ."

"*Kennedy*," Andrew said tersely.

"Thank you, the *Kennedy*. Anyway, you seem to take delight that you will be steaming up and down the west and east coasts of South America showing, as you say, the flag. But what you don't seem to understand is the effect your ship has on the people of that region."

"I'm not a politician," Andrew said. "I go where I'm ordered. But I think I understand the purpose my government has for sending the *Kennedy* around the Southern Hemisphere. We see our national security as being threatened by the rise of communist insurgencies in these areas and, yes, to allow that to happen would be destabilizing to Mexico."

Rita couldn't control herself any longer. "Oh, very good *Commandante*, for one who merely follows orders without thinking."

Jorge gave her a reassuring look. She smiled back and then turned to Andrew and adjusted her glasses as if they were gun sights. Watching the two of them take turns at Andrew made Sunny think of a tag team wrestling match. Rita tagged Jorge with a flick of her tongue. "But the point my husband was trying to help you understand is that a show of force from a super power no longer frightens weaker countries, I think. It only makes them hate you the more, don't you see?"

"Look *kid*, a long time ago I accepted the fact that the world is never going to be crazy about Americans. Sometimes nations have to go it alone when it comes to what they see as their national interest."

Andrew turned to David again for support, but David just turned up his drink and took a long swallow. "Anyway," he continued, "you know what bothers me about this conversation? It's ya'll. Both of ya'll think you really understand America, but ya'll don't. America is basically a pacifist country. It takes a hell of a lot to get Americans mad enough to fight about anything. Look at the Iranian crisis. If we had been a country of trigger happy militarists, we'd have bombed the shit out of 'em after our hostages were released. We don't go looking for fights. Don't have to. There are plenty of them around. We've had war declared on us, you know. Yeah, for quite a while now. A low intensity war by the Soviets. It's a cheap way of wearing us down. Terrorists groups hit us from the right and left and from within, all supported and funded by Moscow. Subversions go on in our backyard right under our noses. Groups that wish us harm. So, what should we do? Do nothing? Hell no. We'll continue to send ships to the far reaches of the earth to let those who wish us harm know that we're not going to be easy.

"So, ya'll can think what you want. But ya'll really don't understand anything about us. We live by the rule of law. And that law is based on one document, the Constitution. And the main tenant of the Constitution is that our government's first duty is to protect its citizens. Nothing else takes precedence over that mandate. Government must do that before it does anything else. And if it fails to protect its citizens, then it breaks its covenant with them and they have the right to dissolve the government and establish another. That's what we're all about. Us, me, the military, protecting our people and their interests as we see it. Not how ya'll do, or anyone else."

Rita ran her tongue around her lips and gazed at Andrew as if she were deciding whether he would be something good to eat. Seeing her wet tongue move slowly around her mouth gave Andrew a rise. He wondered what she would be like giving head.

As if reading Andrew's mind, Jorge touched Rita's shoulder. A tag. Rita acquiesced, but still gave Andrew the eye.

Jorge began. "But you have still missed the point. There is nothing fundamentally wrong with a nation having a strong patriotic military government. In my country we have such a military, but we do not flaunt our power at the weaker nations around us as you are planning do with the *Kennedy* . . ."

In a flash Sunny's fists banged down on the table, almost knocking everyone's drinks over. Her sudden action startled even Andrew. There was a fire in her voice as she spoke. "Have you two been asleep for the last ten years? My God, have you been so cloistered behind the walls of your villa that you have not seen what has happened in our country? The military: patriots?"

"Well, patriot is a relative term, I think," Rita said, leaning over the table toward Sunny. "Besides, you now have American citizenship. I would think Argentina's troubles should be less and less of a concern for you."

"The fact that I have American citizenship has not taken away my love for Argentina, nor has it caused me to become blind to the fact that it has sunk into the abyss of terror. Do you no longer remember our friends who were dragged from their beds in the middle of the night never to be heard from again? Do you no longer have concerns for those we grew up with, those who we once called brothers and sisters, who have been missing for years?"

"There have been excesses, yes, I will admit this," Jorge said, his brow furrowed. "But can you not remember what Argentina was like before the military took over? Do you not remember the bombings, the assassinations? It was anarchy. Did you want us to go the way of Uruguay?"

"Uruguay?" Andrew said. "David, what does he mean by Uruguay?"

But again, David did not offer an answer. Instead he just gave Andrew a look of unconcern, shook his head, and continued to sip on his drink.

"Uruguay is a country, *commandante*," Rita said, her smile turning into a smirk.

"He knows that," Jorge said to her testily. "Let me explain, *commandante*. In 1968, Uruguay was a free democratic country. It had the highest standard of living in all of South America. Its people were literate, its incidence of deaths at birth low. But the fever of Marxism infected a small group of artists, lawyers, and doctors."

"Just after Feltrinelli published the first popular printing of *Doctor Zhivago*," Rita interjected loudly.

Jorge seemed to ignore her interruption like he would an insect bite. "Anyway," he continued, "these creatures formed a terrorist group known as the *Tupermaros*. Following the teachings of Carlos Marighella, they terrorized the country with assassinations, bombings, and intimidation. And as Marighella predicted, the democratic government was unable to put an end to the anarchy. The military took over."

"And now it is a military dictatorship," Sunny said. There was sadness in the tone of her voice.

"But there is a fundamental difference between the government of Uruguay and our *junta*," Jorge retorted. "The government of Uruguay is there to stay. It intends to enslave the population for as long as it can. Our *junta* wish to remain in power only until the Communists are rooted out of Argentine society. Then they will turn the government over to the civilians."

"You really believe they will give up power?" Sunny asked, shaking her head. "Jorge, you are an intelligent man, yet you deny the evidence all around you. The *junta* have used the recent events in Uruguay to justify their own reign of terror. They have tricked you and others into supporting wholesale murder. They tell you they are fighting Communists, but the truth is they have tortured and killed people whose only crime is to have had the courage to speak out against them, people who have cried for the return of democracy to Argentina."

"Reign of terror," Rita said contemptuously. "You have been listening to your American professors too long."

Sunny stiffened. "Ask the mothers of the *Plaza de Mayo* about terror. Ask them about their missing children. Children, our friends, who because they were members of some campus club, or any other innocuous organization the *junta* saw as a threat to their power, were seized, sent to *Los Estados* and never heard from again. Oh, how naive you two are."

"And what good have they done with their pathetic weekly marches?" Jorge asked.

"At least they have the courage to do something," Sunny said.

Jorge's face became flushed. "What do you really know about the *junta?*" he asked. "Have you ever met any of the generals? No, of course not. That would be too much for you to do. But if you had, as I have, you would find them very different from you believe them to be. They are patriots who love Argentina as much as you do. They know of their critics, and there are many, but they remain firm in their beliefs. They have promised me and the other landowners that once the Communists have been purged from our society, they will back civilian elections. And I believe them."

"And why on earth would you believe them?" Sunny asked with a look of shock.

"Because," Jorge said proudly, "my family and the others have always controlled the military."

"Jorge, for the sake of God, no one can control evil," Sunny replied.

"You don't know what you are talking about," Jorge retorted. "You listen to the lies of your friends, friends who have not *disappeared* but are instead in hiding for fear of being arrested for their acts of subversion. You talk of terror, you . . ."

Sunny suddenly bent low over the table, and with a fist clenched in Jorge's face, said through her teeth, "They take them up in helicopters in the middle of the night and push them over the River Platta. Alive!"

Suddenly, Jorge changed shape right before David's eyes. Before he had been squat and sweaty, but in an instant he was thin, wiry, and old. The glasses he wore had been replaced by a black cloth patch that was strapped across his forehead and covered one eye. The slicked back hair was now close cropped and gray. The tight fitting gray suit had turned into black pajamas.

Slowly, as though coming out of a deep coma, he began to recognize the features of the figure before him. But why would Jorge want to become the District Chief? He had killed the District Chief in a fit of rage. Shot him dead with a pistol right between the eyes. So why become a dead man? The District Chief turned to him and stared at him maniacally with his Cyclops eye. Then, in flawless French, the District Chief began to speak.

"Captaine."

Yes, the District Chief had spoken flawless French.

"Remember? What he is saying to our wife, I said to you long ago. Remember? Terror is legitimate when used by a movement to achieve ultimate victory over its enemies. Remember? I had just shot her in the head. It was to make a point to the others. But I said it was justified. I shot her in the brain without passion, without hate. Doesn't he sound just like me? You must be just. Justice should be merciless without passion, without hate."

Red. Everything was turning red. David suddenly jumped up and pushed the table aside. Drinks and ashtrays flew across the floor, causing the nearest patrons to flee from their tables. For a second, he froze as if he were stunned and confused by what he had just done. Then he reached over and grabbed Jorge by the shirt and effortlessly drew him up to his face. Jorge, trembling and his face contorted with fear, offered no resistance. For a moment, David just stared at him, a breath away. Then he whispered, "You don't know what terror is."

He turned to Sunny and gave her a cold stare, but Sunny was too stunned to move. This was a side of David she had never seen before. She found herself trembling. Then just as suddenly, he let Jorge go and headed for the door. Sunny grabbed her pocketbook and, not looking at the others, ran after him.

Jorge just stood there shaking, his fists clenched, silent. Rita reached for his hand, but he pushed it away. "Goddamn it!" he screamed.

Andrew sat back with a wide grin on his face and fired up a Black Jack, blowing some smoke toward Jorge. "You were saying, Poncho?"

Chapter 4

The meat, hanging on a hook, swayed provocatively back and forth. Blood dripped from it. No one noticed it at first. They were all too tired from the trek through the wet underbrush, and when the clearing had appeared they had been grateful and had stopped to rest. The jungle could play tricks with even the most experienced of warriors. Every soldier worth anything knew this and never took the jungle lightly. Sounds, smells and, most of all, sights, became distorted in the maze of its darkened colors. So the meat just hung there, not more than ten feet from where they stood, dripping, oozing, dangling, staring at them with accusing eyes, dark and blood red. A quick breeze, a palpitation from the nearby rice water, blew across them and the meat. Force was the first to hear it. He swirled around with his rifle aimed sightlessly in the direction of the noise. The others scattered and did the same. But the meat paid them no attention. It just swayed gently from side to side, staring at them.

"What the hell?" Keaton said in amazement, slowly dropping to one knee on the soft jungle floor. The rest of the team cautiously lowered their weapons and began to crouch.

All except him. He could not move; what he was seeing had seized him with horror and disbelief. "You were supposed to be in Cambot!" he screamed, his fists angrily clenched. "In Cambot, safe. What are you doing here?" He lunged for the meat, but Force tackled him to the ground and the others muffled his cries. He struggled to free himself from their grips. Doc's hand covered his face so tightly he couldn't breathe.

From where he was he could see Keaton, who seemed confused and bewildered; he kept turning his head first to the meat then to him as if he could not make up his mind what to do. "Let go of him," Keaton ordered. His voice was like a gunshot. The others immediately let go.

"*Dai Uy*, do you know what you've done?" Keaton asked, his face contorted by a mixture of anger and amazement.

He was so choked up that he was speechless. He just turned away from Keaton and the others and stared at Jude's lifeless body as it twisted slowly above the ground.

Then the same sinking feeling hit all of them at once. They were standing in a clearing just a few yards from a rice paddy dike. Several palm trees with their precious coconuts hanging precariously from them were at one end of the clearing between them and the dike. Jude's body hung from an A-frame made of bamboo.

Why had he been placed directly in their path? Why had he been shown to them at all? he wondered. The sick answer hit each of them with the force of a landmine. The VC wanted them to do just what they were doing now. And be killed.

"Ambush!" David screamed as he dove to the jungle's floor and crawled to the safety of the apartment bathroom.

Chapter 5

Georgetown University
Washington, D.C.

Father Martin Perez's ministry was the student body of Georgetown University. As the counselor and psychological therapist for the university, his days were spent listening attentively to the troubles of young men and women of that cosmopolitan institution of higher learning and helping them through the difficult process of self healing.

He worked out of a comfortable office near the dean of students in Healy Hall, the refurbished historical administration building. His office looked comfortably lived in; it was. Perez usually slept nights on an old couch tucked away at one end of the room. His high-back, brown leather counseling chair was sunken and worn. And along with dozens of student files, scores of books filled the numerous shelves built into the dark, wood-paneled, high ceiling walls. The office always smelled musty, with a trace of good tobacco. On his desk were several open books with an assortment of markers, each slowly making its way toward the last chapter. Perez was well educated, holding a PhD in clinical psychology from Harvard, the diploma for which he displayed proudly on the wall behind his desk. He had a thin, long face with heavy eyebrows that almost hung over his brown horn-rimmed glasses and he had a habit of pursing his lips and looking upward before speaking, especially when contemplating profound thoughts.

"It's a problem of stress," he pronounced thoughtfully in a clear, forceful voice as he gazed at Sunny through a thick fog of tobacco smoke. "The psychological community is just now identifying an illness that is peculiar to Vietnam veterans. We call it delayed stress syndrome."

Sunny relaxed and sank back into the deep leather of the chair Perez had offered her. "Delayed stress syndrome," she said thoughtfully, not looking at Perez.

"Yes. The operative word is delayed," Perez said authoritatively as he puffed away on his pipe. "It's actually Freudian, you know. The greater part of a man's mind lies in the realm of the Id, the unconscious. When a person experiences a traumatic event which is too stressful to be dealt with on the conscious level, that trauma is repressed into the unconscious where it lies dormant. The traumatic event is experienced in the form of a thought. A thought, in its purest form, is energy. And energy cannot be destroyed."

Perez talked as if he were giving a lecture. He pursed his lips and started to rock back and forth in his chair. "This concept is important if we are to understand what is happening to your husband because, if a thought is energy and energy cannot be destroyed, then it follows that the traumatic thought stored away in the far, uncharted regions of the Id can live on forever, never dying as long as it stays hidden in the unconscious part of the mind.

"The Id is an animal which is ever seeking gratification of its two primary impulses: the wish to seek pleasure and the wish to destroy, even seek death. All thoughts that are trapped in the realm of the Id become a part of one of these two impulses. Even though the Id is unconscious, it is constantly trying to invade the conscious world. But between it and the outside world, stands the Ego. The Ego must fight a continual battle on three fronts. First, it must fight off the recriminations of the Super Ego, our conscience, assuming one has a conscience. Secondly, the Ego tries very hard every minute of the day to maintain a harmonious relationship with the world. In other words, to stop us from walking out in front of cars or making bad judgments and so on. But in a very real sense, its hardest task is to keep the Id impulses in their place which, as I have said, is in the unconscious."

His pipe had gone out, and he carefully lit it again. "If an unconscious traumatic impulse is very strong, it can dominate the Id. In fact, the Ego will have to work overtime, you might say, to keep the impulse from reaching the conscious world and wreaking havoc in a person's life. The Id knows only gratification. It does not possess reason or caution. In a very real sense, it is a psychotic monster. There is a time in every day when the Ego is at its weakest, and that is when a person is sleeping. During sleep, the Ego is most susceptible to the Id's strong impulses."

"Nightmares?"

"Exactly. Unconscious traumas barely at the conscious level, but enough to cause sleep disturbances. In Vietnam, our soldiers were faced with a war that gave them no clear-cut moral guidelines. They were asked to do things that were ostensibly moral, or at least within the parameters of military conscience, moral. But on examination from hindsight, many veterans began to question that supposed morality and ultimately found their actions to be profoundly immoral."

"Can my husband be helped?" Sunny asked, leaning forward in the chair.

"At this late stage, it takes an enormous amount of time, but it can be done with therapy," Perez replied in a subdued tone.

"Father, I have never doubted myself, but in this I feel inadequate. I don't even know where to start. I have tried to get David to talk to me, but he resists."

Father Perez put down his pipe and slowly stood up, his great concern evident on his narrow face. He folded his large hands behind his back and walked slowly over to a large globe sitting next to the window across from his desk and stood quietly beside it as if to contemplate one of the many places he had been on the real earth. Then he pursed his lips. "You are very intelligent. How far will you go to help your husband?"

"I will go as far as I have to."

The rich, pleasant smelling pipe smoke hung like a morning mist at chest level across the darkening room. Sunny found the smell of it reassuring. It reminded her of her childhood, of her father. When she had first come to Father Perez some weeks before it had been as confessor to priest, but now she had opened up to him and he had responded to her anguish as a friend. And in the process, she learned from him a part of his past that few others knew.

"Yes," Perez said with a far off look, "I was what the troops called a sky-pilot, a chaplain. I was with the Forces in the Delta." He had been there at the same time David had served. As he talked, Sunny began to realize he and David had many things in common. But most of all, both men had tried to become intellectuals as a way of dealing with their own personal hells.

"Have you ever met this Keaton, this man you have told me whose name David sometimes calls out during the dreams?" Perez asked anxiously.

"No. I don't even know his full name."

"Our green beret teams were quite close. Authority stemmed from respect more so than from rank. I can't help but believe Keaton might somehow be the source of David's trauma. We need to find him, if possible."

"That might be impossible," Sunny replied. "He has to be at least seventy years old by now. He might even be dead."

Perez rubbed his chin. "There's another aspect of David's nightmares that causes me some concern, and that is the fact he moves around a lot during these episodes. Overt movement indicates to me that these impulses are so strong they take over control of his autonomic nervous system, and that's not good."

"Isn't he just sleepwalking?" Sunny asked hopefully.

"No. Somnambulism is a distinct sickness not related to the type of trauma David is experiencing."

"Then why does he move?"

"I don't know. But I fear he could definitely hurt himself. You said he talks to someone in the dreams."

"Yes, but he has never called out a name, other than Keaton's."

As he stood next to the globe, he could no longer hear Sunny's words. He became lost in his own memories.

His military past was not his only secret. There was another one, darker and more threatening.

He had returned to his Jesuit brothers from Southeast Asia lean and crew cut. But unlike David, he had not been able to keep what he felt inside. His nights had been spent crying in the arms of fellow priests who could not understand the things he spoke of, but who had at least listened. He had spent his days in quite meditation and deep study of the scriptures in hopes of regaining the confidence he had exuded before his first hot LZ. His superiors had thoughtfully let him recover for a full year, then had sent him off to Harvard for his PhD. At Harvard, as he was locked securely in his ancient dorm room and immersed in the deep mysteries of the human mind, questions had arisen, troubling questions for which he could find no satisfactory answers. Question, scientific method of inquiry, answer. His Harvard professors had taught him there was an answer for everything. Scientific truths were as sacrosanct as any theology. So he had kept searching for an answer, begging for an answer. There had to be an answer. But he could find none. The existence of Jehovah contradicted the exactness, the purity of science. How could the laws of nature co-exist with the laws of the Bible?

In the quiet dark of a Harvard dorm room, Martin Perez had come to the conclusion he had never shared with anyone.

"Father?" Sunny asked plaintively, seeing the far away look on Perez's face.

Perez turned to her. "Next week," was all he said.

Chapter 6

David stood hunched over like an old man, his face almost against the windowpane. It was a cloudy night sky he faced, and that made the empty apartment seem all the more lonely without Sunny. A storm had been coming toward Washington for days. It was out there, in the distance, over the dark waters of the ocean, coiling, brooding, and gathering strength. Like a haunting memory, muffled thunder resonated against the windows. *Artillery fire*, he remembered. Lightning flicked and snapped across the storm's mass. *Spooky and Puff on a monsoon night*. Next flash, and I'll count – Flash! One, two, three, four. Boom! It was only five miles away. *Late at night while you're sleeping, Charlie Cong comes a creeping around.*

He lifted the glass of dark liquid to his lips and sloshed the whiskey into his mouth. It exploded and burned going down. Sullenly, he gazed at the bottle and damned himself for drinking. He had promised Sunny he would never lose control of his drinking again. But hell, he had promised her a lot of things. But Sunny was different from most people. She believed people could rise above their condition if they were willing to work hard and had faith. That was why he knew she was hurting inside, for she loved a man who had lost the will to fight and had no faith in anything, least of all himself.

He took another drink. When had it started? When was it he had begun to run from his fears? *Berlin*, he said to himself.

After Vietnam, the Army had stationed him there. And after a while he began frequenting the bars and cellars at night time in that city that never slept. It was at the *Egg Shell* that he had met Lena, a young Swedish student. Her only mistake had been falling in love with him. How could she have known he hated himself so much? After she had run screaming from his life, a succession of German girls, nocturnal carnivores picked up from various dark corners of the city, replenished his need for indifferent companionship. The sex became stranger and more depraved with each new bed mate, and the escape mechanisms he enlisted with gusto each night had graduated from Napoleon Cognac to the most mind-mangling marijuana that could be purchased on the Kufurstendam.

The effects of living life in a revolving door – by day *STRAC* army officer; by night laid back, smoked up, eater of women for dinner Captain Midnight – began to take a toll on his ability to think rationally and, at any given moment, to separate the two people he had become. The demands that came with being an officer became more difficult as the weeks passed. Just getting through each day had become a continual test of his sanity, and at night he drifted into a craziness that rivaled that of the day. Lying on the bed in his darkened apartment on Pritchardstrasse, all sights, sounds, and sensations were heightened and distorted. He would gaze dully at the rain slapping against the window and forcefully order the girl between his legs to blow Jude away, just like a good soldier should.

It started to rain. The reconnaissance of the storm had reached him, just like he had known it would. Everything in his life was being threatened. The past had come back. But why now? The past had faded and dimmed, the future had held promise. But now the dreams, the nightmares, the screaming meemies in the dark of night.

The monks had been right. Everything revolves. Life, time itself, is a circle. No one ever escapes the past for very long. Sooner or later, it has to be dealt with in one way or the other.

He let the drink fall from his hand. His mind found Sunny again.

She doesn't understand, he thought. *She believes in the mystic, the cosmic omnipresence, the God, the Jehovah-Head. Goddamn it Sunny, what the hell. What's happening to us is not being controlled by your Johnny-come-lately. He's not that old. No, my fate was foretold by those ancient rustics lying dormant on their concrete slabs. You Sunny, me, Andrew, we are all part of this swirling madness called humanity. Life, the universe, atoms, us. We all interact. None can exist without the whole. And like balls on a pool table, we roll around in life governed by the strike of the stick. No God, no law; the luck of the draw. The monks knew this. They tried to tell me. Life, like the stars, evolves by revolving. Nothing really dies. Not souls, not matter, not deeds. Everything comes back to the surface sooner or later. And it's simply the luck of the draw when your number comes up. Oh, Sunny, we're in the shit real deep this time.*

Chapter 7

San Francisco, California
January 1982

>The Lord has made all things for Himself,
>Yes, even the wicked for the day of doom.
>   Proverbs: 16:4

Two heavyset men stood to either side of the cringing man who postured shakily in front of the large desk. Behind the desk, the dark figure did not speak but started the gorillas with a nod. Instantly, the heavies began slapping the cringer across the face and the shoulders.

"Oh, God, Doctor. Don't. I'll get it . . . ahh . . . no," the cringer said with a squeaky voice.

"Let him go," the man behind the desk commanded. The heavies, like robots, obeyed.

The cringer raised himself up and, placing his hands on the desk, began his prayer. "Doctor, I didn't know that whore would hold out on me. She was giving head on the side. It happens with the out of town ones, the younger ones that come off the highways. They don't understand responsibility like the downtown girls. They . . ."

"Shut up."

"Yes, Doctor. I'll shut up, yeah, I will . . ."

"You hired her, didn't you?"

"Yes, Doctor, I did. Yes, it was me. But, I mean, you should see her tits . . . and she's only seventeen and tits like that. But head's her specialty. Gets lots of compliments, she does. Can do ten, maybe twenty tricks a day."

"How long?"

"Well, yes . . . how long? Maybe a month. Yes, a month. Uh, no. Maybe two months. No. It's been a month."

"Shut up."

"Yes, I'll shut up." The cringer's voice trailed off into a whimper as he saw the girl being dragged toward him from a darkened corner of the large bedroom that was also the Doctor's office. She struggled uselessly as she was roughly pushed by another heavy in front of the desk alongside her pimp. The cringer gave her a meek sideways glance. She had been gagged and her hands were tied behind her back. She wore a white slip with nothing underneath, and was barefoot. It was as if she had been abducted right out of her bedroom. He turned back to the man behind the desk.

"You will pay for her part of the money."

"Oh, yes, Doctor, I'll pay. Do it right away, yes, today. I will . . ."

"And you will pay for your mistake in judgment."

The look of fear and apprehension on the pimp's face turned to one of terror. He began to cringe even further below the front of the desk.

"Do you know how long it takes to strangle a person to death?" the Doctor asked.

The pimp froze.

The Doctor sat silently, enjoying the effect the question had on the pimp. Contentedly, he watched the pimp's face turn ashen, revealing his sudden realization he might be dead in a few minutes.

The pimp's mouth was so dry he could not answer.

"It takes a long time," the Doctor continues, "depending on how tightly you hold the person's neck."

The cringer swallowed hard.

"Make up for your mistake. Strangle this cheating bitch!" the Doctor ordered.

The girl started to struggle, but the behemoth holding her simply turned her toward the pimp, offering her to him like a meal. Then one of the heavies snatched the gag from her mouth. But before she could cry out, the cringer was on her like a wild praying mantis, his delicate hands squeezing at her throat with what strength he had. Her eyes began to water and her tongue protruded from her mouth. A gurgling sound filled the room along with the grunting of the pimp.

The Doctor looked at his watch until one minute had passed. The girl was still struggling, trying to hold onto life. He understood what she was thinking now. *No, this isn't really happening! It'll stop in a minute.* But soon she would realize she was going to die, and her autonomic nervous system would take over in a panic, a futile last exertion of will. One minute and thirty seconds. *She knows.* Her struggle took on a fierce jerking, spasmodic movements. But the pimp held on to her throat, grunting even harder as his frail body struggled to hold onto the writhing girl. At the two minute mark, the girl's will to live left her. All that held her up were the huge arms of the man holding her and the pimp's hands. Her eyes no longer focused on her killer, but gazed dully ahead into eternity. A few seconds later, she went completely limp.

The holder, sensing death, looked at his master, who nodded. The holder let the dead girl go and she fell onto the floor, the pimp still on top of her, still choking her. The Doctor motioned to one of the heavies who quickly pried lose the pimp's hands from the girl's throat and placed him again in front of the desk.

The pimp was sweating and panting heavily. He had the depraved, desperate look of an animal that had just killed for his supper. But there was something else there hidden just beneath the sweating and the fear. It was contempt. *Contempt for himself*, the dark man thought. *Now he will obey without question. For he does not enjoy killing.*

"The money by midnight."

The pimp nodded and was led away. The heavies lifted the girl's lifeless body in an effortless motion and carried it out of the room. It was once again dark and quiet.

Now that his day's work was done, he could think. He could ponder his earlier visitor and the message he had brought. *Why had he come after all of these years? Why make contact now? Was there a hidden meaning in what he had said?*

"Doctor, excuse for the interruption, but there's a man outside, an old gent who says you'll see him. I don't know who he is," the bodyguard said in a dull monotone.

He looked up, perturbed. "Tell him I'm busy. Find out who it is, then tell him to be gone. And don't bother me again with this off the street stuff. Only appointments. You understand?"

"Yes, Doctor," the guard said hurriedly and left.

A moment later, the guard returned. "He said to tell you 'Phoenix.' I don't know."

He dropped what he was reading on his desk. "He said what?"

"Oh, he said 'Phoenix' sir."

The word, like a bullet, shot through his mind and found its imprint in its dark recesses. A synapse, and the memories started to rush forth like blood from a wound. The evil, the death, and the spawning ground for the demon-self he had become. Phoenix had taught him the ways of evil, the thousand ways to kill. Phoenix, where he learned to sell his soul for lust, for promotion, for advancement and, yes, for lucre. Phoenix had changed him. A metamorphosis from healer to killer, from human being to animal.

"Let him in," he said with reserve.

The door opened and the guard ushered in an old, but still rugged looking man with short cropped, gray-white hair. The man's face was barely visible in the darkened room, but he recognized its jut jaw, its rock like features. Predatory. Forceful. It chilled him when the man's steel gray eyes met his. Without looking, he motioned the guard out. The door closed. He offered the man a chair with a gesture, but it was refused.

"I'd have thought you'd been long dead by now," he said with a trace of apprehension in his voice. *What does he want from me after all this time?* he thought. *How did he find me? What does he know of my business?*

"You seem to have come a long way for a man with little ambition." The man's voice was raspy, but not sickly.

He had a sudden hot flush of anger, but it just as quickly cooled. The old man had always told him he would have to learn to control his hot temper if he was going to make it in the civilian world. Back then he had not welcomed the advice, but as time wore on, he had taken it to heart. "One must adjust."

"I can see you've adjusted very well."

"Where have you been all these years?"

"Around."

"Why have you come to me? What is it you want?"

"Do you remember when you were with the Special Forces?"

"A hundred years ago, eh?" he began, but a stare from the gray eyes stopped him. "Yeah, I remember Special Forces. Best time in my life."

"Do you remember the *covenant?*"

The covenant. Hearing the word froze him. "You need money?" he quickly asked, hoping that was what the old man needed. Money was an easy thing to give. It was what he knew. But the past was long dead, like most of the men who had made the dark promise. A promise made when their lives seemed at an end. If it was money, he could give it. If it was anything else, the old man could go fuck himself.

"Not money."

The voice suddenly sounded powerful. It had a resonance of strength that seemed unnatural. And it was as if the old man was reading his mind. He thought of summoning his guards but, no, this old fool was not armed. His men would have searched thoroughly. Besides, the son of a bitch had to be seventy years old. But the old man seemed to be reading his mind again. "Are you going to deny the promise you made?"

"It depends," he said contemptuously. "I'm a businessman now and my time is valuable . . ."

"You're a gambler, a pimp, a drug dealer, and a murderer."

"Goddamn you! Get the fuck out of here before I have you thrown out. Who do you think you are talking to me like that in my own office?"

The old man raised his hand. "I just want there to be honesty between us. I know you. I've always known you. You are of the earth. There are things that are going to happen soon that you are to be a part of. Things that go beyond your worldly needs for wealth and power."

"I'm not a member of the team any more. You understand? I'm my own boss now. I do what I want to. Now, what do you want?"

"I cannot tell you more now, but soon, very soon. Will you honor the covenant?"

He did not answer directly, but the answer to the old man's question was in his eyes. Instead, he stood, exposing his huge body to the old man as if to frighten him. "Don't push it. Nam was a long time ago. Most of us are dead, or crazy."

"The others will come."

The words sent and electric shock through him. "The others are alive? You know where they are?"

"Soon I will contact you again," the old man said, turning. "I know the way out. *Some* of us do."

He lit his pipe, took in several deep breaths. The powerful narcotic instantly began to dull his senses. After a few moments, he sank back into his chair, his eyes staring blindly into the darkness of his cavernous office. Phoenix. The death, the horror, the faces – John, Julio, Jude, the bastard *Dai Uy*, Keaton. *Keaton. After all these years why have you come back? Why have you placed yourself before me so I can cut your throat?*

Chapter 8

The sound of the drums was far off in the night, but each minute coming nearer. It was a comforting sound. It meant help was out there, hovering over the darkened jungle, searching for them as they hid below. As they lay in a circle, the darkness covered them like a blanket. Each man kept silent. No one dared speak, for the prowling and sniffling of other creatures could be heard probing their perimeter searching for an opening.

The Viet Cong officer knew that if his men were going to close in for the kill, it would have to be now, for the drumbeats were ever approaching, and he had suffered their wrath before. As soon as his crawlers returned to him, he at once became decisive.

He lay face down, the stench of rotting flesh filling his nostrils, causing him to fear he was about to throw up. He could feel Keaton's jungle boot barely touching him. He gripped the stock of his weapon. The selector switch was on full automatic. He wanted them to come. If they would come, it would hurry up and be over and then maybe everything would end. The thought of it possibly ending made him no longer afraid. It was something like jumping out of an airplane. Once you were out the door, there was nothing to be afraid of. Either your chute opened or it didn't. *So come on, you motherfuckers. I've got something made in America for you.*

Like a bat, he sensed something coming at him in the blackness, and instinctively he raised the barrel of his weapon to ward off the phantom. His bayonet caught the naked leaping figure in the groin; his unseen enemy let out a yell and went limp. Quickly, he let the mess slide off his bayonet.

Before he could check the body for signs of any remaining life, apparitions began leaping like wild animals everywhere. In the total darkness, men began slashing at one another, and only the fact that some were clothed and some were not distinguished friend from foe. He did not move from where he was but struck out in the darkness from side to side and from front to rear, hoping to stick something again. The adrenalin in him was revving him up so high he felt like he was going to burst open. Then like a drum roll, he heard Force's machine gun start to kick open. With that, a flare went off and the fighting became even more fierce as the antagonists, now able to see each other, became more accurate with their blows.

As he watched Keaton cut open a screaming enemy's throat, he was hit. It felt like something had punched him with a great amount of force, so hard it knocked him to the ground. A white burning sensation seared through his thigh. He looked down, but couldn't see anything. Then, as if in slow motion, he looked up at Keaton only feet away and, strangely felt as if he were watching someone he scarcely knew.

A giant of a man, Keaton stuck his bayonet into the belly of the man who had attacked him and let him drop, then slashed another attacker open and left him disemboweled at his feet. Turning quickly, he cut open two others with a short burst from his weapon. "Hey, 'atta boy, Keaton. Cut 'em loose," he yelled.

Then he felt a hand turn him over onto his back. Above him, a hairy figure, sweaty and trembling, raised a knife. "I'm glad," he said. But a quick pop from a rifle butt knocked the attacker's head against his stomach, and instinctively he grabbed the hairy figure by the throat and began to choke with all the strength left in him.

Then from above, the drumbeats turned into the whoop-whoop-whooping of Sea Wolves.

"Oh God, Sunny!" David screamed.

"I'm here because my wife wants me to see you. I don't believe in psychoanalysis. I think in most cases people are capable of helping themselves. But right now? Well, you know her. She's told you everything. You know what's happening to me."

For a moment, Perez continued to puff lazily on is pipe and said nothing. "Start with what you're thinking right now," he began, his voice firm and controlled.

He knew why David had come to him, and it was not for therapy. Sunny had told him of the horror of the other night. David had totally lost control of himself. Now she was afraid, and that was what had forced David to come to grips with the reality of what was happening to him. The nightmares had shown him what could happen. They had shown him he had no control over it. No, David was not there for therapy, not even for advice. He was there to save Sunny from the dreams.

"I'm thinking I hope you can separate your priestly need to save my soul from what I really need – some good advice."

"Is that what you need?"

"Yes, that's what's needed," David shot back. *Was it? Even now, could he keep on lying to himself?* What he needed was an answer, not therapy, an answer that would explain the meaning of the dreams.

David gave the old office a quick once over. She was there; he could sense her presence. Maybe she had sat in this very chair and poured out her heart to this man. Maybe she had cried out to her God. Is this why she had chosen this priest? He didn't know, but he did know they both shared a mental intimacy with Sunny. Andrew would say they had both mind fucked her. So he was here.

Father Perez sat impassively waiting for David to speak.

David took the cue from the look on Perez's face. "I've been having nightmares about my combat experience," he said warily.

"Why don't you tell me about the dreams?"

David got up and walked over to the large globe Perez loved to study. "I once had high ideals about what duty meant. I once considered it to mean more than following orders or carrying out what your commander told you to do. Because I knew sometimes something inside a person takes over when he's faced with either following orders or doing what he knows is the right and moral thing to do. And there's the conflict."

"Are you saying duty forsakes honor?" Perez asked.

"But when you do the honorable thing and your men get killed, then you face the harsh reality of duty. Duty knows no honor. For honor lets the humanity of men cloud their judgment, stops them from carrying out their duty, no matter how harsh that might be."

"Are you saying men who are guided by their conscience to do the honorable thing in times of conflict make bad officers?"

David gave Perez a cold stare. "Once, a long time ago, I let my conscience stop me from doing my duty and a lot of people suffered because of it. I won't ever let that happen again."

"Is that what you dream about, some mistake you made in combat?"

"Sometimes, but that's not why I'm here. I almost killed my wife the other night. I had my hands around her throat choking her to death when I woke up. We don't even sleep together any more. But you know that. You sit there in your *Rogerian* pose, knowing that. Now, why don't we quit this intellectual discourse and get down to the meat. I'm acting out my dreams and I don't know what to do about it. Can you help me? Can you do more than pray for my soul?"

"Look, Major, you came here for help. I'm willing to give it. But you must understand from the outset that to think it can be done overnight is unrealistic. If you're willing to work with me, at the pace I set, I believe we can find out what the problem is and together work toward a solution. If you're not willing to work, then you can leave right now. Do we understand each other?"

David returned to his seat, nodded respectfully, and slumped back in the chair.

As Perez began to speak, he had a stern look on his face. "The first thing we are going to have to do is come to an understanding, and that is this: you tell me the absolute and complete truth about what you are thinking and feeling and I promise to listen and keep what's said between us confidential. Agreed?"

"I'll try," David said reluctantly.

"All right, then we shall, as you say, get to the meat." Perez shook out the bowl of his pipe with a bang against a large silver ashtray. "Now, nightmares are common among Vets, but you are correct in your fears. Occurrences of physical violence during nocturnal traumatic disturbances are rare. Therefore, to allow ourselves to get to the real Id impulse that is precipitating this violence, I must ask some pointed questions and you must answer then fully and succinctly."

"I'll answer them, but I don't really think you'll understand what I'm saying," David replied.

"Why? Because you think one who hasn't experienced combat cannot adequately relate to it?"

"I couldn't have said it any better myself."

Perez smiled to himself. Sunny had not told David. He got up from his deep chair and walked over to his desk, bent low, and opened a bottom drawer. Then he straightened up and held up what first appeared to David to be a crumpled piece of green felt. But as Father Perez held it closer, David felt an unexplained wave of relief come over him and at the same time a twinge of embarrassment. He reached out and took the object. Its green cloth felt old and worn. Its yellow and red striped flash had lost some color and the silver captain's bars in the middle of the flash were tarnished.

Perez offered him coffee, and after they had sipped in silence for a while, Perez put down his cup and began again. "The horror we saw each day seemed to become routine after a while, but that was an illusion. We protected our sensibilities and our psyche by dulling our senses. That was a necessary part of our everyday survival, similar to camouflage. The sudden resurrection of these locked away thoughts can be explained by your experiencing a series of stressful events, or seeing something that reminded you of Vietnam. Any trauma has the potential to stir the unconscious," Perez said. He pursed his lips authoritatively and adjusted his glasses.

David shook his head. "I've experienced none of that. It, the dreams, started several months ago. At first, they were similar to flashbacks, just scary spurts of light, noise, and images. Then after a while, each dream was a part of an experience, each part just as horrible as the other. But I don't know what started them."

Perez rubbed his chin. "There must have been something."

"No, nothing. They just started all of a sudden."

"And the dream is progressive, unfolding?"

"Yes, but each episode is as horrible as or more horrible than the one before."

"Tell me everything. You must leave nothing out."

David had kept the darkness of the past from everyone he knew, especially Sunny. He blamed himself for the loss of his team and for what eventually happened to its survivors. At first he was hesitant to open up to Perez. He started out with half-truths and denials. The two men parried and thrust like fighters until the dam inside of David that held back the wall of emotion was weakened and began to crack. Perez sensed what was happening to David and pressed on.

"Why couldn't you shoot Jude? He was a traitor," Perez said, his voice controlled and concealing the excitement he felt.

"I don't know. The gun, it was so heavy," David replied, wringing his hands.

"Oh, come on. That's feeble. How much can a small pistol weigh? Why couldn't you shoot? You had shot men before. Killing was something you were adept at doing. It was your job. Now stop and think. Really think. What – what stopped you from pulling the trigger?"

"The *presence*," David said faintly, not looking at Perez.

"The presence? What presence?"

"The one in my dreams."

"The one in your dreams? I want to know what stopped you then, when you were in Vietnam."

"In my dreams, there's a voice. A powerful voice. The presence behind that voice was there in the jungle that day. It pushed my hand down. It was what stopped me from shooting Jude. It clouded my sense of duty. If I had shot Jude, the VC would never have captured and tortured him and never would have been able to find and ambush us. Now can you see why the dreams are so terrifying. The presence nearly destroyed my life once before. Now, after all of this time, it's here again, taking over my life, trying to destroy the only thing I have that is worth living for. You tell me what it is. You tell me how to make it go away."

Perez swallowed hard. "I don't know. It will take time. I told you it would take time."

"How much time? Can't you see that time is running out for me?" *And for Sunny*, he thought.

"David, sometimes we humans explain the unexplainable by attributing to it mystic origins. In reality, when we hear voices in our dreams, we actually are hearing ourselves. As the years have passed, the feelings you had that horrible day have been lost. The presence you think was there in the jungle on that fateful day, the presence you think comes to you now in your dreams, was and is, in reality, your own good conscience. That's all. And you should be proud you had enough of one then too stop you from committing murder. It's natural that you blame yourself for the loss of your team. You were their leader."

"You're a priest, right?"

"Why, yes. What . . ."

"Nothing." David turned his face away from Perez. "I just want an answer," David continued. "Why is this happening? Why now? Can you help me? Can you?"

Perez stood up and walked over to the window and drew back the curtain. The day was cloudy. The leaves of November, left by negligence, blew wildly across the grounds carried along by the wind. He turned and looked sadly at David. "I . . . don't know if I can help you. But I am willing to try." Perez did not see David nod, nor did he feel his quiet leaving. He felt heavy and tired. There was so much he did not understand about David's dreams, and this troubled him. His dream incidents did not exhibit the etiology of delayed stress syndrome. Even so, there had to be a logical scientific explanation. There had to be.

Chapter 9

Blackstone, Virginia
February 1982

> Trust in the Lord with all your heart,
> And lean not on your own understanding;
> In all your ways acknowledge Him,
> And He shall direct your paths.
>
> Proverbs 3:5-6

Night was coming in quickly like a *fast mover*. It first darkened the tree line past the cornfield and then spread to the highway that passed by Slaw's Café and Sportsman's Store. Chip held onto Mary's hand as they sauntered across the wet and musky smelling field. What was left of a three day snowfall was patch worked with the stubble of summer's harvest past.

Chip was thin and hard. He was in his late thirties, but his brown, close cut hair gave him the appearance of a much younger man. He had a narrow face etched with noticeable light furrows caused by being too near the center of conflict during another more disquieting time in his life. It was an honest face though, and one that rarely betrayed emotion. Mary was a slight girl, ten years Chip's junior, his wife for several years. They were both hard people, as hard as the cornfield they rented for a percentage of the crops they worked long hours to raise.

Slaw's, located two miles outside Blackstone proper, was a gathering place for the local townspeople and farmers and was a haven for the area's hunters and fishermen. Slaw's served home cooked meals that were affordable and delectable and, after a hard day's work, Chip and Mary were more than happy to let Mr. Slaw take care of their supper for them. Chip shook the cold off and Mary rubbed her hands together as they took a booth. Mr. Slaw ambled over and perfunctorily offered them a menu, which they waved off.

"Want the special?" Slaw asked with a knowing grin. He had known Chip since he was a scruffy little boy who hung around the tanning shop listening to wild tales the hunters told as they glorified their day's contest.

"Yes, and for Mary too."

Chip sounded tired. Last season had been tough and they would have to make up for the loss in the coming crop. And though they tried not to talk about it, the hardship they would have to endure to make this year's crop pay off was constantly on their minds, like a wound that refused to heal. They ate slowly and in silence.

It was full dark when they began to make their way back to the farm. The air was crisp and thick. Overhead, a twinkling blanket of stars provided a breathtaking contrast to the dark woods. Silently they walked, the air from their breath hanging in the air. After a short while they began to smell the wood from their house's stove and could make out a faint glow from the light burning inside. From the edge of the woods to their house lay a flat patch of grass no more than fifty yards across. Hand in hand they began to cross.

But after a few yards, Chip suddenly stopped. He seemed to freeze in place, hardly a muscle moving. Mary was frightened; she had never seen Chip act like this. He crouched low, his eyes intently searching the wood line. He was like an animal ready for the kill. For the first time in their life together, she realized he could be a dangerous person, and she shivered at the sight. Slowly he reached for her waist and brought her around behind him, his body shielding hers. She nearly cried out, but common sense told her to be silent. Slowly, like cats, they moved step by step toward the house. As they approached the front porch, Chip froze again. This time Mary sensed he was ready to attack. But attack what?

"Chip, would you really hurt me?" spoke a voice, raspy and low.

Chip hesitated for a moment then straightened up. "Is that you?"

"Who is it? Who's out there?" Mary nervously whispered in Chip's ear. Then out of the corner of her eye she saw a movement, a dark figure standing on the porch.

"Yes, I am here. We must talk."

"Honey," Chip said, "it's all right. You go on in and make some coffee. This is a friend."

"I'm not going anywhere until you tell me what's going on. Who is he?" Mary said loudly.

"Trust me. Please go in. We'll be there shortly."

Mary could see her husband's eyes in the cold starlight. There was no sign of fear in them. In fact, there was the trace of a faint smile on his face. Slowly and cautiously, she left them and walked toward the house, but before she entered the door she gave the tall stranger standing in the darkness beside her a determined look and firmly said to Chip, "If you need me, holler." She went inside.

"You've chosen well, Chip."

"I was lucky, Keaton. Don't you want to go inside? It's cold."

Chip detected something about Keaton that was unfamiliar. He could not put his finger on it, but there was something about his presence that was unknown.

"No, we must talk, then I must leave you. You'll make an excuse to your wife?"

How does how know I'm married? Chip thought. *And how did he know where to find me after all this time?* "I'll tell her."

"How did your harvest turn out?"

"Not too . . . why are you asking this?" Chip responded.

But Keaton wasn't asking; he already knew about the harvest. Chip suddenly felt afraid.

"Don't fear me, Chip. I was always your compatriot, and I always will be."

"Why are you here? Are you in some kind of trouble? That's it. What's happened?"

"If I were in trouble, would you help me?"

"You know the answer to that."

"But you're married now, with responsibilities."

"My wife sticks with me, I stick with her."

"For you, there would have been no other kind of woman."

"It's the covenant, isn't it?" Chip asked apprehensively.

"Yes. It's the covenant."

Chip hung his head and sighed. He had purposefully forgotten about the covenant just as he had driven the jungle from his consciousness. The covenant: the death pact, the life giver. Chip looked around him as if to give his farm the once over in the darkness. If he left now, they would never survive the summer. "Keaton," he said, "the farm can't survive without me. My wife alone can't handle the work it needs. I have to consider her."

"Something is going to happen soon. Something of purpose, of value to many others. Something a man like you must take part in. I need you. Others need you even more. When we made the covenant many years ago, we knew there might come a day when a plight might bring us together again. We were, in many ways, naive about what we were doing, for it was done for a purpose already conceived. Now, that time has come. Will you join your brothers?"

"Who's left alive? Me . . . you. Julio and John never even made it to body bags. Not many of us are left to do anything. Look at you. You're over seventy. And me, I'm tired."

"There are enough," Keaton replied coldly. The tone of Keaton's voice had a finality to it. Whatever it was Keaton wanted him to do had already been planned out. Keaton never left anything to chance.

"Things are different now. I'm different now. Mary's dependent on me. If I left her with the burdens that we have, it would leave us destitute. She doesn't even know about Vietnam, about us and the covenant. I'm not about to leave her. She deserves better than that."

"Yes, she *does* deserve better. Your word was given long ago. Shall you shame your character and not honor it?" Keaton's voice thundered like a mortar round.

Chip turned around and headed toward the house. At the door, he stopped and, without turning back to Keaton said, "You're still welcome to come in, but I can't go. If you need money, we have very little, but I'll give you what I can."

"Your crop was a failure last season. Now, a new season approaches. A season with a different harvest as its reward. Don't let the land lie fallow, Chip. Think about what you're doing. Do you think I've come only to take? I come to give. I come to honor the covenant."

Chip stopped.

"You are a follower of the *Son*, and yet you still doubt. Trust me. No harm will come to Mary." Keaton's voice was soft yet powerful and alluring. Chip wanted to reach out and touch the voice.

He turned back to face Keaton. In the darkness he searched for the face, that old familiar safe harbor where he had many times sought refuge from the storms of fear and self doubt. But Keaton was gone. Vanished. He ran back into the yard and looked right and left, but only the cold stillness of the night was there. Had he been a specter, the ghost of a distant past? No, Mary had seen him too. He began to shiver as a fear as powerful as any he had known in combat overtook him. He looked up at the stars. The answer was there. But just as they were not made of papier mache because of *His* respect for our intelligence, nor was Chip's answer to be easily given.

Chapter 10

```
Port Stanley
Falkland Islands
April 2, 1982
```

> And they rose early in the morning and went up to the top of the mountain, saying, "Here we are, and we will go up to the place which the Lord has promised, for we have sinned!"
> Then Moses said, "Now, why do you transgress the command of the Lord?" For this will not succeed.
> "Do not go up, lest you be defeated by your enemies, for the Lord is not among you."
> Numbers 14:40-41

Captain Enrico Alvarez was proud of the marines. In less than two hours they had advanced from the edge of the Bay to the old weather-beaten church in the town's center.

At first light, just as the dawn was drifting away toward the mainland, the battalion had scooted off the landing ships in large turtle-like amphibious armored vehicles, tread across the short, choppy stretch of water between the ships and the port and, with a roar, enveloped the town. At the outskirts of the sparse settlement, there had ensued a fierce firefight with the small detachment of Royal Marines. Three of his men had been killed. But after assessing the situation, the Governor

General of the Islands had ordered the marines to surrender. This they had promptly done without provoking a further serious incident. So far, the war was going as planned and was as pleasant an occasion as a gentleman could want.

Alvarez was a handsome man. He had a tan, narrow face accentuated by jet black hair, combed straight back. His eyes were black and deep and his lips were full. He loved good wine, good food, and good cigars. And often, women; plenty of women. But his great passion, his great love, was Argentina. All of his looks, his intelligence, his effort and labor were reserved for her. As he stood next to his jeep surveying the movement of the marines, he made a striking figure dressed in his camouflage SAS smock, his naval fatigue pants, and high topped boots. He carried his Beretta high on his hip and wore his peaked naval officer's hat so that its shiny bib was just at eye level. He looked the leader. But just as looks can be deceiving, so was the purpose for his presence in Port Stanley.

Even though, ostensibly, he was a member of the marine detachment and a naval officer, he was not their commander. Captain Alvarez, forty-seven years old, the son of wealthy parents, and friend *accompli* of the *junta*, had since 1976 been the Chief of Security and Commander of the feared State Prison located on the island of Los Estados. Los Estados was the first step in a sojourn through hell that finally ended in the River Platta for hundreds of missing Argentineans, the *desaparecidos*. Alvarez was the tour guide.

A *dirty war* had been commenced to save the nation from the communist-inspired anarchy that had destroyed Argentina's neighbor, Uruguay. He fought his country's enemies with a zeal that epitomized religiofication of a cause. His cause was Argentina, his way of life, his very being. And if it took the death of hundreds of men, women, and children, agent provocateurs, or misguided souls to maintain Argentinean society, so be it. He did not think of himself as a cruel man. He did not enjoy torture and he did not participate in rape. There was no passion in the way he carried out his duties, and this was what made him the most dangerous man in Argentina – for the lack of emotion that characterized his dark endeavors excluded any possibility of reprieve or remorse for his victims. He could mutilate and kill as easily as he could make love.

He moved away from his jeep as the commander of the marines approached. The commander, a tall, thin colonel, was neatly dressed except for his boots which were caked with mud. No salute was exchanged, even though on the face of it the colonel outranked Alvarez; they simply exchanged nods. "We have secured the last boathouse on the dock. By the Virgin, we have succeeded. The Malvinas are ours once again. All Argentina will be in fiesta by tomorrow night, captain." The colonel and Alvarez embraced.

"This is a great day in history. We took them back and there were few casualties," Alvarez said, grinning from ear to ear.

"I will radio the general so the troops can start their landings," the colonel said, disappearing in the diesel smoke of the dozens of American made armored vehicles that were starting to line up along the narrow streets.

The marines seemed in good spirits. Soon the Army troops would start to arrive and they would be back on the transports heading for the mainland. The marines had done their job well. This for sure would be the conclusion of his report to the *junta*.

As Alvarez lit a cigarette, three marines approached him with a leftenant of the British Royal Marines. The young officer gave him a snappy salute which was returned just as smartly. Alvarez offered the leftenant a cigarette, an English Player.

"Thank you, sir," the fair haired youth said.

Like his fellow servicemen in the air force, Alvarez admired the British. "My pleasure," he said in almost flawless English.

"How long will you be staying, sir?" the officer asked earnestly, without a trace of sarcasm.

Alvarez smiled. "Forever."

The officer saluted again and was led away.

Forever, Alvarez said to himself. *Forever? The generals believe that Thatcher will not attack us. Eight thousand miles, they say. Their economy is in too much trouble, incapable of sustaining the financial base for fighting a war with an eight thousand mile supply line. The generals have been right about many things. But have they been right about the British? Only time will tell.* He rubbed his chin. *For now*, he thought, *I will celebrate like everyone else. Tomorrow I must start to eradicate all those who would help the British against us.*

Alvarez got into the jeep and motioned for his driver to head to the airstrip where C-130 aircraft were starting to land. As the driver started the jeep, the sun broke through a tear in the overcast sky, throwing the reflection of the church steeple across the jeep. For a moment, Alvarez felt a knifing chill as the sudden flash of light fell over him. The driver seemed to feel it too and gave Alvarez a startled look. "It's all right, boy," he said quietly. "God has always been on our side."

Chapter 11

Fort Myers Officers Club
Washington D.C.
April 2, 1982

Nothing puts the hum in the military like a war. The gathering of the staff and ladies of War College faculty had been planned to say hello to new members and goodbye to those who would be leaving soon: a *hi-bye*. But the news from the South Atlantic had stirred their intellects and captured their imaginations. Tonight, they would talk war.

Normally, Andrew loved these get togethers. They drew Boombas like Corvettes and suntans. But tonight, in addition to the flirtatious fantasies about with whom he might be sleeping after a night's hunting, he also had an unwelcome sense of self-importance because what had taken place in the South Atlantic would make him the center of interest and the sought-after conferee of the party. The reason for his soon-to-be-experienced fame was that the *Kennedy*'s sailing orders included a trip around Cape Horn, a mere three hundred miles from the Falklands, a thirty minute, six hundred mile an hour supersonic roller coaster of a ride in a F-18, and that had put the glow on him, that eerie light that foretold the possibility of his being near the mouth of the beast. The fact that he might soon be eaten alive made him all the more interesting.

This was a formal affair. The women wore low cut cocktail dresses, with just a little breast showing. The Army officers, confident and controlled, wore their dress blues, a replica of the old cavalry uniform: dark blue, almost black coat with yellow epaulets; white shirt and black bow tie; light blue pants with gold stripes. The Marine officers, their blue coats split down the middle exposing a dress red breasted coat, moved nervously about the throng, their hands on slick sabers that barely touched the polished marble floor. Standing by themselves, preoccupied with technology, were the Air Force officers, razor sharp in sky blue, bow tied dinner uniforms adorned with tiny silver wings. Naval officers like Andrew stood erect and detached in white high collared uniforms holding drinks with hands protected by white gloves. Tonight they had cast off the camouflage fatigues and subdued flight suits worn to protect them in combat for Christmas tree uniforms adorned with rows of brightly colored ribbons and shiny badges that blinked and flashed as they walked under the chandeliers that hung low over the large ballroom.

Andrew stood at the end of the room next to a huge fireplace. A Marine Harrier pilot was fast-pitching him about what would happen when the British Sea-Harrier met up with the French made Super Etendard of the Argentineans, and as far as the Marine was concerned, the French jet was no match for the Hawker-Sidney. Andrew wasn't sure about the Marine's thesis and really didn't give a damn, for as the evening moved forward thoughts of pussy and fighting had given way to one worry – the whereabouts of Sunny and David. And the later they were, the more worried he became.

The Marine pilot pressed on. "The one reason they'll win in a dog fight is that they'll turn on a dime. All the pilot has to do at the right moment is vector his thrust away from a frontal angle of attack and – swoosh! The Etendard will overfly him and – zap! Right in the ol' cross-hairs. Blow the motherfucker all to hell."

"Look, there's no use in getting your hopes up. There's not going to be any fight," Andrew said sardonically.

"What?" the marine officer shrieked, looking at Andrew as if he had thrown water in his face.

"Eight thousand miles! You think the British are going to travel that distance to fight a war over a bunch of sheep? Get serious." Andrew took a sip of his drink as the Marine turned on his heel and left as if he had gotten wind of a bad smell. "Don't go away mad," Andrew said sarcastically.

Where were they, he wondered. Something had to be wrong or they would have been here by now. Formal functions were part of the military workday. In spite of everything, during the last couple of weeks they had been able to come to grips with their situation. Andrew knew how difficult it had been for both of them, David faced with the night hell of the dreams and now Sunny, her homeland in chaos. He took another slug of his drink. The damn Falklands landing. No telling what had gone through Sunny's mind when she heard the news. He just shook his head. *Sunny.* He still had a problem imagining her as anything but American, but Argentina was her homeland, where her family still lived.

Then he saw her standing in the entranceway of the ballroom. She was alone for the moment and she seemed disoriented, caught up in the confusing commotion between the officers and their wives as they mouthed insincerities to each other. She was searching the room, and he knew instinctively that she was looking for him. Tonight she appeared especially vulnerable and frail.

For a moment, he entertained the thought of going to her. Instead, he fought back the desire and walked to the window with his back to the dance floor. He stood there, silently watching the reflection in the glass for a glimpse of David's arrival. And as he waited, the thought came to him that now, more than any time in his life, he wanted to get back to the sea, to the fighter jets he loved.

"Andrew," Sunny said. David now stood beside her, noticeably nervous.

"I was beginning to worry about you two. Need a drink?" Andrew asked, avoiding Sunny's eyes.

"No, not yet," David said. He hated social functions. "All here?"

"All except for our fearless leader."

"Yes, I thought he'd be here with bells on."

"You have heard the news, Andrew?" Sunny asked, taking him by the hand.

He could feel her warmth even through the glove. She looked tired and, though she tried to hide it, worried. One look at her face and the realization of what she was going through hit him like the cold air that had come over Haiphong that time when he ejected from his burning jet. Unfortunately, she was caught in the middle of this thing. If the landing evolved into a full scale conflict, America would quite naturally side with the British. Because she was Argentinean by birth, everyone would assume her sympathies would be with her countrymen and that would affect David.

"Andrew?"

"Nothing's going to come of this. It'll be over in a couple of days, weeks at the most. As soon as the Brits and the Gauchos realize the price this thing is going to cost, they'll settle it through diplomacy."

Sunny gave him a half smile. Before she could speak, a voice boomed.

"Attention!"

A short, stout man entered the room with a woman, his thin, frail wife. They moved with forced politeness from group to group, smiling, shaking hands, and patting people on the shoulders.

"Fearless leader," Andrew said slowly, holding his glass up in mock toast.

Major General Barney Knott, the commander and president of the War College, disliked his assignment. He thought of himself as a commander of armies, not classrooms. Rather than here, bogged down with academics, he'd rather be commanding the 101st at Ft. Campbell or the 82nd at Ft. Bragg. But Knott had learned a long time ago what waves were, and his career had been characterized by calm waters in the face of authority.

As if he had heard Andrew, Knott came straight over to him and swatted him on the shoulder. He gave a disdainful glance toward David then let his eyes rest for a second on the swell of Sunny's breasts. "Well, Lieutenant Commander, any thoughts on what you might be seeing down there in the South Atlantic?" Knott asked in a booming voice that was meant to catch everyone's attention.

Knott's baiting hit Andrew in the head like a hammer. This was why he did not care to be the hero of the ball. "No sir," Andrew responded. "I don't believe we'll see anything. It'll be winter by the time we arrive, you know, and I hear the visibility is very poor."

There was a slight murmur from the crowd.

"I think you'll see more than you realize if the thing gets as big as I think it will," Knott stated flatly.

"You may be right, sir," Andrew replied accommodatingly.

Knott took in a deep breath and said to everyone in the room, "This war could be a Godsend to us. Many of our theories about combined arms operations will be tested and what we learn may prove valuable in future planning." He stopped, letting everyone gather around. Then as if he was giving a formal lecture, Knott began again, turning to one officer, then another. "An officer's most important duty in peace time is to train his men to win the air-land battle. Training. That's an army's primary duty. It can't be evaded or subordinated to any other consideration. If all of you believe in and accept this premise, which side will prevail in the Falklands? Let us discuss this with openness and frankness, and then we'll eat and dance."

"The Argentineans have several factors that favor their side," said a tall intelligent looking Army colonel. "They have the proximity of land. The mainland is only three hundred nautical miles from the islands, making air resupply quick and safe. They can control the waters around the war zone with an aircraft carrier, several cruisers, and submarines, and they have a modern air force that can remain over the target area long enough to control the airspace above the battle. If they are well led, I believe they will win."

"I think you have to consider that the Argentineans have not fought a war in nearly two hundred years. Experience will be a key factor in this conflict's outcome," interjected a Marine major who sported a curling mustache.

A rather young and sturdy Army lieutenant colonel recently assigned from Special Forces raised his hand as if he were in a classroom. Knott recognized him with a nod. "I think the key to the eventual outcome, to which the general has already alluded, is training. Whichever side has trained best will prevail," he said.

"That simple?" countered the Army colonel.

"Training an army is never simple, but the level of training will influence the outcome," Knott interjected authoritatively, excited by the sparing. "The British army is one of the best trained in the world. Their officers and noncommissioned officers have experience and a dedication to duty that will carry them forward when all else fails."

"Are we to assume Argentine officers lack dedication?" the colonel asked. "After all, they've always considered the Falklands, the Malvinas as they call them, to be a part of their country. They have never recognized British sovereignty over the islands, just as Mexico has never recognized our sovereignty over its northern territory. To their way of thinking, this is a patriotic action of almost religious significance."

"As I see it," interrupted a square-jawed Navy captain with short cropped red hair, "the real key will be the ability of the Royal Navy to successfully put a landing force ashore and afterwards maintain control of the waters surrounding the islands. This they can do with their Sea Harriers and submarines."

"Yes, but the landings will have to be conducted in a harsh climate with rough seas. The Argentines will have air superiority, which will make the landing extremely hazardous," an Air Force major said, emphasizing his point by striking one of his fists into the other hand's open palm.

"But you are all forgetting one most important aspect of this war, and that is the logistics of supporting a prolonged conflict with an eight thousand mile supply line," an Army major from the Quartermaster Corps said haughtily. "This war simply cannot be supported for a very long duration. The British will have to strike fast and win quickly before the Argentines sever that line."

"Considering all of the salient points you have all so intelligently raised – the control of the sea, the air, and the ability to sustain the operation – once the two armies are joined on the ground, what will eventually decide the outcome of the war?" Knott asked, hoping to guide the conversation back to where he wanted it.

"I still think, all things considered, the lack of experience and training will be the key factor. The Argentineans simply do not have the requisite experience or the leadership in their officers corps to beat the British," the Green Beret officer said, picking up on Knott's cue.

"Exactly. Exactly," Knott said enthusiastically.

"The lack of training played no major part in the first Arab Israeli war in 1948," the Army colonel said, resolutely looking Knott squarely in the eyes. "The Jewish people were fighting for what they saw as their homeland," the Army colonel continued. "Nothing could have defeated them. We couldn't defeat the Viet Cong, and no one could stop what happened in Iran. Are we forgetting what we teach our junior officers – the only thing that cannot be defeated in war is a group of determined men?"

The others started to nod their heads and murmur approvingly to themselves. Even Andrew smiled. The colonel's point had hit home. Every officer in the room believed that when the chips were really down, their own gut courage would pull them through. To deny the colonel's averment would be to deny the noblest part of their own characters.

"Of course, that has to be taken into consideration, as patriotic fervor on the part of any nation must, but we are practitioners of the art of military application. If we are to learn from this endeavor, we must coldly set aside any emotional interference with our thinking and apply the knowledge we have of our profession to logically predict the outcome," Knott replied. "But you may be right, colonel, other factors may be present," Knott continued. "So in the interest of fairness let us assume, for the moment, that the Argentineans will not set aside emotional fervor and that their emotional fervor it will be the driving force behind their invasion. How far will it take them? How much emotional fervor will it take to overcome a lack of training and experience? Fortunately, we have in our number, as many of you know, an Argentinean who might be able to enlighten us with firsthand knowledge of what her countrymen might be thinking at this time. Mrs. Elliot?"

It had been on the hillside of Nui Ta Bec when David first experienced the paralyzing effects of fear. What was it the doctor had said? People don't freeze because they quit thinking. No. They freeze because they start thinking so much and so rapidly the brain can't effectively process all the thoughts. And when that happens, like any good computer, the brain shuts down. So when the world started churning up around him on Nui Ta Bec, all he could think to do was to pull the trigger of his weapon, not to first flick the safety switch off. Nothing had happened then, and nothing was happening now. Unfortunately for Sunny, the attack had come so suddenly and so unexpectedly David had succumbed to the same paralysis that had hit him on Nui Ta Bec. He could see her standing there, but he couldn't move to help her. His mind raced for an appropriate response, but doing so left him standing there like so much dead weight, useless and indecisive.

"General, my countrymen will not take back the Malvinas," Sunny answered firmly. She stood facing Knott, her head held high, her eyes not leaving his.

Knott sensed a power in her that was unfamiliar to him. It made him wonder what she saw in a man like Elliot. But despite his momentary respect for her, Knott was a man who thrived on conflict. He pressed on. "That's a pretty definite statement, isn't it?" he quipped, turning to the others and laughing.

"Yes. But it is the truth."

The room fell silent. *What was wrong with this woman? This was a general she was talking to.*

"The colonel there says the retaking of the Malvinas is a 'holy cause' to your people," Knott replied.

"He is right," Sunny replied. "The Argentinean people have always felt the Malvinas, the Falklands, to be a part of Argentina. Just as we Americans consider the Hawaiian Islands to be a part of America."

"*We?*"

"Yes, general, I am an American citizen. As I was saying, this cause has always been a part of our national conscience. But what has happened now, this morning, is not holy in the sense you think."

"And what sense is that?" Knott quipped.

Sunny smiled at Knott, but ignored his insult and turned to the colonel. "You are right. At first there will be great enthusiasm for this venture among the people. Even within the armed forces there will be fervor for war. This will last for a time – until the British attack, and they will attack – and when they do, we will lose our will to fight. We will see that God is not with us."

"Let's leave The Almighty out of this, Mrs. Elliot. I don't think He'll take sides in this one," Knott said sarcastically.

From around the room, laughter broke out.

"It's hard for me to believe you would question the need to have God on a nation's side during wartime, general," Sunny said, quickly turning to Knott.

The laughing stopped. *Why was she confronting the general?* The room fell completely silent.

"Religious views respectfully aside, you do admit your former countrymen will lose this war?" Knott asked, not hiding his anger at being challenged.

"Unfortunately, yes."

The door was open and Knott charged through. "Why unfortunately?"

"Because . . ."

"Maybe because you find it hard to support any nation that opposes Argentina?" Knott paused, letting his statement hang in the air. "I can see that must be a real problem for you, Mrs. Elliot. You know, it takes more than reading the Constitution to become an American, and that's because this country stands for things foreigners will never understand."

"And just what *does* America stand for, general?" Sunny asked quietly.

God, she might be beautiful, but she's stupid, Knott thought. "Do you know what power is, Mrs. Elliot? No, I can see you don't. America stands for power, young lady. Power projected with military might and economic strength." He threw back his head and let out a booming laugh. "Hell, the whole world is jealous of us. You can be anything here, lady. All you have to do is work for it. But you must know this. After all, you wanted to be an American didn't you?"

Andrew lessened his grip and his glass left his hand and smashed against the polished floor. Knott gave him a sharp look as the assembled officers and wives winced at the sound of the glass's destruction.

But Sunny spoke up before he could say anything. There was a tone of authority and confidence in her voice. It unnerved Knott to hear a woman talk like this. "Argentina will lose because, as a nation, it has lost its honor. Its sense of purpose has been channeled into the service of greed and evil. But the sad part of this ill-advised venture against the British is that many brave men will die needlessly, and that is what I meant by saying it is unfortunate."

"Soldiers are expected to die," Knott said. "No," he continued, "Argentina will lose because it's not powerful. It's a third rate military power taking on a country that understands discipline and duty, not because it's lost its honor."

But Sunny would not back down. "You think I don't understand power. Well, you are wrong, general. I know power for what it is – a corrupter of men. A narcotic that, like greed for wealth, darkens men's souls. America is a powerful nation. A nation *should* be powerful, but if it uses that power unjustly, it will eventually fall out of favor with God. A nation *should* be prosperous, but a nation whose people are driven solely by the need to obtain wealth will lose its sense of purpose, its honor. Its people will lose their ability to care for one another and for other nations less fortunate than they. Their moral fiber will decay and they will become divided within and easy prey for the more powerful, the more resolute. General, you must only read history to see where America's future lies if it follows the wrong path. No nation has ever survived whose people became victims of its marketplace, whose leaders were preoccupied with obtaining wealth and power. I fear for America, general. I fear *it* does not understand power."

"If that's the way you feel, why did you become an American?" Knott asked spitefully.

But Sunny didn't answer him. All at once she became aware of how quiet the room had become around her and realized she had gone too far. She had brought David into this. Knott was his superior. Again, she was involving others without their consent. She dropped her head and looked away.

Knott's face was flushed and sweaty. "Major Elliot, your wife seems ill," he said, giving David a cross look.

Then his eye caught a flicker of light as Andrew lit a Black Jack. Soon, foul smelling smoke began to form around Knott's face. "*I'd* like to hear why she became an American," Andrew said. "That is, well, unless we big tough men are terrified of what she has to say. Anybody here scared of this little lady?" Andrew said, puffing furiously on his cigar.

Knott's face became contorted with anger and the assembled officers fell away nervously waiting for him to explode.

But Sunny knew this had to be stopped, if not for David's sake, for Andrew's. She lifted her head. "No," she said flatly, "the general is right. I am not feeling very well." She turned, took David by the arm, and silently and awkwardly while the others gave them curious stares, they left.

At the entranceway, David looked back for just a second, but it was long enough for him to see Andrew's face. He recognized the look. He had seen it before in a dark and desperate land far, far away.

Chapter 12

**New York, New York
January 3, 1982**

> How have you helped him who is without power?
> How have you saved the arm that has no strength?
> How have you counseled one who has no wisdom?
> And how have you declared sound advice to many?
> To whom have you uttered words?
> And whose spirit came from you?
>
> Job 26:2-24

"In the valley of the, ho, ho, ho, Green Giant!"

The copilot grimaced as the booming voice of the pilot filled his flight helmet. Fortunately for the air controllers at Kennedy and the passengers, the aircraft's radio had been switched to intercom. Jake Arrado was the pilot, but for the moment, entertainment was his game. Each time he took off from Kennedy on the ferry run to the Pam Am building, he would dip below the Manhattan skyline and skim the Hudson. It was a great show he put on for the passengers.

Years ago Jake had nervously sung the same jingle while he was extracting MACSOG teams out of dangerous, dark Cambodian messes surrounded by dense, dank forests. Now he extracted rich people who were in a hurry to get somewhere so they could make a profit, and the forests had been replaced by skyscrapers.

His aircraft, a surplus Sikorsky HH-53C, was a refurbished, reworked, and overhauled helicopter that had been used during the war to rescue downed pilots in Indian country. It had a top speed of well over two hundred miles an hour and could carry thirty combat troops, or twenty civilians. During the war, downed Air Force pilots had dubbed the HH-53C the Jolly Green Giant because of its size and because it could take hits and still fly.

"Roll Tide, roll," Jake said as he flicked the cyclic stick and banked the chopper toward the World Trade Center. A gentle tug at the collective handle, and the big giant gained the altitude it needed to line up for the approach to the top of the Pan Am Building. Jake adjusted his flight helmet, a nervous reflex from the days when he had more hair. Now that he was balding and had put on a paunch, the helmet bothered him more and the seats of the aircraft were harder to strap into.

"Want to take her in?" he asked his youthful copilot.

The young man nodded.

"You have the aircraft," Jake said and turned his attention to the fireball in the distance that was sinking behind New Jersey. He figured he was still capable of having feelings so long as he found the setting sun a marvelous sight. After two disappointing marriages which had left him the father of four children, lonely, and broke, the fact that he could feel anything was in itself a miracle.

"Landing gear down," the copilot said perfunctorily. "Three green." Three green lights. The gear was down. The big bird flared to a landing.

Once on the landing pad, Jake felt a sense of anxiety wash over him. When he was airborne, he was above it all, above the world and its craziness, its misplaced priorities. But most of all, above his own troubles. The copilot let the engine idle. He would be getting off and sleeping over in town. Once the passengers and the stewardesses disembarked, Jake would fly the aircraft back to Kennedy where it would be refueled and prepared for the night run and another set of pilots. He watched carefully as the copilot and two stewardesses left the pad for the elevator. When they were safely inside, the ground crewmen gave the all clear sign. Slowly, he revved up the big turbines, then pulled and pitched. The lumbering giant was, in reality, an agile and responsive aircraft and up it went.

He headed out over the Avenue of the Americas and the open area above the Hudson. Even though he was still airborne, he felt apprehensive about going in. All he could see ahead of him through the windscreen was another lonely night. He couldn't land.

"JFK tower, this is Ferry 34 on squawk 118.5," he radioed into his mike.

"Ferry 34," responded the controller in a flat, detached voice.

"I'll be ten miles southeast at two thousand to shoot some approaches."

"Roger, Ferry 34."

He looked at the fuel gauge. He could fly for another two hours, but how would he explain the extra flight time to base? There really was no rush for him to land. The maintenance crews would not start to work on the ship for another hour. He could tell them he had been having trouble with the hydraulics and needed to put some G-stress on the system. Yes, that was it. They never questioned a pilot when he needed to test the aircraft for a safety hazard. Satisfied, he banked the chopper toward the open sea. As he left the seven-mile limit, he switched on his night lights. Outside the craft two rotating beacons, one under the belly and the other on top of the aircraft along with a strobe light, warned other aircraft of his approach. Inside the cockpit he switched on the red dash lights to protect his night vision. As the world darkened around him, he seemed to lose any sense of the aircraft moving. Only the engines' droning sound evidenced the aircraft's life. In violation of FAA rules, he switched off his radio.

Alone in the darkness, he started muttering a mantra. *All life is sorrow. To die is to live.* Here in the darkness, he had control of his destiny. Down there, life was only an illusion where no one really had control over anything. Stay in the helicopter – stay in control. If he wanted, he could stay in the helicopter for the rest of his life. All he had to do was keep on flying. And what if he did just keep flying? In a few short hours, his life would be over. Would it be that bad? Had he not lived a full life? He had seen the world. He had fathered children – left something of himself behind. It was not like he would be leaving them destitute. His life insurance made him worth more dead than alive.

And wasn't drowning one of the least painful ways to die? You really just went to sleep. How had it happened? How had he let it get this far? How had his life slipped from the palm of his hand? Decision time.

His eyes were still sharp as an eagle's and he still had quick reflexes and strong muscles despite his added weight. So even with the helmet blocking most of his peripheral vision, he was still able to see the figure move toward him. Instinctively, he reached out with his right hand and pulled the man down toward the copilot's seat. With almost acrobatic ease, the man fell into the seat. Jack reached up from the man's arm to his shirt and tightened it near the neck. Then as the eerie red light closed around the man's features, he couldn't think of anything to say or do. As if an afterthought, he pointed toward the copilot's helmet. The man put it on and turned his head toward Jake.

"Reminds you of *Ba Chuc*, doesn't it?" the man said, looking out of the window into the darkness whirling by at over two hundred miles per hour.

"What . . . what are you doing here, Keaton?" Jake asked, not believing what he was seeing.

"You remember when you were with the team, your second tour, how we used to fly in at night, and how we likened flying in the darkness to being in a time capsule?"

Jake did not respond.

"It doesn't seem like you're going anywhere, does it?"

Jake turned away. *What did he want after all this time and why had he come after him?*

Then he felt a hand gently grip his shoulder. It felt warm, almost reassuring.

"But we are, you know. We are."

"What do you want, Keaton?"

"You've gained weight."

"You noticed. Look, what do you want?"

"I just want to talk to you. For now."

"Look, couldn't you have met me at my base instead of up here? Look at this;" Jake said feigning surprise, "I'm almost sixty miles out. I've got to turn around and head in. Put your safety straps on, okay?"

Keaton snapped his safety straps together then asked, "Why don't you just keep flying?"

He gave Keaton a sharp look.

"It's hard to know where you're going, especially when your past clouds the way, Jake."

"The past is all we've got. You ought to know that. Now, what do you want with me?"

"You're wrong. The future is what gives meaning to life – the future and all of its infinite possibilities. If you only knew what's out there waiting for you Jake . . ."

"Keaton, goddamn it, what do you want? I haven't seen you since they washed us out. Now all of a sudden here you are, the ghost of Tet past. Shit!"

"We're sixty miles over the ocean. Do we keep flying, or do we turn around?" Keaton said with a knowing smile.

Jake took one look at Keaton and started to shiver. "Fuck you!" he hissed, and banked the chopper hard to the right. The G-forces flattened them against the seat as the aircraft came about one hundred and eighty degrees. "We're heading in. You happy?" The aircraft corrected its weight once Jake aligned it with the azimuth that would take them into Kennedy. As soon as he trimmed the controls and set the throttle, he turned to Keaton. "The jungle's over there," he said, pointing west. "Ten thousand miles away. But every day, every night, it's still right here." He put his finger to his head. "Can't leave it behind, Keaton. I tried twice with two good women, but I couldn't keep it together. I tried taking normal jobs, but each time I got so bored I thought I'd lose my mind. I mean, can you see me flying a desk? Almost became a cop once, but I knew I'd kill somebody first chance I got. Now look at me. My life's a mess. You say the future is where it's at. Shit, tomorrow's the future and when it comes, it's the past all over again." Jake let out a laugh. "Now here you come out of the blue, the Past Man himself, to tell me about the future. Keaton, when I land this thing, I want you to walk away and don't ever come back. You understand?"

"Don't you want to know why I've come?"

Jake gave Keaton a stern, agitated look.

"It's time to honor the covenant."

Jake shook his head from side to side. "No, Keaton. No. That was a long time ago. I'm not going to get involved with you or any of them again, especially if it involves *him*. So just get the fuck out of here if you know what's good for you."

"Your life has no meaning, Jake. You live in darkness. For you, the covenant will be a life giver. You must live up to your word and honor the promise you made to the others, even if it touches *him*."

"To hell with him. He's responsible for everything, for the whole damn thing. If I ever saw him again, I'd have to kill him."

"He has suffered too. He's no better off than you."

"You know where he is?" Jake said, clenching his teeth. "Tell me. Where is he?"

"In time, Jake. But for now, know that what I will ask of you will be dangerous."

"Dangerous? You mean dangerous like this?" Jake pushed the cyclic stick forward. Instantly the big chopper plunged downward into the darkness over the ocean. Negative G-forces crushed against the aircraft's super structure lifting Jake almost out of his seat. His stomach felt like it was in his throat. "He says it'll be dangerous. You think I give a damn about dying? I don't give a damn about anything," Jake screamed above the whining of the turbine engines. Outside the rotary blades popped and cracked as the chopper spiraled faster than gravity toward the unseen surface of the sea. Suddenly, everything – time, motion, sound, images – stopped. Jake could no longer hear the death screams of the helicopter. It was as if his mind's eye had switched to slow motion. Keaton turned toward him and smiled, and when he did, a glowing light, warm and soft, emanated from around him. Jake could see Keaton was not afraid, and somehow this quelled his own fear.

Then Keaton spoke. "No, Jake. Your life will soon be fulfilled. Your courage will find favor and your name shall be known for honor and righteousness and you will be able to stand in the light of men once more."

But it was not Keaton's voice that he heard. He could see Keaton's mouth moving, but the words were not his. Jake felt a strange calm come over him. The voice was powerful, yet at the same time warm and reassuring. He wanted to reach out and touch the voice.

"Ferry 34, JFK Center. Do you want to declare an emergency?" The crackle of the air controller seemed to startle Jake. "Ferry 34?"

Jake pulled hard at the cyclic and the collective. His stomach went from his throat to the bottom of his pants as the chopper leveled out. Instinctively, Jake regained altitude, and when he checked his instruments he hung his head. "I'm sorry, Keaton. You didn't deserve that."

Keaton touched Jake.

Jake radioed his position to JFK Center and the controller set him up for a radar vectored approach. By all logic, he should be dead now. What was it that had saved him? Had it been the call from the aircraft controller? Had it been the calming effect of Keaton's words? Then he remembered the radio had been turned off. Had he switched it back on in the confusion? Had Keaton? He did not know. It had all happened so fast. But the voice . . . it was not Keaton's. Jake shook his head.

"When we land, I will not see you for a while, but I will meet you when it's time," Keaton said.

"Why can't you tell me what's going to happen?"

"Because the completeness of the thing has not yet been worked. Besides, you will sense it as the time for action approaches."

"One thing. Will it be because of him?"

"No, another."

"Good, because I'd have to kill him."

"He's already dead, Jake."

Chapter 13

> Who can find a virtuous wife?
> For her worth is far above rubies.
> The heart of her husband safely trusts her;
> So he will have no lack of gain.
> She does him good and not evil
> All the days of her life.
>
> Proverbs 31:10-12

```
Georgetown University
Washington, D.C.
```

From the very beginning of David's session, he had broken into a litany of self degradation. He was a coward. He was indecisive. He was self-centered. Sunny was too good for him. Each time David spewed out streams of self disgust, Perez simply pursed his lips and adjusted his glasses. He even tried the therapist's ploy of nonsensical, interrupting dialogue to disrupt David's train of thought because something had happened that deeply disturbed, albeit fascinated, him: David's nightmares had suddenly stopped. But David was on a roll, and he was not going to quit until he got to the bottom of himself. "You know, we were going to make love last night," David said. "Well, I couldn't get it up. Does that surprise you?"

Perez again said nothing.

"Doesn't surprise *me* anymore."

"Did you read the paper this morning?" Perez asked. "It seems there was very little loss of life in the Falklands. There's even talk of settling the matter diplomatically. So maybe there's hope yet. Should make your wife sleep a little easier."

David turned stone faced for a moment as though he were contemplating saying something, but then he gave Perez a nonchalant look. "You know what really amuses me about the other night? Andrew. You know, my friend Andrew. Well, he actually gave me an opening. All I had to do was take the first step. Andrew actually called their bluff. All I had to do was charge in there behind him, but I couldn't. All I could do was follow Sunny out the door."

"Again, when did they stop?" Perez asked, then fired his pipe.

"About a week ago," David replied sullenly. "Does this mean we stop, or could they start again?"

"The night of the social, had they stopped prior to that night?"

"No. I don't exactly remember the date they stopped, but I don't remember having any nightmares after that night. Why is that night important? Is it because I've been rambling on about what happened? Listen, how could what happened at the party cause me to stop having the dreams? That just doesn't make any sense. Besides, why are you so concerned about the dreams stopping? Isn't that why I came to you, to find out why I've been having the dreams and stop them? Look, maybe you've been successful. You ought to be happy."

David gave Perez a quizzical look. "You're not, are you? You're disappointed because they've stopped. I'll be damned!" David let out a laugh. "You want me to start dreaming again."

"Nonsense. Of course I'm glad you're having some peace of mind," Perez said, somewhat agitated.

"No, my dreams interested you. You saw something in them, didn't you? Something that had nothing to do with my therapy. What was it? Go on, tell me. What fascinated you about my dreams?"

The Psychical apparatus, the concept that the mind has three parts – the ego, the id, and the super ego, was first proffered to the world by Freud. For several decades, the theory of the apparatus had been the gospel of the psychiatric profession, but along with other sacred cows, it had been attacked and vilified during the mindless purges of the sixties and early seventies. "Touchy feelies" were in. Members of the Me generation could do no wrong in their total denial of personal responsibility for their lives. Exposing one's genitals in Big Sur was more meaningful and more uplifting than exposing one's innermost secrets on an analyst's couch. *In a Gadda da Vida, Honey!* If David had come to him then, Perez would have told him to get in touch with himself, his surroundings, even change his diet. He might have even given him a mantra and started him on the road to enlightenment. But the age of adolescence eventually burned itself out like its rock stars, and with it went the touchy feelies. A new age of reason dawned in its vacuum. Freud, after all, had been right. No one and no thing can escape the past. The past has to be dealt with sooner or later. Perez had repented and accepted the theology of the apparatus. The key to David's future lay in understanding his past. And David's past was locked away in the deep recesses of his unconscious self. The dreams had stopped. Was this the quiet before the storm? Would the repressed David who had not so long ago killed without remorse, take up the sword again?

David was right. He *was* fascinated by the dreams. They portrayed a telling truth. Outwardly, David's ego was fragile, insure, even petulant. But Perez believed David was, in reality, a time bomb that, for some reason he had yet to figure out, had failed to explode. So Perez had to be careful. David had to be handled gently. Ever so carefully, Perez would have to dismantle him piece by piece, or someone might die in the explosion, and he feared who that someone might be. No, David wasn't yet ready to be confronted with the truth about himself.

"Tell me about Sunny," Perez said.

"If we were in Germany and you asked me to tell you about something, I would think you were asking about its size, its shape, color, and so on. Want to know what she looks like with her clothes off? No. Then I guess we'll do it American. Let's see. You want to know what I think of her as a person. Right?"

"How about when you met?"

"When we met? Well, what if I told you I wasn't the one who brought us together, that it was she who first fell in love with me," David said proudly, half grinning. "So, priest, what do you think about that?"

Perez just puffed on his pipe as if he hadn't heard David.

"You don't believe that, do you? I wouldn't believe it either." David got up and put his hands in his pockets. Looking out Perez's window, he began to speak softly. "You see, I'd given up on ever loving a woman the way other men do. Because of the way I was and the things I had done, I used women as a diversion, an escape. Surely Sunny had to have sensed that. When we first met, I desired her. I wanted to take her the way I had taken so many other women. But the more I tried, the more she resisted. Usually when that kind of thing happened – and it didn't happen often, I knew what I was looking for in a woman – I would just break off contact. And I tried that with her, really I did. But she persisted in seeing me. She said she loved me, that she didn't understand it herself, but she loved me."

"Did you believe her?"

"Not at first. I eventually allowed myself to believe it, after I overcame my fear of her."

"Why were you afraid of her?"

"Because if I hurt her, did something to her that I later couldn't live with . . ."

"What made her so different from the other women you'd known that you'd be so concerned for . . ."

"Jesus! Have you ever loved a woman? Before you became a nun, did you ever entertain the thought of what a woman could be like?" David was almost shouting.

Perez shifted uneasily in his chair. His thoughts drifted to Claire and how her body had felt against his. Smooth and silky, and hot.

He had met her during a forum on Middle Eastern terrorism sponsored by the university's Walsh School of Foreign Service. She was a wispy girl, honey blonde and intelligent. It had begun innocently enough. They had simply sat together during the lecture. When he looked back on the meeting, he unhappily concluded it had been mere chance, not divine predestination, that had brought them together, and that had made knowing her all the more painful.

He was a brave man. Anyone who had known him in Vietnam could attest to that. But the first time he was alone with Claire and looked deeply into her eyes and saw her fire, he trembled. For most of his adult life he had worshiped and loved an intangible, unseen deity whose touch he yearned for but had never felt. But the realization that loving another human being would be far more demanding than a passive God brought about in him insecurity he had never before experienced. Human beings were not as forgiving as God. They demanded more of each other and were judgmental. Their needs were sometimes emotional, defying all logic. He had feared having to learn a new way of dealing with life.

She worked at the Air and Space Museum and had received her post graduate degree in astronomy from Cornell. Even though she was intelligent and quite mature, she found herself devilishly excited by his not too indiscrete visits. From the very first, the thought of sleeping with a priest excited her in an almost death defying way. She thought childishly that it would be like making love to God. She envisioned their relationship as being like one of those in a quickie romance novel where the winsome wench brings the disillusioned man of God down to earth with a shot of thigh and a flash of tit. Only, after a while she came to understand he was not pursuing her because of any repressed sexual desire. And unlike the man of the cloth portrayed in the paperback novel who, after sipping the wine of passion, returned to the light refreshed and renewed in spirit, he was falling in love with her. She began to feel a guilt that was as overwhelming as it was unexpected. She forbade him to ever see her again.

She had asked him many times why he still wore the turned collar now that the ways of the world were as meaningful to him as being deep inside of her. He gave her every answer except the one she knew to be the truth: being a priest meant he didn't have to play by the rules. Even in 1982, the garments he wore evoked respect and awe. If he quit the Order, he would be just another Washington psychologist with office expenses, housing, subsistence, and income tax to pay. But wearing the cloth meant he could live for free in a comfortable place, eat good food, work in esteemed surroundings, and belong to an organization that provided security. Maslow would have understood. He was trying to become self-actualized, and he was almost there. All he needed was love.

"I'm sorry," David said sincerely. He bit his lip for a moment, then continued. "Look, there was, is, something about Sunny, a purity, a decency very few people possess. I was afraid of what loving me would do to her. I wanted to keep her away from me, keep her away from being . . ."

"Soiled?" Perez said quickly.

"Yes. All right."

"Is that why you were surprised to see her persist with your relationship?"

"No. It was because of her belief in God. I've never known anybody with a belief as strong as hers except . . ." *Jude*, he thought. "You're a priest. Don't you understand?"

"Understand?"

"I thought one of the tenants of Christian theology dictates that true believers turn their faces away from all that is evil."

"Something like that."

"Then why did Sunny marry me? Why didn't she just let me leave her when I wanted to? She knew I was an atheist, that I would never believe in her God, your God. Don't you see why her loving me just didn't make any sense? Sunny would never violate her God's laws for another human being, no matter how much she cared for him. And marrying me violated God's law."

"Maybe she thought she could convert you."

"She's never tried that."

"Look, David, Sunny's only human. No matter how much she believes in God, the fact remains that she is still a frail human being, subject to all the pressures and temptations that trap other human beings. You've put her on a pedestal, where men usually put the women they adore. Yes, I agree with you. Sunny is a remarkable woman. She's bright and beautiful. She possesses an admirable sense of morality and, as evidenced by her experiences in Argentina, she has great moral courage. But David, she's not better than you. You are worthy to have someone love you and to love. She married you because she loves you. It's as simple as that. You're a handsome man; some would even call you dashing. She found in you an irresistible attraction she couldn't overcome. All her life she had fought the military. You are a military man. Unconsciously, you became a surrogate for the Argentine military. You took the place of all she had hated. It was like she had no control over it and if she controlled you, subconsciously she could control her fear of the military, a fear she had had all her life. Face it David. Sunny isn't a god, nor is she a handmaiden of the Lord. She is just a woman driven by impulses normal to most human beings."

"Are you saying she married me out of fear?" David asked with a look of puzzlement.

"In a way, yes."

"And you discount what I've said, despite what you know about her and her love for God."

"I know she loves God. I'm not questioning that. I just don't want you to feel there was some divine design behind your marriage. If I'm going to be able to help you, I want you to be able to see what your problems are from the standpoint of reality."

"I would never ever think some divine design was behind our relationship. I might see it as happening for some other reason, but not in any mystic sense. But I have to say, I can't understand why you would scoff at the idea. You're a strange sort of sky-pilot."

Perez stood up and put down his pipe. Maybe it was time to drive to the heart of the beast. "I want to put you under hypnosis."

"Why?"

"Because maybe it'll help you."

"Not good enough."

Perez gave David a cold stare. "I want to put you under hypnosis. It will help you."

"How will it help me?"

"It will speed up the therapeutic process."

"Okay. I'll do just about anything to get this over."

"I want you to just sit back and relax," Perez said, adjusting his glasses.

"Aren't you going to have me stare at some swinging watch?" David asked with a smirk.

"This isn't Hollywood. Now, when I tell you to begin, I want you to look at me and start counting backwards from one hundred to one. While you are counting, you will find it will become boring and your mind will start to wander. Try as best as you can to concentrate on your counting. Try to free your thoughts from anything but the numbers. You may also find you are becoming tired. This is natural, so don't be alarmed. Just keep trying to count. One other thing. If I ask you a question, you may answer, but once you've finished, continue to count. Are you ready?"

"Yes, but what if I shut my eyes?"

"It won't matter. Begin."

"100 . . . 99 . . . 98 . . . 97." It *was* boring. Into the eighties, David's mind began to wander. *Sunny, Sunny, forgive me* . . . "81. . . 80 . . . 79," . . . David could sense Perez's presence, but strangely he was afraid to look into his eyes. Then, darkness . . . "71 . . .70," . . . darkness everywhere. Perez was right, counting backwards was damn boring, and it could make you really tired. "84 . . . 83 . . . 85 . . . 88." *What was she doing?* "69." *She was running, tripping, crawling along the ground, Sunny!* Of course, it came to him, he was asleep. He was having one of those nightmares where you are really awake but can't move. You are awake and wanting to move but you are still a part of the dream. *Come out of it!* "69 . . . 40." *I have to get . . . somebody to help me! . . . David!* The voice. *David!* The voice. It was warm and loving. He wanted to touch the voice. *Yes, I'm here.*

"David," Perez said softly.

"Yes, I'm here."

"Do you remember your nightmares?"

"Yes."

"Do you remember hurting Sunny?"

"Yes."

"Why did you hurt Sunny?"

"I don't know."

"Did someone tell you to hurt Sunny?"

"No."

"Isn't it true that someone talks to you in your dreams?"

"Yes, someone talks to me."

"Who?"

"I don't know."

"Is it Keaton?"

David didn't respond.

"Is it Keaton who talks to you?" Perez repeated.

"I don't know."

"Is it Keaton who talks to you?" Perez said again.

"I don't know."

"Yes, you do know. Is it Keaton? Think hard. Clear your thoughts. Keaton. You have called to him in your dreams. Remember. Remember. Is it Keaton? Keaton appears in your nightmares, doesn't he?"

"Yes, he lives in my dreams."

"Have you seen Keaton recently?"

"No, he died a long time ago."

"How did he die?"

David grimaced and clenched his fists.

"How did he . . ."

To his astonishment, before Perez could repeat the question David's eyes opened wide. His face became dark and contorted.

"David, you will wake up now!" Perez quickly commanded. "David . . ."

"I killed him!" David screamed.

"David, wake up!"

"I killed him! I killed him! I killed him!"

"David . . . David . . . David!"

Chapter 14

New Orleans, Louisiana

> Behold, I send a messenger,
> And he will prepare the way before me.
> Malachi 3:1

The week before, Mardi Gras had gratefully evaporated like some huge belch from a wino's stomach. Life in the French Quarter seemed to be returning to some semblance of normal, which meant the cuckoos would remain dormant until the first winds of spring blew the stench from the open gutters out to sea.

Bill Force, like all cops, hated Mardi Gras. Muggings, thefts, and assaults tripled as the annual onslaught of merrymakers descended on New Orleans like carnivorous locusts. And what they left in their wake was trash and money. Nor could Force understand why anyone would want to stay in the Quarter for more than a couple of days. He came unwrapped after spending just a night there. But in his heart of hearts, he really loved New Orleans. The Mississip', the Ponchatrain, and the Quarter. Even its smell evoked in him a sense of pride in being part of something unique and unequaled anywhere in the world, sort of like he used to feel when he was in Special Forces. As the patrol lieutenant on the night shift he commanded all of the uniformed officers in and around the Quarter. Other similar Lews commanded different sectors of greater New Orleans, but the Quarter was his domain. After eight at night, after the big boys at headquarters had left for home, Force ruled. Nobody did a damn thing unless he approved it. It was like being the god of the crazies. A shower had just ended. The clouds that had brought it were hanging lazily over the mouth of the Mississippi. There was a clear, dark blue sky in their place. A yellow bomber's moon, full and bright, hovered over the city like a well-fueled gas lantern. At some point, the nuts would be on full automatic.

Force was a huge man, six feet seven inches tall and every inch muscle. He could give a cold, bone chilling stare that quieted even the most ravenous gutter creature, but he was not given to quick temper. Instead, he let his adversaries vent and spew until he judged them vulnerable then, like lightning, he struck. And when he did strike, it was quick and bone crushing. He expected high standards from his men, standards they knew he also set for himself. And in a tight situation, they knew he would go with them the whole nine yards. Being a police officer meant more to Force than simply having a career. Wearing the star and crescent badge of the New Orleans Police Department was a way of recapturing lost honor.

He parked his light blue and white cruiser next to a police barricade sign at Bourbon and St. Louis. As he exited the vehicle, he turned off the car radio and switched to the radio attached to his belt. He called headquarters for a radio check and informed them of his location, or his 10-20 in the vernacular of the police radio. A few street vermin were slithering up from the puddles along the sidewalks, but for the most part the Quarter seemed quiet for 2:00 a.m. on a Thursday. Most of the jazz houses were winding down. It had been a slow night, and it cost too much to keep the waitresses on station. Even the flesh holes were clothing their people and sending them out to fend for themselves. The expensive restaurants had long since shut down for the night. An occasional car veered past the streets that were open to traffic. Except for a few stragglers, the Quarter was deserted.

He stopped in front of the Ramada Inn on St. Louis. It had once been a convent and was shaped like a square fort that took up one entire block. During the turn of the century, nuns had sunned themselves in its huge courtyard. Now a swimming pool provided a similar pleasure to less clad ladies of different mission and purpose. The main entrance was lit with four large gas torches that hung over the large doorway.

The first things Force noticed were that the door was slightly open and there was no doorman. Force knew an officer was just around the block on Bourbon, and he called him. But a sixth sense told him that to wait for the cavalry might cost the settlers their lives. He drew his service revolver and slowly opened the huge wooden door. Inside there were several steps that led to the foyer and the registration and office area. Quietly, with his weapon held at chest level, slightly drawn toward him, he slowly climbed the stairs.

At the top of the stairs and to the right was the restaurant. He could hear muffled voices coming from inside. He then turned his attention toward the registration desk on his left. Like a huge alley cat, he ambled over to the counter. A quick look over it and his worst suspicions were confirmed. Lying on the floor was a Latino man whose throat had been cut. Force bit his lip and chewed his fist and backed away. Behind the registration desk was the office. Slowly, he pushed back the door, and then quickly whirled around the corner. No one there. Unless the bandits were robbing each room, which was unlikely, they could only be in one other place. He quickly moved back to the top of the stairs and positioned himself where he could see inside the dining area.

With a sudden swoosh, the huge front door opened. A young officer, out of breath, came to a quick halt upon seeing Force's upheld hand with his finger to his lips. Force motioned for the officer to follow him into the dining area and indicated with a point where the danger was. There was no time to call anyone else, and following good procedure, they turned off their radios to keep the robbers from hearing the crackle of nighttime New Orleans police radio traffic.

There were two entrances into the kitchen area. The young officer positioned himself next to the entrance that led out of the restaurant, down the stairs and out into the street, while Force maneuvered himself next to the far entrance. Both entrances had swinging doors. Force could see the anxiety on the young officer's face. For a second, their eyes met and at that moment Force felt a familiar sensation, one he had felt many times before in the heat and confusion of a fight when brothers in arms took comfort in their shared fears, their shared danger. It comforted him. But the sanctity of the moment was shattered by the sharp report of gunfire from inside the kitchen. "Stay and be ready!"

he commanded the young officer as he slammed through the swinging door.

His camera eye instantly assessed the scene inside. Not more than ten feet from him was a young girl face down in a puddle of crimson blood. Standing over her naked body was a young male, readying his smoking revolver for another shot. Two other women, also naked, were kneeling in front of a larger man who was about to execute them in the same manner. The quickness of Force's entry had caught the killers by surprise. The executioner of the girl lying on the floor scarcely had time to raise his revolver before Force put a round in his shoulder and another in his face. The other killer bolted for the door where the young officer waited. Force fired, but he missed, and then headed after the man. Outside he heard two shots. As he burst through the door, he saw the young officer sprawled over a table, his service revolver lying at his feet. All he could think about was what they taught at the academy about lag time. Force headed down the stairs and out into the night.

His momentum carried him out the huge door onto the sidewalk where the burning torches made him an easy target. Parts of brick and dust hit him in the face as a bullet ricocheted off the old wall of the Ramada, followed by the sound of additional gunfire. He slammed against the concrete sidewalk and rolled over into the gutter. The crack had come from the other end of the street. Instinctively, he aimed his weapon in that direction just in time to see the shooter turn and flee in the direction of Jackson Square. Quickly, he lifted himself out of the dirty water and started after the shooter at a dead run.

Then it occurred to him that no one at Headquarters knew what was happening. He switched on his radio. "104, a 10-53 just occurred at the Ramada at St. Louis. One officer down, several victims present. Am in pursuit of one male black wearing a white T-shirt and blue jeans toward Jackson Square. Shots fired, officer needs assistance!"

Jackson Square was normally a dimly lit place, but the full moon had cast down a death pallor that draped the park and the St. Louis Cathedral like a white shroud. He was reminded of one of those movies about the Blitz of London where air raid sirens could be heard wailing across the city. Only now, it was the sound of the sirens from the police cruisers that were screaming toward his location from all over New Orleans. When a fellow cop was in trouble, all the stops were let out.

The courtyard in front of the cathedral, where during day magicians and other street entertainers fascinated the crowds of tourists, was made of solid stone. At night, except for an occasional bum, the courtyard was empty. He crept along the row of shops on Orleans until he reached Chatre then sprinted across the street until he reached Pirate, an alley that led past the cathedral into the courtyard. Pirate was covered by the shadow of the cathedral, and this allowed him to move quickly.

He stopped at the edge of the huge iron gates that protected the entrance of the church. Then his eye caught a speck of light near the entrance to the park, a flash of moonlight reflecting off the barrel of a gun. He leveled his weapon and fired three rounds. The sound was deafening. In the darkness, hundreds of pigeons took flight, making a staccato fluttering sound that reverberated off the walls of the old buildings that surrounded the square. He used the sound to cover his charge across the stone courtyard. Reaching the gate and the point where his rounds had hit, he hoped to find a body, but there was none.

"Shit!" he said under his breath. Then he spotted another reflection on the grass. It was moonlight reflecting off a wet surface. He bent down – blood. He smiled. He looked around and quickly surveyed the park. The statute of Andrew Jackson was framed in the gray light of several old spotlights. The suspect would not be near the statute.

Then he thought he heard a sound, something brushing up against the row of bushes near the far end of the square. Hunkered down, he headed in the direction of the sound. He decided he would use the statute for cover. If he ran straight for the statute, whoever might be on the other side would not be able to see him. Once behind the statute, he could get off a shot at the bushes. He reached the statute and crept down near its base. Slowly, he circumvented it until he reached a position just over Old Hickory's horse. He raised his head past the base ever so slightly to get a better view, and that was the last thing he remembered before the moon went black.

At 6:00 a.m., Force's head hurt. The Tylenol had helped some, but he had caught a hard blow. As he sat at his desk filling out the report he would have to file on the incident for the Chief, he couldn't make up his mind which hurt more, his head or his pride. It was his sector, and there were two dead civilians, one dead police officer, one dead suspect, and another suspect had gotten away. It had been a bad shift. No one seemed to be placing the blame on him, not yet anyway. Experience told him, however, that there would be a lot of questions he would have to answer. But he felt confident he would have the answers to all of them, except one: Why had the robber allowed him to live?

"Lieutenant." It was the desk sergeant.

"A man left this letter for you shortly after the shift started. I asked him if he wanted me to call you back to the station to read it, but he said it could wait 'til the shift change."

"Did he say who he was?"

"No. He was an older man, I'd say sixties at least, gray hair, but kinda tough looking. He didn't say anything else."

"Thank you," Force said. "I'll read it in a minute, soon as I've finished this report."

"Lieutenant," the sergeant said again.

"Yes." Force looked up at the sergeant.

"You did a good job. You saved those girls' lives."

Force didn't say anything. He just smiled at the sergeant and looked back at his report.

Once home, Force eased himself into his favorite chair. The clock on the wall told him it was 10:00 a.m. Normally, he would be fast asleep by now, but he was too keyed up about the shooting, and there was the nagging puzzlement of why he was still alive. In time, he would deal with the shooting, but the only way he would ever come to grips with the fact that four people had just died and he had not joined them would be when he confronted face to face the robber he had wounded.

The letter. He had almost forgotten. He reached into his back pocket and pulled the crumpled plain white envelope out and opened it. The message was written in clear handwritten script:

I will come back to you soon
that the covenant will be honored.

Force let the paper fall from his hand and slumped back in the chair. Closing his eyes, he saw the flames coming toward him once again.

Chapter 15

Buenos Aires, Argentina
April 18, 1982

It was a Sunday morning, overcast with rain expected. Captain Alvarez had caught a slight cold and had sequestered himself in his apartment. Spread across his bed were the files of several leftist agitators he needed to review before he approved the seizure and detention of the suspects. Since the capture of the Islands, dissident unrest had increased. Intelligence reports indicated that several communist cells intended to take advantage of the nation's preoccupation with the British menace to try to create a state of anarchy in the countryside. Of course, that would not be allowed to happen. He studied each file separately. He reviewed the charges made against each suspect for a legal nexus and then evaluated the folder's data for further intelligence activities. Each file contained a picture of the accused. Their faces were so innocent looking, so vulnerable. He was especially fascinated by the young women. Why? How had they come to be mixed up in these crimes? Had some been in love? Had they been misguided by their professors? If so, that was being corrected. Or were they just stupid females who had been taken in by men who thought with their dicks? Such a waste of young lives.

Records were important. Future generations would want to know how the country had protected itself during this time of peril. But the records of these unfortunates would never end up in the military war archives along with battle plans and dispatches. This was a *dirty war* Alvarez fought. He received no accolades for his work, no recognition. There would be no record of the acts he carried out in the name of Argentina. Likewise, there would be no record of the fate of Argentina's enemies. Like a body floating in the River Platta, they would simply vanish out of sight.

As awful as he felt, Alvarez continued to work for time was of the essence. He had been given special instructions by the generals to complete all of his security assessments as soon as possible and take the necessary action. For today, the Honorable American Secretary of State Alexander Haig would meet with the *junta*. It was known through Washington sources that Haig would deliver to them an ultimatum from the Reagan administration to withdraw from the Malvinas or go it alone. American public opinion was in favor of the British cause by a wide margin, which meant America was now a potential enemy. This fact made Alvarez's job all the more important and more difficult, for many Americans lived and worked in Argentina and many more visited the country every year. Each was a potential source of intelligence for the Americans and, in turn, the British. He would have to quickly identify potential threats and neutralize them. But he also knew that even though he had to act with haste, he had to be careful not to make a mistake that might bring America into the conflict.

He was proud of the counter-intelligence apparatus he had established. Prior to 1968, he had been assigned to naval intelligence with the mission of counter-intelligence against Chile and Peru. But in 1968, terrorist activities against the civilian government increased from three a year to three hundred. In a secret report to the government he warned that unless action was taken against the left wing organizations operating in the country, a state of anarchy would soon exist. But the civilian government was too timid to act. Assassinations, bombings, and kidnappings became so commonplace that the papers no longer gave their occurrences front page coverage. By the end of the year, the people were marching in the streets screaming for order to be restored. A right wing faction of ex-army officers heard their cries and acted.

With the backing of the military, they overthrew the government in power.

The new government had promised to end the anarchy in the streets and restore order to everyday Argentine life. But shortly after the government made this promise, terrorist activities started up again. The old men who made up the new government soon realized that the renewed terrorism had to be dealt with quickly and decisively or they too would be replaced. Alvarez's report, which detailed the establishment of a counter-terrorist organization made up of loyal armed services officers who would follow orders without remorse or question and rid Argentina of the vermin who ate at her honor, was welcomed with enthusiasm. He was ordered to set up the counter-terrorist unit and to command it. He would report directly to the president and to no one else, and was given complete authority to save Argentina from the communists. This he was pleased and happy to do.

During the first year of the unit's activation, terrorist activity had fallen off sixty percent. His men, dressed in civilian garb and driving ominous green sedans, had literally scooped suspects off the streets. The civilian government couldn't have been more pleased. But the Roman Catholic Church was not. The Church fought the government from the pulpit. Mass became, in essence, a human rights happening throughout the country. Finally, the government capitulated and declared that the war against terrorism had been won. The counter-terrorist unit had been disbanded, and Alvarez had been transferred to desk duty at the Naval Academy, where he had languished in constant depression and preoccupation with thoughts of suicide.

But a force outside of Argentina would eventually determine Alvarez's fate. From his exile, dictator Juan Peron had watched events take place in the country he had ruled for twenty years. Peron still lusted for power, and the lesson of what anarchy could do to a democracy had not been lost on him. If terrorism could bring his sleeping country to the point where its people were afraid to go out of their homes, then terrorism might bring a cry for a government that could make the streets safe again. The present government had lied to the people because it would rather face the wrath of the left than the wrath of God. However, Peron had no such inhibitions. From his villa in Mexico, he had plotted and woven intricate webs of intrigue and murder. He had financed terrorist groups from the right as well as from the left, and the end result had been a nightmare of terror that had left the streets of Argentina blood red. In 1973, Peron had returned to Buenos Aires, the champion of law and order. He had lived only one year as dictator and had died, leaving his second wife, Isabel, to rule in his stead for two years. But she had been so inept that the country had been thrown into another dark night of terror and anarchy.

Finally, all sides had had enough. The military, in a lightning coup, had taken control of the government and had been immediately hailed as the saviors of the country by the people, the press, and even the Church.

But like all dictators, they were insecure and paranoid. The *junta*, as they became known, were determined to rid the country of left wing terrorists and maintain the adoration of the people. Alvarez and his unit had been resurrected. The unit had been designated the *El Grupo Proteger*, the protection group. It had been given complete authority over all domestic security. Inherent in its mandate was the authority to arrest, imprison, and execute the enemies of Argentina without formal charges and without trial. Alvarez had been given the responsibility not only of recruiting its personnel but also of establishing its headquarters and detention facility. For his headquarters he had chosen the Naval Academy located next to the Platta River on the outskirts of Buenos Aires, an innocent looking structure that resembled a quite, elegant school building. And for his instrument of terror, he had chosen a trio of turn-of-the-century marbled mansions built long ago on the island of *Los Estados*, literally at the end of the earth, by cattle barons as places of refuge and escape from the constant turmoil of Argentine coups.

He had learned from his previous experience that secrecy has its virtues. No longer did his men pull the enemies of the state from their beds in the middle of the night causing outcry and condemnation. His men now used a more subtle approach. Everyone had a favorite pastime that occupied some part of their week. It might be a soccer game, or a restaurant frequented, or a visit to a part of the city that refreshed the spirit. A good intelligence man knew his prey's weaker, unguarded moments, and when that moment arrived he tore his prey from the arms of security and ripped him apart. All over Argentina, men and women left their homes on innocent journeys only to never be heard from again. Everyone knew of someone who had just unexpectedly disappeared, vanished off the face of the earth. But where, no one knew. When a family complained to the local police that their loved one was missing, the beauty of the operation really blossomed: the police had no knowledge of the group's action, and therefore actually investigated the complaint. Which in turn, because of their ineptitude, actually helped cover up the actions of the group. So the fate of the *Disappeared Ones*, as they were called by the press, remained a mystery. Many people wondered if the group had been reactivated, but no one knew for sure.

He took a sip of wine. *This is interesting*, he thought, as he held the picture of a woman in his hand. *Yes, this is most interesting. But she's no threat now. She's not even here. But . . .* He searched the information in the folder. *Yes, of course.* He put the folder down and rubbed his chin contemplatively. What did she know now that she lived, as Che had said, in the heart of the beast? Maybe there was a way to find out. Could it be done? Yes, of course it could.

He searched the folder further until he found what he was looking for. A name.

Chapter 16

Who is this who darkens counsel
By words without knowledge?
Now prepare yourself like a man;
I will question you,
And you will answer Me.

                    Job 38:2-4

Nashville, Tennessee
March 19, 1982

Pratt Goldman, PhD, took a deep breath, stretched his muscles against his thin frame, and flopped down into an oversized leather chair. Lazily, he propped his black polished Johnson & Murphys up on his large cherry wood desk. With a flick of his finger, he unbuttoned the neck of his white Gant oxford cloth shirt. His silk blue and white Yves St. Laurent tie was open at the collar. The top half of his gray Hart, Shaffner & Marx suit was thrown rather carelessly over the back of an empty chair next to his desk. The legs of his pants had fallen back from his shoes just enough to expose his Ralph Lauren argyle socks – gray, red, and blue checks. He ran his hands through his graying, dark hair and interlocked them behind his neck. His wedding ring and his college ring, with its Phi Beta Kappa engraving, gave a click as they met.

A flick of sunlight caught his attention as it fell between several fast-moving clouds that filled the last sky of winter. Tomorrow brought the advent of spring. He slowly turned his youthful appearing, thin face toward the large curtainless window that comprised one wall of this spacious office. The sunlight was a welcome sight for the gray winter had stayed unusually long. There was another quick darkening and then a shot of sunlight again. This time, it hit his face at an angle that illuminated an ugly scar that ran for four inches across his forehead. The students who filled his office for the afternoon's Socratic Method session were for a moment startled at the sight of their professor's disfigurement. Most of the time the scar was concealed behind a flop of hair that fell across his face. Must have been a car accident, some of them thought. Others were reminded of the dueling scars of pre-war German youths.

Ever alert, Pratt sensed a momentary change in the mood of the students that caused him to stiffen. "Is there something below?" he asked pointedly.

A pretty raven-haired child flowed over to the window. Below, her fellows were moving purposefully from class to class. Many still wore the down parks that were "in" this year. The winter wind still had a bite to it. "No, Dr. Goldman, just class change," she purred.

But for a moment she had a feeling of being watched, a presence below, a presence that was strong and alluring, yet not threatening.

"Hmm. Well, let's begin," Pratt said.

Vanderbilt University had procured for itself a large part of western Nashville and considered itself a bastion of enlightenment in a sea of local yokels desensitized to all that was intelligent by the shrieking opium of country music. Vanderbilt isolated itself from Nashville in the same way Berlin isolated itself from the affairs of the Federal Republic. Elitist thinking and attitudes hung about the coiffured grounds of the tranquil campus like tear gas. Pratt, like the rest of the faculty and student body, never ventured too far away from the shadow of Kirkland Hall. He lived just off campus with his wife of ten years and his two small daughters. He had taught at Vanderbilt for almost four years. Next semester, he would be up for tenure. Tenure would mean he could stay. Tenure would mean some stability in his life. But tenure for philosophy professors was as rare as the Silver Star he had nailed to his wall.

The raven-haired young woman floated down to the floor and leaned against a bookcase. Her companion sat down next to her and gave her his hand, which was accepted. Still, she felt the presence. It was just outside the window. Below.

"Philosophy is religion," Pratt said, enthusiastically laying the question before them. It was their cue. They would be required to develop a dialogue centered around the statement.

"Religion is philosophy," a flaxen-haired youth said from his perch atop a table.

"Excellent. Now expound."

"A philosophy is a way of thinking based upon assumptions that are unprovable. Religion is unprovable."

"Is religion unprovable, or is the existence of the central core of any religion, the existence of God, unprovable?" queried the raven's companion.

"God? It is obvious that one can prove that religion exists. A simple drive down any town's street proves the existence of religion," answered the raven. As she spoke, she felt sudden warmth, an almost tingling sensation flow from her skin. She looked to her companion for explanation, but he seemed unaware of her experience.

"Then God is philosophy?" Pratt asked.

"Before we can make that statement, you must prove that God does not exist," the raven said. "For if God does exist, his way of thinking is not philosophy, but law. The existence of God would eliminate the possibility of one philosophizing his laws, for to do so would be to go against God. Likewise, those who would make philosophy their God would be committing a mortal sin."

"But proving the existence of God is impossible," the table percher said. "So what you say is irrelevant, which supports the view that religion is merely a way of viewing life based upon unprovable presumptions. A philosophy."

"And there are a myriad of these religious philosophies encompassing the entire globe. They have divided nations and families and have wreaked havoc upon man from the earliest times," the raven's companion interrupted loudly.

The raven shot him a disapproving look.

"Don't stray from the subject," Pratt said, raising his voice. "We are not debating the effect of religion on the life of man. We are exploring two divergent assumptions: whether religion is a truism or a fallacy."

"I don't agree," the raven said pointedly. "If we are to understand the true nature of any man's philosophy of life, we must know his feelings about the existence of God, for men who believe in God see the world and their place in it in ways much different from unbelievers."

Outside, the wind rubbed its hands across the windowpane. The raven turned her head toward the sound and smiled.

"Lenin once said that religion is the opiate of the masses, and he was right. People who believe in God use religion like a crutch. If a person believes an unseen force controls the universe, then he can assume he has no real control over his own life, which can be very convenient in that it relieves a person of all personal responsibility for what happens to him. It's sort of like the ultimate welfare state," the percher said, obviously proud of his own wit.

"Cosmic welfare, far out!" chimed in the companion, grinning at the raven, hoping to regain favor.

Pratt raised his hand as if to signal that Socrates would have been displeased. "Religion – the existence of God, has always troubled the great thinkers of the world," Pratt said with a tone of authority, sitting up in his chair. "Those who believe in the existence of a living God see him as being unimaginable, yet at the same time they believe him capable of controlling all that is imaginable in the universe. It is quite a contradiction, one that is at the very heart of our debate. It is a contradiction to believe in an all powerful deity who is responsible for the very creation of the universe, the first cause, the ruler of all, and at the same time to see him as a personal God who lives in each man's heart guiding his every action. The belief in God as the first cause, the great scientist, is philosophy. The belief that God speaks to man and dictates his every action is theology. Philosophy and theology are not the same. The former is the basis for reasoning the order of nature. The latter is the basis for religion."

"Are you saying it's not whether one believes in God, but how one views God's relationship to man that's important?" the raven asked, a look of incredulity on her face.

"Yes. How does that make you feel?" Pratt asked, folding his hands behind his neck, his eyes boring into the raven.

"It makes me feel empty. What you're saying is, you can accept the universe was created by something, a god by any other name, but this god is nothing more than a cold hearted orb. That this god does not care for the life he created, does not share kinship with us, does not need love or worship, and has given us no guidance on how to conduct our daily affairs. He just created the universe and all the life in it then left it alone. You're saying you can accept the fact God created the planets, the stars, the thousand wonders of the vast void around us with such scientific attention to detail, such minute care, but is incapable of caring for each one of us personally, that we're alone in this vast universe, left to our own devices to live and die and never know our creator, never meet him face to face. I can't accept that."

"But why can't you accept that?" Pratt asked with a half smile.

"Because if mere existence is all we have, then life is without hope."

The other students gave the raven surprised looks. They had never heard her speak in this way.

"Nonsense. Life always has hope," the percher said tersely.

"If all you have to look forward to is death, it doesn't," replied the raven, giving the percher a resolute look.

"Is it the finality of death that makes you afraid?" Pratt asked, looking for a hint of reluctance.

"I'm not afraid of death because I know it's not final," the raven said. "It's not fear you hear in my words, but unwillingness. I cannot accept that the universe created itself. I cannot accept that whatever created it, God if you will, has simply abandoned his creations to their own futile devices. I cannot accept that God has not given man a set of laws to abide by."

"And how has he done this? Through the prophets? Through The Buddha, Jesus, or some obscure writings left to emotional and unintelligent interpretation by every religious zealot who envisions himself as having the true meaning of his God's divine will for man?" the percher said, his face flushed with emotion.

"God speaks to men through their hearts. Even if there were no writings or words from prophets, God's will would still be known through simple feelings. When a man does something that's wrong, he needs no law to tell him he has committed something that's wrong.

He feels in his heart the wrongness of his act. Where do you think that feeling of the heart comes from? It comes from God himself," the raven responded.

"No, it comes from *The Force*," the raven's companion said cynically with a laugh.

"Quiet!" Pratt said. "We speak in intelligent terms here. If you can't honor that, then leave."

The companion was startled by Pratt's rebuke.

The raven continued. "But, Dr. Goldman, I do agree with you that man has taken the wonder of God and created theologies which have perverted his simple truths and his divine wisdom. Man has come to worship theology instead of God, evil theologies that have separated men instead of bringing them together. If God were in this very room, he would tell you that theology is the philosophy of Satan and religion is its byproduct."

"Satan! Ah, there's another creature we should discuss. If there is a God, then there must be a Satan, true?" Pratt surprised himself at how quickly he had begun to attack her statements.

"Yes, I agree. Satan lives."

"You are a Roman Catholic, or a Protestant maybe?" he asked, leaning toward her, his face aimed at her like a rifle.

"I don't attend church. I worship the Lord in the secrecy of my heart and thoughts."

"Well, do you claim you have a special relationship with the Creator?"

"No. I have the same relationship with Him all men have."

"And what is that?"

"Faith."

"That's my point. On what have you based your faith? There must be some body of knowledge that has enabled you to have a special insight into the nature of the Creator that others do not have."

"I only know what I feel."

"And that is . . ."

"Dr. Goldman, what are you doing?" The raven startled Pratt with the sharp tone of her voice.

God, what's happening, he thought. *What am I doing?*

As he stared at the tiny creature curled up on the floor, her image suddenly began to change. A misty essence began to envelope the office, clouding his sight. All at once, he was hot and wet with perspiration. Then he felt something in his hand. He looked down. *Damn.* He was holding a knife. In the next instant, he found himself standing over the girl. A look of stark terror was on her face. Blood ran slowly down her leg from a gaping cut. *Did I do that?* he asked himself. *Yes, and now I must finish it.* He stooped down and grabbed her hair. Her head fell back, exposing her smooth neck. He put the sharp blade against her throat and slowly started to cut the skin. But as her blood started to trickle from her neck, he heard a sharp rap from behind. Instinctively, he swirled in the direction of the sound. The rapping began again. He let the girl's head go and she fell away like a lifeless doll.

"*Shall I?*" a voice muffled and distant asked.

"*Shall I?*" the voice asked again.

Slowly an eerie yellow light began to brighten the room. The mist seemed to evaporate and the dead girl at his feet was once again the raven. She was staring him with a look of wonderment.

"Dr. Goldman, are you all right? Shall I open the door?" asked the percher.

Pratt fell back in his chair and gave consent with a wave of his hand. The percher opened the door. Pratt slowly raised his head to see who it was.

For a moment, he could not speak. He knew he was all right now. The homicidal ideation had left him and he had regained his reason. And yet, what he saw in the doorway couldn't be real either. He looked around. This was his office and these were his students. It was real. He did not take his eyes off the tall figure when he spoke. The tone of his voice was apprehensive. "Leave us, students."

The percher and the companion slowly got to their feet and sidestepped their way past the man in the doorway. Neither of them spoke as they left.

The raven slowly got to her feet and picked up her books. She gave Pratt a questioning glance then started to leave. But as she entered the doorway, her eyes met those of the man. In that instant, she felt an overpowering urge to touch this stranger. As if reading her thoughts, the stranger put his hand on her shoulder. A warm feeling, invigorating and powerful seemed to flow through her body with his touch. She wanted to smile, but strangely she found she could no longer look him in the eyes. It was as if she knew she was in the presence of something wonderfully powerful. But there was something strangely familiar about this man, as if she had been in his presence before. She lowered her head and quietly left.

"Do you still call yourself a son of Abraham?" asked the old man in a powerful voice.

"What do you want, Keaton?"

Chapter 17

> Those who war against you
> Shall be as nothing,
> As a nonexistent thing.
> For I, the Lord your God,
> will hold your right hand,
> Saying to you, "Fear not,
> I will help you."
>
> Isaiah 41:12-13

Alexandria, Virginia

"I wish I could talk you out of this," David said. The frustration he felt was evident in the tone of his voice.

Sunny stopped folding her clothes and put her arms around him. "David, they are my parents. I must go to them and do what I can." She knew what he was experiencing – a feeling of helplessness that was the result of his years of guilt. "I know you can't go with me. You're an American officer. With this war, it would be impossible for you to go to Argentina."

"Why not wait a few days? Maybe they're just being questioned and will be released in a few days."

"David, I know the methods of the secret police. If they think no one will protest the taking of my parents, then they will jail them indefinitely. They will become lost. No, I must go at once and protest. I am an American citizen now, and the wife of an American Army officer. My protest will carry weight. Nothing will happen to me."

David reluctantly sat down on the bed.

"And besides," Sunny continued, "Jorge and Rita are accompanying me. Their family ties with the *junta* will be security enough."

The doorbell rang and David got up and opened the door. Jorge and Rita gave him an icy smile as they pushed past him and joined Sunny. David could hear Jorge and Rita saying something to Sunny, but it was in Spanish.

"Jorge, do you think this is a wise thing for her to do?" David asked, leaning against the bedroom wall.

"I think she must go to Argentina. To do nothing would be to abandon her mother and father. You cannot expect her to do that," Jorge said.

"No, she has a moral obligation to help them, I think" Rita said, adjusting her glasses. "Yes, you must understand that though. Yes?"

"But both of you know what kind of record she has with the police. What's to prevent them from snatching her up when she arrives at the airport in Buenos Aires?" David asked.

"There are two things to prevent such an action," Jorge said. "First, she is the wife of an American army officer and an American citizen. To seize her would cause an international incident, which is exactly what the *junta* do not need at this time. Second, I am not without influence in my country. As long as my wife and I travel with her and lodge her, she will be safe."

"David, Jorge is right," Sunny said, taking David by the hand. "I will be safe."

David lowered his head.

"I know you understand. They are my parents. I must try to help them."

"But what did they do?"

"It doesn't matter whether they did anything. The *junta* do not need a reason to pick up and detain anyone. What does matter is now that it's happened, someone must come to their rescue. And I am the only person they have."

"But there's a war going on there!"

"I know war, David. I have been at war with the *junta* for many years. This ill-conceived venture in the Malvinas will preoccupy the military. They will not have time for two old people and their daughter. In many ways, if this had to happen, it could not have happened at a better time."

"There are things that you do not know," Jorge said to David. "Trust us to know Argentina and its politics better than you. Your wife has courage. Respect that and don't make her trip any more difficult than it already is."

"Yes, your whining like a baby doesn't make her task any more the easier, I think," Rita said sarcastically.

David's face became flushed. "Look," he said angrily.

But Sunny stepped in between him and Jorge and Rita. "Please, this is my home and David is my husband. Friendship aside, I will not allow you to show him such disrespect." Her voice was quivering with emotion.

"I apologize for myself and for my wife," Jorge said, somewhat insincerely. "This is a difficult time, you understand."

David would not look at either one of them.

"Well, Sonia, we must also prepare for the trip. We will meet you at Dulles in the morning," Jorge said, taking Rita by the arm.

"Jorge," Sunny said, touching him, "thank you."

Then Jorge and Rita smiled and left without saying a word to David.

It was one of those rare, placid spring nights. The air was crisp and peaceful. Overhead, a meadow of brilliant twinkling stars stretched across a clear cerulean heaven. It was as if God was telling man all was well. David and Sunny leaned against the sill of their apartment's bay window, concealed by the darkness around them. Below, past the dark waters of the Potomac, the lights of Washington broke the serenity of the night. And out farther, toward the sea, they could make out the dim lights of Annapolis. From their perch, they could see far away, farther than they had ever been able to see before. But what they longed to see most was beyond their power.

"Wonder if the people in Buenos Aires are seeing these same stars?" Sunny asked introspectively.

Even in the darkness, David could see the beauty of her simmering hair as it fell protectively around the rise and fall of her breasts. Her naked skin radiated the starlight into a silky smooth cloak that outlined the curvatures of her body. Her eyes did not turn to David but seemed to be searching for something far away in the distance.

"Are you sorry you married me?" David asked.

Sunny turned to him, startled. "David?"

"I feel like I've let you down. I don't mean the nightmares. Other ways."

"What is happening to us now started long ago before we met. I don't blame you for that. The important thing is that we are facing it together."

"When you married me, you weren't in love with me, were you?"

"I love you now. That's what really matters."

"I could sense it then, but I was so desperate for your love it didn't matter. I guess I thought you would learn to love me."

"David, why are you saying these things? You've no reason to doubt my love for you."

"I'm sorry. I'm just depressed because you're leaving. I know you love me now. I guess I'm afraid of losing you."

"No, that will never happen."

"Sunny . . ."

"No." Sunny reached up and took his hand, and together they became one as they lay back on the bed. David's lips met hers as he entered her. Her body became part of his as he took her in his arms and thrust himself deep inside of her. He kissed her face and neck, then the nipples of her breasts. "David!" she cried, her head turning from side to side as he penetrated her again and again and again. She ran her tongue over his face, lips, and neck. Her body burned with a wet heat that made her feel faint. She pulsated with his every motion, matching his movements, savoring the pleasure. *Why do I have to do this?* she cried to herself. *Why must I leave him?* His thrusts into the deep recesses of her belly were coming faster and faster until she felt a wall of electricity begin to build up in her stomach. *David, my love, don't let me leave. Stop me. Tell me I can't go.* "David!" she screamed as the dam in her burst, causing her to jerk so hard David could hardly hold her.

How long have we been asleep? David wondered as he awoke. He looked at the clock. Four in the morning. Sunny felt him move and in protest snuggled even closer.

"You awake?" he asked quietly.

"Yes, but I don't want to be," she replied lazily. "What time is it?"

"It's not time yet."

"I don't want to go back to sleep," she said, sliding away from him and out from under the sheets. "I can sleep on the plane," she said with a tone of sad reluctance in her voice.

He watched her disappear into the kitchen. He heard her ask him if he wanted coffee. He heard himself reply yes. But his mind had taken him back to their first encounter. It had been innocent, quite accidental. Afterward, he had mused their meeting and falling in love had been happenstance. He had even laughed at her notion that they had been predestined to marry. But now he let himself wonder if perhaps she might have been right. Had they been brought together for a purpose? And if so, to what purpose? Better still, for whose purpose? He threw back his head and shut his eyes. When they returned to the window sill, daylight was still a couple of hours away. The stars were still there but had wandered across the heavens as the night passed.

Sunny reached out to David. "I want you to know something. I was in love with you when we married. What you sensed was only my confusion about loving you. I could not understand how it had happened so fast, but now I do. Now I understand it all. You were once a man after God's own heart. And even though you have abandoned Him, He has never left you, not for an instant. A father doesn't abandon a child he loves. God wanted me to love you. He has allowed me to become a part of His plans for you, and that makes me proud. It makes me feel important. David, I know you can't understand why I must go to my parents. But know this – I can no more abandon them in their time of peril than you would abandon me."

He turned away from her pleading eyes and stared out into the evaporating darkness. He wanted to tell her she was being foolish. He wanted to tell her the fears he had about her leaving. He wanted to tell her he was angry – angry at her for leaving him and angry at himself for not stopping her and for being so weak. But he said nothing. He just let her go.

Chapter 18

Moreover I saw under the sun:
In the place of judgment,
Wickedness was there;
And in the place of righteousness,
Inequity was there.

I said in my heart,
"God shall judge the righteous and the wicked,
For there shall be a time there for every purpose and for every work."
Ecclesiastes 3:16-17

Andrew fired up a Black Jack. "You know," he said between puffs, "it takes a good eight hours to get there."

David threw back a shot of Andrew's Jack Daniels. It had a mellow burn to it that caused him to wince. "I know. But she should have called early this morning," he said darkly. It was becoming dark outside. He walked over to the window. "We moved in here for the view, you know." He strained his eyes, hoping to see past the clouds that had formed in the distance.

"Look, I'll go out and get some food," Andrew said. He knew what David was thinking, and he was beginning to have the same fears.

"I'm not hungry," David said, turning to the phone. Since well before midnight he had been pacing all over the apartment, but he had never taken his eyes off the phone for very long. It was as if he and the phone were attached by an unseen umbilical cord. It had become the focal point of the apartment. His hopes rested on its every possibility. At times, he found himself marveling at how this little piece of plastic and wire could connect him in an instant with the woman he loved a world away. If only it would ring.

"I used to have the same feelings," Andrew said, not looking at David. "Just after I landed I would run up to the flight operations room and check on the rest of the wing. It never failed. Every mission, there would be one or two who would still be unaccounted for when I got there. The waiting's the hardest part."

"I should never have let her go," David said introspectively.

"Think you could have stopped her?"

"Maybe I should have tried at least."

"You didn't?"

"No, not really."

Andrew winced and put the cigar between his teeth. "Shit, David!"

"Andrew, don't," David said, sitting down the glass of whiskey. Thunder began to sound far away in the night. Another big one was brewing out to sea. "I couldn't have stopped her and you know it. You know her as well as I do."

"You're right. She doesn't think like us."

David smiled. Andrew knew Sunny well. And even though he would leaving for the fleet soon, something deep inside told him that he and Sunny would always be close to Andrew.

It was midnight. The witching hour, David used to call it when he was a kid. Andrew had left earlier after extracting a promise from David that he would phone him, no matter what the time, when Sunny called. It was raining. Water made little streams across the window glass. David sat in a chair in the dark apartment gazing out the window. Intermittently, a flicker of lightning seared through the storm like a ghostly finger, illuminating his face in the window. And each time he saw his image, he knew he was getting older.

As the hours grew long and he drifted from consciousness to sleep and back, he was bothered by one singular, disturbing thought: who was Sunny? Who was this woman he had married? A woman he loved so passionately, yet a woman with whom he had so little in common. It was as if at times she was two different people. There was the woman in bed who made love without restraint, who satisfied his every desire like no woman he had ever known before. Then there was the woman whose love for her unseen God was so fierce she would readily give up her life for Him. But was she really two different people, or was she a woman whose capacity to love was so great she could give her body and soul unselfishly to the point of indifference to her own well being? He did not know. All he knew was that when he was inside of her, he felt whole, complete, and unafraid. The burning desire he had to be a part of her life, to smother her with affection, to be loved by her, was so intense it controlled his every thought. No, he may never know why she had chosen him to share her life.

But what had dawned on him in these dark waking hours was the realization and acceptance of the fact that what he felt for her that was much stronger than love. What he also felt for her was a feeling he had had only a few times in his life. It was a feeling that was humbling, yet at the same time reassuring. It was respect. For Sunny possessed all of the characteristics of a leader. Had Keaton and team known her, they would have followed her anywhere. Andrew knew this. And so did General Knott. Sunny was not ordinary. She stood for something. Something all men desire.

He was asleep, yet he could feel Sunny's presence.

Sunny was near, so close he would only have to reach out to touch her. But standing between them was another presence, an angry creature filled with venomous hate. He could sense its lust for her.

"Sunny!" he screamed.

She turned to him but shook her head, telling him not to come near.

He tried to lift himself up, but each time he reached for her it was not his but the scaly, thorny arm of the creature that nearly touched her. She screamed, a terrifying scream that sent the creature writhing with delight.

"You must not come to me, not yet. You are not ready to come to me," Sunny cried.

He turned to the creature then back to her. "Now I understand. It can only get to you through me."

Angrily, the creature turned toward him and exposed its hideous face. He froze with fear.

"David, go to her," the creature hissed.

He turned to Sunny, but she motioned for him to go away.

"David. You must go to her," the creature growled. "You must."

Then it began to scamper around him like a dog, barking and growling. It smelled of everything that was putrid and decaying, a smell made him feel sick. Suddenly, the creature stopped. It cringed and began to howl, a shrieking, fearful cry that pierced his ears. Not far in the misty distance he could see what had terrified it. There stood Sunny. She was alone, yet he could sense she was not afraid. A light emanated from all around her – a warm light, alluring and powerful. And he was drawn to it. Then he began to understand. The creature was afraid of Sunny; for all its power, it was terrified of her.

He heard a soft ringing. It sounded like a church bell, the very church bell that had once called him to worship as a boy. *Mother. If only he could see her again. Mother.* The ringing became louder and louder. The creature turned in the direction of the bell, startled by the sound. It cringed with each tone, and he could see that it was terrified of the sound. Slowly, the bell's tone changed from a chime to a series of shrill notes.

He jerked up out of the chair, breathing hard and his body wet with perspiration. Strangely, he felt sick to his stomach. The phone rang again and again. Quickly, he picked up the receiver. The crackling of thousands of miles of electricity told him in an instant it was Sunny calling from Argentina.

"Sunny!" he cried, almost yelling.

"David." Her voice sounded different.

"Sunny?"

"No, David. How can I say this to you? They took her. They took her from us when we got off the plane. There was nothing we could do. You must believe me. There was nothing we could do."

"David – David!"

PART TWO

The Leader

The Prophet's Lament

Oh Lord, how long shall I cry,
And You will not hear?
Even cry out to You, "Violence!"
And You will not save.
Why do You show me iniquity,
And cause me to see trouble?
And plundering and violence
Are before me;
There is strife, and contention arises.
Therefore the law is powerless,
And justice never comes forth.
For the wicked surround the righteous;
Therefore perverse judgment proceeds.

The Lord's reply

"Look among the nations and watch –
Be utterly astounded.
For I will work a work in your days
Which you would not believe,
Though it were told you."
Habakkuk 1:1-6

Chapter 19

```
April 25, 1982
Grytviken, South Georgia Island
```

Late in the afternoon, the winds died down. While this had eased the misery of the combined force of SAS Royal Marines, and Special Boat Services troops who were moving rapidly across the rugged terrain, it had also taken away an effective cover for the noise they were making as they trudged over the rough rock strewn terrain. This worried their commander, an SAS officer. In the early hours before they landed, a fierce naval barrage had softened Argentine positions around their objective, the small fishing village of Grytviken. While this barrage had resulted in the deaths of quite a number of the Argentineans, it had also alerted them to the impending British attack. Now the dying of the winds lessened what chance of surprise they had left.

As the force of seventy-five weather beaten but highly motivated Britishers neared the outskirts of the village, they changed their formation from a long column to two groups. Their final coordination line would be the rock wall that comprised the southern boundary of Grytviken. At the FCL, they would halt, make any tactical adjustments, receive any last minute instructions from their commander, then envelope the village in swift fashion.

"Wall's coming up, sir," a youthful SBS sergeant said to the SAS captain.

"Good."

He jumped up on a rock for a better view. Through his field glasses he could make out the wall some three hundred yards ahead of his advancing column. He radioed ahead an order to halt at the wall, and then he moved to the front of his men at a fast pace, his heart pounding with excitement.

The troops had taken up positions along the length of the wall. They were a tired bunch. The trek had fatigued even the heartiest of them. As the SAS officer looked both ways up and down the wall, all that he could clearly make out were the clouds created by the breaths of his seventy-five men, reminding him of a herd of horses on the cold morning of a hunt. The SAS officer raised his head above the wall. Through his glasses he surveyed the cold gray village. It appeared to be deserted. An evening mist was forming around the grassy spots along the streets. A thick fog would be an advantage to the Argentineans, so he would like to attack now. He stood up, raised his Sterling machine gun, and cried, "All right, lads. Let's move!"

"No, sir. Look!" cried a junior officer to his right.

"What?" The SAS officer was astonished his order had been questioned. Then he saw that his men were standing, waving their weapons in the air and cheering. "What . . . what?"

Finally he saw what they were cheering about. All across the village white flags were being waved by the Argentineans. "Well, damn it all," the SAS officer said in exasperation. The first land battle for the Falklands had been won without a single shot having been fired.

Chapter 20

The National Defense University
Washington, D.C.

America had just recovered from four hundred forty-four days of frustration. Revolutionary Guards of the Army of God had taken fifty-four American embassy employees hostage in Tehran, Iran. In response, the Carter administration, against the advice of the hostage negotiation experts, had made the fate of the hostages the focal point of its foreign policy. The more importance America placed on the hostages, the more valuable they became to the Iranians. After a while, they became too valuable to give up.

By violating the first principle of hostage negotiation – never make the hostages themselves the negotiating issue – Carter, *et al.* had given the Ayatollah Khomeini a catalyst with which he was able to bring together all of the politically divergent groups present in Iran and focus them on one central enemy: the Great Satan – the United States of America.

When the Administration had finally realized that prayer, love, and diplomacy would not gain the hostages' release, a desperate attempt had been made to rescue them. But after three years of systematic emasculation by the Administration and the Congress, the armed forces, when ordered to carry out a rescue operation, had been unable to emulate Germany's GSG-9. Instead of success, there had been a disaster as lack of intelligence information, inter-service rivalry, and outdated equipment had led to the fiery deaths of several American servicemen in the Dasht E Kavir. After news of the deaths of the servicemen and the failure of the mission, the morale of the American people had sunk.

So when a source at the State Department told a cub reporter about an Army major's wife who had been taken hostage by the Argentinean secret police, the story had made page twenty-four of the *Washington Post* and had been allotted only two paragraphs. But there were those who had read the paper and found the piece important.

"Major Elliot," General Knott said with a look of impatience, "explain to me why you didn't inform me about what happened to your wife before you went to the damn State Department! My God man, don't you understand what chain of command means?"

"Sir, I didn't think this was an Army matter," David replied.

"Oh, that's weak. Really weak. Who in the hell do you think you are? That uniform you're wearing doesn't come off at five o'clock. You sleep in it, you bathe in it, and you take a shit in it. You're a soldier twenty-four hours a day. You are Army. You belong to us. And I'm your commanding officer. You owe me your loyalty and your respect. Hell, how would you feel if one of your men had something as serious as this happen to him and the way you found out about it was by reading about it in your morning newspaper? What if DA had called me before I learned about this? They'd have thought I was a damn idiot!"

David sensed something unfamiliar in the tone of Knott's voice. It was fear; Knott was afraid, he realized, and he felt himself somewhat strengthened by Knott's vulnerability. "If I embarrassed you, I apologize. But I had to try to see what options were available to me."

"And what did you find?"

From the look on Knott's face, David realized he already knew what State had said, but he related the experience just the same.

"Their first comment was that the war would complicate things, but while I waited they immediately put in a call to our embassy in Buenos Aires and told them what had happened. There was nothing they could tell me at that time. I called this morning and they told me the Argentineans had told our embassy they'd never heard of my wife. They were politely told to keep checking."

"But you think they're lying?"

"Of course. I know she left for Buenos Aires. If she was safe she would have called by now. Why would her friends lie about her whereabouts?"

"Yes, why?"

"I don't understand what you're implying, sir."

Knott sat back in his chair and folded his arms across his chest. "Isn't it true your wife was, what we used to call in the sixties, an agitator? That she was an enemy of the Argentine government?"

David fought hard not to grimace. Now he understood what had happened. DA must have received information from State about the incident. DA had checked out the story with the CIA. Their agents in Argentina had confirmed the story, but had added information about Sunny's background. When the file had hit State's desk, it had been flagged. Sunny was a naturalized citizen with a past history of subversive activities against a government friendly to America. Questions must have been raised concerning what her motives were for being in the middle of a war zone. And based on their information, conclusions had been made about her political affiliations. The Argentineans probably had told State she was a communist. State had called DA back and had told them that, as far as they were concerned, it was an internal matter. Then DA had called Knott and had told him to keep David in line until the war was over.

"God, I love this country," he said out loud without thinking.

"What?" Knott said.

"Sir, my wife is not a communist," said David emphatically.

"Who the hell said anything about her being a communist? I simply asked you if she was an agitator."

"I guess if you categorize her . . ."

"Major. Just give me an old fashioned, straight forward, nondescript answer."

"My wife protested against the military *junta* and their methods, yes."

"Is that why she went back, to protest the war?"

"No. She returned because her parents had been arrested. She went down there to find out what she could about them. That's all."

"Why were her parents arrested?"

"Sir, I don't know."

"It would seem subversion runs in her family."

"Sir, my wife has been illegally arrested. She is an American citizen. Doesn't that count for anything?"

"First, Major Elliot, we don't know if your wife has been arrested illegally. In fact, we don't even know if she's been arrested at all. What we do know is that she is a known enemy of the government of Argentina, a person who in the past has caused it considerable problems. All of a sudden she comes back to Argentina when that country is right in the middle of the biggest damn war it has ever fought. What would you have done if you had been the authorities down there? As for her parents, we don't know anything about them except that your wife said her parents had been arrested illegally. Why couldn't it be, Major Elliot, that they were *legally* arrested, huh?"

David just threw up his hands.

"That's what I thought," Knott said with a smirk. "Now, I'm going to give you an order. You are an American officer. You serve under the authority of Congress and the President. Your wife has willingly subjected herself to the dangers of a war zone and, for whatever reason, she has dropped out of sight. The United States cannot become involved in this affair anymore than it already has. You are not to go to the State Department and stir up any more trouble. Let them handle this matter through diplomatic channels. Understand?"

David nodded.

"Further, you are to report to me personally any information you receive concerning your wife's whereabouts and her activities. Understand?"

"I understand, sir. But again, my wife is an American citizen. Are we just going to sit back and do nothing?" David gave Knott a look of incredulity.

"What would you have us do? Mount some sort of military attack to free her? Shit, has your brain gone dead? Can't you remember what happened when we tried that sort of thing during the Iranian crisis? Nobody's going to put the American people through that again!"

Knott's face turned red. David had seen him upset before, but never like this. Knott turned away from David toward the window. "We sent those boys on a suicide mission." There was a scienter of disgust in Knott's voice as he spoke. "It was disgraceful. And do you know what got them killed? Politics. The President and the Congress were living in Disneyland. Why couldn't they understand how dangerous the world is? How disliked we Americans are? They had disbanded our intelligence network, which had left us virtually blind all over the world. Damn pacifists! No wonder they were so damned shocked to wake up one day and find Iran in chaos.

"So they asked those brave young men to make up for years of their neglect and stupidity. And when the mission failed, they were shocked. They were shocked to learn our equipment was outdated. They were shocked to learn our training was inadequate. So they started to look for someone to blame. But do you think they blamed themselves? No. They blamed us."

Knott suddenly stopped and swallowed hard. He had gone too far with David. This was, after all, a man he might soon be disciplining. He turned back and spoke slowly, as if carefully choosing each word. "Of course, we in the military sometimes can't see the big picture. That's why the politicians . . . uh, the civilians, have control of the government. And that's the way it should be. Anyway, you have your orders and I expect you to follow them."

General Knott then walked back to the window, his back turned away from David. He spoke softly, in a compromising tone. "Look, Elliot, I know this is hard on you. You remember," he let out a little laugh, "I've met your wife. A beautiful woman. But," Knott stiffened, his body suddenly becoming ramrod, "you've got to remember who you are and what you represent. We . . . we officers, aren't like everyone else. We stand for the country's ideals and laws. If we don't show discipline in our own ranks, how can we expect it from our men? It's going to take discipline to face up to this situation you're in. But you can do it. Just remember your duty. Just think about what you're going to be teaching others about duty, and you'll know what to do."

David heard himself utter the words, but it was as if it wasn't he who was saying them. No, it was someone else. But the words were said. They came out like a rush of air, a pent up feeling that suddenly found a way to escape and, once it was out, unleashed itself with a vengeance. "You're not worthy to be an American."

Knott suddenly turned and lunged at David with an angry, hateful look of utter contempt on his face, his fists clenched in rage. He started to strike David, but caught himself and stopped. His body was shaking, his face drawn tight and flushed. "Listen," he said through his teeth, "it's your own damn fault your wife's in this mess. You should've stopped her from going back down there. You knew she might be in danger, and yet you let her go. What kind of man are you, Elliot? What kind of man would let his wife be put in that kind of danger? If you'd been more of a man, she'd be safe now. But you're not. You sit there and whine. 'General, she's an American; can't we do something?' You make me sick. Now, get the fuck out of here before I forget who I am!"

Once outside, David leaned against the hall wall feeling dizzy and sick. Students passed him going to classes, but he was oblivious to their presence. He ran his hand over his face, which was dripping with cold perspiration.

Now it was clear to him. He now understood the meaning of the dreams. Payment time. How much were the lives of his dead men worth? What would be the price for the years of suffering of those left alive?

Knott had been right. He should have seen it coming. He should have stopped her from going. The dreams should have been a warning to him that the time for payment was coming. Yes, it was time for him to pay. And only Sunny's death and the suffering it would bring him would satisfy the debt.

Chapter 21

> David arose from a place toward the south, fell on his face to the ground and bowed down three times. And they kissed one another; and they wept together, but David more so.
>
> Then Jonathan said to David, "Go in peace, since we have both sworn in the name of the Lord saying, 'May the Lord be between you and me, and between your descendants and my descendants, forever.'" So he arose and departed, and Jonathan went into the City.
>
> 1 Samuel 22:41-42

Oceana Naval Base
Virginia Beach, Virginia

The second principle of hostage negotiation is never allow the hostage taker to become frustrated. While in some instances frustration can be a valuable learning experience, in most cases its ultimate manifestation is violence.

And Andrew was both frustrated and angry. The State and Defense Departments, even the news media, had all turned deaf ears to David's pleas for help. All the doors had slammed shut. No one, it seemed, cared about one American caught up in a far away war. The thought of Sunny rotting away in some South American shit hole and nobody willing or able to do anything about it, least of all himself, had nearly driven him mad.

"David, why did you let her go?"
"I had no choice, what could I do?"
"Had no choice? She is your wife."
"Jorge assured me."
"Jorge is a pimp."
"You know she's not like us. You know that."
"That's right, you bastard. She's too good for you."
"But not too good for you, right?"
"You motherfucker."

Like most fighter pilots, Andrew possessed a dual personality. On the ground, he was jovial, talkative, and a little lazy. He joked a lot, told rude stories, and indulged in Jack Daniels and Black Jacks. But in the air, a metamorphosis occurred; he became a cool, intelligent, aggressive hunter who tenaciously stalked his prey until his instinct told him the time was right to close in for the kill. And right now, he felt like killing something.

He adjusted the chin strap of his UT orange and white flight helmet and flipped down its sun visor as he anxiously awaited the tower's go to start his take off roll. His twin engine F-18A Hornet fighter idling near the end of the runway seemed to sense his need for the air and purred suggestively.

He had arrived at the naval air station a week before to start his transition training in the Navy's newest fighter aircraft and for sea duty. An absence from flying for nearly three years had taken a toll on his reflexes as well as his psyche. But it had taken him only four days of steady flying to get back in the cockpit, and now he was ready. It had been a bad dream, the War College, but now he was back.

His run up was long complete. "Tower, Old Hickory," he radioed briskly.

"Old Hickory," the tower radioed back. The voice coming through his flight helmet was that of a woman. For a moment Andrew tried to imagine what she looked like.

"What are ya'll doing up there? What's the holdup? The longer I sit here the more taxpayers' fuel I burn up," Andrew said, strapping on his oxygen mask.

"Old Hickory, be advised two Israeli Kifirs on final."

"The Children of God."

"Old Hickory, you have traffic?"

"Negative," he replied.

To his right, he could see the two delta winged Israeli-made jets coming in low and slow on simultaneous approach, dark exhaust fumes trailing behind each. He made a mental note to look up the two Jewish fighter jocks at the club that night. The jets touched down with a roar.

"Old Hickory, clear," said the tower.

"Thank ya', darlin'," Andrew said, pushing the throttle slowly forward and positioning the aircraft carefully on the white center stripes of the runway with his feet. He powered up. The jet lurched forward and started down the runway at a terrific pace. At seventy-five knots, he gradually moved the control stick toward his stomach. The agile aircraft deftly responded. Andrew had the "light touch."

Outside, the roar of the two Pratt and Whitney turbofans was deafening, but inside the cockpit Andrew could detect only a slight muffled hum. At ninety knots, he switched on the afterburners and the jet burst up off the runway, leaving two black contrails in its wake. He withdrew the flaps. A second later, he brought up the landing gear. Cleaned up, the jet started to gain speed rapidly – two hundred fifty knots, and only eight seconds since he had taken off from the runway. He banked the aircraft left as he exited the pattern. Three thousand feet below, the city of Virginia Beach was applying its first suntan oil of the day.

"Tower, Old Hickory. Leaving your scope for area Tango Delta," Andrew radioed, still climbing at a rate of thirty thousand feet per minute.

"Roger, Old Hickory, Tango Delta."

Tango Delta was a two hundred square area over the Atlantic that was restricted against commercial and private aviation. Naval fighter aircraft used it to practice high speed combat maneuvers. It had its own special air-ground control group that coordinated all aircraft inside its perimeter.

"Tango Delta control, Old Hickory," Andrew radioed after switching frequencies.

"Old Hickory, clear." The control had his flight plan.

"Roger," Andrew said, extinguishing the afterburners.

He leveled off at twenty-five thousand feet and switched the controls of the aircraft to the inboard ailerons. Airspeed five hundred forty knots. He lifted up his flight helmet's sun visor. The sky around him was two-toned – at sea level a gray blue, while above it was almost black, so dark he could see the stars even though it was already midmorning. Visibility at this height was forever. Far off toward the south, fat patches of white clouds floated over the azure sea like mushrooms. "God," he said softly.

He was thankful the Hornet was a single-Aviator aircraft. The F-14A Tomcat had a radar intercept officer who normally rode in the back seat, but these new aircraft put the responsibility of flying and fighting back on the pilot, where it belonged. The inside of the cockpit was about the size of the driver's side of a Porsche. Every control, every instrument, had been placed by the engineers at McDonnell Douglas where any pilot, no matter what his size, could touch them, even in a tight high-G turn. Andrew's view of the world around him was not inhibited by any part of the aircraft. The wings and power plants were well to his rear. Looking to either side was like looking down a steep cliff. He could see all the way to the ground. To his front, the pointed nose filled with sophisticated electronic equipment was the only visible evidence he had of the aircraft around him, and it was slanted toward the ground so that it did not obstruct his view. So when he put the aircraft through its paces, it seemed to him as if he were in a highly instrumented box, with no engine sound, no external sign of his aircraft's movement. Only the whirling motion of the world outside and the harsh effect of the G forces assured him he was in control of the events taking place around him.

He had now become a part of the aircraft, more machine than man. He could even tell what his craft was thinking. And it did think. It knew how far it was from home, or how long it would take to get where it was going. It knew when it was hungry or tired. It knew when it could no longer fight a good fight. It even knew if part of it was sick. All of these things its computers were programmed to communicate.

There was a constant dialogue between the Hornet and Andrew. The machine used lights, gauges, sounds, and graphics to tell him about its condition. It even had a television camera located in its nose that gave him a view, in the center of his instrument panel, which he could adjust for close up vision of the aircraft he was engaging. He responded to all of the Hornet's messages by a touch of his fingers or feet.

He rolled the Hornet upside down and dove toward the sea in a split-S maneuver. His G-suit began to puff up. The negative G-forces lifted his excess body weight but not Andrew, for he was strapped in his ejection seat so tightly only his arms, legs, and upper torso could move. The sky left his windscreen and became the sea and then the sky again. He banked hard right. This time he was pushed down into the seat.

And while the world twisted and turned outside the canopy, his mind engaged itself in polyphasic thought. On one level of consciousness he was flying the Hornet, but on another level he was thinking of what he had done to David. David had taken leave, gone into seclusion, rarely leaving his apartment. To anyone who asked why, he explained his need for privacy during this difficult time. Actually, he was suffering from severe depression and was following Perez's orders.

"My doctor told me not to see anyone," David had said.
"Who?" he asked.
"I said my doctor. Now leave."
"You'll see me. You've got some explaining to do."
Oh, Sunny, forgive me.

He lowered the nose to gain speed then pulled back hard on the stick. The Hornet noised up, starting its loop. But when the angle of attack reached the peak of the loop, directly straight up, he switched on the afterburners. The jet shot up like a rocket, pushing him back with a violent jerk. At this angle, the engines were producing more pounds of thrust than the plane weighted, which meant he could, if he wished, keep going until he left the earth's atmosphere, never to return again. The sky became darker and darker, the stars more clearly defined with each passing second. *How far can I go with this?* he wondered, as he began to run out of air.

David had gone too far. Andrew had hit him in the mouth, causing him to go sprawling across the apartment's floor. David had tried to get up, but Andrew had kicked him in the face and he had fallen back hard. This time David had not tried to get back up. Instead, he had just leaned back against the wall, blood trickling from his nose.

"I hit a nerve, didn't I? Admit it. You love her, don't you?" David had asked.

Andrew realized this was going too far. The Hornet was beginning to yaw, which meant the air was too thin at this height to support the wings. Both engines began to cut out, which meant they were oxygen starved. A quick glance at the altimeter told him the story: sixty thousand feet, well above the Hornet's service ceiling. He pushed the stick forward and inverted back toward the blue sky. Almost, this time.

Why did I hit him? What's wrong with me? Andrew asked himself as he leveled off at forty thousand feet. *He is my friend. He hasn't been well. I just – why didn't he stop her? Shit, how could he have stopped her? I couldn't have stopped her. Why did I think he could have? Sunny, I'm so sorry. I know you'd be ashamed of me if you knew what I did.*

He put the Hornet in a sixty degree bank. At this steep a degree of turn, the Hornet's weight would increase with every passing second. He would have to increase his speed in order to maintain altitude. He added power and the G-forces pushed him down into the seat. The flesh of his face sagged, deforming his features, but his G-suit absorbed most of the weight, preventing his blood from leaving his brain.

Guilt was an emotion foreign to Andrew. So when it overcame him he had nothing in his past to draw upon to help him cope with his feelings. All he had been able to do was to strike out irrationally at what was available: David. It had been easy to blame David. He was her husband, and in Andrew's world husbands were supposed to be in charge. So instead of standing by David, helping him cope with the reality of losing Sunny, he had smashed his face. This morning, he had not liked what he saw in the mirror.

He began a power drive. As the Hornet gained speed, the airframe actually began to whine. He could not hear the screams of his plane, but he could feel them. At forty thousand feet and eight hundred fifty knots, it would take only twenty seconds to crash into the ocean.

He could picture her again, there in the center of his radar screen. She was wearing a gaily colored dress, flowers, blue, loose, revealing her tanned legs. But then she had looked away. Was she afraid? Did she know what awaited her in Buenos Aires? She had to have known something was going to happen to her. In his heart, he knew she had relied on him to pick up the pieces when it happened, and he had let her down. Had let David down. Had let himself down.

He slowly pulled back on the stick and the Hornet gracefully pulled up from the dive and leveled off about a thousand feet above the ocean. After he had recovered from the negative Gs caused by the sudden deceleration, he edged the fighter even closer to the surface, only about a hundred feet. As he increased his speed to five hundred knots, the placid water below turned into a blue blur.

Sunny was alone. She had known what the odds were of her being arrested, but she had taken the chance. But then, her whole life in Argentina had been one big chance. Even so, Andrew could understand what she had done. He had done the same thing many times before. Sometimes you have to take chances to win. It was like diving into a bombing run. Sometimes you made it out, sometimes you didn't. This time, they had shot her down. Now she was alone and in danger. And no one would help her.

He gained altitude and requested a radar vector from Tango Delta Control to Oceana NAB. It had been a good flight, plenty of thinking, plenty of Gs. Five miles out from the runway, a yellow light blinked and a beeper sounded five times: the outside marker. The Hornet was telling him he was correctly lined up for his instrument approach. He pushed up the sun visor. Sunny was gone from the cockpit, but he could still sense her presence. She was there, in the cockpit, in his mind.

Then a horrible reality settled in on him. It had been there all along, so obvious he had conveniently refused to recognize it. In just a few short weeks, the *Kennedy* would be sailing near Argentina and he would be up there leading air patrols in the most powerful fighter plane in the world. Yet he would be powerless to help her. She would be so near, but so far away. He could feel the anger in him rise again as he slammed the fifty-nine thousand pound airplane against the runway.

Chapter 22

Alexandria, Virginia

All nations are class societies. This truism is the one incontrovertible characteristic which all nations share. Equally true is that when people come together in one place for any length of time there will naturally evolve a division of social standing. It is a *lex non scripta* from which no one has ever been exempt, although both communist and democratic nations have insisted to the contrary, proclaiming their forms of government have swept away all class distinctions. This, of course, is a lie on the part of one and a false assumption on the part of the other.

There are in any nation, regardless of its religion, geography, or socioeconomic status, three classes of people: the rich and powerful; the vast majority; and the poor, who are often illiterate and always disenfranchised. And even though the rich and powerful control every aspect of a society, they are dependent upon the other classes for survival, for they are too small in number to feed, fuel, or even fight for themselves. In order to survive, they must milk the other classes.

The rich and powerful obtain the necessary services they need and the protection they require by granting to the vast majority limited and controlled access to the inner sanctums of power and knowledge. They create in this grant the implied promise that perhaps one day, if they are loyal, certain individual members of the vast majority may be admitted to their class. Sometimes it is a promise that is disguised in the trappings of patriotic fervor. And the belief in the truth of the lie is made stronger by the fact that some members of the vast majority actually do become rich and powerful. From the poor, the rich and powerful exact the means to obtain their food and fuel. They also draw from them a pool of common labor to perform such menial tasks as are required in any society. The rich and powerful secure this servitude by making certain the poor are at all times dependent upon them for their very survival. Grants of food, shelter, health care, and security are given carefully and selectively in order to keep the poor in awe of the power the rich have over their lives. People who are preoccupied with survival have little time left for anything else. And so, ironically, the rich and powerful of a nation are always its most vulnerable, its easiest to overthrow. They must be ever vigilant, never allowing themselves to be too comfortable in their wealth, never allowing their power to lull them into a false sense of security. The vast majority must be ever satisfied and the poor ever hungry. Otherwise, the rich and powerful will find themselves in a fool's paradise.

Jorge was at first afraid of David. But Rita had sensed from first sight that he was vulnerable, that his hunger for information was far greater than his need to unleash his frustration. So, she had let him in when he appeared unannounced at their door. He now had in his hand the strong drink Rita had prepared for him. It had calmed him, just as Rita had wanted.

He had never intended to blame Jorge and Rita for what happened to Sunny. Rita understood this, even if Jorge remained suspicious. All he really wanted was an answer, and some hope.

Rita sat next to Jorge across the room from David. Their apartment was spacious, large for Georgetown, imitation colonial but expensive. There was a blue flowered couch with splashes of grey and purple, thick cherry wood night stands, round cream-colored lamps. A painting of Jorge's father hung over the fireplace. It was late and they had been asleep when David arrived. Rita was in her red nightgown, her nipples showing through. Jorge wore pajamas that made him seem all the more plump. He was not happy with this encounter but had accepted its inevitability. Rita was more curious.

"I should have come sooner, but I wasn't sure how I would act. Then I realized what happened to Sunny must have been a shock to you too," David said apologetically to Jorge.

"It happened very quickly. She was standing next to us at the baggage counter when . . ."

As Jorge told the story, David could see her standing there. He could see the look of acceptance on her face. He could even imagine what her captors looked like. *Go on, Jorge*, David thought. *Bring her back to me. Let me see her once more.*

". . . two men dressed in business suits took her by the arms and led her away from us. I tried to protest . . ."

Liar, David thought.

". . . but it did no good. They paid me no attention."

Rita spoke up. "David, it was as if she knew they would take her. She made no attempt to free herself. She did not even cry out."

No, she wouldn't, David knew.

"I made inquiries. My family made inquiries. But she had simply vanished," Jorge said.

"Yes, simply vanished," Rita echoed.

"Jorge, I'm not trying to insult you when I say this, but even in Argentina people don't just vanish without a trace. There has to be some agency, some governmental entity that knows her whereabouts. For God's sake, she's an American citizen."

"Has your embassy been able to locate her?" Rita asked confrontationally. "I think not. Unfortunately, Sonia has disappeared . . . just like others have."

"Rita, shut up!" Jorge shouted.

"It is true," Rita said sternly to Jorge. "I will not lie to him."

Then she turned to David. "The Group has taken her," she said.

"The Group?"

"Yes, the Group, the organization responsible for internal security in Argentina. They have the power to arrest and detain without warrant and without due process anyone whom they suspect of being a threat to national security."

"And Sonia had been identified as an enemy of the *junta*," Jorge said. "This was many years ago. Long before she met you and long before she came to America to study."

David slumped back in his chair. "I knew of her past, but somehow I thought all that was over."

"Nothing is ever over as far as the *junta* are concerned," Jorge said, looking up at the picture over the mantle.

"It's the war," Rita said. "It's made the *junta* paranoid. That's why they seized her parents. A ruse, of course, to get Sonia back into Argentina. She would have been written off as gone and good riddance, but the war . . ."

"But what possible use could she be to them now? She's been away so long. She would have never gone back except for the arrest of her parents."

Jorge and Rita were strangely silent, giving David blank looks.

In an instant it registered with him like an artillery barrage. "They wanted her because she is married to me?"

"Who knows what motivates them?" Jorge replied irritably. "But they released her parents shortly after she was seized."

"Sunny always thought . . ." David stopped himself. "I thought you, your family, had influence with the *junta*."

"Events have been taking place very fast in Buenos Aires," Jorge said. "Our military officers seem to have lost their senses. It's as if they have forgotten those who put them in power in the first place. They have closed their ears to sound advice, to wise counsel."

"They are out of control," Rita said angrily.

"They will regain their composure once this time passes," Jorge said, trying to rebuff her.

"Why do you still cling to the myth that our families can influence the generals? They have been given the reigns of power and now they refuse to let go. Jorge, can you not see that, even now? Tell David what happened when your father made inquiries with the army concerning Sonia."

David turned to Jorge with a demanding look, but Jorge remained silent.

"He was told he should keep his interests separate from matters that the Group deemed in the interest of the people of Argentina," Rita said when she saw Jorge would not answer.

"What will happen to her?" David begged.

Jorge's brow furrowed. "When we, our families, first learned of the

Group, inquiries were made with the *junta*. Assurances were given such an organization was needed to guarantee that what had happened in Uruguay would not happen in our country. We were promised nothing would happen to innocent people, only to leftists and anarchists. Only those who actively opposed Argentine society would be detained. You must understand that historically the relationship between our families and the military has been one of master and servant. So, at the time, we did not feel threatened by the existence of the Group. Military officers come from what you call the middle class. To be commissioned in the armed forces, one has to obtain permission from three groups of power: the Church, the military council, and the Families. From that point on, if a man is selected to become an officer and is loyal and patriotic, the Families see to it that he and his family live a lifestyle commensurate with his position."

"And so you see," Rita said, leaning toward David and exposing her breasts, "the officers who now rule our country live in nice houses, drive expensive cars, and have fat bank accounts. All thanks to the Families."

"And yet this madness with the Malvinas has apparently blinded them to whom they should owe their loyalty," Jorge said nervously.

"They are out of control," chimed Rita.

Jorge reluctantly nodded his head in agreement.

"What's going to happen to her?" David asked firmly.

Jorge rubbed his chin. "We still have connections with some of the younger officers in the *junta*."

"Those who realize who pays their bills," Rita said.

"Through them we might be able to locate her," Jorge said.

"No!" Rita snapped. "We know where she is."

"We don't know for sure," Jorge responded.

"We know. We know the Group. We know their methods."

"Where is she? Tell me, damn it!" David shouted, tired of their bantering.

Jorge took a deep breath then let his words out. "Los Estados."

"And where is that?" David had heard the name before but could not remember where.

"It is a detention facility located at the southern tip of the country. It is a desolate, barren island. You can only get to it from the air – the seas are too rough. The Group isolates and interrogates all political prisoners there before taking them to the Naval Academy in Buenos Aires."

"Where they're murdered," David added sardonically.

"So long as she's in Los Estados, she will be alive. They only interrogate there," Rita said reassuringly.

"How can you be sure?" David asked, hope filling his voice.

"They are very organized. They have a method, a procedure for doing things, a procedure from which they do not deviate," Rita said, a far off look on her face.

David shook his head in disbelief. She was talking as if the Group was a baseball team.

"Look, we know it's hard for you to understand what has happened in our country," Jorge said. "We find it hard to understand it ourselves, but we will still try to help. We will still make inquiries. Perhaps if the *junta* hear that some of the Families are interested in Sonia, they will spare her."

"How long can we expect her to stay on Los Estados?" David asked tonelessly.

"It usually takes them around two months to fully interrogate a prisoner before they are sentenced," Jorge replied.

"How do you know these things?" David asked, finding it incredible that Jorge could know so much about the inner workings of an organization as sinister as the Group.

Jorge wet his lips and ran his pudgy fingers through his slick hair.

"Jorge?"

Rita put her hand out as if to stop David from approaching her husband. "You do not understand," she said. "You cannot understand what things were like during the time of anarchy. There were bombings, assassinations, and extortion. Something had to be done. Jorge did what he did for Argentina. No one at the time thought the *junta* would go so far."

"You were a member of the Group?" David asked, completely astonished.

"I was an informant."

David had sensed from the moment he entered their apartment that Rita was sympathetic to what he was experiencing. Now he understood.

It was not sympathy but empathy. Just as Sunny had been outside the norm of Argentinean life, so had Jorge. For patriotic reasons, he had betrayed friendships and confidences he had himself fostered, and the end result had been that many young lives had been snuffed out.

But David could empathize with Jorge, and that was something not even Rita could have imagined. He told them about Phoenix.

"Just as you thought the Group and its work was necessary, we too thought our cause made us necessary as well. And like you, the things we did seemed perfectly logical at the time, at least within the parameters of our societal setting. But with us there was an added factor. We were in a desperate and alien environment, removed from everything that was familiar and natural to us. In order to survive, we had to adapt, get down deep and lose ourselves. A British mercenary I knew called it 'going native.' We became a part of everything around us, an environment where there were no laws and no societal norms based on morality. We were in a jungle made not only of vegetation but of history, where there was only one rule: survive. And we did what had to be done to survive."

David then took a drink.

"You seem to have developed your rationalization well," Rita said without sarcasm.

"Can any of us remain sane without rationalizing our lives?" David asked rhetorically.

"You understand the reason for the *junta* forming the Group, don't you," Rita stated knowingly.

David gave her a half smile. "Yes, I understand why. It was the ultimate way of expressing their paranoia, of controlling their worst fears."

"What were they afraid of?" asked Jorge, bleary eyed.

"Of losing control," David replied.

"But they had the power."

"No, not really," David continued. "Your laws stood in their way. As long as you had a government of laws, their power was limited. Laws always do that to governments. So, when you legitimized the Group you, in effect, did away with a government ruled by law. We did the same thing in Vietnam when we formed Phoenix. I guess we thought we had to fight fire with fire."

"Like I said, you have developed your rationalization well," Rita said again.

"It helps if you can do it," David said, taking another drink.

"How about you, Jorge? Been able to rationalize the killings you took part in?"

Jorge concealed his face with his hands.

David smiled and held his drink up to Jorge in a mock toast. "Now, tell me about Los Estados. Ever been there?"

"Of course. The Families used to own the island," Jorge said as if he were talking to someone who should have known.

David again shook his head in disbelief.

"As I said, it's a barren place, or was before the Group took it over. An air base has been built there for the Navy. It's a large strip with several support buildings and hangars nearby. The compound used by the Group is composed of three villas, each a short distance from the others."

"How far?"

"A hundred yards or so."

"All fenced in with watch towers, I suppose?"

"There is no need for a fence. There's no place to go. If someone did escape, and that has never been done before, they would die from exposure or be eaten by wolves."

"Wolves?"

"Placed there by the Group."

David grimaced, then laughed. "Sounds like my kind of guys. Tell me more about the Group. Who's its leader? What kind of man is he?"

"We do not know his name. He is said to be young and handsome. We believe he is a naval officer. His identity is a state secret," Jorge said.

"He is said to be from one of the Families," Rita said, "but he has the complete trust of the *junta*."

Why do I ask? David thought, biting his lips. *I know all about him. I know what his values are. I know how he thinks. We're all alike, aren't we, Keaton? We leaders of the damned. We members of a fraternity of death bringers.*

". . . is why he is feared. His men obey his orders without question

... David, are you listening?" Jorge said, seeing the far off look of David's face.

In David's mind's eye, he could picture this leader. *He thinks himself to be all powerful. That happens when a man thinks himself to be above the law. But then, he is above the law. He can kill anyone he wants without fear of retribution. What power!*

"David?" a voice asked. Maybe Rita's.

Yes, I know him. I know how he thinks, what he values, what he fears. He and I were once so much alike. The Group has done this to him. Phoenix did it to me. Jude could see it, even if I could not. He kills those he wants. I killed those I wanted. What power! And now he will kill Sunny, and with her, me. What power!

"David!" It was Rita.

"Sorry. I was just thinking," David said groggily, putting his drink to his lips. "I was just thinking I would like to meet this man some day."

Chapter 23

Lockharts Café
Mahned, Mississippi
May 13, 1982

A dark highway runs past the east gate of Camp Shelby near Hattiesburg. It coils like a black snake through the De Soto National Forest where annually thousands of National Guardsmen train during the summer. A half mile outside the east gate sits a small café, a conglomeration of trailers attached to a wooden house. For almost two decades the café has been a watering hole for the Army of the South, an oasis of air conditioning and cold drink in the desert of mosquitoes, fire ants, armadillos, and snakes, a refuge from the searing heat and powdery dust of the nearby training grounds. Its name is Lockharts.

The night was hot, muggy, and windless. The smell of the nearby swamp putrefied the stale air, and the acrid aroma of kudzu was everywhere. Nighttime in Mississippi.

In the dark dead of night, the only source of light for miles around was the cafe's yellow sign. It covered the trucks and Army jeeps filling the gravel parking lot with a yellow pallor. Occasionally a truck would fly by on the dark highway or a jeep would emerge from the access road across from the café leading into the deep forest where night training was being conducted, but aside from these flashes of movement, the world around Lockharts was seemingly dead. The sight of the huge black man dressed in the uniform of the Mississippi Highway Patrol caused heads to turn and voices to grow quite as he entered the café.

The café patrons had already segregated themselves. The locals, with their assorted baseball caps, Buck knives, and tobacco were on one side of the room. The guardsmen, dirty, uniformed, and with their M-16s loaded with blanks, were on the other. But there had never been a fight between the two groups since Lockharts opened. Mrs. Lockhart was revered by both locals and guardsmen alike, for everyone knew that her heart, her pocketbook, and her doors were open to one and all, and there was only one rule of the house: be friendly.

The café was dimly lit. Smoke hung at chest level. The bar was at one end of the room, tables and booths were at the other. The trooper appeared to be looking for something.

Mrs. Lockhart left the bar and ambled over to him. Just as she started to ask him his business, George Jones began his song. "Officer," she shouted in greeting, "can I be of help?"

"No."

The trooper took a seat at an empty table near the door. Mrs. Lockhart gave him an inquisitive look that the trooper returned with a cold stare. She shook her head and went back to the bar.

The trooper gave the room the once over. Plastered, tacked, nailed, or taped all over the walls were the insignia and unit crests of nearly every unit in the Army and of the Tennessee, Alabama, Georgia, and Mississippi National Guards. *Typical Army hole*, he thought. It reminded him of places he had been before.

Heads had turned back by now and the talk had once again risen to a level in proportion with the output of the jukebox. Besides, whatever the trooper wanted was his business. In Mississippi, nobody messed with cops, even if the cop was black.

At one end of the room occupying three tables were nine guardsmen. They were eating, drinking, and laughing. Lying in neat piles near their feet were their web gear, helmets, and M-16s.

Once he had unobtrusively counted the rifles, the trooper left.

Connely, a nineteen year old guardsman from Brownsville, Tennessee, started up the five-ton truck. The diesel engine kicked over with a hum and a whine. Its grinding noise stopped the chirping of the crickets. It was as if they could sense something dreadful was about to interrupt their peaceful night.

"Ya'll keep ya' seats back there," Sergeant Maney yelled to the squad seated in the covered cargo area of the truck. The soldiers in the rear just laughed.

Connely turned off the highway and onto the access road. After he had shifted gears, he adjusted the rearview mirror, using as a reference the fading yellow sign of Lockharts. Then he noticed something strange: a blue light.

"Sarge, look at this!" he yelled above the engine noise.

"What?" Maney shouted.

"There's a cop behind us."

Maney checked the side view mirror. "This is a military reservation but hell, pull over."

The soldiers riding in the back exchanged curious looks as the truck ground to a dusty halt. The man driving the black sedan, which had a magnetic flashing blue light affixed to its top, stopped about ten yards from the rear of the truck and switched on the car's high beams. The soldiers turned away from the harsh lights.

The trooper stepped from the car, leaving the driver's door open. At the rear of the truck, he stopped. "All you men climb out of the truck and line up at the tailgate," he ordered. Then he walked up to the driver. "Please step out and come around the back you two over there." Maney and Connely did as they were told and joined the others at the truck's rear.

The trooper walked back to the front of the car and stood in front of the bright lights that were blinding the soldiers. Sergeant Maney stepped forward, his hand held over his eyes.

"Look officer, what's goin' on here? We're military personnel and this is a military post."

It was deadly quiet. The trooper did not answer.

One of the soldiers started to ask Maney something, but a sudden blast from the trooper's shotgun tore his jaw off. The Remington automatic self-feeding shotgun was in the hands of an expert. The second shot lifted Maney and threw him against the truck. Connely fell face down in the dirt, but he no longer had a face. The others were blown apart where they stood. It took all of nine seconds.

The trooper nonchalantly walked back to the car and pushed the trunk release button. He threw the hot Remington into the trunk and took out a burlap bag. Quickly, he took off the uniform and stuffed it into the bag. Underneath he wore shorts and a t-shirt. He slipped on a pair of tennis shoes and pulled the plug on the blue light and dropped it in its case on the front seat. He was not worried about the noise. Anyone who might have heard the firing would think it was the guardsmen.

After he lit an expensive Havana cigar, he took the bag and walked over to the pile of cooling bodies. Carefully, he put their thirty round magazines into the bag. He climbed up into the cargo area of the truck and stuffed the dormant M-16s into the bag. He found two other automatic rifles in the cab of the truck. Returning to the Cadillac, he threw the bag of rifles in the trunk and slammed it shut. In three hours he would be in Birmingham. There he would stay and visit with a woman he knew. Then he would go to Richmond Hill, like Keaton had told him.

You must arrive at the mansion not later than the 15th of May. You must bring with you seven automatic rifles, with clips, and ten thousand rounds of ammunition. This is what you must do. There, the covenant will be honored by each one.

Doc took another puff off the cigar. He reached inside the car and pushed in the light switch. The forest became pitch black, covering up the evil scene around him. Overhead, a black, moonless, star speckled sky spread across the horizon, mute to the violence that had just occurred. He became very still and, sure enough, the crickets started their chirping. He smiled.

Keaton had said get the weapons, but had not said how. He could have bought them, but this way the FBI would be hot on their trail. This way, everyone would be looking for them. *No, Keaton, this gathering is not going to turn out like you think it will. I'll see to that. I have set in motion this night the means of your death and that of the others. I will finish what I should have done before. The covenant be damned!*

Finally, he walked over to the bodies, took a sharp Buck knife from his pocket and, bending down over one of the dead guardsmen, neatly cut off a shoulder patch and stuffed it into his pocket.

Chapter 24

```
HMS Hermes
400 nautical miles from San Carlos
May 13, 1982
```

There was gale force wind whipping around the bow of the British aircraft carrier *Hermes*. The deck crew, wearing thick water resistant parkas and face masks to protect them against the stinging spray, had just armed and cleared the two Sea Harriers sitting on the flight deck. The pilots were anxious to lift off, but their air officer, waiting patiently for the ship to turn into the wind, had not yet given them clearance. Under most weather conditions, the Sea Harriers could lift straight up and fly off with full power on any azimuth regardless of the wind's direction. But in this storm, a strong gust of wind could slam them into the flight deck while they were hovering, so as a precaution the Harriers would conduct takeoffs from the elevated forward deck to give them the thrust they needed to overcome the wind.

The *Hermes* was especially vulnerable to Argentine air attacks because, unlike her American cousins, she had no early warning radar aircraft to alert her of attacks well in advance. The Argentines had a particularly deadly aircraft in the French-made Super Etendard and the Los Estados airbase was only an hour's flight away, so the *Hermes's* first line of early warning defense was the Harriers and their brave pilots.

Flight Leftenant Steed fidgeted nervously with his mortar board, a map holder strapped to his leg. He felt as if he were cocooned inside his aircraft just waiting to be blown over the side of the ship. "Come on, will you!" he said into his mike.

"Blue Pair, you say something?" replied the air officer laconically. He knew what the two pilots were feeling for he had been in their situation himself.

No answer.

Flight Warrant Officer Harding had the same feelings as his leader but was a little older and a little wiser. He had ice water for blood.

The air officer watched patiently as the wind direction finder slowly shifted in the opposite direction of the ship's heading. Finally he said, "Blue Pair, you are cleared for lift."

"Roger," Steed said as he powered up and the little jet started its slow roll down the ramp. As he gained speed, he vectored his thrusters downward and the jet slowly lifted off the deck. Behind him, his wingman Harding dutifully followed.

When the jets reached an altitude of three thousand feet, the air turbulence ceased. They were still a thousand feet below the ceiling of the clouds. Steed radioed Harding and informed him they would stay at this altitude and circle the vulnerable carrier at a distance of two hundred miles before they rose above the clouds. He gave the same message to the *Hermes*. The temperature of the air outside the Harriers was ten degrees below zero. It would become progressively colder as they gained altitude. Below them, the Antarctic waters would freeze a man to death in two minutes.

Steed banked the jet toward the rising sun. He glanced at the Harrier's clock. It was 0800. He was twenty-four years old and had wondered all his young life what it would be like to fight an air war like his grandfather had done in 1939. He was confident he would soon find out. "Nothing low. I'm climbing on top," he radioed to Harding.

"Roger," Harding replied. He was positioned to the right and behind his leader. His attention was focused on the trailing edge of his leader's right wing, not ahead or to the sides, not even on his instrument panel. Whenever his leader's wing moved, he moved with it. He was always careful to keep the same distance between his aircraft and the wing of Steed's aircraft. Formation flying is an exercise in exact distances. The two stubby-winged jets shot up through the clouds. Harding backed off a little but kept the same airspeed. In the thick mist laden haze, neither pilot could see the other, so heading and airspeed were important. Neither one could go faster than the other or change direction.

In a flash, the world outside Harding's canopy changed color from gray to a brilliant bright blue. Steed's altimeter indicated he had reached an altitude of forty-one thousand feet.

"Oh, nice!" Steed exclaimed.

"Roger," Harding replied flatly through a contented smile.

For an hour, they flew a pattern that circled the exact position of the *Hermes* below. At this altitude, the air was smooth and crisp. Steed almost hated to return to the carrier. The world seemed so serene at this height, but his fuel gauge was demanding his attention. One hour's fuel left. Time to head down. The VORTAC radio direction finder gave him the carrier's position relative to the azimuth he was flying.

"I'll be banking west now," Steed radioed Harding.

He rolled the aircraft over, leveled off, and started a standard rate slow power descent toward the gray rolling hill-like clouds below. As the two aircraft entered the clouds, Steed decreased his angle of attack, thus slowing his aircraft's speed.

Then, Harding's jet slammed into Steed's right wing and exploded with a brilliant flash of light. Steed could only see the flash for a second before it was consumed by the mist.

As he began a high-G tumble toward the dark ocean, Steed instinctively reached for the ejection mechanism but, as his hand felt for the pull ring, he let it go. At least, he figured, in the aircraft he would have a casket.

Chapter 25

New Orleans, LA

It was a dark and melancholy night, cold and lonely. Outside, a quiet rain fell on old streets and blackened houses. Everyone in suburban New Orleans seemed to be asleep. Unlike their neighbors in the French Quarter, they had jobs to go to in the morning.

Force lived in an apartment on St. Charles Alle next to Tulane University. St. Charles was pre-Napoleon. Old money ornate marble mausoleums housed the affluent of New Orleans society. The Alle was severed down its center by a flower laden median on which traveled the famous English racing green St. Charles trolley cars. When he was in no particular hurry, he indulged himself and rode the car to the French Quarter precinct that was only two blocks from the end of the line. His apartment was small but handsomely proportioned, with high ceilings and a bay window that hung over a perfectly tailored sidewalk. Normally, anyone living on a police lieutenant's salary could not have afforded to live in a neighborhood like St. Charles, but he worked an extra job at a bank.

He had packed everything he thought he would need for the trip into two military bags, one aviators used to carry flight helmets and a duffle. Both lay waiting on his couch. Keaton had been specific: seven sets of web gear; belts with straps; first aid pouches; ammo cases; and canteens. *So there are seven of us left.*

He had secured to his web gear his special holster that held his Sig Sauer P-226, a K-bar knife, and a rolled poncho. He kept his personal effects to a bare minimum; he believed in fighting light.

He stood next to the bay window. The apartment was dark. On a nearby table lay his service revolver wrapped in its holster belt. He blinked as a twinkling light caught him by surprise – the reflection in a car's light from the Alle below. It reminded him of a time before when a twinkling light had been a warning of danger.

He and Jude had been in a rubber assault boat near Mizen Head, Ireland. About this same time of night, they had parachuted into a dark and choppy sea. In the pitch black, the lighthouse at Mizen Head had sent them a warning of danger, of treacherous waters ahead. Had he just received another warning of danger yet unseen? A peril submerged in the unknown of the future like a jagged rock beneath the surface of uncharted water? Or was it simply reminding him of who he was and what he stood for? And what he would become.

Force was a police officer. And what that meant to him no one else could ever fully understand. He had sworn an oath to live by a code based on honor and unselfish public service. So far, he had been true to that code. So far, he had been able to lose himself in its tenets, even to the point that the code had formed the very traits of his own personality.

So far.

He had come back from Southeast Asia a broken man filled with shame and hate. Hate for himself. Hate for them. Hate for *him*. It had nearly driven him mad, the hate. He could have gone either way then. A bullet in his own head or a bullet in someone else's.

Each night the images of his own disgrace came like apparitions in the dark, haunting him, reminding him of how effortlessly they had broken him, of how easy it had been for them to cause him to spill his guts about everything he knew. And *how* he had talked! He had given them names, numbers, locations, dates, plans for future operations, methods. He had served it up to them, had become their waiter: *more water, sir?* All it had taken was for them to nail one of his testicles to a table, and the reward they had offered for his cooperation was to hack it off.

And so for him, becoming a police officer had been an act of personal salvation and not merely a choice of vocation. Only by giving himself completely to the idea of a life based on complete selflessness had he been able to lift himself out of the mire of the darkness of self-pity and doubt and stand in the light of men once more.

So far.

He opened a desk drawer to secure his service revolver.

Would Keaton ask him to betray what he stood for? Would the covenant he had sworn to so long ago pit him against the code of honor that now formed the basis for his whole being? Would he be forced to choose between the two?

He started to slowly push the drawer shut, but then he saw what was beneath his gun, what he was about to leave behind. He reached down and gently lifted up *his badge*. He gazed at it as if it were a child needing affection. Tears welled up in his eyes as he brought the badge to his lips and kissed it.

He put his badge in his pocket then took the object that had been under it and stuffed it into his duffel bag. If he was going to face the others after all this time, knowing what each of them knew, he would need it for strength, for what it stood for. He would need its old magic once again. He would need his green beret.

He sucked up his gut and disappeared into the rain like he had done so many times before in far away dark, evil places. Richmond Hill, Georgia was two days away, and Keaton was waiting.

Chapter 26

```
Nashville, Tennessee
May 13, 1982
```

According to Freud, intellectualization, a form of finding neat, airtight, logical explanations for unacceptable thoughts, is necessary if men are to sometimes do the abnormal but necessary things that must be done in order for civilizations to exist. Adolph Eichmann, protégé of Himmler, had carried this defense mechanism to its apex. Eichmann had reasoned that the killing of thousands of Jews was necessary in order to protect the rear lines of communications of the advancing German armies as they pushed ever deeper into Russia. Pratt Goldman had reasoned that Phoenix was necessary to protect the similar interests of the American forces in the Mekong Delta. In other words, the blood never stained his hands.

Even before his formal schooling, Pratt had educated himself in the deep mysteries of Freud, Kant, and Jung. Yes, we are animals, trapped by our genetic origins, forever dominated by our pasts. Yet, through denying our emotional, basal impulses with applied logic, we can escape the curse of our animal beginnings. He had disciplined himself to approach every difficult situation logically. If killing had to be done, then there had to be a logical explanation for it. Everything, even murder, is done for a reason, not on a whim, or on an impulse, or to satisfy some animalistic desire.

Each day of his existence in the dark jungles of Cambodia and Vietnam had been an exercise in neatly packaged, easily justified behavior. When they had been taken prisoner, he had logically reasoned that to resist would be stupid and illogical. So, without being asked, he had volunteered himself as informant and confessor. Afterwards, the VC had beaten him for show and because he was weak.

From the minute they had been captured, he had known the other men eventually would break. And he had been right. All, under the most inhuman and gruesome torture, had spilled their guts. And so, what he had done next had also been logical. *This madness has to stop*, he had told himself then. None of it was logical anymore. So, once he had rested at headquarters in Chau Doc, he had reported the team's confessions to his supervisors, turning his friends' moments of weakness into his own salvation. They were all secretly drummed out of the Army with honorable discharges. But unknown to the rest, he had been given a medal for service to his country, a fact that, to this day, none of them knew.

Quite logically then, he thought, Melanie should have understood and dutifully accepted his explanation after he announced to her in cavalier fashion that he would be "going somewhere away" for a few days. Or perhaps he assumed that, after having lived with her all of these years and after she had borne him two children, he knew her. He should have seen the fallacy of that assumption. After all, did Melanie really know *him?*

Apparently not, she confessed when he tried to explain about the covenant. He was shocked at how swiftly her personality changed when her secure world was suddenly threatened. He was also surprised to discover she could cut as deeply and as easily as he.

"And what do you suggest the girls and I do while you're off visiting your friends?" she asked angrily, her lips trembling.

"I think you're making a lot more out of this than it deserves," he replied matter-of-factly, not bothering to even get up from his chair. "Really, you're acting as though I've never gone away before. I mean, how many times did I go to seminars last year? Three, maybe four? You didn't raise hell then."

"Don't do this!" Melanie screamed. "Don't talk down to me like this. This is not the same thing and you know it."

"God," Pratt said, exasperated. "Look, it's just for a couple of days. I don't have to work right now. There's money in the bank. You can pay the bills as well as I can. You can take care of the children and the house. I just don't understand what you're so damn upset about. I shouldn't be gone more than a couple of days. I'll meet the rest of the guys and then . . . I'll come home. Understand?"

"You son of a bitch. You sit there and tell me about some damn macho blood pact you and a bunch of freak psychopaths made years ago when you were in the middle of that damn war. Then you tell me that some old man you thought was long dead suddenly shows up in your office and tells you to buy seven sets of fatigues, boots, winter jackets, and ski masks, obviously for somebody to wear. Hell, it's spring time! Then you top it off by telling me you're leaving tomorrow. You bastard!"

"Look, you've got no reason to mistrust me."

"Trust isn't the issue here. It's priorities. What's more important to you? The girls and me or this damn fool meeting?"

"I think that's an unfair question."

"My God. He thinks I'm being unfair," Melanie said sarcastically, then laughed. She threw up her hands and started walking around as if she were alone. "You have worked hard, you're about to be up for tenure. We have a nice house, friends. We're finally out of debt. And you don't seem to see the seriousness of leaving your family and heading off on some fool adolescent adventure that might get you in trouble. And you think I'm just supposed to understand? 'Oh, it's all right,'" she said, acting crazy, "'pack up and head off for the war again, old sport. We'll be waiting with open arms for your return.' Bullshit!"

"Listen! If I thought there was anything at all to this damn meeting, I wouldn't go," Pratt said harshly. "That old man, Keaton is his name, is about seventy years old. Hell, what can a seventy year old man do?"

"Be president."

"Melanie, there are only seven of us left. It's just a reunion. Look, I'll even tell you where it's at: a place called Richmond Hill, Georgia. You know what's in Richmond Hill, Georgia? Nothing. We'll get together, talk, get drunk, and I'll be back in a couple of days. Hell, would you be so upset if I got together with some of my old fraternity brothers? Of course you wouldn't"

"But the uniforms? He even gave you sizes," Melanie screamed, exasperated she could not reach him.

"You know as much about that as I do."

"Doesn't that tell you something?"

"What it tells me is that an old man wants some uniforms for some friends of his."

"What did you think when this Keaton came to you? Didn't you question anything about what he was asking you to do, especially after all this time?"

No. There had been no questioning. Keaton had talked and he had listened. There had been something unnatural, even alien, about Keaton's demeanor. Something final. His request that Pratt join the others and honor the covenant had been more than a demand. It had been put to him in the form of a challenge. It was as if Keaton knew about his betrayal. No, not even he could have known about that. But it was as if Keaton was daring him not to show up.

"The covenant is your last chance."

"Last chance at what?"

"To pay for your life. To escape the darkness."

"You don't think I took that promise seriously, do you?"

"No, I don't."

"Then give me one good reason why I should join you."

"To know what will happen."

And that had been it. He had stayed all of five minutes and left in his wake instructions on what to bring, when, and where.

But there had been something else. It had been thirteen years since he had last seen Keaton, but the memory of his old mentor when recalled was as vivid as a nightmare. The visitor who had shuffled into the sanctity of his office was an aberration of that remembrance. Keaton was an individual who had been cut of common stuff. Well-traveled and possessed of great experience, he still had been a man who had no formal education beyond his study of the art of soldiering. His lineage was sturdy and hardworking, but unremarkable. His language had evidenced his military life: straightforward, precise, not given to adjectives. Abstract thought had been foreign to his existence.

But the Keaton who had suddenly appeared in his office like a specter from a long dead past had spoken with a powerful, chimerical voice. There had been an alluring assurance about his presence, an aura of strength and, yes, knowledge. So strange, so addicting, this Keaton had a narcotic-like omniscience that he could not escape. It was an anomaly he felt the need to explain.

Yes, Keaton, I will join the others, but not because of the covenant, and not because I seek to be forgiven for my actions. I need no forgiveness for my actions. I will go, as you said, out of simple curiosity. I want to know what simple things the others have done with their lives compared to mine. I want to look at them and laugh.

"Pratt," Melanie said earnestly, "if you leave, the kids and I won't be here when you come back."

He threw back his head and laughed. Who the hell did she think she was fooling?

Chapter 27

**Blackstone, Virginia
May 13, 1982**

Mary's soft hair fell over her shoulders and across her cheeks like a blonde waterfall, smothering Chip with a silky, strawberry scented essence, and flowed across his chest as she moved softly over him, kissing his forehead and face. They were wet kisses, moistened with her tears. For, with the coming of the dawn, she knew he would slip from her grip and leave her for a rendezvous of uncertain reason.

Keaton had once again appeared in the dark of night. And it had been she who let him into their home. The first time Keaton had appeared to them on that dark, cold winter night past, she had dutifully left them alone and afterward did not press Chip for an explanation of who Keaton was and what he wanted. She had thought Chip would tell her when he was ready, but he never had. Each time she had probed close to the subject, he had waved her off or smiled and told her it was Vietnam. He never discussed Vietnam.

So when Keaton had suddenly appeared again, she was not about to let him escape. Nor was she about to leave him alone again with her husband. She had stood quietly to one side, studying the presence before her. He was tall and old with a craggy rock face, steel gray eyes, and close cropped gray hair. He wore a dark gray suit and a gray-black overcoat. His shoes were worn and unpolished. At first glance, he had appeared to be just another old man who had come in off the street, but there had been a translucence about him that caused shivers to go up her spine. As he and Chip had talked, she had tried to interject herself into their conversation. They had talked about things she had never heard Chip talk of before: a covenant, honor, and a *Dai Uy?* But it had been evident from his demeanor toward her that Keaton was not going to let her in. And although his explanations to Chip's inquiries had been halting, even nebulous, Chip had seemed to accept without question what Keaton had to say.

To her surprise, Chip had not seemed interested in Keaton's motives or the strangeness of his one request: Chip was to buy five army issue immersion heaters. Immersion heaters, Chip had told her, were gas fueled heaters used to cook food. The heater was placed inside a steel drum and surrounded by water. The heater put off a great amount of heat and boiled the water at the same time. Once he had bought these heaters he was to meet Keaton and some other men in an obscure little town on the east coast of Georgia. Never mind that to do this would cost more money than they could afford. Never mind that what he wanted Chip to do sounded like a request from a mad man. Never mind, hell! She had torn into Chip.

"First, I want to know why."

Chip raised his hand as if to quieten her while Keaton pretended to look away.

"No, Chip. Our marriage is a fifty-fifty proposition. I have a right to know what's going on here. I have a right to know what you're getting us into."

Chip turned to Keaton. "She's right. We've always shared. Can't you tell us?"

Tell us? My God, Chip doesn't know any more than I do, she thought. She turned angrily toward Keaton. "Listen, before I let my husband go off with you or anyone else, I've got to know what he's getting himself into. Now, you tell me – us."

She glared first at Chip, then at Keaton, then back at Chip.

Neither returned her look.

"My God. What's wrong with you, Chip?" she screamed, exasperated. "I can't believe what I'm actually hearing. This old man comes into our house and tells you to just pack and meet him somewhere and oh, by the way, bring military items with you, will you? And you say, 'Why yes, sir!'" She hung her head. "This can't be happening. We are up to our necks in debt. We've got to plant crops in the field this week. We almost lost everything last year. Oh, God, am I losing my mind?"

"No," Keaton said softly.

Chip brushed aside the hair from Mary's face. She seemed to accept it now. Her anger was gone, but in its place was fear and uncertainty. She understood he had to go, but not why. Men were different; no matter how hard women try to fight it, men were different. But what would she do without him? There were bills to pay, and the crops.

"Go to Mr. Slaw. Tell him what's happened. Don't tell him everything, though," he said close to Mary's cheek.

"I don't know everything," Mary replied quietly.

He propped himself up on a pillow against the headboard of the bed and turned his face toward the window frame, past Mary's nude body. Outside, an early morning mist had risen. A mist not unlike the one which had been present on the last day he saw Jude alive.

"I want you to understand that I'm not proud of everything I did over there. I guess that's one reason I never talked about it much with you. I love you too much for you to think anything bad about me."

He got up and walked to the window. As he began to speak, he put his hands against the windowpane and stared across the field. "We were pretty tight, the bunch of us. Rank didn't get in the way either. Everybody knew who was in charge. I guess after so many near calls, you get close to guys like that. And I guess that's how the covenant came about."

"What do you mean by the covenant?" Mary asked.

"Well, before the covenant, there was Jude. He was one of our team. Jude thought we were God's hosts. You know, from the Old Testament. The Army of the Lord. Jude saw everything in the world in terms of good and evil. He believed good and evil were constantly fighting each other for the control of men's souls, for the control of nations and peoples. To him, Vietnam was part of that fight. We were the Lord's hosts and the communists, not just those in Vietnam but all over the world, were the forces of darkness. I know it sounds silly and naive, but he believed it."

He turned and looked at Mary for some reaction, but she was expressionless, her eyes fixed on him. He turned back to the window and continued. "Jude felt atheism, communism, and totalitarianism were put on earth by God to test righteous men and righteous nations. He believed we were engaged in a life and death struggle with those evil forces, and that we, the American people, were losing. He used to say the emergence of America as a nation was no accident, that God had put America on this earth to fight evil. At the time, I dismissed him as a religious fanatic. I even used to laugh at him at times. But now? Anyway, he thought we were losing the fight because evil, Satan if you will, had won over the soul of America."

"Do you believe him?" Mary asked, but he did not answer her.

"Jude said Satan never attacked the weak and evil – they were already his. Instead, he went after those who could hurt him most: policemen, teachers, ministers, and most of all, America's leaders, its businessmen and its politicians. He said the evidence of what was happening was all around us. All we had to do was recognize it. The marketplace had become corrupt and devoid of morality. All businessmen cared about was making a profit, not their employees, not the country. And our political leaders had become the servants of big money, the people who were paying for their campaigns and who owned them."

"Honey," Mary said, grabbing him by the hand and pulling him against her, "we aren't a part of all that sickness, of those people and their world."

"Are we blameless? I wonder," he said, running his fingers through his hair. "Jude used to say the world was Satan's and that an age of darkness might soon set upon the world unless Americans changed their ways, unless we woke up to what we were becoming."

"He must have been an interesting man," Mary said.

"Yes, but he did some things he shouldn't have done. He took everything too far."

Then he paused for a minute. Mary gazed at him with a quizzical look on her face and waited silently for him to continue.

"Everything changed in 1968. We were given a mission called

Phoenix. Phoenix was a CIA program. What we did was target VC leaders and then assassinate them. No trial, just shot them based on intelligence information. Before Phoenix, our team had gone out and trained the local units in our area and provided medical assistance to the people in the nearby villages. But when we were ordered to carry out Phoenix, all of us changed."

Mary was hesitant about asking, but the temptation was too great. "Did you . . . did you?"

"I made my peace with God long before I met you."

"But the covenant?" Mary asked again, even though in her heart of hearts she was afraid of what she would hear.

"In Jude's mind, Phoenix had destroyed us, and Satan was the architect of Phoenix. So he did something desperate. He betrayed us to the VC. He told them when we were going to carry out a Phoenix mission in this little village called Tri Ton. He sent our mercenaries, Kit Carson Scouts we called them, in first to draw the fire. Jude had no respect for the scouts. He saw them as evil men who would kill anyone for pay. I didn't agree with him about our scouts. Anyway, he hoped if enough of them got killed headquarters at MACSOG would pull us out. Well, to him it sounded good. But one of our guys went a little crazy and charged in after the scouts and was killed. Jude fell apart, begging for forgiveness and all. We barely got away with our skins."

"What happened to him?" Mary asked softly.

"When he saw John die, he lost it. Right in the middle of the attack he charged into the kill zone in an attempt to save John and was hit by enemy fire. We eventually got it all from him, what he had passed on to the VC. We had this leader, a Captain named Elliot. According to doctrine, he was supposed to execute Jude for being a traitor. But he didn't have the stomach for it. Instead of letting one of us do it, he told Jude to go over the border into Cambodia and just disappear. That didn't happen though. Jude got caught by the VC. They put two and two together, found our trail, and circled around and trapped us. It should have been over then but, instead of killing us, they took us prisoner, and that's when the covenant came about."

As he continued to talk, images of the team's capture and subsequent torture, long repressed to the darkness of his unconscious, began to escape into the light and synapsed across his brain in vivid detail.

He lay face down on the muddy jungle floor. His hands were tied behind his back and his bare feet were caked with mud, his boots having been stripped to keep him from escaping. He felt groggy, as if awakening from a deep sleep. He sensed he had been moved. He could no longer hear the Sea Wolves. His head hurt. Slowly, he turned his face and saw Keaton lying on his side trussed up a few feet away. He could not see the others in the darkness, but could hear the slaps of rifle butts against their bodies as their captors roused them and lifted them to their feet. Then he heard a sharp command given by someone in authority. Two strong arms lifted him up. Almost effortlessly, the VC dragged him and the others into the depths of the dense jungle as it started to rain again. Every once in a while, he thought he heard one of the team say something, but immediately a slap and a smack hushed the sound.

He and the rest of the team and were being hurried deeper and deeper into the tangled abyss that was the Cambodian jungle. After what seemed like forever, their captors stopped and let each man fall helplessly to the jungle floor. He was thirsty. He wanted water so badly, he would have drunk his own urine. After a few minutes, he was able to slurp rain water that had accumulated around his face. It tasted wonderful! Then their captors went about their business again. This time, their movement was more purposeful, faster and more deliberate. He sensed they were nearing their destination, and he was right. Ahead in that wet darkness, he could make out their destination – Nui O.

He and the rest of the team were trudged up the mountain's side and secured in a dark and dank cave. Once they were in the cave, they were thrown into a pit that had been dug in the cave's floor. The pit had a circumference of nearly fifty feet and was fifteen feet deep. Their only light came from a flickering rag torch soaked in coal oil that had been embedded in the ground at the edge of the pit. When the men of the team looked up, all they could see was a darkened earth ceiling flickering wildly from the reflection given off by the torch. Every few minutes, a flop-haired guard would peep over the side and the pit and give them a mocking grin.

Doc was the first to venture to speak. "I wanna know now, is anyone wounded?"

Each man quietly responded "no."

"I sure could use some water," Pratt said with a parched voice.

"Think Junior there understands English?" Force said, looking up at the guard.

"Not likely," Keaton chimed in.

"You got a plan?" Force asked Keaton.

Keaton sat down and leaned against the wall. "No, I don't. What I don't understand is why they took us prisoner." It was as if he was talking to himself.

"Did anybody see *Dai Uy* and Julio?" he asked.

"They're dead," Jake responded flatly

"We don't know that," Keaton said quickly.

"Well if the *Dai Uy* ain't dead, he sure as hell should be," Jake replied.

"Can this shit. We gotta figure a way outta this mess," Doc said, feeling his way around the wall. "We gotta put our heads together and figure this thing out."

As if one of their captors had overheard what had been said, a bamboo ladder was run down the side of the wall. Several guards stood above them with AK-47s at the ready. Two of them suddenly slid down the ladder and grabbed Force. He struggled until one of the guards kicked him in the solar plexus, then he bent over and fell to the floor. A rope was quickly thrown into the pit and the men below tied him up. With a grin and a signal, the men above hoisted him up and over the top of the pit. The ladder was withdrawn and the men above disappeared. After a few minutes, they heard Force let out a blood curdling scream.

Then for what seemed like a very long time, there was an eerie silence. He and Pratt and lay huddled next to each other. Keaton paced back and forth. And Jake and Doc leaned up against opposite sides of the wall. No one spoke. They were too tired and too scared. Each knew that whatever Force was facing awaited them as well. Then, with a sickening thud, Force fell hard against the floor of the pit. Two guards peered into the pit and began to laugh.

Doc, the team's *Bac Si*, was the first to rush to Force, but realized there wasn't much he could do to help him when he saw what the VC had done. Force's pants had been removed and in the flickering light he could see that one of Force's testicles had been hacked off. Blood was everywhere, and Force lay moaning and began rolling from side to side. Then Doc began his work. "Keaton, you and Chip sit on him. Keep him on his back." He and Keaton did as they were told. Doc then took his bare foot and applied it to the jagged skin of Force's scrotum to stop the bleeding. "This'll take a while," Doc managed to say. Once the bleeding had stopped, Force lay against the pit's wall dehydrated and in pain.

Jake was next to go up the ladder. They returned him an hour later, his face bruised and bloody. He lay on the ground, not moving, his eyes open but not focusing on any of them. After a while, he managed to pull himself up and crawl over to the side of the pit. But still he said nothing.

"You know none of us is going to make it out of here alive, don't you?" Pratt said to them.

No one replied. Each knew Pratt was right. This was the end of the mission. No more escapes just in the nick of time. No more Jolly Green Giants. No more nothing. Rank, promotion, mission, the Army. Nothing mattered any more. The gun was at the backs of their heads and its hammer had been pulled back.

"Do any of you remember what Jude said?" Keaton asked, desperation evident in his voice.

"Yeah," Jake said meekly, answering for the others. He was sitting up now and staring hopefully at Keaton.

"He knew something. I can see that now." Keaton said, standing in the middle of the pit. He looked up into the flickering dark of the cave's ceiling and raised his hands upwards. "God," Keaton prayed, "if you will let me and my men out of this, I give you my word that I will do your will and look after each one of them for the rest of my life." His voice was loud and pleading.

Force sat up, managed a feeble smile, and said, "I give my word too."

Doc fell to his knees and cupped his hands together and upward and said, "I too give my word."

He and Pratt raised their hands upward and, in unison, said, "I give my word."

"Count me in too," Jake said, then fell to the ground and passed out.

Then the VC came for him.

He was tied down tightly to a wooden chair with thick rope, each leg lifted up by two guards. Then he saw what was about to occur. In the flickering light, he could see one of the guards flipping a Zippo. Then the guard held the flame under one of his feet. Pain soared from the sole of his foot throughout his body. He screamed so long that he eventually passed out from lack of breath. Two loud slaps across his nose woke him. Then the lighter was set aflame under his other foot. After he was revived again, he told then everything they wanted to know in halting, breathless detail.

After a time, the VC had finished with all of them. Each realized what they had done and each knew what would happen next. They were hurting, hungry, thirsty, afraid, and ashamed as they lay quietly around the floor of the pit waiting to die.

Pratt was the first to hear it. It sounded like rolling thunder coming at them from a distance. As it came closer, they sat up and exchanged questioning looks in the dim light. The sound came closer and closer. Then the ground began to shake, and the rumbling sound was so loud that some of their eardrums burst. Overhead, the ceiling of the cave began to fall in large chunks of earth and rock. Jake rolled away just before a piece landed with a thump where he had been.

Keaton knew what it was. "Arc Light!" he screamed.

All around them dust and debris began to fill the cave's air and they began to cough and gasp for breath. They looked up and saw the guards were gone. Instinctively, he spun Keaton around and then turned around so that his hands met Keaton's. It took some time to loosen the kemp bonds, something they had not been able to do with the guards ever present above. After a few minutes, Keaton had his bonds off and then he untied the rest.

They pushed him to the top of the pit. No one was to be seen. He lowered the ladder for the rest. And holding onto Force, they made it out of the destroyed cave, and they made their way down the side of Nui O and into Vietnam.

"We made it back to our headquarters at Chau Doc where we were stood down for a few days." Chip stopped speaking and a look of shame came over his face. Mary started to say something, but he began speaking again. "Then we were arrested. All of us. Charged with violating the military code of justice by giving information to the enemy. It was true, of course. We were guilty. But the Army didn't want any stench, so we were given honorable discharges for the good of the service."

"And Jude?" Mary asked.

"The VC tortured him to death."

"How did the Army know about what happened after you and the others were captured?" Mary asked, but he just shook his head.

"I don't know. I really don't."

Mary helped him pack. No, she didn't understand why he had to leave at this time in their lives. But he was her husband. Something was happening in Georgia, something she sensed was important. He was her husband, and she would stand behind him for they, too, had made a covenant.

"One thing I didn't mention before," he said as he stood at the door. "Our captain was blamed by the others for everything because he didn't shoot Jude."

"Did he break under the torture too?"

"He wasn't even with us. When the VC first ambushed us he was wounded and the VC left him for dead. If he'd been with us, he would have cracked, too."

Mary followed him to his truck. At the window, she kissed him. He looked at her, touched her face, and smiled.

"Jude knew something we didn't. He could see ahead. What happened to us, to him, all happened for a reason. I'm going because I want to know what that purpose was. And if the answer is in Richmond Hill, Georgia, I'll find it."

Chapter 28

Los Estados Prison
May 13, 1982

> Now, it came to pass at the end of seven days that the word of the Lord came to me saying, "Son of man, I have made you a watchman for the house of Israel; therefore hear a word from My mouth, and give them warning from Me:
>
> When I say to the wicked, 'You shall surely die,' and give them no warning, nor speak to warn the wicked from his wicked way, to save his life, that same wicked man shall die in his iniquity; but his blood I will require at your hand.
>
> Yet if you warn the wicked, and he does not turn from his wickedness, nor from his wicked way, he shall die in his iniquity; but you have delivered your soul."
>
> Ezekiel 3:16-19

A jet whirl of cold wind blew across the hard frozen ground between the Headquarters building and Internments One and Two. Captain Alvarez bent at the waist and leaned forward as the gusts, filled with stinging snowflakes, whipped against his face. With one hand he kept his parka's hood closed and with the other he maintained his balance as he trudged purposefully toward Internment Two. The grounds around

Los Estados prison were barren and flat. The fierce Antarctic winds that blew in from the cold sea formed the ground's snow into anthill-like piles scattered irregularly across the dead brown tundra. The air was filled with a constant rushing sound which, after prolonged exposure, could deafen a man.

He passed the helicopter that had brought him in from the mainland two days earlier and gave it a nervous sideways glance as if to make sure it was secure. He never stayed at Los Estados for more than three days at a time. There was too much to do on the mainland. The helicopter was his only way out. During the winter there was a lifeless quality to the landscape that depressed him. Few people ever visited Los Estados of their own free will. Even his men, wary of the effects of the winter, hardly ever ventured outside. Then there were the wolves; they had to be fed.

He gratefully pushed open the thick wooden double doors of Internment Two and entered the foyer. A guard sitting at his desk post just inside the great hall snapped to attention at his approach. Gracefully, he slid off his parka and handed it to the guard, seemingly without taking notice of his presence. The wind could be heard even inside the thick marbled walls of the huge villa. It reminded him of the sound the elevated trains from the subways of New York made when he had visited that city as a boy.

The great hall of Internment Two had been used at one time as a reception room for dances, weddings, and other gay social festivities of the aristocracy of Buenos Aires. It had once vibrated with the sounds of laughter and music. Now the hall housed the guards who oversaw the entrance ways to the villa's former great rooms where prisoners were now interned. The hall was brightly lit by three immense chandeliers that hung from the villa's roof. Ornate, with garish baroque paintings of voluptuous baby-faced women in various suggestive poses, the paintings were the only remaining evidences of the former owners of the villa, the land barons who had revealed their intention for these retreats with their taste in art. Center to the room was a winding wooden staircase that led to each floor. The second and third floors were formed like a horseshoe starting from the villa's entrance rearward. A banister of beautifully carved oak outlined each floor. There were nine bedrooms on each level, each with its own bathroom and entrance. There were two sitting rooms, a dining hall, a study, and a library on the ground floor in which were stored the Group's record section. The basement, with its dank rock walls and partitioned cells, was where most of the torture took place.

Internments One and Two together held sixty-one prisoners who were transferred intermittently from interrogation to the Naval Academy in Buenos Aires where they were executed. Interment Three housed his men. With arrests taking place at the rate of twenty a month, Los Estados was filled to capacity nearly year round, with each prisoner staying four to six weeks, depending on what information the prisoner was believed to possess.

He sat his peaked cap down on the guard's desk. The guard quickly and officiously hung it on a rack, a command presence for all to see.

"The key to 13," he curtly ordered.

"Yes, *commandante!*" the guard replied, handing Alvarez the ancient key.

As he slowly made his way up the winding staircase, Alvarez's head turned to the southeast as another roar of sound supplemented the wind. Super Etendard and Mirage jet fighters were taking off from the newly constructed naval air base at the far end of the island. *The naval aircraft are attacking the British fleet again*, he thought. Only a week before they had struck first blood by sinking the destroyer *Sheffield* and shooting down a Harrier jet.

The wooden doors of the guest rooms had been replaced by steel doors with bolt locks secured by a simple turn key. At the top of each door was a sliding peep hole through which it was possible to view the prisoner before entering. He slid the plate covering the peep hole aside and with one eye looked in. It was his habit to observe each prisoner before he entered. Once he had entered a cell and found a prisoner who had been dead for two days. The stench had upset his stomach.

There was a simple mattress secured to the floor and clearly visible from the peep hole. There was no other furniture. The walls were yellow and dingy, having been stripped of their gaily flowered wallpaper. The hardwood floor was dull and dirty, its veneer having long ago been rubbed away. The bathroom was doorless. It was not visible from the peep hole, but it had been stripped of anything detachable. Its faucet, commode, and shower were still intact but had no running water, the water being controlled from the basement. The room was lit by a single bright ceiling light that was covered with wire mesh and was always kept burning. The glass in the room's two windows had been replaced by Plexiglas. There was a small wire covered central heating outlet near the ceiling. The heat was turned on only during times of interrogation.

As he gazed through the peep hole, he could see her react to the influx of warm air. Instinctively, she rose from a fetal position on the mattress and stood on her toes, raising her arms up to the vent, hoping to channel the hot air downwards toward her naked body. He smiled. This one was not like most. She had an almost animal-like will to survive. Grudgingly after all because, due to their traitorous activity, these people were less than human, he found himself admiring her obstinacy the same way a hunter admires a prey that gives him a particularly hard time before it is shot.

By now she knew what was about to happen. Whenever the heat came on, her pain would begin. But for a moment she was able to experience a quick moment of pleasure. Pleasure and pain – Freud had been right, he mused. But today she was not scheduled for torture. Yesterday she had been water boarded. Tomorrow she would be shocked with electric current. Today she would be questioned. It was a simple routine: torture and question; torture and question. And once the prisoner had learned the routine, it was reversed.

He shut the peep hole and unlocked the bolt and pushed it back. Then he carefully opened the door and entered the room, slamming the door loudly behind him. The girl swung around and backed up against the wall shivering. *From cold or from fear?* he wondered.

"Sit down on the mattress," he ordered her in a loud voice. He then placed himself in front of her, his legs spread apart, his hands interlocked behind his back. A sickly half smile spread across his face as he stared down at her. Then, with a hesitant motion, he petulantly took a white handkerchief from his pocket and meekly coughed into it. The room smelled of unwashed human skin. There was also the scent of urine and feces. *Oh, damn*, he thought, chiding himself for not having her sprayed down before he arrived.

He did not ordinarily take part in the interrogation of prisoners. He had experts in the Group for that. Men who enjoyed their work.

But this one was different. Perhaps it was because she was an American. Or perhaps it was because she had escaped from him once before that he found her case personally interesting. He had, after all, orchestrated her return to Argentina after reviewing her file.

He noted that some color had begun to return to her cheeks. But her extremities – her fingers, toes, nose, and lips, were still bluish. Her long black hair was tangled and fell behind her back. Her nipples were hard and withdrawn. She was surviving the cold well, he noted. Even without heat, the thickness of the walls and the warmth that radiated from the center of the villa kept the temperature of the cells a constant fifty-eight degrees. Very uncomfortable, but not enough to kill, unless one was already sick or ready to die.

She sat quietly, her legs folded under her buttocks, shivering, her teeth involuntarily rubbing against each other. She did not look up at him but instead fixed her icy gaze at some memory of happiness only she could see. She had learned to disassociate herself from her surroundings, he surmised. Disassociation was common among prisoners. It was a last ditch effort defense mechanism against the reality of the hopelessness of their situation. So she had gone inside herself; had escaped from the cell to the sanctity of her spirit.

"Sonia," Alvarez began firmly, "look at me. Look at me."

She slowly raised her eyes, once bright but now faded black and dull from sleepless days and constant pain. Eyes imprisoned by dark, hollow sockets. Mournful, pleading eyes, which had once searched for substance rather than form in others, now mirrored the awful futility of that quest. Eyes that had once searched for someone she could trust, someone like her, now betrayed the reality of paranoia.

"Good. Now, answer my question. You remember my question, Sonia?"

But it was not truly a question. Interrogation is an art. The key to its success is keeping the subject's mind trained on a single thought, a single request for information, and a single fact from which the prisoner was not allowed to deviate, or escape from, or had the time or the strength to form a defense against. Answer, or pain; answer and no pain. It was really quite simple.

"What is your husband's occupation?" he asked.

"I've told you," Sunny answered faintly. "He is a teacher. Nothing else."

"At the United States War College?"

"Yes."

"Did he know of your acts of subversion against your country?"

"He knew very little of my life here."

She started to lower her head. The mere act of holding her head up for any length of time was tiring and painful.

"Look at me. Look at me!" he shouted. Painfully, she did as she was told. He began again, his voice monotone, unyielding. "I find that unbelievable. You loved each other?"

"We love each other."

"Don't contradict me!" he snapped.

Sunny instinctively turned her head as if to accept a blow to her face, but only words came.

"When he fucked you, you must have talked to him. You must have given him your thoughts just as you gave him your body. No? Do you think I am stupid? Now, what does he know?"

"My husband knows I was a protestor, but that's all he knows. He is not political. He is a teacher."

"Your husband is an Army officer, a major, is he not?"

She nodded and, without thinking, lowered her head. With an effortless motion, he kicked her just below her breast bone. Her mouth opened wide, but only a rushing sound of escaping air came out. Her eyes rolled up in her head. She grasped her stomach then rolled over on the soiled mattress and began to cough as her body jerked and convulsed spasmodically.

He waited a moment, letting the shock to her body subside, then grabbed a handful of her long hair and lifted her upright. "Sit up and look at me," he said through his teeth.

Her face was drawn and contorted in a mask of all encompassing pain. She felt like screaming, but was paralyzed by a deep sucking feeling below her rib cage. She could hardly breathe. Mucus flowed freely from her nose. And though she tried to control it, she felt herself urinating.

"You filthy, traitorous bitch," he hissed. The sight of her disgusted him. No longer the beautiful woman from the photograph, she seemed to have lost all of her human traits. But that was the beauty of the interrogation process. After a while, they all lost their human qualities. Day after day they became filthier and more horrid looking. And after a time, they lost their identity. Killing them then was the only humane thing a civilized man could do.

But Alvarez only pretended to be angry. In reality, his show of anger was for Sunny's consumption. The theatrics were for whatever result they could coerce. After all, one cannot be competent and passionate at the same time.

"What?" he asked.

She had made an only faintly discernable sound, almost a whisper. It had passed with a hiss from her blue lips as she had found his eyes.

"What?" he asked again, almost allowing himself to become agitated at her unresponsiveness.

"He is coming . . ." she uttered, with air barely coming out of her mouth.

He stood up. The expression on his face changed from one of mild exasperation to unmistakable satisfaction. So, now it came. The truth. "When will he come?" he asked evenly, smiling.

Sunny took halting breaths, holding her stomach with her hands, and began to forcefully swallow to keep from throwing up.

"Look at me!" he screamed. "What does he know? Who are his contacts here? When will he come?" He pounded away at her, repeating his questions over and over again. Her head began to swim as the room's walls started to revolve around her in a slow, swirling motion.

"He will come for you," she managed to say again.

"Who do you mean by *you?*" Alvarez asked with a smirk.

Sunny was dizzy, her vision blurred. Standing over her, the dark threatening figure of Alvarez was immense and powerful. His anger lashed out at her in his words. Could it be that he had not understood her?

"Who will the United States come for? General Galtieri? Admiral Anaya? Who?"

There was an intonation in his voice that evoked in her a familiar terror. Not just a feeling of terror. She had been afraid many times before. No, Alvarez had conjured up the remembrance of a distinct presence, one she had been near before. Then, like a shot in the back of her head, she recalled the day. *I know you*, she thought. *You. The presence. That day on the commons. You and that presence are one and the same. Evil. Pure evil.* "He will come for you," Sunny said, summoning all the strength she had left in her, her eyes boring into his.

He took a step back. For a second there was something there in her face, a look that sent a chill, icy, stinging cold up his spine. He laughed nervously. Then it started. Uncontrollably, his knees began to shake and his lips to quiver. All at once a sick feeling came over him. He felt the lunch he had just eaten start to come up.

That look. He had seen it before, and he knew what it meant. That same look had been on the face of the priest.

He agreed to personally take care of the arrest of the priest. It was a most delicate matter. The Church was not informed of the Group's involvement in the affair because the Generals greatly feared a confrontation. The Generals had come to him solicitously, their hats literally in their hands. But he had been gracious. Normally, the Group would not have been asked to dispose of an errant member of the clergy. In the past the Church had gone to great pains to show the *junta* it could discipline its own. But this cleric had gone too far for the Generals to ignore. This priest had helped secrete two students who had attempted to assassinate the commander of the Argentine Air Force, General Dozo. The attack had been poorly executed and had failed.

The Group's informers had traced the would-be assassins to the rectory at the priest's church. In predatory fashion, he and his men descended on the rectory, but the priest and the two men had fled to the sanctuary adjacent to the rectory. He cautiously entered the narthex after his men had beaten open the church's old wooden doors. The sound of their boots slapping against the polished concrete floor filled the nave as they briskly approached the altar where, kneeling in prayer, were the two wanted men. And with them was the young priest.

Slowly, the priest rose and, after making the sign of the cross over the heads of the two men, turned and faced him. The placid look on the young priest's face was somewhat disarming. Could it be a look of subterfuge, even ploy? Disdainfully, he averted his eyes from the priest's stare and motioned for his men to seize the would-be assassins.

Then he turned back to the priest and was puzzled by the look that remained on the priest's face. There was no fear there, no apprehension. Instead, he realized, it was a look of acceptance, and something else: expectation

As he gazed into the priest's smooth, fearless face with its mocking smile, its sky blue eyes that seemed to be silently laughing at him, a creeping feeling of alarm sent warning signals over his entire body. Yes, this priest knew something was about to happen. Something had been planned, put into motion, finalized, and this priest was eagerly awaiting its advent.

He stiffened when a white, hot light began to glow with fierce intensity and outlined the priest's face. From the altar, his men seemed to blow apart as the light met them. The would-be assassins evaporated. In a flash, the light reached the priest. He could not move. All at once, the priest's body was lifted up into the air. His arms were outstretched, as if he was nailed to a cross. His thin, blonde hair began to burn as it flared up from his head.

But in this frozen moment, it was the priest's eyes that he would remember, even in his dreams. Those eyes never left his face, not even as the priest blew apart. Their look of triumphant victory would be forever etched in his psyche. Then came the rush of wind and the horrific noise of the blast. All around him flew particles of human bone and flesh mixed with what was left of the altar and pews.

Without his knowing it, the priest had saved him by shielding him from the blast with his own body. When he came to, he was lying outside the burning church. Those of his men who had remained outside the church were standing around, their hands in their pockets, feeling useless. Groggily, he rose up and surveyed the scene of destruction and confusion around him. *What kind of man would destroy the house of God?* he asked himself.

Now Sunny had that same look on her face; of this Alvarez was sure. She knew something. Something had been planned, something that had already been put in motion. But when would it happen, and what would it be? She had not gone to America for study. No. She had gone to America to plan a return, and somehow this American she had married was the key to her plans.

He reached down and grabbed a handful of Sunny's hair and effortlessly lifted her from the mattress. The look had left her face. In its place was again the contorted agony of pain.

"I will be here waiting for him," he said defiantly. "And so will you."

Sunny could hardly speak, but she was trying. Alvarez was bending back her neck so hard with her hair that her mouth would not shut, and he could just make out her words.

"What was that?" he asked quickly upon hearing her faint words. Effortlessly, he slammed her to the floor with a whip of his hand. "Speak up. I can't hear you."

"Save yourself," she said between whimpers.

He took a step back from the battered figure huddled on the floor. For a moment, he was taken aback by her words. Then cautiously he bent down over her and smoothed back the hair from her face. "Oh," he said maniacally, "you mustn't concern yourself with my safety, my lady. No, there are others whom you know who are in more need of your worry than I. But it *is* touching, really touching, that you should care. And to show you how much I thank you for your concern, I am going to allow you a moment of pleasure for your effort."

He stood up and beat the door with his fist. Presently, a guard opened the door.

"Bring the hose and wash her down. Then tell Emile I allow him this one as a reward for his work."

Sunny managed to raise herself up on her elbows and began to sob and shake. Her mouth hung open, but she could not speak.

Alvarez threw back his head and laughed. "Save yourself," was all he said as he slammed shut the door.

Chapter 29

Washington, D.C.
May 13, 1982

It was a warm and friendly spring night, clear and moonless. Over the city, a star filled crystalline sky spread across the horizon. Silently twinkling, it was as distant and unattainable as the peace it belied. The universe, after all, is a violent place.

Father Perez took grateful notice of the absence of humidity as he strode down Constitution Avenue toward the Lincoln Memorial. Usually during this time of the year the moisture from the cooling Potomac River inundated the air with a wet stickiness that caused the clothes of most Washingtonians to cling to their skins. But earlier a fresh breeze from the river had swept the air clean. He took long, rhythmic strides and puffed purposefully on his old pipe, leaving aromatic contrails in his wake, as his mind, invigorated and relaxed from the exercise, went over detail after detail of one case after the other.

It was his habit to take this long, meditating walk at least three times a week, rain or shine. Taking the Metro at M Street to John Marshall Park, he would disembark and start his trek down wide Constitution Avenue past the National Gallery of Art, the Museums of American and Natural History, the Washington Monument with its ever present ménage of inhabitants, and the Ellipse, where joggers ran at all hours under the watchful eyes of the National Park Service Police. He would end his exercise at 23rd Avenue where he would hail a cab and return to his room in the rectory at the university.

He had never been afraid to walk down Constitution Avenue this late at night, and not because the Metropolitan Police had pairs of officers at most major intersections. No, the real reason he was unafraid was because he knew muggers would not attack someone wearing the turned around collar of a Roman Catholic priest. Even muggers were aware men of the cloth had nothing of worldly value to steal. It was late and quiet. The normally hyper populace of the Capitol seemed to have all gone into hibernation for the night. The only sound he could hear was the clop, clop, clopping of his size twelve shoes as they struck the sidewalk.

He had all but forgotten David's case. It had taken the back burner to other more pressing, if easier, cases. Students with depressions brought about by too much studying for final exams, students with thoughts of suicide prompted by the unexpected knowledge of the results of that studying. Then there were the constant anxieties brought about by love affairs. Students helplessly in love with the wrong people, students unable to cope with feelings foreign to their nurturing, students who had been jilted by lovers far away who could not last out the long months of separation, students pregnant. And then there were those who were just lonely and needed someone to talk to. Occasionally breaking the monotony, a student would come to him who was having problems with reality. But for the most part, he dealt with the mundane. He shook his head.

What had happened to David had been unfortunate, but life no longer presented any surprises to Perez. For him the unexpected had become commonplace. Peoples' horrible predicaments no longer aroused him or caused him any great concern. Had not Freud said a therapist's first job is to be indifferent to the patient's plight? How else could a therapist truly develop a logical understanding for a patient's problems unless he remained emotionally detached from the patient as a human being? David's case had interested him. That was true. It had taken him to new heights as a professional. But David had stopped coming once Sunny had been taken prisoner. He had tried to persuade him to come in for further therapy, but David had refused. So, quite professionally, Perez had written him off. A therapist never forced a patient into therapy. Entering and staying with therapy was always within the purview of the patient.

But Perez could not let go of Sunny. The memory of her pleading eyes, her selfless fear for David, was etched in him. A thousand times he had chided himself for letting her get too close. Freud would have been displeased. Still, every time he read or heard about what was happening in the South Atlantic, images of Sunny rushed forth, despite his futile attempts to forever suppress her memory.

He stopped. It was to his left across a grassy knoll that led to the Constitution Gardens that he sought to go. The site was under construction, due to be finished next November in time for Veterans Day. Placing it here, only a short walk from the Lincoln Memorial and the reflecting pool had been the most thoughtful of ideas. Where better to heal the hurt of a generation than near the resting place of that immortal binder of the nation's wounds? He stepped over the construction tapes and trudged up the knoll, his hands behind his back, his pipe firmly gripped between his teeth. It was dark, and more than once he found himself tripping over an unseen mound of dirt or a left over brick. Reaching the top of the cut in the knoll he made his way around to the proposed entrance.

As he rounded the bottom of the knoll, he experienced the same kind of feeling he had once had upon entering the sanctuary of a church. There was an aura of reverence already here. Even with only the sides of the dark V scarring the landscape, the eventual shape of the monument could be understood. A simple V cut into the nape of the knoll on which the name of every American killed in the Vietnam War would be etched into slabs of polished black marble. A V for Vietnam, not for victory. Later, he had been told, a statute would be placed away from the base of the V just at the edge of the Garden's sparse woods, depicting a Black, a Chicano, and a white soldier emerging from the jungle dressed in the combat regalia of the war. That might be nice, he thought. People liked images. But this? What a magnificent idea. Elegant in its simplicity. It will be America's Wailing Wall.

It was quite, almost tomb-like as he surveyed with a critical eye the work being done on the memorial. After all, he reckoned, this was his memorial too. For part of him had died in Vietnam along with the

58,000 men and women whose names would forever be a part of this landscape.

In the jungle he had learned to sense when he was being watched, the feeling that someone in the dark is shining a light on you. You knew when you were exposed. So he stiffened when he began to experience that familiar feeling.

He took the pipe from his mouth. "Who's there?" he said loudly, turning his head in one direction then the other, but the darkness gave no hint as to the whereabouts of the suspected onlooker. For a moment he felt a little foolish. *Must be getting old*, he thought to himself in a self-consoling way. Then a sound. Someone was walking in the darkness near the trees. *Just a soul like me out for a stroll on a warm spring night*, he hoped nervously.

He understood anxiety. He had studied its affects on the nervous system. Anxiety was to the body like gasoline was to a car: fuel. Too much fuel and the car's engine ran hot. Too much anxiety and a person hyperventilates, or worse. The key to fighting anxiety was to be able to identify its cause, localize it, and then deal with it in a positive manner. Treating anxiety could be easy or difficult depending on which type of anxiety a patient suffered from. If a person is afraid of something in the dark say, or someone or something unseen but heard moving around on a dark night near them hidden in a clump of trees, that type of anxiety, or fear, is called free-floating anxiety. If a person is fearful from free-floating anxiety, he would be difficult to treat until the thing causing his fear is identified, localized, made an identifiable object. When the source of a person's anxiety is identified it can be dealt with. In other words, a therapist's job is to turn free-floating anxiety into object anxiety. A person might be just as fearful, but it was easier to treat him if he knew what he was afraid of and could fight it one on one.

He intellectualized that in order to overcome his fear he had to face whatever it was near the woods. He put his pipe in his pocket, ran his hands through his hair, and tromped off rather noisily in the direction of the footsteps. He was once again thankful there was no humidity in the air. In a situation like this, the last thing he wanted was for his glasses to fog up. That had happened once before, and it had been disastrous, as he painfully remembered.

The canal ran along the base of Nui Co To, Superstition Mountain. It was a shallow canal, only six feet deep, built for sampans to ply their trade with the small hamlets at the water's edge. Nui Co To was not really a mountain. It was more or less a pile of rocks and dirt a thousand feet high, formed ages ago by the slow, steady nudging of the South China Sea against the Mekong Delta. It was a part of the Seven Virgins Mountain chain, similar geographical freaks rising up from the otherwise flat Delta. It was early morning, near dawn. A lethargic green mist hung low over the canal and the adjacent jungle. It had been raining for most of the night. The brief respite from the constant downpour of the water was welcomed by the men moving quietly over the canal in slithers of boats.

There were three sampans, each carrying three men. He was in the second boat. They seemed to float effortlessly down the dark, still canal, each carried along by a Cambodian bandit using a muffled oar. No one dared speak, for the night was filled with those who sought their lives.

Earlier, during the day, he had visited a dying major at the O'Lam firebase to administer last rites. The young major had died with only one regret, and that was not having even once seen his newly born daughter.

The other Americans were advisors who were heading for Chau Doc for a stand down. Travel during the day was too hazardous, and an air extraction was out of the question. The North Vietnamese Army had dotted the mountain with antiaircraft weapons that had withstood numerous air strikes. Stealth seemed the safest way out. For his part, he would be glad to see the old French hotel that headquartered MACV Advisory Team 64. But for now, there was nothing he could do except sit crunched up in the center of the sampan and let the bandits, who were being paid handsomely for their efforts, guide them to safety.

He shivered. The morning chill was upon them. Even near the equator, it had a bite. Despite the darkness, he could tell something else was blurring his vision. He took off his glasses and saw the mist had fogged the lenses. He took out a handkerchief and tried to wipe the moisture away, but it was no use. As long as they stayed in this humidity-filled mist, his glasses would be of no use to him. He folded them up, put them in a case, and stuffed them securely in one of his fatigue's side pockets.

He was now, for all practical purposes, blind. Still, when the flashes of light appeared above him, his eyes picked them out of the darkness, causing his head to turn in their direction. The flickering lights were far away on the crest of the mountain. For a moment, he was fixated on their frequency. Then he let out a gasp as all around him the placid canal water began to erupt in geyser-like splashes accompanied by the familiar whizzing sound of large caliber bullets hitting the water. Finally, from the crest of the mountain, came the poc, poc report of a heavy machine gun. He froze with fear.

Then suddenly, rolling down from the mountain top, came hundreds of small hot-white fireballs traveling at horrific speed, each one following the other like the licking tongue of some fire-breathing dragon. The gunner had loaded tracers and was walking them over the killing zone. The red hot rounds spewed and hissed as they hit the water. Some burned brightly for a second or to before they embedded themselves into the muddy banks of the canal.

"*Phu kit!*" cried someone in the first boat.

The bandits started rowing furiously down the canal. Unless the North Vietnamese Army gunner had a starlight scope, and that was unlikely, he was either reconnoitering by fire, or had a listening post nearby and was being guided by someone who had spotted the sampans. It did not matter. Their only hope of escape was to get past the mountain as quickly as possible.

He began to pray out loud. "Our Father, who art in heaven, hallowed be thy name . . ."

As if in defiance, a dragon tongue covered his sampan with a fiery shower of tracers. The bandit rowing the sampan let out a blood curdling scream and fell over the side of the boat. The bandit went under the water so fast that he and his traveling companion could not find the body, even though they frantically splashed around in the muddy water with their hands.

He looked up just in time to see it. Cloaked with a fuzzy iridescence, the sampan to his front evaporated as a hailstorm of tracers cut the boat and everyone in it to shreds. He quickly turned around, only to see that the boat that had been following them had already disappeared.

Then it started, that gut wrenching, paralyzing fear that attacked him every time he came under fire. "Not now. Oh God," he screamed. It was a combination of a sickly feeling in his stomach that made him want to vomit and a churning in his intestines that made him feel like defecating. He fought to keep control of himself.

He swallowed hard, retrieved his wire rimmed granny glasses and wrapped them around his ears, and turned to the advisor next to him and said, "We have to get into the canal and try to make it to the bank." He could just make out a nod from the advisor.

He knew if they could make it to the bank they could hide until the morning then make their way to Chau Doc and safety. Both men rolled out of the sampan into the excrement filled water and started swimming for the bank. About halfway to the bank, the mist rolled over them and he lost sight of the advisor. Around them the tongue of the dragon still licked and hissed with a ferocity that seemed to him unnecessarily cruel. He stopped and found he was in a deep part of the canal and had to tread water. His jungle boots made each kick difficult. To his amazement, he found himself tiring very fast. It had been at this point that his glasses fogged up again and he lost sight of everything around him. All he could see was the mist and the lapping water as it splashed in his face.

Then he heard the unmistakable sound of a man thrashing desperately in the water. "Father, please. Where are you?" the advisor called. The voice sounded panicky and wet, as if the man was having a difficult time keeping the canal water out of his mouth.

He searched, but he could see nothing. "Where are you?" he shouted, reaching out to this front. But there was nothing there.

"Father, please. I'm . . . I'm drowning. It's over my . . ." The voice trailed off.

He swam in what he believed to be the direction of the voice, but again, there was no one there.

"Father. . . please . . ." The voice was mixed in between splashes.

"Oh, Jehovah! Where has your love gone?" he cried out as he tried in vain to brush aside the mist with a splashing motion of his arms. But the blackness over the face of the water would not subside. As he prayed to his God, the splashing stopped. And in its place there came a sickly gurgling sound. "Ahhhhh!" he screamed, his fists clenched in rage, his arms beating wildly toward the heavens.

Perez stopped at the edge of the woods near the first blossoming dogwood tree. There, standing not more than ten feet directly in front of him, was a tall figure dressed in a gray overcoat. For a moment he was alarmed by the sudden appearance of the man. But after a quick overlook of the immediate area told him they were alone, he regained his composure.

He reached inside his pocket and retrieved his lighter. Effortlessly, he fired up the pipe with his Zippo, illuminating the man's face. It was an old face, craggy and leathery, with short cropped gray hair. He felt his fear leave him.

"Nice evening," Perez said, the pipe between his teeth.

The old man took a couple of steps in his direction and dug his hands deep in his coat pockets. "Spring," was all he said. He had a deep voice, telling of age, but there was a hint of power there. Maybe the man had once been a singer.

"It'll be a fine memorial when it is finished," Perez stated authoritatively, looking around the darkened site and waving his hand suggestively.

The old man took another step toward him. He was now close enough to see Perez eye to eye. "You feel comfortable here," the man said flatly. It was a statement, not a question.

He was struck by the old man's steel gray eyes. For a moment, the sight of them caused him to shiver. They were the eyes of a wolf. "Do you come here often?" Perez asked, hoping to get some small talk started so that he could conveniently break off this encounter and leave.

"You are Father Martin Perez of Georgetown University," the man said evenly and with a knowing smile.

The pipe almost dropped from Perez's mouth and he was seized by a sudden urge to run away or to cry out for help. But the swiftness of the stranger's words had stunned him to the point of paralysis. All he could do was let his mind race for an appropriate response.

As if sensitive to his predicament, the stranger spoke again with a quiet, calming voice. "Do not be alarmed. You are familiar to me, and I mean you no harm."

Perez felt the tension begin to leave his body. "How is it you know me? And how did you come to be here? Have you been following me? If so, I feel it's an invasion of my. . . "

The stranger raised his hand as if to quiet him. "Now, listen to me. We have not much time."

A look of sheer awe came over Perez's face. *Who is this man?* he thought. *How could he . . . what does he mean?*

"I know of your fear, but after I tell you who I am you will understand," the stranger said, his hand still raised.

Perez did not reply. He stood still and silent, waiting breathlessly.

"I am Keaton, friend of David."

Perez breathed hard and blinked as his glasses started to fog up from his own nervous perspiration. There were too many questions that needed answers. David had told him under hypnosis that he had killed Keaton. If this man was Keaton, then what of David's statement? After he had brought David back from his hypnotic state, he had dared not mention Keaton for fear of causing a recurring episode of the trauma David had experienced. And David had ceased coming to the sessions before he could probe into the matter any further. Secondly, if this wasn't Keaton, who was it? And even if this was Keaton, when had he talked to David? How did he know he would be at the memorial this night? He was as confused as he was fearful.

"Why do you still fear me?" Keaton asked reassuringly.

Yes, why do I fear him? Perez asked himself. *Maybe it is because this was all so unexpected, so sudden. Or maybe it was became it made no sense.* "What do you want?" he asked forcefully. Object anxiety had to be fought head on.

"Can we walk?" Keaton asked.

Yes, walking would help. He motioned for Keaton to lead the way. Keaton gracefully nodded, and together they slowly made their way into the canopy of the hackberry and dogwood trees.

Perez started. "When did you last see David?"

"Some time ago," Keaton answered calmly.

"I am most concerned about him, especially after what happened to his wife. By the way, have you met her?"

"I know her," Keaton replied softly.

"And David?" Perez asked. "He will be all right, if he receives the therapy he needs," he added, not thinking.

Keaton stopped and turned to Perez. "Therapy?" he said.

Perez caught himself. *Why did I mention therapy?*

"Therapy is not what he needs," Keaton said sharply.

Perez became flustered. "Look, Mr. Keaton, I am glad to have met you. I am also pleased David sent you to see me. But my time is valuable, and I would be less than candid if I did not tell you that I am somewhat agitated at the method by which you chose to contact me. You could have easily made an appointment at my office. I value my private time and . . ."

Keaton raised his hand toward Perez and gave him a stern look. "In two days' time a group of specially chosen men will gather in a town called Richmond Hill on the east coast of Georgia. On the outskirts of this town, there is a place known as the Ford Mansion. There will these men meet. David has no knowledge of this gathering. However, each of these men is known to him."

Perez gave Keaton a questioning look. "If David is not aware of this meeting, why are you telling me?"

Keaton was silent. A dark look came over his face.

"Look, I think you and I have nothing further to say," Perez said angrily and started to walk away.

"Martin!" The tone of Keaton's voice was chilling.

Perez stopped and turned around. "Who are you?" he asked very fast, his eyes wide.

"Do you not now know me?"

Perez swallowed hard. "No, I don't know who you are, and I don't know what you want of me. Now, please leave me alone. Tell David I don't know what his reason for doing this was and I don't care, but if he thinks he can start playing games with me, he's wrong. I intend to go to the authorities if this happens again."

Keaton reached out and pointed a finger at him as if it were a sword. "Martin, in two days' time David must go to Richmond Hill. It is of utmost importance that he rejoin the others. More is at stake than you can possibly understand." Keaton's words seemed to emanate from the tip of his finger and their effect was to go through Perez like a dagger.

Perez suddenly felt faint and reached for a limb of a dogwood to steady himself. In one swift motion, he tore his glasses from his face and turned angrily to Keaton. "You . . ." But Keaton was gone. "You'll not get away so easily," he said fitfully then let go of the limb and started after Keaton down the paved walkway that ran through the garden. But after a few yards, he could find no trace of the old man and stopped, holding his hand against his chest. He was breathing hard and sweating. "Come back!" he cried out. "Where are you?"

But there was nothing in reply except the stillness of the dark woods. He stood unsteadily, his long arms rigid at his sides, his fists clenched in anger. *What was the purpose in this?* he kept asking himself over and over. *Why, David? Why?*

Chapter 30

Before he slipped into the abyss of his subconscious, David wondered why he was experiencing another nightmare. At his conscious level, he reassured himself it was merely another dream, and that if he would just be patient he would eventually wake up. Still, with every passing second, he found himself falling into the dark waters of a familiar terror. Like a drowning man, he desperately grasped for anything that would keep him conscious. Eventually though, he went under.

He surfaced to find himself entombed in a coffin made of a smooth glass-like substance. He tried to sit up, but the space that enclosed him was too small and cramped for him to move anything but his arms. Panic seized him and he began beating frantically on the ceiling of the coffin with his fists, but the smooth surface wouldn't budge. He was trapped. Buried alive.

Strangely, he began to notice he could see all around him. Then he looked up; the coffin was transparent. To his amazement and relief, he could see the world outside of the coffin. It seemed he was being shot through space like a rocket. Outside, streaks of white, wispy clouds were passing by at terrific speeds. The sky was bright blue and endless.

What an incredible view, he mused. A sharp beeping noise caught his attention and he looked down to see that the coffin had an instrument panel. He grinned. This wasn't so bad.

Then he heard a voice coming from the other side of the instrument panel. "David, isn't it wonderful?"

"Andrew?" It *was* Andrew, wearing his flight suit and helmet and sitting in front of the console of the instrument panel, his head turned in his direction. Instead of his usual grin, Andrew gave him a wry, knowing smile. "Wait a minute. Why are you smiling? The last time I saw you, you kicked me in the face," he said incredulously.

"It's really peaceful, David. Once you understand what it all means."

Outside the coffin, there was a roar of wind and the sky began to revolve away. In its place appeared a gently rolling kaleidoscope of land. Hills, green and dotted with small trees, puffed up here and there. Streams, blue with white patches of froth, snaked harmlessly across the emerald green plain patched with fields of brown and gold. This glorious terra firma seemed to flow effortlessly across the face of the glass.

"This isn't a coffin. It's a jet fighter!"

"Yes, David. It's wonderful, isn't it?" Andrew said contentedly.

"I don't understand."

"Not many do. Only a few will ever let themselves understand. But when they do, it's pretty wonderful."

The view outside the glass suddenly turned black.

"What's happening?" he cried.

"There is darkness that's spreading over the earth, David. Unless it can be stopped, it will smother the light of man. But stopping it will be difficult. For its doctrine is powerful and its call is deceptively pleasant to the ears of the naive and the guilty. Many already know its perverse teachings. The land has only one hope. Sunny knew this."

"*Knew* this? You talk about her as if she is dead. Don't talk about her like that. She's not dead!"

"David, there are only two forces in the world: good and evil. And there's no in between. But unfortunately we've yet to learn that the struggle between the two can be deceptive in its nature. We turn our heads from the truth before us by adding meanings where there are none. We appease evil by legitimizing it with our laws. Our misconceptions about freedom of choice have caused us to forsake our brothers everywhere. We've not yet learned, David, that freedom means responsibility. Responsibility to others, to ourselves. And most of all, responsibility to Him. The lust for lucre and power has changed us to become hollow and evil. We've lost our way, David. We've lost sight of the reason for our existence. And in doing so, we are helping snuff out the light. But Sunny knew all of this. She was a light in the void."

It was so dark he could not even see his hand before his face. "Please turn on the light. The darkness, the darkness . . ." he begged Andrew.

"I know, but this is what it will be like. No one will have any choice. No one's thoughts will be their own. People will live life like slaves to *Them*, the *Masters*, coming and going, living and dying, at their pleasure."

"This is just a dream. This isn't reality!"

"A dream? This *is* reality for your brothers all over the earth. This is now. This is what Sunny endures!"

He started jerking violently against the straps that held him against the coffin-seat, but it was no use. "Got to get out of here! Got to stop this dream, now." Angrily he lurched forward with his arms outstretched reaching for Andrew's flight helmet. "Andrew . . . stop this!" he screamed. But Andrew was beyond his reach.

The flight helmet turned away from him, then turned back again. But the face inside was no longer Andrew's. "Jude!"

"Yes, David. Look up. Tell me what you see." Jude's voice flowed over the coffin surrounding David with a resonance of power.

He looked up. "I don't understand it," he said wide eyed. The darkness of the void above was broken here and there by flashes of red fire. Lightning inside a thunderstorm? And with each flash, he swore he could hear a high pitched wail above the rushing wind outside the cockpit.

"No, David," Jude said. "Not lightning. What you see are the souls of men who have succumbed to the *Ruler of the Earth*. Do you still not understand?"

He barely shook his head.

"He was given the Earth and all in it for his domain. Those who worship power, wealth, and lust: the things of this world – are his until the end of time. And do you know where they are doomed to spend eternity?"

Before he could answer, Jude reached across the instrument console, grabbed his jaw, and turned his head toward a bright fireball that hung in the cold space above the earth. "Energy, David. A soul is pure energy. It can never be destroyed. How would you like to be inside of that?" There was terrible thunder outside the coffin.

"Where are we going? Please, I need to know," he asked, tears streaming down his cheeks.

"We are going to *Him* from whom you have turned your face." Then the helmet turned away from him.

"Who, Jude? Who are we . . . ?"

The flight helmet again turned again, and he was frozen with fear upon seeing the face inside. "Keaton! Why you? Don't look at me with those eyes. No . . . no . . . it can't be you. You're . . . Ahhhh!" he screamed and began slapping his hands against the hard, smooth glass.

Slap, slap, slap . . . rap, rap, rap. David shot up in bed. He was breathing hard and his body was covered with sweat. He turned to the door in the hallway. *Rap, rap, rap.* He looked at the clock on the night stand: 12:30 a.m. Who could it be at this time of the morning? Sunny! News of Sunny.

He jumped up and stumbled down the hallway. He quickly opened the door and, to his disappointment and amazement, there stood an angry Father Perez. "What do you want?" he asked in an unfriendly tone.

"I have the same question," Perez replied harshly.

"Look, it's late. And I don't feel like playing mind games with you now. Now, what is it?"

Perez gave David an impatient look. "Don't try to pretend you don't know why I'm here."

"Has something happened?"

Perez sighed with disgust and pushed his way past David and into the apartment. Reluctantly David signed with just as much disgust, turned on several lamps in the living room, and motioned for Perez to take a seat. A chill was on the room so David shut the open window. Perez's anger seemed to have left him, albeit his face was furrowed and dark.

"I had a visitor tonight," Perez announced in hopes of eliciting some betraying response.

David didn't answer; he just crossed his legs and yawned.

"Do you know an old gentleman, tall, muscular, gray hair, with the eyes of a wolf?"

David licked his lips and shook his head no.

"No? Well he knows you."

"How so?"

"He served with you in Vietnam."

A look of faint interest came over David's face. "What's his name?"

"Keaton."

As Perez watched, David's face turned ashen. He tried to imagine what images of personal hell that name evoked.

"Yes, Keaton," he said again, carefully.

David paired the nightmare with what Perez had just told him and his lips began to tremble as his thoughts flowed, uninhibited by any doubt. "That's impossible," he said somberly.

A questioning look came over Perez's face.

"Peebles Michael Keaton, Master Sergeant, United States Army Special Forces, shot himself in the head on December 25th in the year of our Lord, 1975," David said flatly.

He had returned from Berlin, grateful to have been chosen to be a member of the War College faculty. He had successfully repressed the horror of Vietnam and had lied to himself about his future in the Army, but illusions always evaporate with the first winds of reality. His did when a long distance phone call from a lawyer in Linton, Indiana woke him from an afternoon nap on a Saturday. Linton, a small farming town, sits dormant in southern Indiana.

He had arrived by mid-morning, exhausted from the drive. He had no trouble finding the funeral home. It was the only business in town that was not in financial trouble. He parked his car in the almost empty lot. Upon entering the large white building, he was greeted by the odor of embalming fluid and the sweet smell of decaying flowers

After standing for a time somewhat forlornly in the empty foyer looking for the right room, he was approached by a pleasant enough looking gentleman – tall, narrow faced, with slicked back gray hair, dressed in a black suit that seemed just draped over his lanky frame.

The man had an affable smile that appeared to be well-practiced. "Who is the party?" the man asked with a solicitously sweet voice.

"Keaton. Peebles Keaton," he replied somewhat awkwardly, extending his hand to the man. "I was his friend."

The man, his eyes closed to slits, nodded his head understandingly and grasped his hand between both of his slick and oily ones. He withdrew his hand from the undertaker's grasp.

"So sad," the man said in a mournful tone, indicating experience with these matters. Grieving was his living. Death was his natural resource.

He followed as the man lamentably led him to a room at the end of the hallway. The room was rectangular and spacious. Two chandeliers hung from a high ceiling, giving the room the appearance of being illuminated by celestial light. There were no windows, and the walls were an off-white cream color, the carpet red. Rows of brown wooden folding chairs started at the back of the room and extended to the front with an aisle in between. Today they were empty. He and the undertaker were the only people in the room.

"Is the funeral going to start on time?" he asked quietly, then felt a little silly for doing so.

"In thirty minutes," the undertaker said sweetly, but with a trace of curtness.

"Do you know a Mr. Martin, a lawyer?" he asked the undertaker.

"You are the executor of the deceased's estate?"

"No. Mr. Keaton didn't leave a will. My name was found on a piece of paper wrapped up in some cash."

"Before you leave, I will prepare a statement for you."

Keaton was entombed in a plain bronze casket that was shut tight. The wall behind the casket and an adjacent podium were embedded with flower hooks, but he was surprised to see there were no flowers anywhere.

"Hasn't anyone been here? Aren't there any flowers?" he asked painfully.

"Oh, do you wish some flowers? I can have them here before the service."

"No, that won't be necessary," he answered, giving the undertaker a hard look.

The service had been short and perfunctory. A minister from a local Baptist church had entered the room and, after giving him a sideways glance and a sickly smile, had read a passage from the Bible, said a prayer, and left for his car. Poor Keaton was a Roman Catholic, he thought ironically. Then attendants from the mortuary loaded Keaton into a black hearse. The whole affair lasted about ten minutes.

The drive from the mortuary took him past closed buildings and lifeless streets to a small cemetery just outside of town where Keaton's casket was rolled onto a drop over a fresh hole in the frozen dirt. It was a cold, gray day. A brisk, chilly wind sent shivers up everyone. The preacher said a quick prayer and departed.

The undertaker seemed in a hurry to return to a more profitable enterprise. But before the undertaker could leave, he grabbed him by the arm. "One thing. Why was his casket closed?" he asked through the chill.

"Oh, well," the undertaker said with the same smile, "Mr. Keaton shot himself in the forehead. It really was a mess."

Perez swallowed hard. "Then . . . who. . . was the man who approached me tonight?"

David forcefully regained his composure. "I don't know. But whoever it was has a cruel sense of humor. Perhaps it was some nut who read about Sunny in the paper. Who knows?"

"Even if that were true, why would he come to me?" Perez asked hesitantly.

"How the hell do I know?"

Perez gave David a stern look. "This is most serious. You must tell me. Did you send this man to me tonight?"

David returned the stare. "No, I did not."

A spontaneous and mutual understanding of an awful reality dawned on them: someone knew a great deal about them both. Someone unknown to either of them. But who, and how?

Perez paced the floor of David's apartment, recalling every detail about the pretender who had confronted him at the memorial site. The man had Keaton's looks and his mannerisms. Whoever had planned this scenario had researched his subject well. But who and why? The same questions were there and neither David nor Perez could come up with any satisfactory answers.

"He obviously knew about Sunny. When I asked him if he had met her, he replied that he knew her," Perez said through a cloud of pipe smoke.

"No doubt," David said thoughtfully, "but how did he know about you? The only persons who know I had been in therapy are Sunny and you, and maybe Andrew, a friend".

"I've never met Andrew," Perez stated.

"No, it wouldn't have been Andrew," David said with a chagrined look. Had Sunny confided in Andrew?

"Are you sure?"

"Yes, he's in Virginia. Besides, he never knew about Keaton."

"Then there's a possibility I feel I have to mention," Perez said, jabbing David's arm with his finger.

"It could have been a member of your old team."

"Ridiculous," David said, giving Perez a sharp look.

"Don't be so sure. Let's look at what we have. A piece about Sunny appears in the newspaper. Innocuous enough, until read by a former team member of yours, one who has held a grudge against you all of these years for whatever reason. After reading the article, a thought emerges in his mind. What if he can turn this tragedy into revenge? The more he mulls it over, the more the plan makes sense. He stakes out your apartment. He follows you to work, to my office. He puts two and two together. Then he revises his plan. He stakes me out. He knows where I go each day. Then when he's ready, he puts the plan into action. He hires someone who knows nothing about you or me or what happened in Vietnam – just an actor, to do what was done tonight."

"But it doesn't make any sense," David said.

"It does if you take seriously this character's last words. He was emphatic that you *rejoin*, yes that was his exact word, rejoin, the others in Richmond Hill, Georgia. And he said in three days time. Now, what do you think?"

"But why portray Keaton? Keaton's dead."

"That was his big mistake. He didn't know Keaton was dead, did he?"

"No. No one knew about Keaton's death," David said.

"Yes, and that's how we'll catch him!" Perez said eagerly.

"But why?" David asked, fascinated, and at the same time surprised that Perez was again interested in involving himself in his affairs. But Perez was involved. For some unknown reason, the culprit of this farce had purposely made Perez a part of his design. Perez was in it up to his neck, like it or not.

"Revenge. It's such a tempting emotion. Humans succumb to its sweet taste as much as they do love, hate, or lust," Perez said indifferently, as if talking to himself. "But why after all this time? You have not been inaccessible. He could have done something to you any time he wanted. No. It had to be that after the reality of Sunny he saw his chance."

"Assuming it is a member of the team, why not just confront me? Why bring you into it?"

"Perhaps he senses that you are vulnerable now. Maybe he feels that because I am . . . was . . . your therapist, you would be more prone to do what I told you. At this point, I just don't know why he chose to involve me. It's you he's after. You are the one he wants in Georgia, not me."

"Somehow my relationship to you is known," David said, and then stopped as if pondering how.

"Did something significant ever happen to the team in Georgia?"

"No. The only time I was ever in Georgia was during my initial training at Ft. Benning."

"Of course. Infantry, Airborne and Ranger schools," Perez said with a tone of familiarity.

"Then it has to be connected with something that happened after the team broke up."

"The team didn't break up," David said quietly.

"Didn't break up?" Perez squinted at David, causing his eyebrows to droop over the rims of his glasses.

"It doesn't matter," David uttered.

Perez reached out and grabbed David's arm. "Tell me what happened to the team, David. Tell me."

"The pain was so damn bad I wanted to scream. But I didn't though, 'cause they were all around us, cackling like a bunch of chickens.

Laughing a nervous sort of laughter, the kind you make when you realize you're alive and probably shouldn't be. They were rounding everybody up. I remember thinking how odd that was. Usually the VC just shot us – the wounded, everybody. They didn't have the manpower or resources to take care of prisoners. I guess the VC commander was afraid of the helicopter gun ships. Even though it was dark as hell, the chopper pilots would have seen gunshot flashes and I could hear them flying around trying to find us in the dark. At the time, I thought they were just rounding everyone up to take us off and shoot us somewhere secure.

"As it turned out, that wasn't true. The VC knew what they were doing. I guess Jude had whetted their appetite. We'd been kicking their asses for over a year and they wanted us real bad. We all had prices on our heads, but now that they had us, they became curious. No, they didn't want to kill us right away. They wanted to get inside our heads, find out what made us tick, find out what we knew. They wanted to know about Phoenix.

"So, I just lay there as still as I could, feeling the pain. I could hear them manhandling the ones left, Jake, Force, all of them. Even Keaton. They were slapping their faces and hitting them with the butts of their rifles. And all the while they did this you could tell they were becoming more excited. After I time I began to realize it was me they were looking for and they were getting angry because they couldn't find me. I could hear Keaton telling them I was dead, but they didn't believe him. They started feeling around the bodies.

"My mind raced for a course of action. I started thinking about how I had found other men who had been tortured. It had usually been pretty grizzly, and I knew I wouldn't be able to stand up very long to that kind of pain. So I slowly pulled out my Webley and waited. I didn't even have the guts to kill myself, but I was willing to make them do it for me. Then the choppers came, Sea Wolves, Navy, and I saw my chance.

"Two of them, a hunter team, flew in and hovered directly over us. I don't think the pilots knew we were below, they were still just searching. But the noise of their hovering concealed the sound of my crawling away into the underbrush. I crawled as fast as I could across that slimy jungle floor. When I thought I was safe enough, I rested. I had to fight hard to control the sound of my breathing. The helicopters had moved on and were hovering somewhere else in the distance so I had to be quiet. Thank God it started to rain again.

"It's funny, now that I think about it, but I was almost thankful I had been wounded. The pain kept me awake and alert. We hadn't slept for two days. You don't sleep while people are trying to kill you. I laid there in the rain, shivering from the cold and the hurt until dawn. Then I started out for Ba Chuc. Ba Chuc was a small Cambodian-Vietnamese town nestled between several of the Seven Virgin Mountains. The Vinh Te Canal ran along its northern outskirts. The Vinh Te was the border between Cambodia and Nam. I decided I'd stick to the canal and follow it with the sun. I don't know how it happened, but I had lost my compass.

"I kept a pretty good pace along the canal's edge. Once in a while, a sampan would float past me, but for most of the morning I was alone. About midday, I started to get tired. I guess I had lost a lot of blood. Each time I stopped to rest, I would cover myself with nipa palm leaves. And I would think. That was the worst part – thinking. I could only imagine what the rest of them were going through. And you know what? I was glad I wasn't with them. How about that? I was glad. I remember the feeling I had about being alive. God, it felt good! I could breathe and feel and see. I didn't feel any shame either. I just felt good.

"The shame came later, though. My men would never have been caught if I had had the guts to shoot Jude. Oh well, I couldn't do anything about that then, could I? They were caught and I was wounded. My instinct to survive was stronger than my quest for honor. Anyway, after the third or fourth stop, I covered myself up and fell asleep. Guess I gave up on thinking.

"I reached the outskirts of Ba Chuc about the time it was getting dark. Took me all day to travel two miles. I was really weak. My pants legs were caked with dried blood and flesh and I couldn't feel anything below my left groin. Thoughts of amputation darted in and out of my consciousness. That scared me more than dying. I knew there was a *Bac Si*, you know, a doctor, in Ba Chuc. What I didn't know was which side he was on.

"The *Bac Si* lived in back of a bar. I don't remember its name, but the people in the bar were having a hell of a time. Might have been a

Saturday night. But I was glad they were having a rousing time because they would be preoccupied with their own debauchery. And I didn't need any attention. I knocked on the back door and after a moment a girl came. And damn it, this girl was as lovely a sight as you could imagine. You know what the beautiful ones looked like.

"She was startled by the sight of me. I guess I did look pretty bad. I told her I was a Co Van, an advisor – they all liked advisors. I didn't have my beret, so she couldn't have known I was with SOG. She let me in. I remember how grateful I was to be able to lay down on that hard bamboo bed. The next thing I knew, I was asleep."

He stood up and started pacing around the apartment.

"It's funny how you can be asleep and at the same time sense what's going on around you. I could feel the doctor treating my wound. I could feel him pull the skin apart and cut parts of it off. That's why the scar looks so bad. He didn't have any anesthetic, so when he started to sew the skin together the pain woke me and at the same time caused me to pass out. Life has a way of evening things out, wouldn't you say?

"I woke up naked, lying on my back in what seemed like a shallow pool of water. You remember some of the richer VNs had shallow troughs in their homes where they washed clothes and took baths? That's what I was lying in. I could feel myself being washed. I opened my eyes and saw it was her. Damn, how ironic. While my team was being tortured, I was being bathed by this beautiful woman. But I wasn't thinking about the team. All I could see, feel, and think about was this girl. She wore a white *ao dai*. Her black hair was tied behind her and fell over her back like a silk tail of a mare. She had one of those round, smooth faces that many of the Delta women had. Her lips were full and wet, and her eyes, it was her eyes I remember. Those emotionless, subservient eyes that tactically transmitted her desire. I didn't have to say anything. She read my face.

"There was one flickering candle on a table at the far end of the room. She floated over to it and blew it out. Even though it was dark, I could see her taking off her *ao dai*. You ever cheat on God and sleep with a Vietnamese girl, priest? No, not you nuns. Let me tell you. Their skin is as smooth and creamy as silk. Their hair smells like spice. And when they make love, their body belongs to you. And I mean belongs to you. She knew I couldn't move, so she massaged me until I was hard. Then she moved on top of me. Oh well, I can see that look on your face. But believe me, priest, what happened that night had nothing to do with sex.

"It felt wonderful. She was so gentle, so careful. I shut my eyes and started to drift like in a dream. Then she stopped. It's strange. I hadn't heard anything. It wouldn't have made any difference if I had. After a second or so, I opened my eyes to see why she had stopped.

"When I saw what was happening to her, I was momentarily stunned. The *Bac Si* had grabbed her hair and wrapped it around her neck and across her mouth. He held her against him and with his other hand he held a scalpel against her throat. She knew what was about to happen. She was staring at me, eyes wide, with tears streaming down her face. It was as if the two of them were staging this for me. With a flick of his hand, he cut open her jugular. Blood went everywhere. The only thing he hadn't counted on was my having my Webley next to the trough. As if by a premonition, the girl had brought it to me. I fired off two shots. One hit him in the chest causing him to release the girl's body. The other got him in the stomach.

"I knew the noise would bring someone, so I slipped on a pair of his pajama pants and left. With any luck, it would have taken him several hours to die. I know what you're thinking. This man had healed me, had saved my life, and I killed him without so much as a flinch. Well, he cut her throat and he didn't have to do that. To this day I don't know why he killed her. I don't even know if he intended to kill me. Maybe she was his daughter and the disgrace was too much for him. Or maybe he was VC and he was ordered to off us both. I don't know. It doesn't matter, does it?

"It took me a week to make my way back to Headquarters at Chau Doc. By that time we were all listed as missing in action. I reported everything I could with as much accuracy as I dared. Shit! You know they gave me a Silver Star and a Purple Heart for gallantry under fire? Hell, what was I supposed to do? Tell them the truth?

"Anyway, the team drifted a few days later. I didn't see much of them at Chau Doc. They were isolated from the rest of us. I tried to see them, really I did. But every time I was told they were being debriefed. You can imagine how I felt. I was responsible for their capture. They were my damn team and I wasn't even allowed to see them. It was only after I protested to the Agency at Embassy House that I found out they had all given the enemy classified information.

"The Army took over the matter from the Agency. The Army always had a hard on for the Agency, and when this slipup came to their attention, they decided to go the whole nine yards. Only, after they started investigating the quality of the information, they got cold feet. The Embassy in Saigon and CORDs stayed any action against the team. It was decided that the operations we had been involved in were too secret to become known at a Courts Martial. The Army was ordered to drop the charges.

"But the Army was going to have its pound of flesh. Even though the charges were dropped, they requested the resignation with honorable discharge of each team member for the good of the service. All except me. I was transferred to Berlin."

"Do you know what happened to them?" Perez asked quietly.

"What happened to them? They all left the Armed Forces. I don't know what became of them. I never tried to find out. The only one I know about is Keaton. I guess he couldn't take the disgrace. No. He could not survive in a civilian world, far off from everything he knew and loved. And all because of me, priest."

David sipped from a cup of coffee as he stood next to the window looking out over the slowly awakening city, waiting apprehensively for the new day to dawn. Today would be the first day. "Well, priest," he said, not bothering to look at Perez, "I think I should go."

"Why?" Perez said, giving David a questioning look. "Because you think by going you can retrieve your lost honor? Or is it because you want something to happen to you to take away the pain?"

"I don't know. You're the shrink, you figure it out. And when you do, keep it to yourself."

"I'll go with you, if you want," Perez said nervously.

David shook his head.

Perez nodded acceptance and quietly stared down at his hands that were folded ever so carefully on his lap. "If you go, you may never come back."

"I should have never come back in the first place."

Chapter 31

New York, New York
May 14, 1982
2000 Hours

> He gives power to the weak,
> And to those who have might
> He increases the strength.
> Even the youths shall faint
> And be weary,
> And the young men shall utterly fall.
> But those who wait on the Lord
> Shall renew their strength;
> They shall mount up with wings
> Like eagles.
> They shall run and not be weary.
> They shall walk and not be faint.
> Isaiah 40:29-31

It was one of those nights pilots love. The air was thick and clear. A bright moon gave form and substance to the land below. The stars were welcoming.

The air traffic controller at Kennedy Center had just come on duty. The large radar screen positioned just behind his computer console imaged in lime green the traffic in his assigned sector, each blip carefully identified by number and type. Also illuminated on the dark oval screen were all air lanes, runway patterns, and instrument approaches within a hundred mile radius. Some controllers monitored low altitude radar, others high. Still others watched the skies within a smaller five mile radius of the runway at John F. Kennedy.

With an air of stoicism, the controller on the distance scope eased himself into the large comfortable chair in front of the console and, with a sigh, slipped on his headset and microphone. With a flick of his finger, he switched the radio from transmit to intercom. He scanned the other radios to assure himself they were on all the proper frequencies. Satisfied he could communicate he made a commo check, switched the radio back to transmit, and readied himself for eight hours of stress. The green glow from the radar screen accented his face, giving him an alien appearance.

Twenty miles out over the Atlantic Ocean and descending from thirty thousand feet, an Air France 747 requested permission to enter the holding pattern.

"Roger, Air France 356. Maintain descent to twenty thousand, hold on entering vector holding pattern. You will follow TWA 241 to 18," replied the controller.

A blip at thirty miles southwest indicated another plane, an Eastern Airline 727 requesting to enter the pattern. The controller expertly put him in line for a landing.

"Ferry 34, your push," the voice crackled through the controller's headset. The controller smiled. Everyone at the center knew Jake Arrado and knew he liked to fly at night.

"Ferry 34," the controller radioed back.

"Ah, Center, requesting clearance to five hundred feet approximately thirty nautical miles at 150 degrees for maneuvers."

"Wait. Break. Eastern 129, Kennedy Center. Be advised helicopter outward approach heading 150"

"Roger, Center," answered the Eastern pilot. Jake would be far below him.

"Ferry 34, flight approved. Contact Tower upon intent to reenter the pattern."

"Roger," Jake replied.

The controller watched his screen. The helicopter would not appear on the screen until it climbed to an altitude of five hundred feet. Just past Runway 21 Right, the blip of Ferry 34 appeared. The controller watched it for a moment then turned his attention to the jets in the area.

Ten miles southeast of Kennedy, the pilot of Eastern 129 spotted the red and green night lights of Jake's helicopter as it approached his aircraft at a lower altitude. Then all of a sudden, he noticed the lights were gone. He checked his on-board weather radar to see if there were any cloud formations that might have obscured the approaching helicopter. It was puzzling, and he wondered what was happening to Ferry 34.

"Center, Eastern 129."

"Center."

"Ah, do you have Ferry 34 on your scope?"

"Roger. I show him approaching you at one thousand feet. Should be almost below you now."

"Center, you have any cloud formations on your scope?"

"Negative. We show clear."

"Center, Ferry 34's navigation lights suddenly went off. I picked them up about five miles out then suddenly they were gone."

"Wait, Eastern 129. Break. Ferry 34, JFK Center . . . Ferry 34, JFK Center . . . Ferry 34."

"Center, Eastern 129. He might be having some electrical problem."

"Roger, Eastern 129. Wait a minute."

As the controller watched the screen, Ferry 34's blip disappeared.

"Eastern 129, Ferry 34 has just dropped off my screen. Can you see him?"

"Negative, Center."

The controller quickly switched to the Coast Guard frequency. "CG 1, this if JFK Center."

"JFK."

"Possible helicopter down fifteen nautical miles southeast from Center at 150 degrees. I will keep advised."

"Roger. I will alert Coast Guard flight 17 which is at present refueling at La Guardia."

"Roger CG 1. Break."

The controller switched back to his main radio frequency. "Ferry 34, JFK Center. Ferry 34!"

There was no reply. The controller wiped the sweat from his brow. Jake was a good pilot. It he left the screen, it was because he was down. "CG 1, JFK Center."

"CG 1."

"I'm declaring an emergency for Ferry 34."

"Roger."

The controller stared hopefully at the area of his screen where Ferry 34 had last been seen, but the blimp would not appear again. Jake Arrado had made a fateful decision about what to do about his life.

Chapter 32

The Ford Mansion
Richmond Hill, Georgia
May 15, 1982

The sun had just gone down, its faint aurora slowly fading against an oblique western sky. The motionless air was humid and stale, filled with the acrid smell of rotting cattails. Beyond the expansive lawn, the black foreboding waters of Ossabaw Sound lapped rhythmically against the reed studded banks. Weeping willows hanging over like repentant sentries silently surrounded the darkened grounds ever protecting the abandoned mansion from the eyes of intruders.

Keaton had said the turnoff the main highway onto the road that led to the hidden mansion would be hard to spot. Its presence was evidenced by nothing more than a spray of dirt lying obscurely across the pockmarked, two lane highway that ran through the sleepy Georgia coast town of Richmond Hill. Doc switched off the lights of the car as he left the highway. *Keaton, I am here. Now it will end.*

The road was dusty and bumpy, and in the dark the only way Doc was able to navigate was by following the tall grass along its sides. His night vision enabled him to pick out the weeping willows ahead and the huge shape of the white columned mansion that stood behind them. Even though he could not see clearly, a jungle sense warned him someone else had already arrived. *The others?* He took his pistol out of its shoulder holster and laid it in his lap. He parked the car under one of the willows. Carefully, not slamming shut the door he quietly made his way toward the mansion. Near the wide, open porch were parked a dark Volvo station wagon and a lighter colored Honda Civic. He pulled the hammer back on his Beretta.

The space between the first two columns that straddled the entrance to the front door was nearly ten feet wide. In all there were ten columns at the front of the mansion, five on each side of the main entrance. Doc was amazed at the size of the mansion. *A lot of money once lived here*, he thought. There were two nine-by-three foot wooden doors at the entrance and both were open. Cat-like and agile for his size, he slowly inched his way into the dark foyer, his weapon aimed at eye level. The foyer was large and rectangular. Rooms adjoined it to the left and right of the entrance. Directly to his front and in the center of the foyer, a single ten foot wide staircase descended from a balcony second level. The floor of the foyer was made of polished marble arranged in alternating white and black squares. From the corniced ceiling hung two large chandeliers. *This was where it all took place,* he thought. *Rich white men and women, eating, drinking, dancing, and laughing.* He paused and grinned to himself. *I could own this now.*

He whirled around at the sound of footsteps coming from the front lawn. He crouched behind one of the open doors. His eyes were wide open, his senses alert. There was a tingling sensation at the back of his neck. His breathing was controlled, quiet. Silently he waited, his eyes aiming down the snout of the Beretta holding the dark, empty space between the gun's sights hostage. It felt good to be a hunter once again. The dark space between the three rectangular, luminous dots slowly became filled with two distinct figures.

They calmly strolled toward him side by side. He could tell by their manner they were not yet aware of his presence. One man was taller than his companion and wore a light colored t-shirt and what appeared to be blue jeans. The other man wore khaki pants and a blue oxford shirt with the sleeves rolled to the elbow. As they neared he could faintly hear them laughing. He lowered the pistol and stepped back onto the porch. Noticing the movement, both men stopped abruptly. Even though they could not see him, instinct told them who he was.

"Well, the Prince of Darkness," said the man in the khakis sarcastically.

Doc shouldered his weapon. "He be here?" he asked, pointedly ignoring Pratt's barb.

"No, he's not here," Force answered hesitantly.

"Ole Force, I'm surprised to see you're still alive. Knew Pratt would be though," Doc replied cynically.

"Well," Pratt said, putting his hands in his pockets and looking from side to side, "he sure picked a hell of a place for a reunion." He smelled heavily of a sweet aftershave.

"Ain't no damn reunion," Doc said quickly.

Pratt took his hands out of his pockets. "No, of course it isn't," he said reluctantly, letting out a sigh.

"He'll be here. Just don't lose your cool until he does," Force said flatly. "Until then, I suggest we go inside and figure out how we're going to stay out of sight until he arrives."

In the darkness Doc just laughed and shook his head. Ole Force hadn't changed. Always had to keep things in their places. And Pratt, he had never liked Pratt. Thought he knew everything. This was going to be a pleasure. He put his hands on his hips and spit. "Where tha hell we supposed to sleep tonight?"

"That wouldn't even have been a question a few years ago," Force said wryly.

"Yeah, well things have changed, big boy."

All three were caught off guard by the approaching lights of a vehicle coming down the dirt road. They each couched low and became still as the vehicle, a dark pickup truck, carefully came to a halt behind Pratt's Volvo. The door opened, and a slight figure dressed in blue jeans and t-shirt emerged. Cautiously, the man moved to the rear of the truck. "Hey, inside," he yelled.

"Shit," Doc said under his breath, shaking his head.

"Chip, over here by the door," Force answered.

The others stood at Chip's approach. "I recognized your voice, Force. Who else's here?"

"Doc and me," Pratt said evenly.

"Keaton?" Chip asked anxiously.

'AWOL!" Doc replied loudly.

"It's good to be with you guys again," Chip said, squaring himself in front of the others, a slight smile on his sweaty face.

For a moment a heavy awkward silence hung in the air. It had been nearly thirteen years since they had last seen each other. As they stood quietly in the dark, each remembered the last distressing time they had stood together. Isolated, humiliated, and betrayed. Then, they had been filled with hate. Some hated the Army they felt had deserted them. Some hated their leader who had let them down. Some hated themselves because they had been so weak. Then they had parted, each secretly hoping to never see the others again. Some had individual feelings of guilt that were too easily mirrored in each others' presence. Some felt they had disgraced their profession. Mutually, they had betrayed their own code of warfare. But alone, each had hoped he might be able to reconcile himself with a world that would never understand what they had been through.

In all the years since, they had kept their feelings inside, afraid to let others know of their anguish. Their experiences had been personal, not to be shared with anyone except the others. Experiences that could not easily be explained to their friends or loved ones, at least not in any manner that made sense to anyone who had not been there. Experiences that had been so horrible, so incriminating, and yet inexplicably wonderful. Experiences, acts committed out of a sense of duty, country or, in some cases, personal gratification and, in the case of one, with purposeful intent. And now, after all these years, standing together in the dark once again, there was a hesitancy to acknowledge their separation had ever occurred. Each had gone his separate way, faced what life had presented, and made an account of himself, all in different ways. But none of that seemed to matter now. In this moment of reunion, time picked up where it had left off in Saigon light years ago. Whales weren't the only creatures who remembered where things had stopped.

Chip made the point that maybe they should be inside. Force went further and had them park their cars out of sight in the trees on the other side of the mansion. Force led them up the stairs to a bedroom directly over the front porch that opened up to the balcony. He had been the first to arrive and quite naturally had scouted out the mansion and the surrounding grounds.

"It's pretty isolated," Force said. "A lot of thick woods to the highway about a half mile in that direction." He pointed east. "The road's the only in that I can tell."

Doc lit a cigar and, without first testing it to see if it was strong enough, leaned against the balcony railing. "It's isolated all right. Just the kind of place some kid wants to come so his chick can give him a blow job. What's he gonna say when he finds us here?"

"He won't if we stay cool and keep our mouths shut," Force replied.

For a moment Force and Doc squared off at each other. In the darkness, the red glowing ember from the tip of Doc's cigar was reflected in their eyes. As they stood there rigid, they seemed ready to spring at each other over something as insignificant as a word. Chip sensed both men had changed. A chasm had developed. They were no longer of like mind and soul. He wondered what divergent paths their lives had followed to have caused this to happen.

"Ah, the prodigal sons return. See you all how they react to each other after so long an absence? All we need now is for Father Keaton to appear and show us the truth and the way. And . . . good night, Tiny Tim, wherever you are," Pratt said sarcastically, his arms spread apart, bending low with a fake bow.

Doc turned to Pratt. "What the fuck do you do to justify your existence?"

"Spread knowledge throughout the universe. Even unto the darker regions."

"Goddamn it!" Doc screamed and lunged for Pratt.

Chip grabbed Doc. "Stop this shit now! Both of you."

"Try that on me," Force said menacingly to Doc.

"That can be arranged," Doc said haughtily.

"Look, I think it's time we start trying to figure out why Keaton brought us here," Chip said eagerly, trying to take their attention away from each other. "I was told to bring some very strange shit."

Force turned away from Doc to Chip. "We were all told to bring something, weren't we? But so what? Keaton knows what he's doing. And you all know why we came. So let's just wait until he gets here. Then he'll let us know what's going on."

"That's not good enough for me," Doc said. "I wanna know what the rest of you brought. I have seven M-16s in my car and enough fuckin' ammo and clips to get us into a damn hell of a firefight." He paused, then said with a tone of disgust, "Didn't any of you damn sheep question what we are being asked to do?"

Silence.

"Immersion heaters," Chip said, letting out a nervous laugh.

"Well now, that's cute," said Pratt. "I brought two sets each of seven complete BDU uniforms, as well as socks, underwear, gloves, wool caps, boots, sleeping bags . . . everything a man would need to fight in the Arctic."

"What you mean?" Doc said through his teeth.

"Parkas. I was told to bring cold weather gear," Pratt added.

Force scratched his head. "Field gear, the whole works, seven sets, and C-rations, enough for seven guys for a month."

"Seven," Doc said as if he was talking to himself. "That means three more of us are comin'."

"Keaton," Pratt said, holding his fingers up in the dark, "and two others. Could be . . ."

"Has to be Jake," Chip said quickly.

"The rest are dead," Force flat flatly. "The rest are dead or crazy."

"That means . . ." Pratt said, his voice said trailing off.

"Yeah," Doc said, his cigar still blazing between his teeth. "The *Dai Uy*."

They returned to Pratt's car to retrieve camping gear.

"I ain't crazy about this," Doc said, taking a sleeping bag from Pratt's Volvo. "No, I ain't. There's got to be a motel, even in this spit in the road."

"It's cheaper," Pratt quipped.

"Yeah, and how would Keaton know where to find us?" Force added.

"Don't give a shit about being found. Don't give a shit about being here," Doc said.

"Then why the hell are you here?" Force asked.

"Same reason you are, baby. I want this contract paid off," Doc said, laughing between puffs on his cigar.

They moved silently from the woods where their cars had been concealed and returned to the second floor of the mansion. No one spoke. The situation itself demanded silence. How would it look to an outsider coming up on them? Grown men with sleeping bags trespassing on the property of another for an unclear and unexplainable purpose. In the dark of the night they would be a tempting feast for a Georgia deputy sheriff, and they all knew it.

As far as Doc was concerned, they had skirted the issue long enough. Propped up against the wall with his sleeping bag at his feet puffing on his cigar, he surveyed the rest with a contemptuous eye. How had Keaton persuaded them to come here? What inadequacies in them had he exposed to make them pack up and leave their lives for this boy scout adventure? Keaton had known what nerve of his to probe. Now it was time for the others to show and tell. If he could end this by daybreak, he could make Atlanta by noon. Keaton had brought them all to one place, and soon he would finally be able to cut himself off from his past forever. After tomorrow, he would be free. "What do you do, Force?" he asked pointedly.

"What do you mean?"

"How do you pay the bills, asshole? What do you think I mean?"

"I'm a police officer."

Doc coughed and let out a deep, loud laugh. "Goddamn, I should've known. That fits you. A fuckin' cop."

"Watch your mouth," Force said through his teeth. "Where I come from, talk like that is unhealthy."

"You know, Doc," Chip said, standing up, "from the moment I got here all I've heard out of you is this bully trying his best to pick a fight with the rest of us. What's your damn problem?"

"I'll tell you what my problem is, boy. It's this whole damn setup. What are we doing here? Huh? Vietnam was a long time ago. Don't any of you shitheads remember what happened to us there? We were sent home in disgrace. The things we had done, the times we had risked our lives – none of that was taken into account; none of that counted for shit. But do any of you think any of those officers who decided our fate would have done anything any differently if they had been put through what the Cong did to us? Hell no! They would've spilled their guts too. But we took it. We ate their shit and left.

"I don't know what happened to the rest of you, but I put all of that behind me and went out and made something of myself. Now, here comes old Sarge after all these years. He calls and we come running like a bunch of sheep. Well, I ain't no damn sheep. I ain't no damn flunky any more!"

"The Doc I once knew was anything but a flunky," Chip said evenly. "He was proud to be in Special Forces."

"Yeah," Force said, "if you feel that way, why'd you show up? You could've told him to go to hell."

"No, he couldn't have," Chip said. "Look at him. He blusters and bursts like a thunderstorm, but Doc could no more have refused Keaton than could I. We all saw him. We all heard his voice. He called us together one more time to honor the covenant. Had we forgotten? Had we fooled ourselves into believing the day would never come when we would be called upon to honor it? That's why we came here. The Army kicked us out, betrayed us, but Keaton never did. Remember, he even tried to take responsibility for what had happened. So, I'm here. I'm here to honor a promise I made when I thought my life was about to end.

Doc spit.

"That's all very fine," Pratt said superciliously, "but I for one have no intention of honoring any silly promise made when we were mentally at the point of contemplating eternity. Jesus, we would have sold our souls to Lucifer to have gotten out of that place. Poor old Keaton, floundering around all these years doing God knows what. Probably boozed up half the time. Who knows what set him off and caused him to come looking for us? Doesn't matter though. I'll listen to whatever crackpot idea he has. I might even enjoy the moment. And then tomorrow, I'm splitting." He paused and smiled. "Don't be too hard on our Black Prince. He no doubt has his own primordial reasons for being here. Probably doesn't even understand them himself. But he's here, so let's all look upon this as a chance to get to know each other again, find out what we've been doing all of these years, and then depart. Hell, I'll even go into town and get some beer."

Force drew up and got close to Pratt's face. "You're an idiot. Do you recall Keaton ever acting foolishly? Of course not. I know what I saw, and what I saw was the same man who pulled me out of hell many a time. There's something serious going down. Now, the covenant may or may not have meant anything to you, but it did to me, and I think it did to the rest of you. Even to Doc. So you'll listen and you'll be respectful. You understand?"

Pratt's lips began to tremble. "Don't threaten me," he managed to say.

"Look," Chip said pleadingly, "this isn't getting us anywhere. Maybe Pratt's right. Let's just relax and wait for Keaton. Then we can make up our minds."

"Yeah, boy, and don't forget your favorite captain. I can't wait to see him either," Doc said, twirling his Beretta around his finger.

"*If* he comes. Remember, he wasn't part of the covenant," Chip said, looking past the others to the dark Georgia night outside the open veranda doors. "And Doc, I don't mind you calling me 'boy.'"

Force sniffed the still early morning air. There was something moving around in the darkness. He stood erect, leaning over the balcony, his eyes straining to see what was out there in the distance from the Sound. How many times had he awakened in the deadly quiet of dark jungle mornings because he had sensed danger from something or someone unseen? Distance and time had not changed him much. He turned toward the dark waters. *It's coming toward us*, he thought. He thought about waking the others, but decided to wait. As he searched the face of the dark water, he was startled to suddenly see a single conical beam of white light spray down from the black sky and fall on the surface of the water. It seemed to come from out of nowhere. Then just as suddenly, it was gone. He licked his lips anxiously.

"Chip," he found himself saying. "Chip," he said again.

Chip shot up like a spring. "What is it?"

"I saw something. Over there, over the Sound. A light. It came on, shined over the water, and then turned off."

"Did you hear anything?" Chip asked, straining to see in the darkness.

"No, must be several miles away."

As they stood there, the light came on again and began to search the surface of the Sound once again.

"Chopper," Force murmured. "A ways off."

The light switched off again.

"Think he's searching for a lost boat or something?"

"Might."

Then they heard it at the same time. The whirling, grinding sound of a fast-approaching machine.

"He's coming our way. I'll wake the others," Force said quickly.

The others groggily positioned themselves on the balcony. All could hear the helicopter, but in the darkness its whereabouts could only be guessed. It seemed to be slowly circling the grounds around the mansion.

"That son of a bitch is gonna land," Doc said, drawing his Beretta from its holster.

"Put that damn gun away," Force said. "We don't know if it's going to land. And even if it does, no one knows we're here."

Then the night sky lit up as bright as day as the landing lights of the chopper came on and its spotlight began sweeping the turf of the front lawn of the mansion. The air began to gust up as the craft flared for a landing. The noise was deafening.

"Not landing huh?" Doc said.

"Let's go downstairs. Hell, we haven't committed any crime," Pratt said

Outside the chopper's engines began a slow whine as power to them was switched off. The air returned to its dormancy as the blades were feathered. Darkness was again over the grounds as the helicopter's lights were extinguished. Cautiously Force and the others emerged from the entrance of the mansion. Even in the darkness, they could tell that the machine sitting defiantly on the front lawn was a huge aircraft.

"Look at the size of this damn thing," Force said quietly.

"I don't like this," Doc said.

After a few seconds, the door on the side of the aircraft opened and a figure slowly felt its way down the retractable steps. Once on the ground, the man seemed bewildered as to what to do next.

"Who are you?" Chip asked loudly.

The man turned, obviously startled, and began to sing. "In the valley of the ho, ho, ho, Green Giant!"

Chapter 33

```
May 15, 1982
0500 Hours
Peeble Island - West Falkland
```

The three Royal Navy Sea King helicopters flew in low using the shoreline of the island for their pilotage. In the darkness, with winds of Force 9 Gale, they maintained a loose formation, one trailing the other. Outside, the temperature was well below zero. The sky was crystal clear. A blessing.

His Royal Highness Prince Edward was unable to relax despite the fact that good Flight Major Wallaby, seated left of him, was now the one driving the Sea King through this murderous weather. Ten hours earlier, the Prince had inserted on Peeble the same SAS troops they were now rushing to pluck up before they froze to death. Then, the sky had been filled with fast moving clouds that hid from view the jagged crags and small hills that presented any pilot with a maze of a flight path. The Prince had expertly driven the craft from the deck of the *Hermes* all the way to the selected landing zone and had not allowed any of his crew to notice how stressful the feat had been. The Prince had bearing.

Now it was his turn to rest. As he gazed at the twinkling stars strewn across the southern sky, he allowed himself to think of home and his family, especially his brother. How worried his brother must be about him now. The news getting to the British people was filled with accounts of the crew of the *Hermes*. Charles was a pilot himself and knew what missions he would be flying. Edward let out a deep sigh.

"Your Highness, we should be approaching the LZ," radioed Wallaby through his intercom. Edward held up his hand and nodded in recognition.

"Blue Flight. This is Blue leader. LZ's coming up."

Ahead in the ink black darkness below, a small green light turned on. Wallaby spotted it.

"You see it?"

"Roger," Edward replied.

"Blue Flight. Green recognition at seven o'clock. Prepare to descend."

The two helicopters following the Prince's veered off in different directions and found a place to hover in the pitch blackness. There they would wait their turn to pick up the SAS men, watching intently for any danger before taking their turn at making a landing on rocky terrain in total darkness with winds gusting up to fifty miles an hour.

As Wallaby started his descent both he and the Prince fixed their eyes on the darkness below searching intently for any sign of the ground. The SAS men were charged with the responsibility of selecting a proper landing site. With their small hand-held green lens lights, they could guide the helicopter to a safe landing.

"I've got two lights side by side," the Prince said.

"I've got them," Wallaby answered.

Slowly Wallaby inched his way down while all along turning the whirling craft into sudden gusts of winds he felt through the seat of his pants. It was harrowing work. Suddenly he felt himself being turned upside down. The helicopter was being turned up on its rotor blade! In an instant, he knew they were going to crash and burn. "Oh, God. We're crashing!" he screamed.

Edward recognized instantly what was happening. "I've got the aircraft."

Wallaby let go of the cyclic and collective and put his hands to his face. He had just experienced what every pilot fears: an attack of vertigo. The Prince had the aircraft.

Chapter 34

The Ford Mansion
Richmond Hill, Georgia

"If you want to know the truth, I don't actually give a shit what any of you think," Jake said tiredly, taking a deep swig from a can of beer then belching loudly, "I don't give a shit what anyone thinks." Jake dressed. in a gray and blue flight suit, was sitting on the ground, his legs folded under him.

"I don't believe this. I mean, look at this thing," Force said incredulously, pointing in the darkness at the dormant helicopter parked a few yards away silently cooling down like a just put up race horse. "You actually stole this damn helicopter? And you're telling us Keaton told you to do it?"

Doc let out a deep, loud laugh.

"You're all here, aren't you? What'd he ask you to bring?" Jake asked.

"None of us was told to steal anything," Force said.

"Jake, did Keaton tell you why he wanted you to meet us here with the helicopter?" Chip asked calmly, sensing Jake was losing control.

"No."

"He didn't tell us, either."

"Then that should signal something to you, shouldn't it?" Jake countered.

"What?" Force asked, agitated.

"That what we're going to do is serious," Jake replied.

Jake's words sent chills running down the backs of the others. The presence of the helicopter added a seriousness to their gathering that they had not anticipated. At the very least, the fact that Jake had stolen the helicopter could make them accessories to a felony. But lingering among them was a thought none wanted to accept, and that was that Keaton had actually told Jake to steal the helicopter. If that was true, it meant what Keaton would ask them to do would be serious. The question then would be if they would do what he wanted.

"Jake, doesn't it bother you that you could be sent to prison for stealing this machine?" Pratt asked, his voice serious and demanding.

"Yeah, it bothers me. If I let myself think about it. But I don't."

Pratt took Chip aside away from the helicopter and spoke quietly. "You know he's crazy, don't you?" Chip didn't respond, so Pratt pressed on. "He was always a little strange. Look at him. He's turned into a juicer. Keaton didn't tell him to steal that thing."

Chip took hold of Pratt's arm. "He doesn't seem crazy to me. A little stressed out maybe, but not crazy. I'm not going to make up my mind about any of this until Keaton arrives."

"Okay, but I'm not going to be a part of this."

"You do what you feel you have to do."

With that, they rejoined the others.

Force sat down next to Jake. The first light of morning was appearing on the horizon past the Sound. Jake's features were slowly taking form. He looked older, heavier and drawn. Force squared himself in front of him. "Listen," he said earnestly, "there's still time. You can take the chopper back and probably nothing will happen. Tell them it went down somewhere. You can make something up."

"Listen!" Jake shouted, and then sprang up with surprising agility. "Listen, all of you. I'm not crazy and I'm not drunk. I came here because Keaton told me to, ordered me to. It was him who told me to take the helicopter. No, he didn't tell me why or what for. He said the reason would be revealed here at this place. Now, I'm going to fly that machine wherever he wants, whenever he wants, and I don't care if any of you come with me." Jake then turned on his heel, threw the beer can to the ground, and went back inside the helicopter.

"That does it for me. I'm leaving as soon as I can get a few hours sleep," Force said.

"Well, I'm glad someone's showing some sense around here," Pratt said, putting his hand on Force's shoulder.

"You're a big talker, Force," Doc said with an expression of hilarity on his face. "Keaton hasn't even gotten here yet and you gonna cut out? Man, what happened to all that self-righteous crap you been putting on us? Gonna leave old Sarge holding the bag, huh?"

"Look, Goddamn it, I'm a police officer. And whatever you might think about that doesn't mean shit to me. I am sworn to enforce the law. I took an oath to stand for something." He paused, his hands clenched in desperation. "It's what I am. I'll help Keaton. I want to help him. But . . . I can't steal. I can't be a part of something illegal."

Chip intervened. "Leave him alone, Doc. Each of us has to do what in our heart we feel is right."

"God, I wish Keaton was here," Force said, the anguish he felt evident in his voice.

"Look, all of you. I say we give Keaton till noon today," Chip said. "If he doesn't show, then each of us can leave and feel no guilt."

"I'll agree to that," Pratt answered cheerfully. "We might even be able to celebrate. The beer's on me."

Force nodded. "How about you, Doc?" Chip asked.

"12:00 noon. I like it."

"What about Jake, the helicopter?" Pratt asked.

"That's his problem," Force said quietly.

Chapter 35

May 16, 1982

The sheriff appeared just after the sun. The written report transcribed during the late hours of dawn by the department's midnight-to-morning dispatcher made for interesting reading over his morning cup of coffee and raspberry filled doughnut.

From what he could decipher from the dispatcher's chicken scratching, it seemed a number of residents near the Sound, mostly farmers and fishermen who were normally early risers, had heard an airplane or maybe a helicopter land or crash in the vicinity of the Ford Mansion. A lot of things were heard from time to time in and around the Sound and the mansion, but the number of calls as well as their close proximity in time made this report worth investigating.

Force was the first to hear the sheriff's car come to a halt near the end of the road. Peering out the window over the balcony, he quietly nudged the others.

"Holy shit!" the sheriff exclaimed, seeing the mammoth helicopter inexplicably sitting on the lawn like some dormant giant grasshopper. With caution, he rolled out of the car and crouched next to the open door, his hand resting on the handle of his still-holstered revolver.

For a second he entertained the thought of having the day dispatcher call for the State Patrol, but he hesitated. What could they do that he couldn't? Besides, he was a politically cautious man. This was his county and the voters had elected him to enforce the law and maintain the peace. Bringing in the State Patrol might be seen as a sign of weakness. And too, if these people were here for legitimate reasons they might just be the sort he would want to help. He shut the car door, adjusted his cowboy hat, and started toward the mansion.

"Morning, officer," Pratt said cheerfully, standing in the doorway, his hand extended.

The sheriff stopped short of the porch and gave Pratt a circumspect look.

"Morning," he answered warily, ignoring Pratt's outstretched hand. "You people havin' a problem?"

"No officer. No problem."

"What ya'll doing here?"

Pratt put his hands in his pockets. "We're visiting . . ."

"*We're?*" the sheriff said, cutting Pratt off.

"Where's the rest of your buddies?"

"Inside."

"Ask 'em to come out, please," he said in a way the other men said shit.

As if they had heard the sheriff's order, the others began to slowly file out of the mansion, rumpled, bearded, and bleary eyed. All except Jake, who was still fast asleep inside the helicopter. The sheriff gave them the once over with a critical policeman's eye, an eye trained to look for the unusual, the out of place, any variation from the normal. Aside from the presence of the machine – it wasn't every day a helicopter landed in the county, even though Ft. Stewart was only thirty miles away – there was nothing suspicious about the men.

The sheriff knew a lot of people. He also had a fair understanding of what made them behave the way they did, which was why he was still alive after all these years. He knew sometimes it was best to try to figure out what cards the other fellow was holding before calling. "I'm Tom T. Taylor. Sheriff of this here county. Where ya'll from?"

"I live in Nashville," Pratt replied evenly, once again extending his hand.

But Sheriff Taylor again paid no attention to it. Instead, he walked up onto the porch and took off his hat. "Whew," he said, wiping his forehead, "it's gonna be a hot one today. What ya'll think?" He put his hat back on and turned to Chip. "You look like you're from around these parts," he said with a wry look on his face.

"Virginia," Chip replied.

"Hmm. Your helicopter there?"

"It belongs to a tour company and was landed here by the pilot. He's inside the chopper," Pratt interjected quickly.

"That so?" the sheriff said, staring at the helicopter curiously.

"Want a ride?" Chip asked.

Sheriff Taylor turned abruptly to Chip. "No, I don't want no damn ride. Want I want to know is what you boys are doin' here on this private property with this machine."

An awkward silence descended. It was almost a malevolent silence, the kind that cloaks the land with the deceit of peacefulness before a storm. The sheriff felt it at once, the danger signals law enforcement officers learn to trust even when their senses lie. With a quick and effortless motion, he flipped off the strap of his gun holster and took matters in hand.

In the dark of the night, men are forced to face who they are. So it had been with David and Father Perez. During the day their minds were occupied with the business of the day. They stood unafraid in the light of the sun, protected from their submerged emotions by companionship and the tasks of work. Even when moments of solitude unleashed feelings of dread and anxiety, the sudden appearance of an acquaintance was enough to scare away the simulacrum of what had attacked the normalcy of their lives. But alone in the night, each was forced to come to the realization of an awful truth – that he was losing control of his life to the gut wrenching, heart pounding, breathtaking affects of fear. And the most horrible of fear at that: fear of the unknown.

In this case it was the unknown purpose of the unknown entity waiting for them in Georgia. For whatever reason and whatever design, they were being summoned. They could only question in anguish who it was that was summoning them and to what purpose.

Both men understood fear, having faced it in combat many times. Each knew the point in time when soldiers are most susceptible to the debilitating effects of fear is before a battle begins and their imaginations began to go wild with thoughts of what could happen to them. This is the fear of the unknown. And no human being can cope for very long with being afraid of the unknown. It is the task of the officer to take this fear of the unknown and focus it on a definable object, such as an enemy unit or a well known enemy commander. Perez called this the art of emasculating the imagination. If an officer is able to do this, then when the battle starts his men will have their energies and fears channeled into meaningful action and, hopefully, victory.

But victory had seemed elusive in Washington. It would have to be sought out. And it would not be found there. Perez and David had known the only way they could break the icy grip of their fear was to come face to face with whatever and whoever was waiting for them in Georgia. They had decided to face the pretender together.

In the late hours of night just before dawn, David pressed on toward the mark. A deep darkness cloaked the earth, interrupted only by the lambent lights of his fleeting auto. Surrounded by the dark, he felt as if they were traveling in a cocoon down a chute into a void of uncertain depth. He wondered where this sojourn would take them, and whether either would ever return. Perez lay sleeping, his head resting against the passenger door, his glasses still clinging to his nose. Just hearing his rhythmic breathing gave David a sense of security. At least he would not be going into this confrontation alone.

Perez woke up as David turned off Interstate 95 and onto the highway that led into Richmond Hill. He cracked open his eyes. David's face was illuminated by the pale green lights from the dash. Across it was etched a look of foreboding.

Perez sat up. "How far are we?" he asked, rubbing his eyes and yawning.

David sighed. "Just a couple of miles. We won't be going through the town. According to this," David held up a piece of paper on which he had written the instructions given to him by a friend at the Smithsonian, "there should be a turnoff to the mansion on the left side of the road."

Perez stared forlornly at the dark countryside, silently questioning whether they would be able to spot the cutoff. David had wanted to arrive in the darkness and take up a position near the mansion on foot so as not to be noticed until first light lest they be easy targets. He shivered on thinking about the implications of that plan.

After a few minutes, David slowed the car. Thick, rough woods had appeared on the right side of the highway. Without either noticing, they had both begun to breath faster. Their muscles tensed and their hearts pounded. Their eyes strained to see in the dark as they searched for the opening in the woods that would indicate the presence of the road.

"There!" Perez shouted.

David nodded and switched off the lights. Slowly, he turned onto the dirt road. "I'm going to park over here in the woods. We'll make out better walking," he said breathlessly.

Perez simply nodded, his mouth too dry to talk.

David wedged the car key under a wheel. "Don't want them to be able to stop either of us from escaping," he whispered.

Escaping, Perez thought excitedly. *My God! He believes they'll try to kill us.*

"But just in case they try," David said almost gleefully, "I brought this along."

Even in the dark Perez could see David was holding a huge revolver.

"It's my Webley. Come on, let's find a hiding place and wait until morning. I can use a little sleep," David said, then started into the woods in the direction of the mansion. Perez swallowed hard, adjusted his glasses, and went after him.

Sheriff Taylor drew his revolver with one swift motion of his hand and ordered, "Ya'll put ya'lls hands on that wall and spread them legs!"

The men stiffened with a start and slowly raised their hands.

All except Doc. Steady and with a cagey eye, Doc measured his chance of taking the sheriff. He was positioned in the doorway: cover. Pratt was between him and the sheriff: concealment. He could draw, fire, and fall back behind the door. If the sheriff was able to get off a shot, he might even hit Pratt. That would save a bullet, but the pleasure of killing Pratt would be the sheriff's, not his. His hand slid discreetly under his shirt and found the cold Beretta.

"What's going on here, officer?" asked a voice coming from the woods.

Startled, the sheriff spun around, his gun now aimed squarely at David's guts. He realized at once that he had just made a huge tactical blunder. He couldn't cover both directions. Cagily, he backed away toward the helicopter. But then he took a second, steadier look at the first man who had unexpectedly come out of the woods and at the man who now stood at his side: a priest. At once, his apprehension turned to embarrassment. *A priest!* He holstered his gun. He felt the tension leave him, and he gave the priest a sheepish grin.

Penitently, he spoke. "My apologies, father. Hereabouts we've had a lot of trouble with trespassers, you understand?"

Perez graciously forgave. "Of course, sheriff. We understand how difficult your job is."

But even as one taut situation ended, Sheriff Taylor sensed another take its place. Again, red lights started to flash in his lawman's head when he realized the men on the porch had been just as surprised as he had been to hear the man speak, and that was odd. He didn't understand it, but he knew definitely they had been surprised, as if they had not known the man and the priest had been there. And now the men on the porch were giving the two men who had emerged from the woods silent harsh looks as if there existed some enmity between them. Something wasn't right about this situation, something not right at all.

He pulled up his gun belt, spit, and walked up to the porch. He screwed his mouth, and turning first to the men on the porch and then back to David and Perez spoke with a tone of impatience. "Now, I want one of you fellas to tell me just what's going on here."

My God, look at them, David thought. *Look at their faces. Did I really think they could ever forgive me? My God, did they plan this thing?* David turned to Perez. *But why would they bring Perez here? That's the only thing that didn't make sense. Perez had nothing to do with Jude. There's something that's not right about this whole thing. But there will be time for answers. First, I've got to get rid of this sheriff.*

David shot a look at the helicopter. "Uh, sheriff," he said hesitantly, "as you can see we are on a sightseeing tour. I can see you're upset because we just dropped out of nowhere, but that's not our fault."

Sheriff Taylor rubbed his chin contemplatively.

"Yes," Pratt said, stepping down from the porch.

"Where's ya'lls tour guide or somethin'?" the sheriff asked.

"As I said, the pilot's on the chopper. He's asleep, but I can wake him if you want," Pratt said quickly.

Jake, David thought.

The sheriff rubbed his belly.

"Look, sheriff, we're all legitimate businessmen, college professors and, well, that man over there is a police officer," Pratt said, pointing to Force.

Force a police officer, David mused.

Sheriff Taylor's eyes perked up. "You an officer of the law?"

"New Orleans Police Department," Force replied proudly.

"See your badge?"

"Here," Force said, offering his wallet.

Sheriff Taylor flipped it open with his pudgy hands. "No badge," he said flatly, not looking up.

"Look under the flap."

The sheriff turned up the leather inner flap. His eyes lit up as the sun reflected off the miniature star and crescent. Next to it he saw a laminated identification card with Force's picture and thumb print. "Well," he said with a sigh, "how long you boys gonna be here?"

For an awkward moment, no one seemed to want to answer, and then Doc spoke. "Be leaving tonight."

"Hmm," the sheriff said, seeming to be satisfied. "Might want that ride before ya'll leave," he said with a sly grin.

"No problem," Chip said, smiling.

"Well, didn't know this place was that famous. Just mostly local people and kids come here, you know. Sort of a different place for folks. Well, I'll be goin', but I'll check back with ya'll later," the sheriff said. With that he left, shaking his head and grinning. *The Ford Mansion a tourist attraction. Damn Yankees will do anything for a dollar.*

Chapter 36

They appeared older, David thought as he stood silently before them, these ghosts from the past, his tormenters, his failures. Time had added weight to them, lessened their hair, and increased the furrows across their faces. But he also sensed that time had changed them as human beings. They were not as they had been before when they had been young, eager, naive, and filled with purpose. What he had failed to do had robbed them of themselves.

In this moment of confrontation, their silent screams of protest struck out at him. He had shared much with these men. They had lived a lifetime together. Were they now going to require him to share with them his last experience? That last unknown jungle tunnel through which all men must pass? He had dreaded this moment but surprisingly found, now that it had arrived, he felt no fear. Standing before them, these men of his past, these men of his dreams, he felt an unexpected relief, as if some great weight had been taken from his shoulders. Time had finally come full circle and, with its advent had swept away the fear and the uncertainty of apprehension.

"I'm here," he pronounced quietly.

"So you are," answered Pratt haughtily.

"And who the hell is this?" he asked, turning his icy stare toward Perez.

David let out a sigh. "You know damn well who he is. Now that we're here, let's finish it."

Pratt was puzzled, but before he could speak Force stepped forward. "What'd he have you bring?"

David indifferently deflected Force's strange question and instead turned to Doc. Doc had never been all that bright, but he had always been truthful. "Doc, why have you brought us here?"

Doc reached inside his shirt pocket and put another huge cigar in his mouth. After he had lit it and taken a few puffs, he spoke slowly to David, the cigar clenched between his lips. "Don't play games. You and your priest friend be here cause Keaton told you to be, just like he did the rest of us. He be not here now, but when he comes, we'll all know what for."

David shook his head, and turning to Perez, gave him an agitated look. Then he suddenly drew the Webley from under his shirt. "All of you put your damn hands where I can see them!" he screamed.

"Well, I'll be damned," Force said with a smirk. "What are you going to do? Shoot us?"

"Yeah, I guess some things never change about a man, huh captain?" Pratt said with a tone of uncertainty.

"It's major to you. Now I'm going to find out why you bastards brought us here, and one of you better start talking real soon because I'm just about at my breaking point." David was visibly shaking. It was obvious to the others that he might shoot them if provoked.

Chip leaned toward David. "Major, I didn't come here to harm you. Keaton asked me to come here just like he did the rest. I don't know anything about this priest, and I don't know why *you* were asked to be here either, so just put down the gun. No one's going to harm you."

Perez turned to David and spoke in his ear. "David, something's terribly wrong here. I can't explain it, but something's just not right about this whole thing."

"Shut up!" David snapped. Perez fell away as though he had been slapped across the face. "All right then. Someone, real slow, tell me what you're all doing here," David said carefully, still pointing the Webley at their guts.

But just as he had finished speaking, he felt a reply against his back that made his question moot: the barrel of a shotgun. "Put the damn gun down or I'll blow your fuckin' guts out." David recognized Jake's voice as he let the Webley fall from his hand to the ground with a thud.

David and Perez sat dejectedly side by side on the steps of the porch with the others hovering over them. Force had David's pistol and Jake still held his shotgun. Doc was strangely detached from what was happening.

"I'd like to put this thing in your mouth and blow your fuckin' brains out," Jake said, taunting David. "And don't you give me the evil eye, priest!"

"Just shut the fuck up, Jake," Force yelled. "There's not going to be any damn killing as long as I'm here. You understand that?"

Jake growled and backed off.

"Major, despite what this juice-head here says," Force said, looking at Jake and then back to David, "none of us came here to harm you."

"Then why?" David asked, his face tightly drawn.

"You really want to know," Chip quipped.

"Indulge me. I've got the time."

"Well, we don't," Pratt said. "Do any of you think that sheriff will continue to believe for very long that lame excuse we gave him? As soon as he starts to let his noon meal digest, he'll be back here for his ride. Or to haul us all off to jail. I mean, look at that damn helicopter!"

"Yeah, where'd you get that chopper?" David asked, turning toward the machine.

"Jake stole it," Force answered.

"None of this is making sense," Pratt said, speaking to Chip. "Keaton told us to meet him here to honor the covenant. I can understand why we came here. But why him? And why the priest? What do they have to do with the covenant?"

"Maybe Keaton wanted to kill this son of a bitch then receive forgiveness," Jake blurted out, then let out a maniacal laugh.

Chip frowned then turned to David. "After we were captured, a lot of things happened that you know nothing about. We made a pact, a promise. It's hard to explain now, but it seemed right then. Anyway, we gave our word that if we got out of that situation we'd come to each others' aid no matter when or where. I guess we never really thought we'd make it out alive."

"To whom did you give your word?" Perez asked, genuinely interested.

"To God," Chip replied without emotion.

"Shit!" Pratt exclaimed, throwing up his hands. "This isn't turning out like I thought. I've got a wife and two kids at home, and I'm leaving."

Force grabbed Pratt by the shirt collar. "You're not going anywhere until Keaton gets here." There was a harsh reality in Force's voice that foretold of violence should Pratt try to make for his car.

Pratt backed away. "We gave it until mid-morning. All of you remember that. At high noon, if Keaton isn't here, I'm leaving. Understand?"

Perez turned to David and David returned the look. Simultaneously, they felt an uneasy peace come over them. David gave each man of the team a serious look. Perplexing as it was, there flashed through his mind the realization that somehow a hoax had been played on all of them. But by whom? And for what? It was time to find out.

David stood up. The others seemed to stiffen, so he spoke slowly so as not to arouse a physical response from anyone. "When did Keaton approach you to set up this meeting?"

"When did he approach you?" Force reproached.

"What if I told you he never came to me?"

"If that be true, how did you come to be here?" asked Doc, seeming to take an interest in the conversation for the first time.

"He told *me* about the meeting," Perez said, standing up.

"Doesn't make sense. Why would he tell you about the covenant?" Chip asked.

"He never mentioned the covenant to me. I was told to make sure David joined you. Nothing else," Perez responded.

"And how were you supposed to do that?"

"I was the major's therapist," Perez replied evenly as he looked at David.

"Oh, that's just great," Pratt said with a laugh.

"He came to each of us at different times," Chip said evenly, ignoring Pratt's remark. "He told us that we were going to be called upon to honor the covenant in some way. He gave each of us specific instructions about what we were to bring. I can only assume that something has been planned and what we brought with us has to do with what Keaton has in mind. You know him as well as we do, major."

Yes, David thought, *I do know him. I also know he's dead. What is happening here?*

"The helicopter?" he asked, turning to the machine.

"Like the man said, I stole it," Jake said proudly. "Keaton told me to."

"And the rest of you. What were you told to bring?"

As each told his story, David listened intently. As they spoke, his mind searched for an explanation. *Perez and I alone were told to bring nothing*, he thought, looking down at the ground, questions racing through his head faster than he could reason. Who had each of them seen, even Perez? There had to be a logical explanation. He looked at his old Rolex: 11:00. Would this imposter appear? How could he and Perez have been so wrong in their assumptions? The team had not brought them here. As far as each of them was concerned, he was just a bad memory. But the nightmares? The dreams? What had it all been for? Had he been wrong even about them? Sunny? What?

Jake had fallen asleep against a tree. No one said anything, thankful for small blessings. Pratt paced nervously up and down the long porch, spreading stains of sweat emanating from his underarms, back, and chest. The sun was already high in the cloudless sky.

"Hate this heat," Doc said to himself, wiping the sweat from his brow. San Francisco was always cool. He looked down at his watch. What if Keaton didn't show up? Should he just take them out now and then hunt Keaton down later? He fingered the shoulder patch stuck deep in his pants pocket. Pratt was right about one thing. That sheriff was no fool. It wouldn't be long before he paid them another visit. He fingered his Beretta's trigger housing and pondered the coming of noon.

Force had been watching Doc closely. He could sense anger just beneath the surface of Doc's expressionless face. He had seen that anger erupt many times before in – yes, criminals he had arrested. What was it Doc was hiding? He felt a familiar fear start to take hold. It was the kind of fear he felt when he got an armed robbery in progress call. *I've got to watch Doc*, he said to himself.

As Chip watched them with mild interest from the steps of the porch, David and Perez surveyed the helicopter. "You never heard any of them speak of this covenant?" Perez asked under his breath.

David shook his head. "No, never. Like I have told you, after what the Army did, we went our separate ways." He touched the empennage of the big aircraft, pretending to inspect it.

"David, I did not simply imagine the man who approached me at the memorial site. After listening to the others, I don't believe they imagined anyone either."

David stopped suddenly and looked Perez in the face. "Are you saying you believe Keaton is still alive?"

"Did you see the body, David? Did you?"

David froze and his eyes glassed over. The cold reality of deceit iced him, freezing tight his muscles, his blood, his very thoughts. Of course Keaton was still alive. Perez had seen him and so had the others. There had been no imposter. He had been had. So had the others. The CIA. Yes, now it was all perfectly clear. Keaton was still working for the Agency. His death had been just a cover, a way of going in deep so he could resurface and carry out some covert operation without being traced. The others? Pawns. He and Perez? Pawns also. "We've been had," he said harshly, his fists clenched, his eyes wide open and staring at the ground. *They deceived and destroyed us in Vietnam when they forced us to carry out Phoenix. Now they think they can do it to us again.*

Perez could see the rage building inside of him. "David," Perez said, taking him by the arm.

But David wrenched his arm away. "Had!" he screamed.

Hearing David's shout, the others jumped up. David left Perez and marched over to them. "You know he's still working for the Agency don't you?" he said loudly.

"Who?" Chip asked pointedly.

"Keaton," David spit.

There was silence as the men exchanged questioning looks.

"Why do you think that?" Force asked.

"Look at the facts. After you left the Army did any of you keep up with Keaton? No. You each went your separate ways and started new lives. But Keaton, like any good operative, went into hibernation until the time was right and the Agency woke him for his next mission, the one he's trying to pull all of us into. And what a cover he had!"

"What?" asked Chip.

"Death!" David told them.

"But we are here for the covenant," Chip said contemplatively.

"Oh, shut up, Chip. Can't you see what the good major here is saying is right?" Pratt said sarcastically. "The covenant be damned. None of us ever took that shit seriously. We were grasping for straws then. I would have sold my mother to them for my life. And don't give me those sanctimonious looks. All of you would have sold your souls to get out of that place." He shook his head and laughed. "The covenant was just what ole Keaton needed to push our buttons and have us show up here. He just used what was already there." He tucked in his shirt. "I'm going home, boys."

"It ain't noon yet," Doc said with a menacing tone.

Pratt looked Doc in the face. "I'm going home."

"I think you ought to stay and hear what Keaton has to say about all this." It was Jake, his shotgun leveled at Pratt's chest.

Pratt let out a nervous laugh. "This is silly. Put the gun down, Jake. This has gone far enough."

"Just sit down over there and give your life ten more minutes," Jake said. The others could tell by the tone of his voice that he was no longer drunk. He sounded like the old Jake, the Jake who could sneak up on a man and slit his throat so fast he couldn't feel his own blood before he died.

Pratt reluctantly sat down.

Jake turned to David. "This is an interesting story, major. Go on and finish it."

David nodded in agreement. "Evidently the Agency had us all figured out pretty well. They had studied our weaknesses and knew what it would take to put us together again for another assignment."

Doc shifted uneasily from one foot to the other. The CIA knew about him?

"So," David continued, "he used your covenant, no doubt genuinely made at the time, to bring you here."

Force folded his arms across his chest. "But why you and why this priest?"

"I wish you would call me Martin," Perez said somberly.

"They, the Agency, figured they needed me too, although I don't know why. Anyway, they obviously knew that at this time in my life I am under some stress, and in their minds they thought maybe Martin could influence me to come here. What they didn't know was that he would up and come with me," David continued.

"What do you think they'll do to me when they find me here?" Perez said nervously.

"Don't worry," David replied with a tone of confidence Perez had not heard in him before.

"Well, they didn't do their research well enough," Jake said, still holding the shotgun, "or they would've found out I'm not going anywhere with you, major. You had your chance and you blew it. To put it bluntly, you can't cut it when the shit hits the fan."

Perez noticed the tacit agreement on the faces of the others as they eyed David. They also seemed to be curious as they eyed David, as if watching to see what his response would be to Jake's challenge. Just seeing the bitter, reproachful looks on their faces told him that what David had said was true. Regardless of what each had told himself, they still connected David's failure in Vietnam with their fates.

"It's 12:00 o'clock," Pratt said defiantly, "and no Keaton."

"He'll show!" Force bellowed.

"And what if he does?" Pratt said angrily. "What if the major is right? Are we going to allow ourselves to be a part of another CIA operation? Jude was right. Before Phoenix, we stood for something. We were soldiers. After Phoenix, what we were was just a bunch of murderers. To me going on another CIA operation would be the same thing as reliving a lie. We can't be a part of something like this. The covenant was what he used to get us to come down here, but it was all a lie!"

"Shut up, wimp," Jake screamed. "I don't buy a word of what the major says. And even if I did, it wouldn't matter. I'm going to follow Keaton, wherever he leads me. I saw him. I saw his face. Don't any of you remember his face? That look? Didn't any of you hear his voice? What's wrong with you all? We lost everything over there. I lost my honor, my sense of purpose, my identity. Now maybe I have the change to get them back. Now maybe I'll be able to look myself in the mirror once again. Yeah, I'll wait. I'll stay here, and if I have to fight it out with the sheriff I'll do that too."

"Jake, listen," Chip said understandingly. "I love Keaton too, but the major has raised questions that Keaton should answer. Why was his death faked? Why didn't he just ask us to help him instead of lying to us about the covenant? We need to know the answers if for nothing else than to ease our minds in the future."

"Fuck the future. The future is now," Jake hissed.

"Look, I don't mind admitting it," Pratt said, "but this is scaring me. Go ahead and call me a wimp if you want, but I don't want any part of what's going on here. I want to go. I am going."

"Pratt, for God's sake," Chip said, touching Pratt on the shoulder. "I've got a wife too. And I love her as much as you do yours, but can't you see it's important we find out what's going on here? You think if the CIA is involved here they're just going to let you go back to your cushy life and forget about what's happened here? I thought you were smart. If you are an educated man, start acting like it. You can't leave. It's just as important to you to find out the truth as it is to the rest of us."

The harsh reality of Chip's words fell on Pratt like a hard rain. Chip was right. If the CIA was involved, he had to know. He already knew too much to be freed from looking over his shoulder the rest of his life. Reluctantly, he sat down on the porch and buried his face in his hands.

Doc grinned.

"Then we wait?" David asked.

The others nodded, even Doc.

"For how long?" Force asked.

"Until he comes," Chip replied.

Chapter 37

The mid-afternoon was hot and humid. The waters of the Sound lay still, devoid of any current that might have brought relief to David and the others from the stale, suffocating air. As the men lay dormant under the drooping willows, they were tormented by swarms of gnats hungering for their sweat and huge flies that bit at their necks. Some tried to doze off, but the insects were ravenous in their attacks.

Wearily, David made his way to the helicopter where Jake was hidden, secluded from the others, alone and brooding with his secret, maligned thoughts. He climbed the extended stairs and entered the spacious cabin of the helicopter. It was hot inside, hotter than under the trees. Jake sat at the end of the cabin near the entrance to the cockpit. Graciously, he offered David a seat with a wave of his hand. He seemed to have gained control over his emotions for now.

"What do you do?" Jake asked, giving David a curious stare.

"I teach."

"Where?"

David told him.

Jake seemed to mull David's response over as if he were trying to make something of it he could slander. After a minute or so, he gave up and opened a beer, and took a long swig. Then quite unexpectedly, he offered David a can. He caught it with one hand. The beer tasted good. Anything wet tasted good.

"Wonder where Keaton wants you to fly this helicopter?" David asked, looking over the cabin.

"I know where he wants to go," Jake said as easily as if he was announcing a preprinted flight schedule.

David shot him a look of sheer amazement. "What?"

"He told me to get together these air charts," Jake said, casually pointing to the briefcase lying at his feet, which David could see was stuffed full of air maps.

"So, where?" he asked anxiously.

"South America."

David felt as if he had been slapped across the face and felt a panicky sickness start to well up in him. He turned to see if Perez was near. No, Perez was walking near the Sound. He began to sweat. "Where in South America?" he heard himself ask without thinking.

"Don't know. Got charts of the whole damn place. Cost nearly three hundred dollars."

"I'll be back," David said. He got up and headed for the door, leaving his beer sitting on the floor.

"Suit yourself, shithead," he thought he heard Jake say as he jumped out of the helicopter, but he couldn't be sure. And at that exact moment, it really didn't matter.

He found Perez deep in thought walking along the treacherously soft banks of the Ossawba. He perked an ear as David ran breathlessly up to him. "What if this whole operation has something to do with Sunny?" he asked excitedly.

Perez rubbed his chin and adjusted his glasses that had slipped down the length of his nose. He looked uncharacteristically disheveled with his turned around collar unbuttoned and his shirt open down the middle exposing a white t-shirt. He gave David a curious questioning look. "Why would you suppose such a thing?"

"What kind of gear have they brought?"

"I know what they have brought, but . . ."

"Jake's got air maps of South America. Don't you think it's more than a coincidence that he should have air maps of South America?"

Perez pursed his lips and frowned.

"Listen Martin, the news about Sunny did make the paper. And even if that wasn't the source, the State and Defense Departments know about her, and you can be sure the CIA knows about the incident too. If Keaton is with the CIA, well, don't you see?"

"David, have you talked to the other men? Keaton visited each of them long before the Falklands War, and long before Sunny disappeared. You must not grasp for false hopes."

David's face turned ashen. He took a deep breath and slumped. "I'm drowning, aren't I? I wanted to think it was possible. Damn! Where is he?"

"It's all right, David," Perez said, putting his hand on David's shoulder. "Let's go back."

"I'm hungry," Pratt stated. "There's a small stop in the road about ten miles away. I'm going to make a run."

Doc thought for a few minutes. "I'll go. You wouldn't want any of these crackers to take a liking to you."

"He's right. No need in both of you going." Force said. "Just get stuff to make sandwiches and such. We don't want to attract any attention," he told Doc.

"No. We don't want to attract any attention by doing something like landing a helicopter here," Doc quipped.

"Just get the damn food and hurry back," Jake said, sloshing some beer down his throat.

"We could eat the C-rations," David interjected.

"No, we couldn't," Force said in rebuttal.

"Get going," he said to Doc. Doc drove off in a cloud of dust that seemed to hang in the humid air forever.

After he watched him disappear behind the trees, David turned to Chip. "When Keaton asked you to come here, did he say anything to you about me?"

"No, nothing. Why?"

"How about you?" he asked Force.

"No."

"He told *me* you were dead," Jake snapped.

David gave Jake a sharp look, cleared his throat, and turned to

Force again. "Do you know anything about what has happened to my wife?"

"No. I didn't even know you were married. Why?"

"Do you know what Jake has in that helicopter?" Force and Chip turned to the chopper and shook their heads. "He has air maps of the entire continent of South America."

"Also, the Southern United States and Central America," Jake added proudly.

"Then that means we're going to Central America," Force said thoughtfully, "or South America."

"If I may," Perez said hesitantly, still feeling like an interloper, "at this time Central America is a very dangerous place. There is an especially bad guerilla war going on in El Salvador, and the Sandinistas are exporting revolution to their neighbors. It would be perfectly logical that the CIA would have operations going on throughout the region in support of friendly governments. It's my guess Keaton wants you to assist him on one of these operations."

Chip nodded. "That makes sense. It has to be. The question each one or us has to ask himself is whether we want to take part in it."

"Count me in, as long as he stays out of it," Jake retorted, pointing toward David.

"There are still some questions I want answered," Force said.

"Well, that's the first sensible thing I've heard today," Pratt said, running his fingers through his hair and looking at David.

"I have questions too," David said haltingly.

"Don't push it, major. Remember, I'm not under your command any more. Just don't push it," Force said harshly, turning away from David. Jake took one look at David's tightly drawn face and let out a cackling laugh.

Doc returned with the food. Hungry, everyone gratefully ate and drank their fill.

"What time it get dark here?" Doc asked, wiping some bread crumbs from his cheek.

"2000 hours, ah, eight o'clock," Jake answered, not looking up from his corned beef sandwich.

Doc looked down at his gold Bulova. It was already 6:00 p.m. *We be here almost two days now,* he thought, *and Keaton's not here. Somethin's not right 'bout this. I got two K's comin' in in two days time. This is gonna' be done tonight!*

"Why did you ask me earlier if I knew what had happened to your wife," Force asked David.

"Nothing. I didn't mean anything by it," David said, looking out across the Sound.

Perez put down his sandwich, reached out from where he was sitting, and grabbed David by the arm. David turned to Perez. There was a stern, reprimanding look on Perez's face. Soon, the others noticed Perez staring at David and found the looks between the two men disturbing.

"Something bothering you two we should know about?" Chip asked.

"David, what harm will it do them?" Perez said.

David turned away from Perez. He wondered if they would listen. But then she was there; he could see her sitting among them. She was smiling, her hair blowing wistfully in an unseen breeze. *Don't be afraid*, she had said. *Okay, Sunny, I'll be humiliated once more for you.* David began.

They were respectfully silent as David told them of Sunny. Even Jake held back his distasteful outbursts. Perez was amazed at how they listened. None of them smirked or traded looks of unconcern. Most seemed to understand David's loss, as if the common bond they had once shared as soldiers still bound them in a mutuality of feeling. Only Doc seemed detached, distracted, apathetic. But Perez noticed something else, which his intellect caused him to question, and that was the longer David spoke about Sunny, the angrier they seemed to become.

"A good wife," Pratt said haughtily. "She obviously has courage, whether she is an agent provocateur or is innocent. But what amazes me is that you are shocked and surprised about what happened to her. What did you think would happen to her down there? Have you forgotten what we used to do for nighttime pleasure in the land of the red fire ant? We would have gotten to her ourselves. Hell, major, you would have shot her yourself if she had been a VC. You expect them to do any different? Patriotism is determined by perception."

"Shut up, Pratt!" Jake yelled.

"Sounds like you make no distinction between good and evil, Dr. Goldman," Perez said. "Certainly, Sonia would be looked upon as a patriot by American standards. You are an American, aren't you?"

"You can go to hell, priest. I am merely making a point to the good major that how you see evil usually depends on what side you're on. During our revolution, the British saw our founding fathers as terrorists. To us, they were heroes. Maybe the Argentineans see the major's wife in the same way the British saw Jefferson and Washington."

"I'm not as cynical as you, Pratt," Chip said. "Somewhere along the line a person has to have the ability to distinguish between good and evil. Major Elliot's wife went to Argentina to help her parents. What she did before coming to America was to help her countrymen fight against an evil regime. To my way of thinking, this country ought to care about what has been done to her. She's one of us. An American."

"I thought you'd grown up some," Jake said, lighting a cigarette. "No one gives a damn about that kind of shit any more unless it affects them personally"

"Exactly," Pratt said authoritatively. "From a philosophical point of view, I would say Americans have become hedonists."

"A hedo-nis?" Jake asked, his mouth screwed up.

"A hedonist, my fine-feathered friend, is one who believes in self-gratification, the pursuit of personal pleasure. When a person becomes a hedonist it's a tragedy, but when a great nation becomes hedonistic, it's a disaster."

Then Pratt turned to David. "Major, all I can say to you is that your tale is sad. But you know, it's hard for me to have any sympathy for you because you're a part of the whole damn thing. You could have gotten out when we did, but you chose to stay. Even knowing how rotten things were, you chose to stay." Pratt had a disgusted look on his face. "No, it's not you I feel sorry for. It's your wife. But at least she had the guts to try to stop what was happening in her country. But you, you just became a part of what was happening to yours."

Chapter 38

> Leadership is the art of influencing others to willingly perform a task.
>
> United States Army

As night slowly cooled the earth, there were those among the team who were beginning to question whether Keaton would ever appear. David listened for a while with interest to their arguments for and against leaving, but increasingly he felt like an outsider, especially when the subject of the covenant was brought up. After a while, he decided to take a walk along the bank of the Sound.

After he has been gone for a few minutes and making sure no one noticed, Doc quietly disappeared into the dark forest. However, it did not take long for the others to question his absence.

"Doc's been a pain in the ass ever since he arrived," Force said, chafing as he stood staring into the blackness of the forest.

"He's already made up his mind to leave. Don't bother with him," Chip said with a tone of finality, turning away.

"If Keaton was really coming, he would have certainly been here by now. We did as we were asked. We came. We brought what we were told to bring. There's nothing for us to be ashamed of. Really, I think we've honored the covenant," Force said, at last giving in to his doubts.

"I agree," Chip said reluctantly. "Who knows what may have happened to him? Besides, I'll bet that sheriff pays us a return visit before morning. We just can't stay here much longer with that helicopter as hot as it is."

Jake stood up and stretched. "Don't worry about the chopper. I made it look like I had crashed at sea," he informed them.

"But what will you do?" Chip asked him in earnest.

Jake looked forlorn.

"You're going to stay here, aren't you?" Chip asked, although he already knew the answer.

Jake nodded.

Force put his hand on Jake's shoulder. "You can't stay here, Jake. Don't you see that?"

But Jake only gave him a blank stare.

With great care, Doc pushed aside each bush he encountered as he traveled through the all-encompassing darkness of the dank forest. With each step, he was careful not to break a twig or crush a pile of leaves and thus prematurely expose his presence, for his prey was very near, and he was anxious for the kill. Yes, he was anxious. He could feel the tension in his muscles. His heart pounded and his body throbbed with the excitement of anticipation. Now he would free himself from his past. In a few moments, he would wipe out the last traces of his old self. Streams of sweat ran down his face and into his eyes as he spied the figure of a man sitting silently on the banks of the Ossawba facing the water. Ever so slowly Doc crept out of the wood line and squared himself behind the sitting figure. He held his breath tight as he raised the cold Beretta and aimed its silencer-extended snout toward the man's head. *This is long overdue, maje*, Doc thought. *You are the one.* His finger tightened around the trigger.

"It is not me you wish to kill," the man said unexpectedly in a raspy voice, not bothering to turn around.

Startled, Doc lowered the gun.

"Yes, it's me," the man said in a slow, whimsical voice.

For a moment, Doc was paralyzed by the sound of the voice, as if its tone had a siren's affect on him. "Keaton?"

"Yes, of course. Why don't you come closer, my friend. Stand over here next to me so my eyes can meet yours."

Reluctantly, Doc did as he was ordered.

"I know what is your desire. You need to kill them all."

The voice was powerful, hot and alluring. Doc wanted to reach out and touch the voice. He wanted to speak, but he was startled by the man's knowledge of his plans.

"Yes, I know the desires of your heart, my friend. One of us betrayed you, didn't he? One of us led you to destruction. Which of us was the coward who told the Army of our weakness? You do not know, do you? So you will have to kill us all to be sure," he said with a grin.

"Why don't you come out and face the others? It be you that brought us here," Doc said, all of a sudden feeling strangely lightheaded.

"Yesss, yesss," the man hissed. "A mission has been planned for you, but not by me."

"Not by . . ."

"Listen to me. I too have suffered at the hands of those who await my return. This thing that is planned is a threat to me and to you, my friend. Oh yes, you are my friend. You and I are one. I hate them as much as you do. Why do you think I would confide in you were it not so? I want them much more than do you."

"Then why not help me kill them?"

"In time. But for now, know that they have powerful allies. We who are of the earth must use the earth to obtain our desires. And so it will be. But for now, you have wealth you are worried about? Yes, I know of it."

The K's, Doc thought. *How could he? He is CIA!*

"Do not worry. I give you my bargain that your wealth will increase if you help me see this thing through."

"Why don't you just do it yourself?"

"I cannot touch anything directly but you, you can do what is necessary. Only, you must not be hasty."

"When?"

"This thing that is planned is yet to be played to its final end. And at that end is where my revenge – your revenge, must be complete. Not now. Not in this place. Do you understand?"

Yes, of course, Doc thought. *Why couldn't I see it before? He was betrayed too. He wants their blood as much as I do. And so does the CIA.*

"Yesss, yesss," the man hissed again, as if reading Doc's mind.

Doc's skin was suddenly cold and clammy. His eyes were fixed, unable to break away from the penetrating stare of the steely, almost glowing eyes of the figure sitting in front of him. He could no longer feel the Beretta in his hand or the heat of the night. All he could feel was the magnetic power of those eyes.

Suddenly the man rose up and stood before him. A cold wind began to blow in from the water and all the sounds of the night became mute. "This is our world, Doc. It is ours to take. All of us who are of the earth, and all things of the earth may serve us. But this thing that has been planned must be destroyed. You will know when the time has come to carry out our revenge. Until that time, you must do what your senses tell you is demanded of you." He smiled, and when he did his mouth seemed a black hole – no teeth, no tongue. "Now, go. This thing will be revealed tonight. And tell no one of our meeting."

With that, the man placed his hand on Doc's forehead. Doc felt an intense heat that burned yet at the same time radiated throughout his body with a satisfying warmth. Then with a turn, the man disappeared quickly into the dark forest.

David walked slowly along the banks, one careful step after the other, his hands behind his back, his head bent low. It was dark, but he could still feel his way along the path others had tread before. The sky overhead was pitch black. Stars twinkled on and off in the humid, still air.

How many times, he questioned, had he been alone on nights like this in far off places around the world? But this night he felt a loneliness that saddened him beyond anything he could have ever imagined. His heart was heavy with the memory of Sunny. During all of those lonely nights he had looked up into the face of the stars and felt a constancy that was comforting in its familiarity. Yes, the stars had always been there. They had always been his compatriots. Could it be, then, that on this night they were there for Sunny as well? Could it be that she could see them now? Could she somehow know that he shared with her, through their magic, this moment of existence? *Sunny, my love, forgive me.*

He stopped. In his path stood a figure, tall, stooped over, and dark. For a moment he felt a twinge of fear and his hand nervously clutched the handle of his faithful Webley. "Perez?" he questioned, his voice a monotone. The figure seemed to be wrapped in a shawl or a cape. And on a night like this, David thought curiously. Then he remembered Perez had no such clothing. "Who are you?" David asked furiously, drawing the Webley and leveling it at the man's guts.

"David."

The man spoke in a voice that was familiar. A strong voice, powerful and alluring. David felt himself raise his hand toward the man as if to touch the voice. This voice, where had he heard it before? "Who are you, and how do you know my name?"

"Do you not know me?"

Oh my God, David thought. *Can it be?* "Keaton!"

"David, we have not much time."

"Wait," David interrupted. He was breathless, his mind racing for answers to a thousand questions, questions only Keaton could answer. "Why have you come back after all this time? Why have you brought us together again? Where have you been?"

"Do not question me, David. Hear my words."

"No. You answer me, damn it!"

"The answers you seek are in the evidence around you. But for now . . ."

He lunged for Keaton, grabbed him around the waist, and wrestled him to the ground. But almost effortlessly, Keaton turned him over and held him down to the ground. Keaton's grip was powerful. "You're strong, old man," he managed to say between his teeth, "but . . ." He threw Keaton over against the edge of the bank then quickly jumped up and kicked at him, but missed. "You're fast, too," he said.

But Keaton did not reply. Instead he caught David's arm as he swung and effortlessly flipped him onto his back. He struck the ground so hard his breath was knocked out. For a moment he was paralyzed, and then he began gasping for air. He could barely see the fuzzy image of Keaton standing over him. He briefly and vindictively entertained the idea of trying to trip Keaton, but the pain inside his rib cage told him the struggle was over. He raised himself on his elbows. "What do you want of me?"

"I shall tell you," Keaton said, dropping the cape from his shoulders. Even though it was dark, David could see a resolute look of confidence across his face. His voice was powerful, almost beguiling. "There was a time in your life, long ago, when you gave me respect. You listened to my word and obeyed my laws. Then you lost faith in yourself."

Obeyed? David thought. *I was his captain. He was my sergeant.*

"Now, you have turned your face from me and have lost your honor. You suffer and are afraid. Have you not learned that nothing can exist without me?"

David was all at once fearful. Who was this before him? Not Keaton. He began to marshal his strength. This person who spoke to him had to be mad. Yes, that was the answer. To pose as his dead sergeant, to summon the others here for some sinister purpose evidenced a malignant will. He searched his mind for a way out. Yes – the Webley. He began to search for it, moving his eyes slowly and being careful not to give away his intention. And there it was, lying at the feet of the mad man. Could he get to it? His breath had returned. He weighed his chances as he pretended to listen.

"Those whom I have called are now waiting. But it is not I who must lead them. It is you."

David looked up at the man. "Oh really? You got them to come here. Why don't you go and face them yourself?" *I'll not play this game*, he thought. *If I can only get to the gun.* "Besides," he said, inching his hand toward the Webley, "have you forgotten about Jude?"

"Do you remember my message to you that there is a darkness spreading across the land? Do you remember now?"

A cold fear froze David solid. The dream. *Who was this man? How could he know of the dream?*

"There *is* a darkness spreading across the land. Its song of sweetness is perverse and wicked, yet pleasantly deceptive to the naive and the guilty. But it can be stopped if men of honor and courage can show the way. If they set the example for others to follow."

With one quick motion, he grabbed the Webley and trained it on the man. "Now, tell me who the hell you are and what you want of us, or I'll kill you."

"Do not be afraid of me, David. For I love you like my own son. For you are a man of my own heart."

He recalled the last night he and Sunny had been together before he had let her disappear from his life. She had spoken those same words then as she lay close to him, her heart softly beating against his. *You were once a man after God's own heart*, she had told him. Slowly he lowered the Webley and let it fall from his hand. All at once he no longer feared the man. "Is that you, Keaton? Please tell me," he said quietly.

"Yes, I am Keaton. Can you not see my face?"

"Now I can. Tell me what it is you want of us. The others are preparing to leave. They think you're not going to come."

Keaton sat down next to him. Close now, David could now make out the features of the man. It was the same gray hair, the same rock jaw and serious look. It was Keaton. Older, perhaps wiser, but it was Keaton. He began to speak, and it was evident from the compromising tone of his voice that he wanted David to relax and trust him. "There was a time after the ambush when your men thought they were going to die. So, they made a covenant. They promised me they would come to each others' aid in times of need. This is why they gather now. They have been summoned to aid a brother."

"Is this a CIA mission?"

Keaton smiled.

"Then let's go to them. They'll do whatever you ask of them. I can see it in their faces."

"No, I must return."

"But you are the one who has the plan."

"I cannot go to them. It is you who must lead them so that they may regain their honor and once again stand in the light of men."

"But it's you they have come to follow. Surely you know how they feel about me."

"You can change that."

"Can I? Look at what's happened to them. Look at what's happened to me. Since the war I've been no good to anyone or anything. I've been living a lie, Keaton. I'm no officer."

"You can change that."

"I can? God, you don't know what's happened to me. I've lost my wife . . ."

"You can change that."

"But I don't know what it is you want them to do!"

"The answer you seek is in the evidence around you," Keaton said, a firm demanding look on his face. Keaton extended his hand to David and as their hands clasped he effortlessly lifted David up. In the darkness of the night they stood facing each other as they had done many times before. "Keaton, tell me what to do!" he yelled.

"You have the means. All you need is the will and the faith."

A strong wind began to blow in from the waters of the Sound. So strong was its gust it blew droplets of water against their faces. Overhead, thunder roared from swirling dark clouds and lightning streaked across the sky.

"Tell me how I can do it," David screamed to be heard above the roar of the wind.

"You must decide," Keaton bellowed.

"Indiana?"

"I was there."

"Father Perez?"

"There is a purpose."

"Will you be there?" David shouted.

"I will always be there," Keaton said, his voice booming.

"Keaton?"

"Be strong and have courage. Do not be afraid, for every place your foot shall tread mine has gone before you." And with that, Keaton turned and disappeared into the night wind.

The sudden storm caught the men under the tree off guard. The low hanging limbs of the willow blew wildly, thrashing them across the faces and arms.

"Let's get to the mansion," Chip yelled.

"I'm going to check on the chopper first," Jake said.

The others ran into the mansion.

Force had earlier brought a battery powered lantern from his vehicle to provide a localized light near the doorway. When he switched the lamp on, it unexpectedly outlined a figure of a man who had previously been hidden. "Jesus, Doc! Let someone know you're around. You scared the hell out of me." Doc just grinned and lit a cigar.

Perez was becoming worried about David. This sudden spring storm had an ominous feeling about it. Nervously, he lit his pipe. "Is the helicopter safe?" he asked Chip.

"Jake may drink too much, but he's one hell of a pilot. And he's a damn fair mechanic. He's not going to let anything happen to his aircraft."

After a few minutes Jake ran inside and stood shaking off the rain. "I saw the good major strolling this way."

"How's the chopper?" Force asked.

"Made in the USA by American workers."

Pratt had been quiet, even sullen. With the weather fast deteriorating, he decided it was time to adjourn this reunion before it got any worse. "Let's call it a day," he said with an air of defiance.

"Yeah," Chip agreed with a nod. "It was good to see each of you again."

"What are we supposed to do with all this stuff?" Force asked, somewhat miffed.

"Get your money back," Perez answered without thinking.

"Why don't we put it to use?" It was David. He was standing in the doorway, faintly illuminated by the fading lamp, a pool of water gathering at his feet as the rain fell from him. Perez sensed something intense in David's manner, a familiar demeanor reminiscent of another place in another time. Perez took a step in David's direction but was halted by David's upheld hand.

Doc lowered his cigar and waited. *Here it comes*, he thought, *so he'll be the one to deliver it.*

"What do you mean, major?" Force asked in a demanding tone.

"A long way from here near the end of the earth is a young woman," David said, his voice powerful and resolute, his eyes looking far away. "An American. She's being held captive against her will. She's vulnerable and alone. Evil men seek her life. And in her hour of darkness she must feel that no one will help her. Soon she will be killed, drugged and thrown out of a helicopter over a dark river to drown."

"My God," Perez said astonished. "What are you thinking?"

"Shut up, priest," Doc said quickly, pointing his finger at Perez.

"Your wife," Chip said, a faint smile on his lips.

"Yes, my wife."

"Well, I can see where this is leading, and I for one am not going to take part in anything as crazy as this," Pratt said, his arms folded across his chest.

"Major, even if we wanted to help you, there's a whole lot of water under the bridge between us," Force said.

Pratt nodded in agreement and leaned over to Force and whispered in his ear. "He's gone crazy. Look at his face."

Force squinted as he scrutinized David's face in the fading light. But instead of the mask of a crazy man, he saw the face of a man hardened by adversity, resolute and steady. There were no maniacal furrows, no gaping grin. He had the look of a man who had come to face his own reason for existence. But there was something else about the look on David's face. Force had seen that look before. But where?

"It's hard for me to believe you would think we would just put our lives on hold, leave our families, and go off on some foolish venture to try to save a woman who is probably already dead," Pratt said harshly.

"Just a minute," Jake said. "You can speak for yourself if you want to, but I came here with every intention of doing whatever Keaton asked of me." Jake stood up and squared off against Pratt. "The covenant was no lark to me."

"Well, I can think of about three good reasons why none of us should even think about going anywhere but back home," Pratt said, his lips quivering.

"Oh? And what are they?" Chip asked, moving next to Jake.

"First," Pratt said, postured before the others as if he were lecturing a class of students, "if we leave in that helicopter we are going to become accessories to grand larceny. Second, it is against the law to become a mercenary. Third, and more importantly, people just can't make governmental decisions such as he's about to ask us to do. What if every American decided he'd take up arms against a foreign government he felt had wronged him? Hell, we'd be traipsing off all over the world killing anyone with whom we disagree. It's the responsibility of the American government to protect your wife, major. Not yours and not ours. And, as we know, our government is reluctant to do anything."

"Shut the fuck up, Pratt. No one feels like hearing your shit," Jake said angrily.

"Keaton asked you all to meet here to honor your covenant, am I right?" David asked. "And you all came, some with every intent of honoring the covenant, some for more personal reasons. But still you came. And not only were you asked to come, you were told to bring with you specific items which we can only surmise would aid in the operation."

"Get to your point," Pratt said testily, looking at his watch.

"I'm warning you, Pratt. Shut up!" Jake shot back.

"You were told to bring fatigues, web gear, weapons and ammo, staples, and transportation. Obviously, what you would need to carry out a mission somewhere," David continued.

Perez studied David as he talked. This wasn't the David he knew.

"But where?" David asked, letting the question hang in the air for a few moments. "The answer is found in the items you were asked to bring. How many sets of uniforms and gear do you have?"

"Seven," answered Force.

"And how many of us are there?"

"Six," said Chip.

"Seven, counting Keaton," Jake countered.

"But if Keaton isn't coming?" David asked with a knowing grin.

"You've seen him, haven't you?" Jake shouted, lunging at David and grabbing him by the shirt. But David did not resist because he could sense it was not rage that motivated Jake, but fear. Fear of failure once again.

As Jake stared wildly into David's eyes, he could see what he had just said was true. David *had* seen Keaton, and now he realized Keaton had once again put his faith in him. Like a breath escaping, the anger he had felt for so many years suddenly turned to remorse. Slowly, he let go of David and began to sob. "I've hated you for so long. I've blamed you for everything bad that's happened in my life. Now I realize I am the one responsible for my life being a failure, not you. But you were a convenient scapegoat, so easy to pass it off on. You were our leader. You had the responsibility to shoot Jude. If you had, maybe we would still be in the Army. Maybe not. Maybe we would have never been humiliated. Maybe we would have. Now, I just don't know any more. All I know for sure is that I respect Keaton more than any man alive. And now I know that he respects you. You and he are one and the same." He wiped his eyes. Standing straight, almost at attention, he said, "That helicopter out there and its pilot are at your command, major."

Perez was stunned. He knew David had planned nothing, yet he did not repudiate Jake's belief. Why? Was he really going to try to get them to rescue Sunny? Could he stand by and see David go through with this madness? He nervously pondered his next move.

David continued, motioning for Jake to sit beside him. "As I said, seven sets of fatigues and gear. But most importantly, seven field jacket-parkas and cold weather gear. It's winter in Argentina."

"Major," Force said, "level with us. Is Keaton coming here?"

David gave each man a resolute look. "He will be with us every step of the way."

Force dropped his head. *The major and Keaton were in this together all along*, he thought. *To free the major's wife? No, wait a minute.* "When was she taken hostage?" he asked wide-eyed.

"About a month ago," David replied, knowing what Force was thinking.

"Keaton came to me long before that. How did he know your wife was going to be taken hostage?"

"He came to me in the dead of winter, major," Chip said rubbing his chin.

David started to reply, but before he could begin Force spoke. "Maybe she planned to be taken hostage."

"The CIA. Damn it major, level with us. What's this all about?" Pratt yelled.

"Does it really matter?" David asked quietly. "What if this is a CIA mission? What if my wife was an operative? What if this had been planned for a long time and my wife's trip to Argentina to help her parents was just a ruse in order to obtain some intelligence information? Would any of that matter? She's an American. And she needs our help."

"What better way to honor the covenant than to help her in her time of desperation?" Jake said, not looking at the others. "Besides, it was Keaton who asked each of us to come. If this is what he wants us to do, then I say we do it and quit arguing about it. Time is obviously of the essence."

Chip stood up, put his hands on his hips, and turned to the others. "Major, do you have a plan?"

"I'm not believing this," Pratt said, biting his lips.

"Hey, boy!" Doc yelled to Pratt. "You ain't green behind the ears as

I recall. You think once you in you can ever get out? You in. They never let you get out now."

Pratt began to tremble. He knew what Doc had said was right. The reality that he would have to see this thing through to its conclusion fell hard on his shoulders. "Oh, Jesus," he said softly to himself.

Doc heard him and let out a laugh. "Better speak to somebody you know, Jew boy."

"I don't want to hear that kind of shit from you again, you hear!" Force bellowed, giving Doc a hard look.

Doc just grinned. *He be the first*, he thought, *and nothing quick and easy.*

In his mind, David could picture Keaton. *Have I done all right?* he asked. *Am I on the right course?* Keaton smiled.

"Yes, I have a plan. But for now, I need to know if all of us are in agreement." As David turned to each man, he received a nod, even from Pratt, although reluctantly. "Good. Now, I must ask of you one more act of faith, and that is that you wait here until tomorrow night. It's important that I go back to Washington to see some people and gather some things. I'll be back no later than midnight. In the meantime, you must prepare everything we need to complete the mission."

Oh, God, what's happening? Perez thought, terrified.

"Doc, you make ready the weapons and ammo then store them in the chopper. We don't want to arouse any suspicions. Force, you put together the uniforms and equipment and then store them. Pratt," but Pratt was looking out the window into the darkness. "Pratt!"

Pratt turned to David with heavy eyes.

"You get together our food and water." Pratt nodded.

"Chip, put the heaters in the chopper and figure out what to do with our cars. Jake, you must start planning our course to Argentina and take it beyond. Figure our refueling points and ways so avoid detection."

"It'll cost a lot of money to fly to Argentina and back," Jake said.

"Don't worry about the money," David said.

"And what of me?" Perez asked meekly.

"The extra uniform is for you. You speak Spanish, don't you?"

Perez swallowed hard.

"Now, be on guard. Pratt's right about the sheriff. If he comes, tell him we have engine failure or something. Stall him until I can return tomorrow night and then we'll be on our way."

David started for the door, but stopped and turned to the others who were watching him intently. "I know this is difficult for you. I know you all have your lives and many of you have families. But I didn't make the covenant. You did. If you choose to honor it, this is a way. As for me, I'll take anyone with me who is still here when I return. I hope all of you are here. I won't let you down this time."

As David left, it came to Force where he had seen the look he had seen earlier on David's face. Keaton had had the same look on his face that cold day when they had last met.

David quickly made his way through the tangled woods, the hard rain beating down across his shoulders. Stopping for a moment to get his bearings he could hear someone running after him. He waited, sensing who it would be.

Breathlessly, Perez caught up to him. His hair had fallen down around his shoulders and his glasses were obscured with little drops of rain. "This is madness, you know," he said imploringly.

"No, it's not madness," David said, grabbing Perez's shoulders with both of his hands. "It's full of purpose and meaning. But you can't see it, can you? I know you now. I see who you are. I see what you've become."

"Don't patronize me. I'm the one who tried to help you become whole again."

"Yes, and for that I am in your debt. But, Martin, what is happening here is beyond reason and intellectual understanding. Look at the whole thing. Look at what's happened around you."

David let go of Perez and backed away. "But," he said, giving Perez a knowing look, "you have to have faith to see it, father."

"Faith!" Perez screamed angrily. "You, an atheist, talk to me of faith?"

"Martin, don't you know now what the dreams were? Can't you understand their meaning? They weren't the product of delayed stress or any other thing found in your books of psychology."

"Then what were they?"

"They were messages."

Chapter 39

May 17, 1982

They had slept long into the morning. None of them had realized how tired they had become. The prior night's storm had freshened the air and blown away the haze and, even though the sun was steadily climbing into the clear blue sky, the air was cool. The chirping of birds and the droning of bees pollinating wild flowers were the only sounds that greeted them as they arose.

Once again, Force was the first to come alive. During the war he had been the second ranking sergeant after Keaton. So, as if picking up where his mentor had left off, he took charge of the others, reminding them of the instructions David had given them. The rest followed his orders without protest.

Perez watched with fascination as the men began to work together. After all this time, although of different temperament and civilian social standing, they each fell back into their old roles without reluctance and once again assumed their military ways as easily and unthinkingly as one rides a bike after many years of abstinence.

In Force's mind, the big question was what they were going to do with their automobiles. After much discussion it was decided they would move them even deeper into the woods and camouflage them. This was the first task they undertook. And a good thing too, because shortly after the last vehicle had been concealed Sheriff Taylor indeed did come calling again.

Today, the sheriff's demeanor was decidedly suspicious. "Never thought this place would be so interestin'," he said with a sly grin.

"It's the helicopter," Jake said as he wiped grease from his hands. "The hydraulic system on the trim tabs is low on fluid and I'm having to purge the system before I can replace it. Shouldn't take much longer."

"How much longer?" The sheriff appeared to be sizing Jake up. During his last visit, Jake had been asleep in the helicopter and his presence now caused the sheriff some confusion at first.

"We'll be out of here by dark," Jake said flatly.

"Hmm. What ya'll boys been doin'?"

"Nothing much. Mostly just sightseeing," replied Force.

"And sleeping," added Chip. "We never figured we'd be here this long."

The sheriff ambled around the mansion for a few minutes as if checking the grounds for damage. Then he walked up to Force. "Checked with your department," he said candidly. "You're for real. They say you're on vacation all right. Seem to think real highly of ya."

Force bit his lip. "I try to do my job."

"Yeah, well, how 'bout that ride now?" he asked, grinning widely.

Jake stepped forward. "Man, I'm sorry, but with the hydraulic system down that'll be impossible."

The sheriff's slaphappy look changed to one of disappointment. "Well, let me look inside at least?"

Again Jake intervened. "Company policy prohibits anyone going on board while repairs are being performed. Insurance, you know."

"Oh."

"But," Jake said quickly, "I'll make an exception in your case."

"Why, thank ya."

As Jake took the sheriff inside the helicopter, Pratt came up to Force. "Thank God we haven't started loading yet."

Force nodded. "As soon as he leaves, get the others over here."

After a few minutes, Jake and the sheriff emerged from the cavern of the helicopter's cabin and, grinning at each other, walked past the others to the sheriff's patrol car. Force motioned for everyone to keep their places.

"Well, I thank ya," Sheriff Taylor said, opening the car's door.

"It was my pleasure, sheriff," Jake said smiling.

The sheriff got into his car and started up the engine. But before he drove off, he leaned out the window and informed them, "I'll check on ya'll after dinner, now." Then he disappeared into the cloud of dust made by the screeching tires of the car.

"Shit!" Force said. "My department knows where I am."

"Don't mean nothin,'" Doc said flatly.

"Doc's right. It doesn't make any difference," Chip said.

Pratt gave each man his uniform and web gear, and each tried on his uniform, including the winter parkas and, after being satisfied of fit, stored them along with the web gear, which they adjusted to their particular height and weight, in their duffle bags. After they had secured the heaters and the food and water inside the helicopter, Doc handed each man, including Perez, his M-16 and ammo.

Force noticed the rifles were government issue. "Where'd you get these weapons?" he asked. But Doc didn't answer him with anything other than a blank stare. Reluctantly, Force backed off. Now wasn't the time for a confrontation, but Force knew that sooner or later he and Doc would have to face each other.

"You gonna accept that gun?" Chip asked Perez.

"Why not?" Perez asked angrily and stormed off in the direction of the mansion.

"What's bothering him?" Pratt asked. Chip just shook his head.

The afternoon passed quietly and uneventfully. They dined on C-rations and water and most took naps while Jake busied himself with fine-tuning the aircraft. He had thoroughly refueled the thirsty helicopter, using the last of his savings, at the Savannah Airport before landing. Happily, he went over every inch of the aircraft, tightening bolts, checking lines, adjusting cables, and measuring fluid levels. As Keaton had instructed, he had also, secreted away enough of the spare parts that might be needed for the most common engine and drive train problems they might encounter. He checked to make sure everything that had been loaded was in its proper place and that he knew where everything was located. He had also hooked up the helicopter's set of FM military radios. With them, he could talk to anything on the ground, in the air, or on the surface of the sea.

Jake was ready. He had worked out the air route they would follow. With its external tanks full, the aircraft trimmed and lean, using only cruising power, he could fly about seven hundred miles between fuel stops. The entire air route from Richmond Hill to a point at the southernmost tip of Argentina would take them five thousand five hundred miles. They would be required to fuel at least nine times, possibly ten if they encountered any unusual situations. They would cross over Florida, the Gulf of Mexico, Central America, and make their way down the western coast of South America. Their first refueling stop would be at the airport in Key West. From there they would fly to the Yucatan Peninsula to a town called Merida, a three and a half hour flight. But this first leg would be extremely hazardous because they would be required to fly dangerously close to Cuban airspace. This meant they would have to drop down below the continental air defense radar cover of the United States and Cuba as soon as they left the Keys and the State of Florida. He was confident he could get by the radar. He smiled contentedly. He had been given another chance, and this time he wasn't going to drop the ball. He fell asleep in the cool cockpit.

Night came, and with it feelings of both anticipation and apprehension. As darkness cloaked the grounds once more the men spoke openly of the difficult task they were about to undertake.

"I have to believe he has a plan that will be sensible," Force said, speaking for David.

"I remember him before Jude," Chip said. "He was a good officer. He paid attention to detail and could always be counted on when things got rough."

"But try to remember what happened to him after Jude," Pratt said. "He fell apart."

"But you've all seen the way he acted yesterday. It was the old captain," Jake said. "Besides, if Keaton trusts him that's enough to satisfy me."

"Father," Chip said, "you've been with him recently. Is there anything we should know about him?"

"Even if there was, I couldn't tell you. As you know, I'm bound by professional ethics."

"Then you're telling us he's okay?" Force asked.

Perez had a chagrined look on his face. "I don't actually know him all that well."

"Then what you doin' here?" Doc asked with a smirk.

Perez sensed there was something menacing about this huge man who puffed lethargically on a thick cigar and gazed at him suspiciously from one end of the room. From the first, Doc had been apathetic about nearly everything. Then all of a sudden he seemed to be more than ready to go on the mission. It was a strange change in behavior, and it puzzled Perez to the point of chancing a reply. "I'm here because David's my friend. I'm going with you because David has asked me to do so for the sake of his wife, who is also my friend. And too, do any of you speak Spanish?"

"You're going as an interpreter? Bullshit!" Jake said. "You're going because, like the rest of us, you have to know. You couldn't live with yourself for not knowing."

Perez adjusted his glasses and gave Jake a hard look. *He's right*, he thought. *I do have to know. I must know the truth about all of this.* He looked away and spoke, not looking back at Jake. "Perhaps you're right, but you must believe me when I say I care for Sonia."

"You think she's still alive?" Chip asked quietly.

"I don't know, but I hope so. For David's sake, and for your sakes. It may well be a trip made for nothing," Perez replied.

"That's okay, father," Force said. "It's a trip we all know we have to make, regardless of personal motive."

The Pontiac Firebird turned off the highway and the driver immediately turned off the lights. Slowly and quietly the car navigated the dirt road until its driver found a grassy place to park. The car's occupants snuggled against each other.

"Roll down the windows. It's hot," the girl said.

Her companion did as he was asked. Then the girl sat up on the edge of the bucket seat and removed her blouse. Her boyfriend swallowed hard and began to breathe heavily in anticipation as he watched the beauty unfold in front of him. Deftly, she unhooked her brassier and let it fall, exposing her firm, hard breasts whose nipples were erect and slightly swollen from excitement. The boy bent over and hungrily took first one then the other nipple in his mouth, sucking them hard and noisily. The girl shuddered and squirmed, running her hands through her long blonde tresses, moaning delightfully.

"Take your shorts off," the boy panted between kisses and sucks.

"No. It's my period," she said, faintly disappointed.

"Shit!" he said, rising up.

But she kissed him on the lips and smiled. "Don't worry. Sit back and let me."

The boy grinned and relaxed in the seat. The girl carefully unbuttoned his blue jeans and with his help slid them down his waist. On her own, she did the same to his underpants. He was erect and hard. She reached down and began to massage him. Hungrily, he found her mouth and they kissed, wet hard kisses.

"Let me," the girl said, as she massaged him faster and faster. The boy let his head fall back against the seat rest and shut his eyes. What had he ever done to deserve what was about to happen? After a few minutes she stopped and spoke to him, her lips close to his chest. "Go ahead. Please go ahead."

Then she heard a thump. She let go and looked up. Blood was streaming down the temple of the boy's face. His eyes were shut tight and his mouth was open. Before she could move or scream, a man's hand caught her by the throat and began to squeeze. Terror froze her stiff. She could feel the life being choked out of her. Her eyes watered and her body convulsed from shock.

Doc felt a familiar feeling as he choked the girl. A twisted smile was etched across his face. A snarl escaped his lips. He hadn't counted on such a gratuitous pleasure. Then unexpectedly, he felt a steel circle being placed against the back of his head. He heard a familiar voice.

"This is the barrel of a Sig Sauer P226 9mm automatic you feel. If you don't let go of her instantly, the last thing you will ever feel will be a bullet tearing through your evil brain." It was Force.

Doc let go of the girl and she fell over in the seat coughing and wheezing.

Force turned Doc around so his back was against the car door. "You crazy fuck! I know you now. Maybe I should shoot you here and now. But I won't, not unless you make me. I'll wait for the major."

"Listen, man. They were about to blow this whole thing. What would we've done if they had overheard us talking and passed that information on to that cracker sheriff? I didn't come this far just to have people waiting to kill us at the end of the line. Now, you think."

"This isn't Vietnam, Doc. Now, get back to the others or I'll use this thing."

Unseen by Force, Doc slowly dug into his pants pocket and took out the shoulder patch he had cut off the dead guardsman's uniform back in Mississippi and let it fall behind him into the back seat of the car. He let out a laugh and headed for the mansion.

Force bent down and felt the boy's pulse. He was still alive, even though Doc had given him quite a pelt. He went around and helped the girl out of the other side of the car. At first the girl was terrified, but seeing the look of concern on his face, she calmed. He put her blouse over her and briefly held her in his arms. "It's all right now. He's gone. Your friend'll be okay. Can you drive?"

The girl, still sobbing and shaking, nodded yes.

"Then get out of here as fast as you can." Force gently picked up the boy and placed him in the passenger seat and the girl quickly climbed into the driver's seat and started up the engine. She gave him a questioning look then tore up the dirt road. He made sure she was well away before he returned to the mansion.

"It won't be long before that sheriff comes here and arrests all of us!" Chip exclaimed. "Doc, are you fucking crazy? Try to kill two kids?"

"Long time ago you all'd understood this thing needed to be done." Doc gave the rest of the men a sideways glance as he stared intently down the black road that both David and the sheriff would have to travel. "What ya'll better do is get yourselves armed and ready in case we have to fight our way out of this one-horse town."

Perez gave Doc a studied look. *Would David still want this man to come with the others?* he asked himself.

"Where the hell is the major?" Force screamed, agitated by David's prolonged absence. "Jake, get the damn engines on that helicopter turning."

"Yeah, I believe it's time to do that," Jake said, then headed for the chopper.

"What do we do with him?" Chip asked Force, gesturing toward

Doc who sat in one corner of the room calmly puffing on a cigar with no sign of concern.

"What do you mean what do we do with him? You want me to shoot him like we thought the major should have done to Jude? This isn't Vietnam, Chip," Force replied.

"This is fucking great!" Pratt said caustically. "We haven't even started yet and we're already at each others' throats. And do you know why?" He paused, letting the others turn to him. "Because deep down inside each of us has the nagging thought that what Doc tried to do just might have been justified under the circumstances. Shit! Before this venture is over all of us are going to be faced with having to kill again."

The whining of the big turbines of the helicopter caught their attention.

"Get on board," Force yelled. "You too, Doc."

Doc got up and stood face to face with Force. *It be not now yet, but it be,* he thought.

Suddenly Perez jumped up. "A car's coming!"

Force, Doc, Chip, Pratt, and Perez ran out onto the porch of the mansion. Perez squinted in the darkness to see who was driving the car.

"It's – it's got its lights off," yelled Force.

Then all five men grew quiet as they heard the wailing of several sirens coming from the direction of the highway.

"We got to get out of here now," Perez said anxiously.

The car screeched to a halt in front of the porch. David jumped out and ran up to Force. "What the hell's going on here?"

"Look, major, there's no time to explain."

"Some police cars jumped behind me as I turned off the road and, as you can see, they're right on my tail."

"David," Perez said imploringly, "we've got to leave this place now!"

David turned in the direction of the helicopter as its six huge blades started to slowly rotate. Its navigation lights winked on. The urgency of the moment finally seized him. "Let me get my bags." He rushed around to the back seat of his car and retrieved a duffle bag and a travel bag. Following Force and the others, he dashed for the open door of the helicopter.

"What about your car?" Force yelled to David, hoping to be heard above the whine of the engines.

"I'll have to leave it," David yelled back.

"Leave it?" Force questioned.

David took Force by the arm. "It doesn't matter," he said with a calm look on his face.

The grass around the chopper, shaded green and red from the navigation lights, blew wildly as the huge blades picked up speed. Outside the aircraft the noise was deafening, so loud in fact that the sirens from the three sheriff's patrol cars that came to a halt short of the humming chopper were drowned out. As Jake lifted the huge machine to a hover, he turned off the navigation lights and aimed its nose in the direction of the flat surface of the Sound. Below, David spotted Sheriff Taylor and several of his deputies outlined by their car lights. As Jake headed out over the dark waters, David could make out sparks coming from the direction of the mansion as the sheriff and his men took aim at the helicopter and began firing.

PART THREE

THE PATRIOTS

For we wrestle not against the flesh and blood, but against principalities, against powers, against the rulers of darkness of this world, against spiritual wickedness in high places.

Ephesians 6:12

Chapter 40

Oh Lord God, to whom vengeance belongs –
Oh God, to whom vengeance belongs,
shine forth!
Rise up, oh Judge of the earth;
Render punishment to the proud.
Lord, how long will the wicked,
How long will the wicket triumph?

              Psalm 94

Jake set the helicopter down on the dew covered tarmac of Key West Airport at exactly 0400 hours. As the team climbed out of the aircraft, yawning and stretching, their only welcome was from a lanky, sandy-haired sleepy teenager working the aviation pumps as a summer job. "You fellas are landing early," the kid said as he hooked the hose from the JP fuel pump to the helicopter's fuel intake port.

"Going to Dry Tortugas. Going to get in some early fishing," Jake answered.

"First time I've seen a travel tour in a helicopter," the kid said as he gave the chopper an admirable once over. "Sun'll be up in about an hour," he continued, turning his attention to the gas pump. "You gonna lift off before then?"

"Yeah, we need an early start," Jake replied. But he was bothered by the fact that one of the helicopter's manifold pressure gauges had fluctuated for most of the trip down. Caution told him he had better wait until light and open up an engine for inspection. This was only the first leg of a long flight. However, it had been the most dangerous in terms of being discovered.

After their escape from Sheriff Taylor, Jake had flown the chopper at low altitudes until he came within radar contact of Jacksonville Center. In the darkness of a moonless Georgia night, this had been a hazardous undertaking. His navigation maps warned him of radio towers and mountains and he circumvented cities, but the thought of power lines and unexpected hills had played with his nerves the whole night. Another worry had been the radar at Atlanta Center. He had no flight plan, and a failure to respond to the Center's inquiry might have caused the FAA to put other centers in his flight path on the alert. To avoid this, he had switched off the aircraft's radar transponder so it would appear as an anomalous blip on any radar screen.

Once Jake had entered the Jacksonville Center control zone, he had switched his transponder on to low power and radioed he was a Cessna twin turbo prop from Valdosta en route to Panama City and requested that a flight plan be filed. Jacksonville had responded as desired. When he didn't appear in Panama City, personnel there would file a complaint against the aircraft for failing to file a flight plan. But by that time they should be in Central America.

David had other worries. After the shootout at the mansion, he was worried about what actions the sheriff would take. He figured that after the sheriff sorted things out in his mind, he would probably contact the FBI in Savannah and relay to them what he knew about the helicopter and its occupants. The FBI would connect this information with the report of the missing helicopter and alert all airports in the southern United States. How much time would they have in Key West? It had only been four hours since they had taken off from Richmond Hill. *It doesn't matter*, he reasoned. Once they took off from Key West, they would be away from the FBI.

His car was another potential problem. Now the authorities knew the identity of one of the helicopter's passengers. How long would it take the FBI to connect him to the War College and to Sunny? Would that eventually pose a threat to the overall safety of the mission? After all, thanks to Doc's nocturnal psychopathic activities, they were all wanted in connection with attempted murder.

"Topped off," the kid announced.

After Jake paid for the fuel in cash David had given him, causing a questioning look from the boy, he taxied the chopper to a parking area near the far runway and shut the engines down.

"I've got to check out this manifold pressure problem," Jake said, somewhat agitated. "Look fellas, this is a complicated machine. If I don't take care of it, it won't take care of us." There was no protest from anyone. The others understood the importance of the aircraft to the mission and to their own safety. Jake was in charge of the helicopter, and what he said was law.

"How long?" David asked.

"No more than two hours," Jake replied confidently.

"Let's get some eats over at that restaurant," Doc said, his stomach growling.

The liftoff of the helicopter from Key West meant they would soon be leaving American airspace. But because they would now be traveling dangerously close to Cuba they were, in reality, only trading the threat of arrest by the FBI for the threat of being shot down by a Cuban Mig.

Jake had been unable to detect anything wrong with either engine. However, experience told him his instruments had not lied. Something was there, something he would have to discover soon.

David rode in the right seat of the aircraft. He watched intently as the coastline of the Florida Keys disappeared underneath the aircraft. "Well, that's it," he said through his helmet's mike.

"Now we're going down on the deck and then head west," Jake said without a trace of nervousness in his voice. He slowly lowered the cyclic stick, and the helicopter began its descent. "Key West Center has our flight plan to Dry Tortugas. I'll switch the transponder off and turn the radio to 128.00, the international frequency."

The sun appeared in the window on Jake's side of the aircraft. It had a bright orange glow to it that reflected a yellow shimmering light off the placid early morning waters of the Gulf of Mexico. It was a cloudless, windless day, which meant Jake would not have to fight any tail or head winds. "Couldn't ask for better weather," Jake remarked as he eyed his instrument panel. David nodded apprehensively. Both men knew they would be clearly visible to any aircraft in the area, and Cuban airspace was twenty minutes away.

The others had made themselves comfortable in the rear cabin. Normally, military aircraft are loud and purposefully uncomfortable. But this Jolly Green Giant, formerly of the Southeast Asia conflict, had been refurbished into a comfortable, roomy, and elegant passenger craft so well insulated against the noise of the turbo fan engines that normal conversation could be easily heard. It also had cabin air and heat.

Perez lit his pipe while gazing absently out the cabin window at the vibrant sea below. The Gulf waters skipped briskly past the helicopter, but he was not interested in the sea. Nor was he interested in the conversation of the men around him. And he was only vaguely aware of the impending danger they faced as the helicopter approached the west coast of Cuba. He was much too occupied with the dilemma in which he had been caught: *why was he here?*

Knowledge takes things from a man, he thought morosely. Yes. It takes away the naivety of mysticism. Belief is pure mysticism. Knowledge is real; it can be touched. But then he grew dark, for this was the real gravamen, the conflict he struggled with. Logically, he should be on his way back to Georgetown. But he had stayed. Why? He did have to know why. Everything about what had taken place was mystical. There was nothing logical or intelligent about any of it. David had been transformed almost overnight from being petulant and indecisive to being strong and resolute, and that transformation was illogical. And David had invoked the mystical as the reason for his transformation. He had alluded to the other men that he had seen Keaton. And what if he *had* seen Keaton? So what? Keaton was just an old man, and probably a government operative. What was mystical about that? And David's loyalties were not fixated on the United States. After what had happened to Sunny, probably they were just the opposite. So why invoke the mystical? Why could David not simply admit he was taking advantage of the situation in order to try to rescue Sunny? Why must David make it something it was not? Again, the invocation of the mystical. Yes, Perez knew the ultimate truth for, unlike the others, he had been in the heart of the animal.

Now he studied the other men in the cabin in an attempt to determine their motivations. This was not a group of crazed freaks,

Jake being the exception. But Perez could understand why Jake was here. Jake had given up on life. No, it wouldn't take more than an hour of therapy to figure out that David had provided Jake with an exciting way to commit suicide.

Force was a police officer. His experience with the police mind told him Force quite naturally sought to be where the action was. But Force appeared to be levelheaded. What was it about the covenant, about Keaton, that would cause him to break the law, violate the sacred code of honor to which all law enforcement officers are sworn, and become an accessory to a crime? Again, the mystical taking precedence over common sense.

Then there was Pratt. Of all of them, Pratt should have been the one most likely to understand the dangers of this foolhardy adventure and to convince the others to face reality. He was an educated man, a Doctor of Philosophy. From the very first, Pratt had tried to reason with the others, to show them that they were acting on their emotions. Even so, Pratt appeared to have given in. Had the others frightened him with their talk of the CIA? Maybe. Maybe not. Most Jews, Perez thought, were very logical when it came to dealing with everyday affairs. Perhaps Pratt had reasoned he had fallen into a trap and that the only way out of it was to go along with the charade for as long as necessary until an opportunity to escape presented itself. Yes, he reasoned, Pratt was a man with whom he could deal with, a man not unlike himself.

Chip was easy. Obviously, it has been simple for Keaton to bring back into the fold. For years, Chip had been looking for a way to achieve atonement for his perceived sins, and for him this was also a way to regress back to a happier time in his life, a time devoid of all worldly responsibility and pressure, like it had been in Vietnam. Perhaps the farming business was not as simple a life as it was made out to be.

He then turned to Doc. Out of the whole lot of them, Doc's presence was the most difficult for him to understand. Doc was an enigma that was sinister and threatening. He stiffened as Doc turned toward him and gave him a cold eyed stare and turned away.

Yes, I came along because I must know why. I must understand all of this. There has to be a logical explanation for everything that has taken place. This is not mystical. This is not cosmic.

Chapter 41

Merida, Mexico

Ten thousand feet over the brown terra firma of the Yucatan Peninsula of Mexico, the helicopter's left engine began blowing puffs of white smoke out the side exhaust port. Jake's suspicions had been confirmed. Chip had been the first to notice the smoke. After he had informed Jake, he returned to his seat and he and the others had eyed the engine's housing and exhaust port with studied, if somewhat morbid, curiosity.

"Merida's ten miles ahead. We'll need to refuel and work on the engine," Jake said perfunctorily to David.

"Any idea about what the problem might be?" David asked, a look of deep concern on his face.

Jake shook his head, even though he was silently going over a list of possibilities.

"Any idea how long we can expect to be in Merida?" David asked.

"We'd better get some hotel rooms," Jake said. "Don't worry major. We've still got a date in Argentina."

David slapped Jake on the shoulder, unstrapped himself, and made his way back to the others.

"Jake says we're going to have to stay in Merida for a few days to make repairs. We'll get some rooms."

The others nodded their heads in agreement.

"Now, it's very important that we stick together," David continued. Our story is that we are on a tour of the Yucatan. We flew in from the Keys. Don't worry about money. I drew out our life savings," David said as he lifted his shirt to expose a black leather wraparound money belt.

"Well, now," Doc said, his eyes lighting up.

Force stood up, his massive size dwarfing the aisle and blocking any passage. "Major, don't you think it's time you took us into your confidence and told us what your plan is?" Chip and Pratt stood beside Force.

"When we land," David responded, not looking Force in the eyes.

Merida, a dusty town of thirty-five thousand, was located twelve miles inland from the Gulf and was the capitol of the Yucatan province. Its main trade was catering to the tourists who flocked to the Yucatan coastline, some of the most virgin and beautiful in the world. There was one dusty main street that ran the length of the town on which were located several hotels and restaurants. Most of the town's buildings were old, dating back to the turn of the century, and Spanish colonial in design with high, rust-colored shale roofs, brown plaster walls, and high windows with bright green shutters. Meridians were polite and hospitable, having long ago come to appreciate the value of foreign currency.

The Merida airport had been constructed with the tourist in mind. It had a single runway two thousand feet long with an instrument landing system that could accommodate most twin engine aircraft. There were a couple of hangars, ample parking space, and a small single terminal building with a control tower affixed to its roof.

As Ferry 34 made its approach to Merida airport, David queried Jake. "We're not in any hurry. The important thing is to make sure the chopper's airworthy. Is it airworthy?"

Jake grinned and nodded.

David looked out the windshield at the brown, desert-like terrain below. *The thirty-first of May*, he thought. *We have to wait until May thirty-first before we can strike. Will we be too late? Will she still be alive? Oh, Sunny. Hold on just a little longer.*

Normally, this part of the Yucatan received a fair amount of rainfall, but this had been a dry spring so far. Merida was situated five miles south of the airport and looked like a cluster of red-roofed buildings that had huddled together in order to protect themselves from the effects of the wind and rain of this savage land. Ferry 34 flared to a landing at the east end of the runway and, after receiving parking instructions from a controller whose English was a mixture of Spanish and East Harlem, taxied to the far end of the terminal next to an empty hangar. A blazing sun welcomed the men as they filtered out of the helicopter, duffle bags in hand.

"Motha', this heat reminds me of Nam," Doc said.

"Let's get to the hotel. I need some sleep," Pratt said as he wiped the beads of sweat from his forehead.

"Let's get to a hotel so the major can let us in on his big secret," Force said in a chiding tone.

"He's right, major," Chip said. "It'll help if we know what our moves will be."

David turned to them. "It's all right. I know you must have fears. But let's wait until we get situated and I'll explain everything," he said to them, a half-lie on his lips.

After the helicopter had been hangared and its precious cargo of weapons and ammo secured, Perez translated the desire for a hotel to an obese taxi driver who had promptly offered his 1962 Cadillac's service to the group.

"Cockroach country," Pratt declared, squeezing in between David and Doc.

The drive to the Hotel Salvacion over a fairly even two lane highway was filled with the constant gibberish of the driver who was obviously pleased he would be collecting seven fares instead of one. "*Theese town, Merida, ees once a place Spaneesh man leeve. You see, many old hees . . .*"

He turned to Perez. "*How you say, hees . . . ?*"

"Historico," Perez said, coming to the driver's rescue.

"*Gracias, se. Historico.* Heestorical. Se. You see many heestorical Spaneesh here, eh Merida," the driver continued happily. No one seemed to listen as the driver, once warmed up, began a tiresome litany about the main attractions of Merida: the town's three hundred year old church located on the square; the bullpens where fighting bulls were raised; and the town's most recent and most famous restaurant, the Plancha, which he claimed Hollywood stars frequented seeking an escape from their adoring fans in North America. What the men were interested in most was where they could shower, sleep, and gather their thoughts. "The Hotel Salvacion. You like, padre?" the driver announced as he jerked up to the hotel's entrance. Perez gave him a forgiving smile. The driver seemed more than satisfied with David's handsome tip and drove back to the airport in a puff of oil smoke.

Force, Pratt, and Chip shared one room. Jake threw his bags in with David and Perez. Doc refused to stay with anyone else and took a separate room. All three rooms were adjoining. After sleeping for several hours and showering, the men met David in his room.

Jake started off by giving a description of the air route with special emphasis on the refueling stops. He was careful to explain that the helicopter needed a complete maintenance overhaul every one hundred flight hours. They had flown seven flight hours since Richmond Hill. The trip to the southern tip of Argentina would take twenty-six flight hours if they flew in a straight line. That left more than enough engine hours to get them back.

"Where is back?" Pratt asked David. "We can't go back to Richmond Hill."

"I can fly you wherever you want. I can take you near Nashville. I can fly you, Bill, to New Orleans. You, Doc . . ."

"It would be best if you flew us to one city," Chip interjected. "Let's say New Orleans. From there we can take commercial flights to wherever we need to go."

"How about the money? I don't have enough on me to buy a ticket," Pratt said.

"Don't worry about the money," David said.

"We can't go to New Orleans," Force said flatly. "All of you are forgetting about our cars."

Doc frowned. *They won't need to be worrying about the trip back*, he thought, amused at their bantering. *Keaton will have an escape route planned for me. Together, we'll make our way back home*. And as for the car he had left back in Georgia, it had been stolen.

"Well, I'll take my chances in New York," Jake said without a trace of apprehension in his voice. David knew Jake had made up his mind to go back and face whatever justice he deserved.

"What about you and the gentile father there?" Pratt said. "Your car's already the property of the good Sheriff Taylor. You can't go back without being arrested."

"Father Perez can take a flight home from Savannah. As for me, I'm prepared to face whatever awaits me in Washington. I'm committed to saving my wife, not myself."

"Oh, cut this shit out," yelled Force. "What are we doing? We should be thinking about what's ahead, not what's going to happen to us once we complete our attack. Now let's have it, major. What's your plan?"

"You're right, Bill. We have to think positively about what we're about to do. We all trust Jake to get us there and to get us back to somewhere safe. Right now, that somewhere is a place called Punta Arenas, Chile. It will be our last refueling stop before we land near an island called Los Estados for the assault. We'll fly back to Punta Arenas and then continue this discussion."

Jake lit a cigarette and offered one to Chip. Doc fired up one his ugly cigars as everyone sat back and listened intently with critical eyes to David as he began.

It was the old David who spoke, the man who had planned the Tri Ton raid, the man who had covered the team's escape on Nui Ta Bec, the man who, before Jude, had been a leader. "Los Estados," he said with a voice that exuded confidence and authority, "is not heavily guarded by the Group."

"This Group, what kind of troops are they?" Force asked.

"I asked my sources that question. What they told me is that the men who make up the Group are specially selected from the three branches of the Argentinean armed forces. They all hold the rank of sergeant or above. The officers are all lieutenants except for the commander, and he's a captain. I'll talk more about him in a minute."

"How well-informed are your informants?" Chip asked.

"Good."

"The opposition?" Force asked again.

"Well trained in police techniques but not much else. They're not a Special Forces type unit. But still, I don't think we should take them lightly. They're mainly . . ."

"Gestapo. They learned well from the Germans," Pratt said matter-of-factly.

"You're right. They go after innocent people, young women and men, even teenagers and children."

"Interesting," Force said, a fire in his eyes.

David smiled. "The leader is the chief inquisitor of Argentina. He's been in the business for some time. He has many deaths to his credit. I will be happy to meet him face to face."

Doc let out a little laugh.

David paid Doc no attention and continued on. "The Los Estados prison is located on a barren island one hundred fifty miles east of Cape Horn and three hundred fifty miles west of the Falkland Islands, which should keep us well out of range of the war. The Argentines and the British have declared only a two hundred mile radius around the Falklands a war zone. Our staging area will be a deserted island named Nueva. Nueva is a hundred and twenty-six miles east of our target. Jake, I estimate it'll take less than thirty minutes to get there and three and a half hours to make it to Punta Arenas."

Jake nodded. "That means after we take off from Punta Arenas we will have just enough fuel to land at Nueva Island, attack the prison, and make it back to Punta Arenas," he said.

"That means," David said, giving Jake a thoughtful look, "we can't run the engines while we wait at Nueva and we can't be on the ground more than fifteen minutes at Los Estados."

There was a disturbing silence as each man contemplated the meaning of David's words.

Then Force spoke up. "Major, why are we landing at Nueva Island? It'll be the dead of Antarctic winter. And if memory serves me from my tour in Alaska, we'll have to keep the helicopter engines warm in order for them to restart because if they don't restart, we'll all freeze to death in the matter of a few hours. It would seem more practical to simply go on and attack at Los Estados and get it over with."

David stood up and rubbed his neck. "First of all, remember we have immersion heaters, so we won't freeze to death. Now, Los Estados must be attacked during daylight. The winds are too treacherous for us to attempt a night landing, and the navigation in and around the accompanying islands would be too difficult in the dark." Once again, in a calm voice, he said only, "We must wait at Nueva Island until the weather will permit a landing."

Pratt blew a puff of smoke out of his mouth. "Shit," he said in disgust, "I need a drink. Anyone want to go to that greasy bar downstairs?"

"Not yet," Force said. "Major, what about the assault itself?"

David opened a briefcase that had been lying on the bed and from it he withdrew a large piece of manila paper. On it was a detailed drawing of Los Estados. He spread it over the bed. "Okay, gather round."

The men complied.

"Here's the prison compound. Three buildings about one hundred yards apart. No guard towers. No fences. This building houses the guards only. These two house the prisoners." He pointed to each building with a pen.

"Which one has your wife?" Chip asked, not looking up from the paper.

"My sources have told me she's in this one here," David said. "It's called Internment Two. The buildings are not constructed like prisons. In reality, they're abandoned mansions that once belonged to rich farmers. There are no special locks or bolts on any of the cell doors, but I don't know which room she's in. So we'll have to find the room she's in."

"Major, won't that take too much time? Opening every cell and at the same time having to carry on a firefight with the Group?" Force asked with a concerned expression.

"There are very few guards stationed at Los Estados because the chance of escape is almost non-existent. The island is isolated and inhabited by wolves. At any one time the prison has a token force of ten or fifteen men."

"Wolves!" Doc said wide eyed.

"Yes. The Group put them there."

"Christ," Pratt said under his breath.

"If we strike quickly, we'll have the element of surprise going for us. It's right in the middle of winter, so there won't be any guards stationed outside the villas. We'll land so that the two villas that house the prisoners will block the view from the barracks building. We can't hit both buildings at once, but a well placed sharpshooter should stop intruders coming from the barracks building. If he's a good shot, we can pull this off. And to answer your question, Bill, we get the key to Sunny's room from the guards. They'll give it to us or," David made a cutting motion at his throat.

Pratt angrily threw a pillow from the room's couch down on the floor. "Major, just who do you think we are, the Memphis SWAT team? None of us has fought in a firefight since Vietnam. I mean, look at us. We're all approaching middle age, and the priest is of no use at all."

"Pratt, I wish you'd just shut up. All of us are in good enough shape to fight for fifteen minutes," Jake hissed.

Pratt's face turned red. "I'm really tired of you always telling me to shut up. Why don't you just get yourself a drink and keep your mouth shut for once."

"Look, both of you stop arguing," Force said.

"I'll pull my own weight here," Perez said to Pratt.

Pratt just looked at Perez and laughed. "What in the hell do you know about combat?"

"He was a green beret sky-pilot," David interjected, causing the others to give Perez a nod of acceptance, but Pratt still gave Perez a questioning look.

"I'm impressed by your plan, major, but I need a drink. Then I'm going to eat. Then I'm going to bed," Pratt said. With that, he left the room.

"I think I'll join the boy," Doc said, putting out his cigar.

"Major, the plan's good," Chip said. "Okay, let's all go get something to eat."

David wrapped up his map then turned to Jake, giving him a look. Jake nodded.

"How do you feel about it now that you know what's going on?" David asked Perez.

"I'll tell you that when I know what's going on."

David let the others leave. Looking at his face in the bathroom mirror, he rubbed two days' stubble on his chin and locked in on his eyes. He hadn't told them everything about Los Estados. He hadn't talked about the Los Estados air base or the miracle he hoped for that would keep its jets from blowing them out of the sky. He put his hands over his face. *Was he betraying them again?*

Chapter 42

And it came to pass, when Joshua was by Jericho, that he lifted his eyes and looked, and behold, a Man stood opposite him and His sword drawn in His hand. And Joshua went to Him and said to Him, "Are you for us or for our adversaries?"

So He said, "No, but as Commander of the Army of the Lord I have now come." And Joshua fell on his face to the earth and worshiped, and said to Him, "What does the Lord say to his servant?"

Then the Commander of the Lord's army said to Joshua, "Take your sandal off your foot, for the place where you stand is holy." And Joshua did so.

Joshua 5:13-15

The Elefante Rosado bar was located in the dimly-lit cellar below the hotel's main lobby. Assembled around its candlelit tables was an assortment of townspeople – those who had money – travelers of differing design and destination, pimps and whores, and those who were just looking for the occasional brawl. The identity of the bar's patrons was protected by a constant chest-level fog of cigar and cigarette smoke that the bar's lone air conditioner could not suck away. Ever present was the foul stench of sweat, stale food, and spilt drink. Placed arrestingly on the wall behind the bar was a pink neon light shaped like a bull elephant drinking from a palm tree-laced watering hole. Its fluorescent effluence served as a homing beacon for patrons whose sense of direction had been dulled by the over-ingestion of the house's fermented cactus plant.

A large crowd had gathered by the time David sank below the tobacco fog and found the rest of the men. A clinking Latin beat blared from a jukebox at one end of the room. Perez said the song was about chickens. A large breasted waitress took their orders, Perez translating. He had removed his turned around collar in deference to Mexican law that forbade clergy from wearing their church garments in public, a futile attempt to suppress the power of the church over domestic life.

"*Hey, caballeros* . . ." tink, tink, tink. Another song clinked out of the juke.

"Where's Chip?" David asked as he peered into the crowd.

"He went with Jake to the helicopter," Force replied.

David understood and nodded.

"Well father, you tastin' the fruit of the vine?" Doc asked as he rolled a large cigar around his lips.

Perez ignored the remark and turned to David. "How long will we be here?"

"It'll depend on what Jake finds inside the engine."

"What difference will that make? You said yourself we'd have to take our time getting there," Perez said after sipping from his tequila. "If you don't mind, I'd rather spend most of that time in a temperate climate."

"He's right," Force said. "I don't see the rush. It'll take two days at the most to get to Los Estados."

"No," David said. "We don't need to take any chances. I want to get as close as possible to Los Estados before we have to make the assault because none of us knows what lies ahead." *May thirty-first*, he checked off in his head.

"I want another drink. Martin, how about you?" Pratt asked flippantly.

"I think I want me one of those women," Doc said hungrily as he eyed two slinky Indian women who, with an air of capitalistic familiarity, had just wandered into the bar.

"There's no place for that," Force stated.

"I got my own room, boy. The man said we'd be here two or three days," Doc shot back, giving Force a cold eye.

"Major?" Force asked, turning to David for a decision.

David gave Doc a hard stare. "Doc's a grown man."

Doc smiled in triumph.

"But Doc," David said, his voice stern and reprimanding, "no slip-ups. We're in too far to turn back. No compromise. You understand?"

Doc drew up his face as the seriousness in the tone of David's voice struck him hard. As he stared into David's eyes he had a sense of traveling back in time. He had seen that look on David's face before; it was the same look he once had when interrogating VC prisoners. It was a look of finality. David turned away from him, and Doc's expression turned into a snarl. A hiss, like that of a snake, came out of his clenched teeth. With a sudden jerk, he grabbed his drink and got up and left the table, disappearing into the crowd by the bar.

"He's going to be trouble," Pratt remarked flatly.

"Leave him to me," Force said.

About half an hour after they had eaten their evening meal, the stranger approached them. "Americans!" the man exclaimed happily, feigning surprise in a voice with a mid-western accent. He stood before them smiling, his hands on his hips. He was a medium sized man, stout, muscular, with short brown hair parted to one side. He had a bright, boyish face and flashing blue eyes. He was wearing a blue oxford cloth shirt with its sleeves rolled up to the elbow and khaki pants. And he seemed to have materialized out of nowhere.

David gave him a blank stare and nodded.

It didn't seem to bother the man that no one had asked him to sit down. He pulled himself up a chair. "I didn't think Merida was 'in' this year," he said loudly in an affable way. "You guys must be hard up for a vacation. Or is it business? You guys in the tourist business?"

"You were right the first time. We're on tour," David replied in a dismissive tone.

Ignoring his lack of welcome, the man continued. "My name's Steelhammer," he said exhibiting a split set of front teeth as he gave them a wide, disarming smile and extended his hand to David. "You are . . ."

"James Wilson," David answered, accepting the hand. Mr. Steelhammer had an iron grip, and despite his jocular manner, David sensed there was something premeditated about his sudden appearance. He put himself on alert. "These are my friends," he said guardedly, waving his hand over the table. Each of the men shook hands with Steelhammer and gave a phony name.

"It's really good to see other Americans here in Mexico. What about this bar? Ever see a bar like this back in the States? I'm sorry; I guess I get carried away sometimes."

"What brings you to Mexico?" Pratt asked as he held his glass to his lips and eyed the stranger suspiciously through his drink.

"The oil business. I work for Exxon. Helping the locals determine whether the area around here is suitable for drilling, you know. The Mexicans are putting a lot of apples in the oil barrel these days. Ha, ha, ha."

"Well maybe their economy needs it," Force said in a disconcerted way.

"Yeah, that's a fact. Pemex, the government run oil concern, is the hot item in Mexico today. The government's putting its hopes for economic recovery on its success. My job's to see that we Yankees share in that success. Ha, ha, ha."

"Well, we wish you luck," David told him, hoping to end the conversation.

"Say, have you fellas eaten yet?" Steelhammer asked, his eyes wide with anticipation.

"Yes," Force replied flatly.

"Oh." Steelhammer looked disappointed. "I'll just order something for myself then." As the others gave him distressed looks, Steelhammer ordered a fajita dinner from a waitress who seemed to know him. "I come here every once in a while. Just to check on what's going on in the region," he said with a grin.

David was intrigued by Steelhammer's use of the word *region*. Businessmen used words like locale, or area, or even territory. Military men used the word region.

Steelhammer ate in a meticulous way, making sure his plate was left neat and orderly and without evidence of food. After he had finished, he seemed to take pleasure in washing down the spicy entree with several beers. Then he patted himself on his firm stomach and lit a thin, black cigar. It was apparent he was in no hurry to leave. Sitting back in his chair, he turned to David. "Saw you land the other day. Nice ship."

David stiffened. The others became still. "As I said, we're on tour," he answered evenly.

"Where's the pilot?" Steelhammer asked with a half smile.

"With the helicopter. Seems there's some problem with the one of the engines."

"Oh, well, I hope it's nothing serious. I'd hate to see your tour ruined."

David didn't reply.

"Where's your tour going?" Steelhammer pressed on, a twinkle in his eye.

"Mexico," Force said flatly.

David gave Force an impatient look. "Yes, we're touring Mexico."

"Not Central America?" Steelhammer asked.

"Mexico," David shot back.

Steelhammer turned to Perez. "What's your line of work?"

Perez cleared his throat. "I'm a clinical psychologist."

"Where?"

"Washington, D.C."

Steelhammer smiled and flicked the ashes off his cigar. "Nice place, D.C.," he said, looking down at the cigar. "Nice place."

"Look, Mr. Steelhammer, we're going to have to excuse ourselves. It's been a long flight and we need to turn in," David said, getting up. "But it was a pleasure to meet you and I wish you every success in your business venture here."

Steelhammer's smile suddenly vanished, and in its place David saw a burning stare. Then he spoke in a voice lacking its previous facetiousness. "Sit down, major. Let's talk."

David had been too startled by Steelhammer's sudden divulgement of knowledge to protest. The others were equally shocked. But his manner was not confrontational, and in a public place, David had reasoned, the best course of action was to do as he wished. They all sat back down. Gone were the jovial mannerisms which Steelhammer had previously exhibited. The smile was still there, but David sensed it was only camouflage for a deeper, more serious intent. As David listened to Steelhammer, he studied his face. Its youthfulness was betrayed by graying temples and a furrowed brow. The blue eyes seemed to stare right through him at something distant, beyond the immediate, on into the future, like a chess player plotting his next move. He was physically in the present but seemed to always be thinking one step ahead. David could also sense the presence of an enormous energy pent up inside Steelhammer.

"I know about you. I know about the helicopter." He waited for a moment, giving what he had just said time to sink in. He put out his cigar. "But let's say, for the sake of conversation, I don't give a damn about what I know. How would that strike you?"

David bent low over the table, his elbows resting on its top. He looked directly into Steelhammer's eyes. "Who the hell are you?"

"Who I am isn't important. What's your answer to my question?"

"Don't play games with this guy, major," Force whispered in David's ear.

"David?" Perez said anxiously under his breath.

"It would strike me as unusual," David answered quietly.

"Ha, ha, ha. That's great!" Steelhammer laughed, slapping his knee.

David, his lips tightly drawn, sat back in his chair. The others were silent, watching David for any cues.

Steelhammer lit his cigar again and, after blowing a few puffs, began. "Look, I don't care what you're up to. Maybe I even agree with your aim and your objective. Right now, I need something you have. And in order to get it, I'll trade my silence."

"What do you know about us, Mr. Steelhammer, if that is your name?" Perez asked testily.

"Easy, easy. I'm not your enemy. If I was, you'd all be in the Merida Federal Jail, which makes this dive look like a resort. As for your question, a few days ago a helicopter, FAA number N-346785, disappeared off the coast of New York. Everyone assumes it crashed at sea. Then a report comes in to the FBI of attempted murder in a town in Georgia named Richmond Hill. And guess how the suspects escaped? In a helicopter."

"We had nothing to do with that," Force blurted out.

"Yeah, a funny thing about that FBI report. One of the suspects, it seems, saved the intended victims' lives. There's something unusual about that, wouldn't you say? But it's not the attempted murders or the stealing of a helicopter that has the FBI hot for these guys. No, it seems several National Guardsmen were murdered down in Mississippi and their weapons stolen. And guess what? The sheriff in Richmond Hill finds one of those guardsmen's shoulder patches in the back seat of the Georgia victims' car. What a coincidence."

"We know nothing about the murders of any National Guardsmen," Force said breathlessly.

David turned to Force. Their eyes met. *Doc?*

Steelhammer noted the startled looks on their faces with satisfaction. *They really didn't know*, he thought. "None of this to makes any sense to the boys at the FBI. The current theory is that a domestic terrorist group, possibly a group called the Covenant Sword and Arm of the Lord out of Arkansas, is responsible. They're checking that theory out."

"What do you think?" David asked warily.

"Well, sometimes different government agencies fail to share information, sort of like inter-service rivalry in the military. Like, the car found at the scene of the crime, seems it belongs to one Major David Elliot, of late an instructor at the War College in D.C." Steelhammer let the words "D.C" come out slowly, turning to Perez with a wry smile.

"Don't worry major. They haven't put three and two together yet. They think you sold yourself to this terrorist group because you went a little crazy."

David dropped his head. *They think I'm crazy. How ironic.*

"Understand one of the guys there is a big cop from New Orleans. That you, buddy?" Steelhammer asked Force.

Force's face contorted with anger.

"Whew!" Steelhammer said cynically, seeing Force's face. "Just keep it in, big guy. Like I said, I'm not your enemy. Anyway, . . ."

"You haven't answered my question," David said firmly.

Steelhammer shot David a hard look. "In this case, major, I know your wife is being held hostage in Argentina and I think you're going to go down there and get yourself killed trying to get her out."

David swallowed hard, a hundred different thoughts racing through his head. Who was this man, and how did he know so much? Now that so much was known about them, would their mission be jeopardized? But most intriguing, why was this man letting them off the hook?

As if understanding the look on David's face, Steelhammer said, "The FBI won't connect your wife's disappearance to any foolhardy attempt to rescue her. Not yet, anyway. They don't think like that."

"Then how did you come to that conclusion?" Pratt asked, sweat pouring down his face.

"Because I *do* think like that. Anyway, it wasn't hard to look up your record, major. Former Special Forces A-team leader. Lost the team in Chau Doc province, late 1960s. You guys were easy to trace too. The police officer, you," Steelhammer said looking at Force. "Your pilot, easy to trace too. I suspect you have a guy with you from Virginia, a farmer. And you," Steelhammer turned his eyes to Pratt, "are a professor at Vanderbilt. By the way, nice place, Vanderbilt. I once attended an Impact Symposium held there. Hmm, but the guy I want to meet is the jerk from San Francisco. He's a known drug pusher and pimp. As I can well see, he's not here."

David shot a glance at Force. *Yes, Doc. He must have left that patch in the car after Force confronted him. But why? And what reason would Doc have to kill those guardsmen? He could have easily bought the weapons they needed. Murder? Oh, God, Keaton, why did you bring Doc back?*

"Look, I'm not here to help the FBI solve a crime. No, that's not within my purview," Steelhammer said with a serious look. "So accept if you will that, for the moment, I believe you guys, at least all of you here at the table, had nothing to do with the murder of those guardsmen. After all, why would you have saved those teenagers' lives if you were culpable? Anyway, you're all big boys. Sooner or later you'll realize what has to be done. And it will be done, won't it?"

"If evidence warrants it," David said flatly. Steelhammer smiled.

"Who do you work for? The CIA? Remember, all of us once worked for the Agency; we know its methods. So just level with us. Why are you going to just sit on this information? Who are you?" Pratt shouted, banging his fists on the table.

"Keep it down, Pratt" Force said.

"Keep it down. Shit. You think this crowd can hear anything? Hell, they wouldn't understand us if they did. In fact, we could kill this jarhead-looking motherfucker right now and no one would ever know it. We could kill him and get the fuck out of here and go back home. No one would ever know," Pratt said, glaring maniacally at Steelhammer.

"Well, major, I can see not everyone came along on this little vacation willingly," Steelhammer said through a half smile.

"He does have a point, though." Force said. "What's to keep us from killing you and getting the hell out of here?"

"Good question, officer. I'll answer it like this. Oh, by the way, the FBI thinks you're a member of the Klan. The CSA and the Klan are like-minded. No. I don't work for the CIA. They work for us. Right now we are involved in a little operation, the success of which is more important to the country than the FBI's need to clear up a crime. As I said, you have something I need. Again, I'll make my offer. How about it?"

"What is it you need?" David asked.

"Your helicopter."

"For how long?"

"I'll need a ride to a place in Honduras. There I'll need you to pick up some people and ferry them to an unspecified location, wait for them for a while, and then ferry them to another unspecified location. You won't be involved in any fighting. So how about it? Ha, ha, ha. What if I throw in the gas money?"

David knew that one of the refueling stops was a town in Honduras called Tegucigalpa. What Steelhammer was asking for was not that far off their intended route.

David turned to the others. "I wish Chip and Jake were here."

"What choice do we have?" Force asked dejectedly.

Perez just shook his head.

"Fuck," was all Pratt said.

"You don't leave us much choice," David said reluctantly to Steelhammer.

Steelhammer sat back in his seat and gave them a wide smile. "Central America's a nice place. You'll like it."

Chapter 43

San Carlos Bay
The Falkland Islands

Naval Commander Pablo Tomba of the Third Naval Fighter and Attack Escuadrilla banked his A4Q Skyhawk jet hard to the left and began his approach to San Carlos Bay at a speed of five hundred fifty miles per hour. Behind him, his two wingmen followed suit. The last light of the day was fading beyond the horizon, but the Bay attack area was dramatically marked by the fires of the burning British frigate *Antrim* that had earlier been hit by several bombs from the brave pilots of the Second Escuadrilla. Another frigate, *Argonaut*, was listing helplessly in the placid waters of the Bay's mouth. But neither of these ships was his target.

The three thousand two hundred fifty ton Type 21 Frigate, *Ardent*, was idling in the southernmost portion of the Bay. Earlier she had been placing exacting gunfire on Argentine shore positions. Now she was about to experience Argentine naval air power at its best. Commander Tomba came in at three hundred feet. Just as the Ardent's thin, knife shaped hull filled his bombsight, he pulled back hard on the joystick. The little American-made jet lurched upward, slamming him against his seat. At the height of seven hundred feet he released his two bombs, each a one thousand pounder, then flipped the jet on its side into a ninety degree bank and headed out over the island for the escape route back to Buenos Aires.

Two seconds into his bank, his jet was buffeted by first one air shock wave then another. Instinctively, he knew his bombs had hit home. "Ahhyee!" he screamed. He would have yelled even louder if he had known that seventy-two of his fellow pilots had gotten through British fighter cover on this day and bombed their targets with devastating effectiveness. However, not all of them had made it back to the mainland.

His smile changed to an expression of horror as he caught a glimpse of a bright orange flash just out of the corner of his eye. His right wingman's plane had just exploded in a ball of fire. A missile, he knew. Instantly, he began an evasive maneuver, twisting and turning, then diving and climbing. His other wingman had darted off to the east. He searched the sky for the sight of him, but to no avail. He would never be heard from again.

Then through his rearview mirror he saw the stubby wing outline of a British Sea Harrier. He banked hard to the right then pushed the jet toward the earth in a split S maneuver, but the pilot of the Sea Harrier clung to him tenaciously. He felt a strong jolt at the rear of his aircraft and the Skyhawk began to yaw from side to side and the joystick felt heavy and sluggish. He checked his instruments; none of them were reading. He knew it was time to get out. He held his arms at his sides and pulled the seat ejection rod. The canopy burst away and his ejection seat shot him up into the freezing air. For what seemed like an eternity, he hung in the air. Then the seat fell away and his parachute opened. Hanging there high over the island, he watched his jet plummet to the ground and explode in a yellow flash. The Harrier pilot swooshed past him as if checking to see if he was all right, and then headed off in the direction of the Bay where now, consolingly to his delight, he could see the evidence of the success of his work as the *Ardent* exploded with a brilliant flash of light that lit up the dark night.

Chapter 44

Las Vegas, Honduras via Merida, Mexico

Jake had found the engine problem, and to his delight, it was minor – a clogged exhaust filter on the right turbine. After a thorough cleaning, he declared the chopper ready to fly. But he hadn't been prepared for David's instructions as to where. None of the men had been prepared for the turn of events.

"If this man Steelhammer knows all about us, you better believe it's possible the Argentineans know about us too," Pratt said, driving home his point to the others gathered in David's room. "So don't be surprised to find them waiting for us when we land at Los Estados."

"I don't agree," Force said. "I don't pretend to know who this Steelhammer is, but if he had intended to do us any harm he could have already turned us in to the Mexicans. No, I believe as long as we play ball he'll keep his mouth shut."

"How do we know we can trust him?" Chip asked.

"I trust him," Force said patiently and without expression. "What puzzles me is Steelhammer himself," he added. "Who does he work for? He said he isn't CIA. Certainly not the FBI. Who?"

Chip turned to David. "Major, I'm not sure about this now. I have doubts that trouble me. We're exposed, out in the open. Maybe Pratt's right. Tell us what to do."

David stood up. "I don't have any idea who Steelhammer works for. But I believe him when he says he'll keep our plans and our whereabouts a secret. He could have turned us in if he had wanted to, but he didn't. His reasons may be personal, they may be professional. He may be working for the U.S., or he may be private. But I don't believe it matters one way or the other. He needs us for some yet to be explained purpose, and I believe if we help him he'll let us go our own way. Besides, what other choice do we have?"

"We can turn away and go home before it's too late," Pratt said firmly.

"No we can't. Doc's seen to that," Force said, turning to Doc who was sitting against the wall smoking a cigar. "I think Doc has some explaining to do."

David turned to Doc. "Did you kill those guardsmen in Mississippi? The weapons you brought are government issue."

Doc stood up. Standing against the wall he seemed even larger and more menacing. He took the cigar out of his mouth and stared at each of the men, finally letting his eyes rest on David. "I don't owe you jackasses an answer to nothin'. I'm here, aren't I? That's what you wanted. Keaton called me just like he did all of you. You don't question his judgment, now do you? So don't ask me no more questions. Understand? Now if you want me to drop out of this little affair, that be okay. I'll go. But unless that be it, I don't want to hear any more of this shit."

David walked over and stood facing Doc. Their eyes met and held. "Listen," he said, "I don't know what you've become. All I know is that I won't let you destroy this mission. If you're a criminal, so be it, but be it back there, back in America. If you killed those men, and I have cause to believe that for some twisted maligned reason you did, someone's going to deal you a hand that is going to be hard to play. But for now, you're in this as deep as the rest of us. You get out of line, you try to sabotage what we're doing, or do something else stupid like you did at the mansion, and it'll be your end. You try, and see what happens. They're six of us. One of us will kill you, and I'll be the first to take on the job. You understand? And as for your going back, you'll go nowhere. Not until after Los Estados. Not until we're successful."

Force pushed David aside. "If you killed those men, I'll take care of you myself."

"Enough of this shit!" shouted Pratt. "Oh, we are so damn sanctimonious, aren't we? So Doc's a killer. Are we really surprised? We're all killers. And we've enlisted in a cause that will call upon us to kill again. So before we start flagellating Doctor Death for his indiscretions, we better start figuring out our own punishments. How about you Chip? Maybe you should burn yourself on a cross? Yes, that'll be a good way for you to make recompense for what you're about to do and be closer to who you'd like to be. And you, good father, forgive us for what we are about to do. Oh, but nay, you took up the sword too. Father forgive yourself? How do you reconcile that M-16 you so willingly carry with the commandments of Jehovah? You there, Force, oh guardian of freedom and liberty, oh Force of my youth, will you afterwards fall on your sword? And sweet Jake, Baron of Beer, how will you do it? Crash into the sea? A true warrior's death. And lastly, the Good Major. What's in this for you? I know, of course. The ultimate redemption of a life of failure and sin. Death in the service of an honorable cause. The best of poetic justice.

"You all make me sick. Of course Doc's a killer. He was turned into a killer. We all turned him into a killer. We all turned each other into killers, and we are confirming that fact by our very presence here in this room. Don't any of you understand this? What's it going to take to make you see the foolhardiness of trying to recapture your pasts and change them? We can't believe in covenants and be rational human beings. And now, along comes this man who just happens to have the resources to know everything about us. And all he wants for his silence is our loyal services. Don't any of you see that once you start down the road to this kind of madness it never ends? We're going to be forced to kill again, to become mercenaries. If you can't see that this man is working for the government, you're blind. They've got us again. They've got us by the balls again. Let's just get out of this now while there's still time and save ourselves."

He fell back against the wall and turned away. "I don't give a shit if you think I'm a coward. I just want to go home," he said, not looking at the rest.

Doc let out a booming laugh. "Look boys, I've got a girl waiting in my room. This shit with this Steel man don't change a thing. We still goin'. And maje, you don't scare me a damn bit. Not a one of you jackasses scares me. Ha, ha, ha." Then he left.

Force shook his head, bent down, and in a seemingly effortless motion lifted Pratt over his shoulder. "I'll take him to the room. He's drunk. As for how I feel, even if I didn't trust him we don't have any choice but to go along with this man Steelhammer. We're in too far to back out now."

"We're all wanted men," Perez said morosely.

Chip nodded. "My mind isn't changed about freeing your wife major, but what we're going to do with this spook Steelhammer makes me nervous. But I guess Bill's right. We don't have any choice." He quietly followed Force out of the room.

"Jake?" David asked.

"One more stop and free gas. Doesn't matter, does it?" Jake said, lighting a cigarette. "Besides, Force and Chip are right. We can't turn back now." He took a drag from his cigarette. "I'm going to the bar."

After the others had gone, David laid back on the bed.

Perez was sitting in a chair at one end of the room smoking his pipe. "You think Steelhammer can really be trusted?" he asked.

David ran his fingers through his hair and took in a deep breath. "Yes, I believe we can trust him. Don't ask me for an explanation why. I just do. He has to be a man with important connections. Look how fast he was about gathering the information on us. Somehow I sense he is working with the government, not the CIA or the services, though he is military. Has it written all over him. An officer. He's with the government. Maybe the National Security Council. You heard him say the CIA worked for 'us.' I don't know right now. We'll know more when we see what he wants us to do."

Perez leaned forward toward David. "Where did he say we were going tomorrow?"

"Las Vegas," David replied with a distant look on his face.

And the next day, Steelhammer took them in tow.

"We're passing over Lighthouse Reef," Jake said as he adjusted the throttle in an effort to lean out the fuel. "The Half Moon Cay national monument is directly in front of us." He checked his air map and his instruments then looked at David for a response.

But David was quietly gazing at the blue and green sea below and the jagged multicolored coral reef with its lonely lighthouse and adjacent monument erected to honor Belize's ancient Mayan founders. "What's that?" he asked, pointing.

Jake looked down and noticed a small warship steaming past the monument, its path marked by a wake of white, foamy sea and a trail of smoke.

"A British frigate," stated Steelhammer. He had come forward and slipped on a pair of headphones and a mike that hung over the cabin climate control console. He stood behind Jake and David holding onto their seats with both hands, a grin across his face. "The Belizeans still depend on the British for protection. Guatemala still claims Belize is theirs, given to them by Spain. Shit never ends, does it?"

"We should enter Honduran airspace in about thirty minutes," Jake said, not looking at Steelhammer.

"Good. That means we'll be in Las Vegas in about an hour and a half then," Steelhammer said, then took off his headphones and mike and returned to the cabin.

"Major, something worries me about landing in the jungle," Jake said.

"Go ahead."

"This bird's not climatized. It's just not outfitted to handle this humid weather. I mean look at it. It's a big luxury ship. Everything it had to protect it from the Southeast Asian weather was stripped a long time ago. I'm worried about the damage that could happen to her if we stay down too long."

"Don't worry, Jake. I'm not going to let anything keep us from our appointment," David assured him.

Pratt was sullen and quiet. He had fallen lethargically into a seat at the rear of the cabin, a look of despondency on his face. He seemed purposely unaware of the events taking place around him as he daydreamed of his children and the life he had left behind. For by now he had come to the realization that he was caught up in this madness without any possibility of escape. And by now his wife must have called the authorities. Yes, by now he was a wanted man. He buried his face in his hands. His life, he surmised, was ruined.

Doc sat across from Pratt but took no interest in him. Patient and cool, he rested, confident that soon he would be unleashed. And from what Keaton had promised, he would profit from the outcome. He had long ago learned to control his hate, his passion, and his emotions. The more the others threatened him, the more he took satisfaction in his secret knowledge of their downfall. Everything had worked out well. The FBI knew who they were and would cast doubt on their actions. The newspapers would slander them. For forever they would be vilified. *Oh, Keaton, my leader, how proud of me you must be. I long to see you again*, he thought.

Force and Chip sat on opposite sides of the aisle and studied Steelhammer with interest as he made some private notations in a small spiral notebook that he kept in his pants pocket. He seemed to be lost in his own secretive thoughts, completely unaware, or unconcerned, that he was being scrutinized.

He looked younger than he had yesterday – a coach planning a softball game, a young officer planning his first attack. When they had boarded Ferry 34 about mid-afternoon, all Steelhammer had brought with him was a flight bag. Instead of his PX pants and shirt, he wore a set of faded green jungle fatigues and a pair of jungle boots, the kind they had all worn in Vietnam. Stitching marks over both pockets and a shoulder evidenced that the fatigues had once been adorned with patches. A convection current bumped the helicopter and Steelhammer glanced up for a moment and noticed the looks Force and Chip were giving him. He smiled, then went back to his notebook.

"Steelhammer," Force said, "what do you do?"

Steelhammer folded the notebook, placed a pencil inside, and stuffed it in his fatigue pants side pocket. "What do I do?"

"Yes, you heard me."

"I do pretty much the same thing as you. I enforce law and order."

"I'm a law enforcement officer. Are you saying you're a police officer?"

"Of sorts, yes. But in a different jurisdiction, larger and less defined."

"You're not CIA, are you?"

"No, I'm not. But you've guessed that already."

Chip spoke up. "Mr. Steelhammer, we're not mercenaries. I just wanted you to know that."

"I didn't believe you were. In fact, were I in the shoes of your friend up there," Steelhammer said, turning toward the cockpit and back again, "and the resources were available, I'd be doing the same thing he's doing."

"He's not our friend," Force said. "He's our officer."

"But you're out of the service," Steelhammer countered.

"He's our officer," Chip said flatly, backing up Force. Steelhammer smiled.

"Who are you?" Force asked again.

"What puzzles me," Steelhammer said, ignoring Force's question, "is how he got you guys to do what you've done so far. From what I know of your backgrounds, you have reason to hate the guy."

"He didn't have anything to do with getting us together," Chip said, obviously pleased with the confusion his answer caused Steelhammer. "We were brought together by another, under another authority."

David and Perez stood unsteadily inside the cramped cabin restroom as Jake negotiated the helicopter through some rough air. Perez looked worried.

"David, we've got to do something about Doc. He's a murderer."

"We don't know that for sure."

"Stop it, David."

"Okay. Yes, I guess you're right. He is a murderer. But what do you want me to do? Shoot him?"

"It may come to that. Look at what we know he did at the mansion and then planting that shoulder patch. He wanted the FBI to believe we were part of what he did in Mississippi and, if he had gotten away with it, a young couple's murders."

"Keaton wanted him to be here. There has to be a reason for that," David said evenly.

"Keaton, Keaton," Perez said contemptuously. "He's just a man. He can make mistakes. All of you invoke his name as if he were a deity. You use him as the ultimate justification for everything you do. My God man, this is a very serious matter we are courting."

But David did not reply. Instead, he shook his head and gave Perez a paternalistic smile that exasperated Perez even more.

"Damn it all, David, what if Steelhammer is a member of the United States government? It means the government is aware of what we're doing . . ."

"And condones it," David said, interrupting Perez.

"You can't believe that, can you?" Perez asked incredulously.

"Martin, you of all people should know there are a lot of things this country is forced to condone in order to insure its survival in this evil world, things the average American on the street might find offensive. But the difference between you and me and the average American is that we know such things are necessary. I judge Steelhammer to be one of those men our government turns to when it needs a dirty job done, one of those jobs that might be offensive to the sensibilities of some Americans yet are undeniably necessary for their survival. Perhaps what he will ask us to do will be an extension of what we are going to do for Sunny."

David stopped and looked out the window and smiled. "He knew from the first what we were up to. And you know, if I judge him right, I'd bet he'd like to go along with us. No, I trust him. He's just an American who was given an important mission to accomplish by his country and, for whatever reason, something fell apart in the execution stage of that mission. Now he needs our help. He has to play by tough rules in his world. He's blackmailing us all right, but that's the only way he can insure our cooperation."

"But he knows about Doc!"

A knock was heard at the restroom door and David opened the door.

It was Steelhammer. "We're over Honduras. Let's talk."

David insisted that whatever Steelhammer had to say be said in front of everyone. Steelhammer, with familiar understanding, agreed.

"We're going to land in a few minutes. Our destination is a clearing about five miles from a town named Las Vegas in the southern region of Honduras. There we will meet a group of people who are refugees, exiles if you will, from their native country, Nicaragua. These people have organized themselves into a fighting force whose main aim is to overthrow the communist regime that betrayed their revolution. I say their revolution because most of the people you will find in this camp fought against the dictatorship of Somoza as guerrillas in the Sandinista Army only to have the fruits of their victory and their dreams of democracy be turned into another dictatorship – not of the right but a Marxist-Leninist one, something none of them could have envisioned beforehand.

"One man in particular, the leader of this group, was a top military leader of the Sandinistas. Once the revolution was successful, and that was largely due to his efforts, he and the others who had hoped to establish a democratic government were exiled by the Ortega brothers. Now he is back in the jungle trying again to free his people."

"Eden Pastora," Perez said.

"Yes," Steelhammer said with a smile. "You're very perceptive."

"I can read."

Steelhammer let out a laugh.

But Perez, straight-faced, continued. "These people you are talking about are the Democratic Front, are they not?"

"Correct. The Revolutionary Democratic Alliance to be exact. Our government feels it is vitally important to support the democratic resistance of Nicaragua. That's my mission, and that's what I am going to ask you to do."

"Specifically?" David inquired.

"Tomorrow night a contingent, a strike force, is going to knock out a power station near the capital of Nicaragua, Managua. It needs to be airlifted in and then transported to a town near the Costa Rican border named, well, that's not important. Anyway, there is where your aviation fuel will be waiting."

"If our government is supporting this operation and you are a representative of our government, then why didn't you make other arrangements for their transport? Surely you weren't just standing around in Mexico waiting for someone to happen by flying a large stolen helicopter so you would extort them into your service," Pratt said sarcastically.

"Of course not, professor. I had another bird, but it was lost over the Gulf, its pilot killed. Anyway, the operation was set. Arrangements with operatives on the ground in the capital had already been put in motion and could not be aborted. I was in the process of obtaining a much smaller bird when you guys dropped in."

"Blackmail, pure and simple," Perez said. "What if we are killed? How will you justify that?"

"Look friend, I didn't plan on you guys being available. I also didn't have anything to do with the decision each of you had obviously made to risk your lives to save the life of Major Elliot's wife. I'm not blackmailing anyone. I'm simply bartering with you – my silence for your help."

"A convenient rationalization," Perez noted, not looking at Steelhammer.

"Father, shut up," Force said. "Let's hear him out."

Steelhammer gave Perez a questioning look. "A priest? Well, I'll be damned. No wonder I couldn't place you."

"Never mind that," David said. "You know we will be at risk. The chopper could be shot down, and then what would become of our original purpose?"

"The Sandinistas have no night-seeing devices, no sophisticated air defense radar systems. Only a lucky shot or an ambush at the LZ could result in the loss of the aircraft, and we have the landing zone secured. Besides, only the pilot will be at risk."

"Wrong!" David shot back. "We all go."

"Jake's not going anywhere without us," Chip chimed in.

Steelhammer could tell by the resolute looks on their faces that these men had bargained with each other to stick together. He liked that. "Okay, fine. I respect that. In fact, I can alter the plan to use all of you and speed up a move that needs to be made."

"What are these guys like?" David asked.

Steelhammer knew David was really asking was whether the guerrillas were competent to lead a night raid such as the one planned. He smiled. "You be the judge of that. But I can tell you that I will be with them all the way."

David nodded.

"Now, I had better get up in the cockpit and guide your pilot in." Steelhammer got up and made his way to the cockpit. At the entrance he stopped and turned. "By the way guys, our operatives say she's still alive."

Chapter 45

```
Las Vegas, Honduras
```

The terrain flowing past under the helicopter reminded Jake of I Corp in Vietnam. Rolling tree-covered hills, brown and green patches of meadow, a trapped lake here and there, and no evidence of human habitation. Mushrooms of cloudy mist hung between saddles in the hills, evidence of a previous rainfall. Not quite a jungle, not quite a forest. An orange sun blazed at eye level outside the window on Steelhammer's side of the cockpit.

Finding himself in constant conversation with Steelhammer, Jake flipped his helmet's sun visor down so as to conceal the fire in his eyes. "Doesn't it bother you that what you're having us do might cost the major's wife her life?" he asked, the passion in his voice barely muffled by the electronic conduit.

Steelhammer turned quickly to Jake. "Yes, it bothers me," he said simply, then turned away and cleared his throat. "You served three tours in Vietnam, didn't you?"

Jake chuckled. "Yeah, and you?"

Steelhammer nodded.

"Thought so. My first tour was as an NCO with the Big Red One. My second tour, after I had gone to flight school and received my warrant officer's commission, I flew C&C with Special Forces operations command," Jake continued.

"You didn't fly with the major your third tour?" Steelhammer asked.

"No, I was his executive officer."

"Unusual for a warrant to be exec."

"Intelligence specialist."

"Hmm. Well maybe you can tell me how he got you guys to agree to be a part of this rescue operation."

"But I thought you knew everything," Jake responded somewhat disingenuously.

"No, I'd really like to know. It seems illogical to me that, given your feelings about this guy, you'd leave your families, give up your security, and risk your lives for him and a woman you've never met."

"It wasn't the major who brought us together. There's another man involved in this rescue, as you call it. He's not here now, but I have no doubt he will be there when we need him. He's the one who brought us together, and for a purpose."

Steelhammer was puzzled. He aimed his face at Jake and waited intently for an explanation. Jake understood Steelhammer's need. Things like this happened in Steelhammer's world. Things like living up to one's word, depending on the honor of others, and relying on another man's integrity. Yet ancillary to each was a reason, a purpose. Steelhammer had to know the reason for their participation. It was central to his character that he understand the motives of men. In his world actions had to be logical, even actions sometimes precipitated by emotion. Jake flipped up his sun visor. His eyes, clear and bright, found Steelhammer's. He told him about the covenant.

Steelhammer turned back to the window and said nothing.

"One other thing," Jake said, grabbing Steelhammer by the shirt sleeve, "if we lose this aircraft on this mission of yours, I will be obligated to kill you."

Steelhammer nodded his head in understanding.

Chip looked dejected as he gazed out the window at the jungle below. Sensing that he was deeply bothered by the turn of events, David approached him.

"Chip," he said softly. Chip turned to him. "Do you really think Keaton would let us come this far and then just abandon us?"

Chip seemed to brighten at the mention of Keaton's name and sat up in his seat. "No, I guess not. But I have to admit to you I've been rather down since we took off. If I hadn't believed in Keaton and his wisdom, I would never have left my wife and our farm." He let out a deep breath. "I'm trying not to think about her. I can only guess what must be going through her mind."

"Are you worried about what people will say about us if we're accused of theft and murder?" David asked.

"No. Mary will know I had nothing to do with any of that, and her opinion is the only one I really care about. What bothers me – and I've tried to tell myself it doesn't matter, but it does – is what will happen to us after we rescue your wife. You know, even if we're successful, we might never be able to go home again. After all, we won't be able to keep what we've done a secret."

David stopped him. "You believe I saw Keaton, don't you?"

"Yes, I believe you did."

"Then trust me. Trust him. I'm not going to tell you I'm not worried about Steelhammer and what we're going to do once we land. I am. But I believe with all my heart that we will be successful. I believe we will make it to Los Estados. And I believe Steelhammer when he says he knows Sunny is still alive."

The telling conviction in David's voice seemed to strengthen Chip. "So, I guess we'd better help Steelhammer out so we can hurry up and meet her," Chip said, smiling.

David smiled back and gave Chip a thumbs-up.

"Steelhammer wants you up front," Perez said to David.

David stood up. The aircraft was rolling gently from side to side as the sun's rays reflected off the hills below and sent upward swift-moving gusts of air through which the helicopter was passing. "Must be getting low," he said as he steadied himself by holding onto the seats on either side of the aisle.

"I hope you know how to handle this," Perez said to David as he passed.

David gave him a sideways look. "Don't worry. Have a little faith," he responded.

In the cockpit David slipped on the headphones and mike.

"Switch your FM radio to 65.45," he heard Steelhammer instruct Jake. Jake did as he was told.

"Roger, done," Jake said. Then he gave David a confident look.

Steelhammer switched the radio sending button from Intercom to Send. "Freedom Base, this is Eagle One, over."

No reply.

"Freedom Base, this is Eagle One."

"Eagle One, this is Freedom Base," replied a voice exuberantly in heavily accented but understandable English.

"ETA five minutes."

"Roger."

"Now, Jake, align the ship on a heading of 300 degrees. The LZ should be marked with smoke."

Jake swung the ship around to the compass heading and started to slow the airspeed. Ahead beside a clearing in the jungle, he spied a wisp of red smoke.

"I identify red smoke," Steelhammer relayed to the station on the ground.

"Roger," came a reply.

Jake aligned the helicopter for an approach. The trick to landing a helicopter is imagining that a string is attached to the helicopter and flows in a straight line to an exact point on the ground where the pilot wants to land. Once that was in his head, all the pilot had to do was slide the helicopter down the string to that spot. Jake started down the string slowly, lowering the collective stick at his right side and screwing back on the power throttle attached to it, and at the same time pulling back ever so gently on the cyclic joystick. Overhead, the big blades began to pop, pop, pop as they fought against gravity. Once again, he was taking the team in.

The ground around Ferry 34 came up suddenly. All at once trees were higher than the helicopter and a swirling wall of vegetation flapped wildly all around them. As the helicopter flared to a landing, David lost sight of the earth as Jake raised the nose to a 30 degree angle of attack. Once they were on the ground, Jake feathered the blades of the helicopter and cut the power to the engines.

"Okay, we're here," he said to Steelhammer after taking off his flight helmet.

"Good job," Steelhammer said and left the cockpit.

Steelhammer left the helicopter first. There to greet him were dozens of fatigues-clad men who almost fought with each other to touch him. David stood in the door of Ferry 34 and marveled at Steelhammer's warm welcome.

"Who is he? A god?" Force asked from behind David.

"They *do* seem to know him," David replied, tongue in cheek.

Once everyone except Jake had exited the helicopter, Steelhammer, who spoke passable Spanish, introduced them to the fatigues-clad men. "These men who are with me are fellow Americans. They have brought with them the machine you see before you. And because of their help, we will be able to strike deep inside your homeland for the first time!"

A great cheer went up from the men.

"These are the freedom fighters of Nicaragua, the Revolutionary Democratic Alliance," Steelhammer said, his hand waving over the men like a wand.

David had the distinct sense of having seen all of this before. And he had. As an advisor in Vietnam, he had fought with nearly every unit of the South Vietnamese forces: ARVN, airborne, rangers, lien doi, and popular self defense forces. This familiar scene had been repeated in nearly every outpost and every Vietnamese village and hamlet. Desperate men showing their heartfelt thanks to foreigners who had chosen to risk their lives for a cause uncertain.

When Jake emerged from the helicopter, the fighters rushed to him almost immediately. Some wanted to give him cigarettes, others food, but most just wanted to say welcome and hail to the man who was skilled enough to fly such a huge wonderful machine. He seemed perplexed for a moment, then the *deja vu* that had overtaken David took hold of him. *Time is a circle.* He took as many of the fighters as who wished inside the helicopter.

"Well, ole Jake seems to have warmed to his popularity," Pratt remarked crassly.

"You jealous, Pratt?" Force asked, stretching his arms.

"Damn, major," Chip said, as he stood hands on hips surveying the camp, "this is just like Nam. I mean, look at this place. Reminds me of a Mike Force base camp."

"It's designed along those lines. I guess it's hard to improve on perfection," Steelhammer said.

Chip returned the compliment with a finger to his forehead.

"Father," Steelhammer said, addressing Perez, "you're going to have your hands busy when I tell them you're a priest. To a man, they're Roman Catholic and their last priest was killed in an ambush a year ago."

"I don't have any of my vestments. I'm not sure how God would feel about my performing mass or giving out sacraments without . . ."

Perez was hushed by Steelhammer's raised hand. "Just between you and me, I don't think God's as interested in methodology as He is in results." Steelhammer was grinning.

Doc chuckled. "Yeah, priest. There be plenty of natural resources here fo' you. So wade in 'em. Ha, ha, ha."

"Shut up, Doc," David snapped.

Doc's face flattened. "Sure maje, sir," he said contemptuously.

"Your gear will be secure on board the chopper," Steelhammer said, "but just to be safe one of you ought to stay with it at all times."

David nodded and turned to Force. "We'll all take turns watching the gear. Make out a roster." Force saluted.

For the remainder of the day, David and the others cleaned their weapons, maintained their personal gear, and took catnaps. Steelhammer had disappeared. Always present around the helicopter were groups of curious fighters, many of whom touched the ship with the type of gentle reverence usually reserved for icons.

Like all jungles, this one hid from the team the fact that the sun had slipped away, so suddenly and without warning, it was dark. In the distance, thunder could be heard. Force looked up at the blue-black night sky. A brilliant spray of twinkling stars turned on and off in the dark heavens. Every so often an unseen blanketing cloud passed through their light like a ghost.

"Rain's coming," he said authoritatively.

David had earlier taken off his shirt. But just as the night had come on suddenly, so had the rulers of the night: the mosquitoes. "I hope so," he said putting on his shirt. "I'd forgotten how bad they were," he said, referring to the mosquitoes.

A slight man approached them. He wore a jungle hat similar to the kind David and the others had worn in Vietnam. Through a toothless mouth he said, "You come. All come. This man," he said, pointing to an even shorter fighter armed with an AK-47, "he stay in plane. Guard your gear."

"Steelhammer?" David questioned.

The man grinned and nodded.

A large hut had been sewn together out of trees and leaves. It reminded David of the kind of hut the Chams used to build up in the Delta near the Vinh Te canal, only this hut was big. He guessed it measured about fifty feet in diameter. In the center of the hut a large hole lined with flat rocks served as a fireplace. Over the fireplace, fashioned out of the skin of a Soviet Hip-type helicopter, was a scoop that caught most, although not all, of the smoke and sucked it out of the hut through a tightly sealed hole in the roof. A huge fire burned. Over it were hung several cooking pots filled with beans, rice, and some meat. Steelhammer motioned for David and the others to sit around the fire.

"Hungry?" Steelhammer asked.

The hut's only source of light were the flames of the fire. Steelhammer sat Buddha-like, his legs folded under him, a patient look on his face. David sensed he was waiting for something, or someone.

"I'm hungry," Doc said, eyeing the food, its aroma filling his nostrils.

"Shortly," Steelhammer said. "The Boss is on his way."

"The Boss?" Pratt asked, his eyes wide with anticipation.

As if in answer to Pratt, a tarp that sealed the hut's entrance was thrown back and two men entered. One stood erect and still, surveying the hut and the men who sat before the fire. The other reverently took the first man's weapon then helped him shake off his web gear. Gently, both were laid against the wall of the hut. Then the second stood back, almost at attention.

Steelhammer stood and saluted the first man. Then he went to him and they exchanged hugs. He followed the first man to the fire and waited until he sat down before joining him.

"This is Commandante Zero," he said.

"Eden Pastora," Perez added.

"Yes. He does not speak English so, Father," Steelhammer said to Perez. Perez understood and nodded.

At that moment, the others suddenly realized Perez was a valuable asset to the team. They were once again in a hostile land inhabited by men of a different culture who spoke a different language. They gave Perez respectful looks as he began to relay Pastora's words.

As Pastora spoke, thanking them for assisting his cause, David could see the years had taken a toll on this slight man. Yes, David remembered Eden Pastora from intelligence briefings in Washington. This was Commandante Zero, the former Sandinista military commander whose *nom de guerre* had become a household word after he had boldly attacked and seized the Somoza government's national assembly in a lightning raid that eventually spelled the end of that regime. He had looked younger then. With jet black hair, a wildly handsome face, and a muscular body, he had stood boldly and defiantly in the door of a jet airplane at Managua's main airport, his beret cocked to one side of his head, and proclaimed that shortly the Somoza government would fall and freedom would be given to the Nicaraguan people. He had been prophetic on the first count and betrayed on the second. Sitting across from him now in the smoky hut, David could see that the muscular body was still there, but the hair was gray and the face was drawn and furrowed, albeit still resolute.

Perez translated. "He says . . ."

Pastora's voice was deep and mellow, almost somber. "What you have done for my people is beyond repayment. The colonel here . . ."

The colonel, David thought.

". . . says we must be most careful with your helicopter and you who fly it."

Pastora gave David a warm smile that mirrored Steelhammer's. "Now, let's eat."

The meal was served by the second man, named Roberto, Pastora's second in command. During the revolution, he had been a personal physician to Daniel Ortega, the El Presidente of The Peoples Republic of Nicaragua. But like his beloved Commandante Zero, he had been betrayed. Now he fought like his leader, out of hand and mouth.

"This helicopter," Pastora said after taking a drink of strong tea, "it is unusual, is it not?"

"On loan," Jake said via Perez.

Pastora laughed, his eyes twinkling in the firelight. "Yes, of course. This thing you do, it is in South America?"

David put down his bowl. A hard rain began to fall. "I think you know what it is we do," he replied.

"Yes, I once loved a woman," Pastora said, his eyes turning away from David. "This woman you love, she is your wife?"

David stiffened.

"We have no secrets here," Steelhammer said defiantly. "I gave you my word that nothing would happen to you and I give you my word this man's word is just as good. Look, I have never lied to these people and I'm not going to start now. Anything but the truth would have not been believed. This way, he will respect your motives."

"He's right, major. I trust this guy," Force said, looking at Pastora. "Remember Chau Got?"

David felt ashamed. Yes, Chau Got, the little Cambodian bandit who had been the Team's Kit Carson scout leader. A man whom he and others had trusted with their lives in that desperate, savage land. And that trust had been built on one thing: honesty. As he stared at the figure of Pastora sitting across from him, he could envision Chau Got. Yes, Chau Got and this man had many things in common; Force could sense it and now so could he – courage, integrity, and truthfulness.

"Yes," he said with telling emotion, "she is my wife. She has fought all her life against a regime not unlike the one of Somoza. She escaped their grip many times, but now she is theirs and her life is at great risk. And we are the only ones who are willing to try to save her."

"An honorable thing," Pastora said through Perez, a fire in his eyes. "We who fight for honorable causes often do so without others understanding our motives. Many in your country perceive me to be a bandit, even a traitor to Nicaragua. They do not understand what happened to our revolution. They do not understand communism. They do not understand who we, of the Revolutionary Democratic Alliance, are. And so, we fight without the support of a people whom we model ourselves after. A people who showed the world that victory can be won over an evil government by determined men and women.

"When I was in the jungle fighting against Somoza and his National Guard, I did not study the words of Marx, Lenin, or Guerverra. No, I studied the writings of Jefferson and read Sandburg's *Lincoln*. We were not communists, at least, most of us weren't, and the ones who were kept their ties to Cuba secret from the rest of us. We are nationalists. We wanted a free and democratic Nicaragua. The thought of freedom and democracy is what attracted most of us to the Sandinista cause. I always thought the Ortegas to be nationalists. I was shocked and hurt when, after we had consolidated our power, they displayed their true color – red."

"How did it happen?" Pratt asked, genuinely interested.

"It was all too easy. After we launched the final drive into Managua in 1979, we could taste our victory, and we hungered for its fruit: democracy. When we established a new government and a national assembly, there were several political parties, one of which was the FSLN, the Sandinistas. And it had been the same during the war. The FSLN was just one of the many factions that had fought Somoza under one joint command. I was a Sandinista myself. But during the war, the Ortegas were careful to conceal from us their true political beliefs, much like Castro did when he was fighting in the mountains of Cuba.

"After the assembly was elected we, the FSLN, proclaimed ourselves to be the military arm of the government. We should have sensed it then – the betrayal. But we did not. We were too drunk with power. After a few months, the Ortegas pushed the other factions aside, sent their leaders into exile, and killed those who opposed them. It was only a matter of time until they consolidated their power by suspending the civil liberties of all Nicaraguans and shutting down the opposition newspapers such as *La Prensa*.

"Overnight, they established defense committees, spies by any other name. And when that was done, the roundup began of everyone who they saw as a potential rival within the FSLN itself. I was tops on their list. But as you can see, I escaped with several other former Sandinistas. And from here, we fight them."

"The church has survived, hasn't it?" asked Chip.

"Yes. The Sandinistas are afraid to directly confront the church at this time, even though they have exiled dozens of priests who stood up to them. One was Father Robello, who was killed last year. The Sandinistas see the church as anti-Marxist. They are right, of course, as Cardinal Obando Y Bravo has told them many times. Ha. But they failed to silence him. However, even within the clergy, opposition is eroding. One priest, Father Cardinal, is the minister of culture. He now resides rather elegantly in Somoza's old home.

"The problem is that the American people simply do not understand what is at stake here in Central America. If they understood that eventually their own security will be threatened by what is happening now, I believe they would support our cause. I think you do not truly see the importance of what we do for Central America." Pastora stood, raising his hands to his face.

"Why Central America?" Force asked.

"The struggle for Central America is in a very real sense a test of the ability of the communist world to defeat the United States on its own ground. We who know the communists believe Central America is the first battleground in the final drive to the heart of America. If the communists can take over Central America, they will have effectively isolated the U. S. from the rest of the hemisphere. And just as important, they will have cut off the main sea route through which soldiers could be sent from one coast to the other." Pastora picked up his bowl of rice and beans and ate as he talked.

"The second battleground will be Mexico. In order for Mexico to be an effective staging area for subversion and the eventual invasion of the United States, it must have its southern flank protected from American invasion and have that same flank secure for resupply and reinforcement from Cuba and the eastern block countries. The southern flank of Mexico is Central America. Once these two battles are won, the final assault on the United States can be a reality. And the genius of all of this is that it is plausible and possible.

"The communists are a determined people. They understand the American mind all too well. And they understand the forces of history. Americans have become conditioned by their fast-paced lives to expect quick results from almost every endeavor they undertake. A book must be read quickly. One's wealth must come shortly after employment. Instant gratification. A war must be won in a short time, or you pull out and leave your allies high and dry.

"The communists do not think like that. They believe that if you wait long enough and are patient, victory will be yours. It took them thirty years to win in Vietnam, but they felt the wait was worth it. They will wait you out in Central America. They wear you down until you once again isolate yourselves behind your nonexistent borders. And when you do that, the wolf will be at your door. History has always been on the side of the patient and the persistent."

After Perez spoke Pastora's words, he pursed his lips. "What you say has some merit, but the majority of the American people are against any military involvement in Central America. And our Congress responds to the wishes of the American people. What would you have Congress do in Nicaragua, vote to support subversion of a popularly-elected government?"

"How did you come to this opinion?" Pastora asked.

"I can read and I can listen. And when I do, I am intelligent enough to make up my own mind," Perez responded.

Pastora continued. "The American people have been told the big lie about what is happening in Central America, especially in Nicaragua. Some time ago, the Polite Bureau of the Sandinista government and the Ortegas recognized that their great enemy was the President of the United States. They knew if Reagan were pushed, he would invade Nicaragua under authority of the Monroe Doctrine. But like most good communists, they had studied history. America lost the Vietnam War on the six o'clock news. The Sandinistas reasoned that if they could sway public opinion in their favor they could hold an isolationist Congress at bay and convince a peace-loving American people that Central America was just another Vietnam.

"A plan was put into effect to cultivate sympathy for their cause with media personalities, movie stars, rock and roll musicians, and other well-known personalities. The movie people were the easiest to win over. Most of them are shallow people whose main interest is in the pursuit of personal pleasure and notoriety. Play on their fragile egos and they will follow any cause.

"But the *sine qua non* of the plan was to cultivate the print and electronic news media. Newsmen by their very nature mistrust government. Vietnam had confirmed the news media's suspicions about government. It didn't take much persuading for the Sandinistas to portray themselves as a small helpless country being threatened by a big bully president. Yes, the American media loved it. Here was the issue many of them had longed for. Life had been boring for them since the 60s. Now, here in their very own back yard, was evidence of the evil president and his evil men.

"They tore into the story hungrily, and the trail of scraps left for them by the Ortegas only whetted their appetite more. Yes, the Ortegas had convinced your media that we who want a democracy for Nicaragua are the evil force here in Central America, not the communistic monolithic regime which has suppressed the light of freedom we fought so hard for. Read column after column found in the newspapers of your country and see what the political pundits are writing. Look carefully at your evening news programs and see how we are portrayed as opposed to the Sandinistas. With that kind of reporting, what other opinion can the American people be expected to have? What other source of information have they had access to? No, the Sandinistas have studied the mind of your newsmen well and have garnered their support. With them on their side, the Sandinistas will have the American public as well. They have shaped American public opinion in favor of a communistic regime whose ultimate goal is to overthrow every democracy in the Western Hemisphere.

"But we here in the jungle have no hard feelings against the American people. For how could they support us with the likes of nightly news anchors and newspaper columnists persuading them on a daily basis that the Sandinistas are a peace loving government that has the popular support of the Nicaraguan people, and that we are a bunch of CIA-led mercenaries who butcher women and children and want to reestablish the old Somoza regime? No, we have no one to tell the American people the truth that we are fighting the first battle of their war for them."

"Why do you continue to fight?" Force asked.

"What else can we do? We can only hope there are enough reasonable men left in the American Congress who can resist the media pressure and understand what's at stake for America here. But, in a couple of years, there will be another presidential election. And that may spell the end of our cause."

"Why?" Chip asked.

"Because," Steelhammer said, interjecting himself into the conversation, "our men of the Party will begin their little minded work."

The rain abruptly stopped.

"But what concerns you is tomorrow night," Pastora said wryly. "So, what happens to us should not concern you now."

Steelhammer took a cue from Pastora's sitting back and produced a map from his fatigues pants pocket. Spreading the map before them, he motioned for the team to draw themselves nearer.

"Now, this will not be an easy flight. We must enter Nicaraguan airspace here." He pointed to the six thousand nine hundred foot mountain, Pico Mogoton. "It will be the dead of night. Fortunately for us, there'll be a full moon tomorrow night during the flight, so pilotage will be enhanced. From the mountain, we'll bank over the lake and approach the outskirts of Managua."

"Where's the power station? I don't see it marked," Jake asked as he surveyed the map with intense interest.

"Here," Steelhammer said, touching the map just to the west of the city. "But you'll have no problem finding it. It'll be clearly marked by its furnace's light. We won't land too close to it, though. About half a mile farther west is a cleared sorghum field. Our people will make it ready for you to land."

Jake nodded, not looking up.

"How long will we be on the ground?" David asked.

"It should take no more than half an hour to move to the station, knock it out, and return to the ship. You and your people will stay with the ship and provide cover."

"Where will you be?" asked Perez.

"Pastora and I will accompany the raiders."

"This will be the first time," Pastora said earnestly, "that we have attempted a strike at the heart of my country. Our success will give the people spirit and show the Ortegas what we are capable of doing."

"And afterwards, you'll fly them to a place in the south of the country. There they'll start a southern front," Steelhammer announced.

"And we'll get our fuel?" Jake asked hesitantly.

"Yes."

"And you'll let us go on our way," David said.

"Yes. You have my word of honor on it," Steelhammer answered, looking David in the eyes.

Chapter 46

Chip was up early. After he had breakfasted on eggs and coffee he decided to take a walk around the camp. He was not rested, having slept a fitful, nightmarish sleep. In his darkest dreams, visions of Mary alone and afraid had torn at his heart, and the morning had brought with it feelings of foreboding.

Ferry 34 had been ceremoniously given a name by the fighters, *El Aguila*, The Eagle. A fighter artist had painted a blue and black bald eagle on the nose of the helicopter, its wings spread apart, its talons ready to snare, its beak open, and its eyes blazing. Jake had taken to The Eagle right away, pronouncing it a fit and proper designation for an aircraft that was about to carry Americans into combat.

"El Aguila!" the fighters shouted.

"The Eagle. Yeah," Jake seconded.

For most of the morning, the team had cleaned their weapons and prepared their gear for the night mission. Pastora and Steelhammer had supervised the loading of The Eagle with a fastidiousness bordering on the maternal. There would be thirty fighters lifted. Each would be carrying enough provisions for three days travel along with personal gear and a weapon. The fighters left back in the camp would move out in the middle of the night under the command of Roberto on a trek that would take ten days of forced march to circumvent Managua and marry up with Pastora's advance party, or what would be left of it, at the new base camp near San Juan del Sur on the Pacific coast just eighty-five miles from Managua.

As Chip, M-16 in hand, trudged through the camp, he took in the sights, sounds, and smells. What he saw conjured up images of places he had been before and his mind began to maunder the past. Yes, this camp wasn't much different from ones he had seen before in places like Tri Ton and Ba Chuc. The faces were different, but the people were the same. Farmers, he thought. Why is it always the farmers who end up fighting? In Vietnam, it had been the rice farmers who had fought the war for both sides. Not the merchants or the educated classes, the farmers. This time they had names like Juan and Jorge instead of Nguyen or Dong. And why was it that the farmers were the center of the conflict? The land. Yes, the land. In the final analysis, it was the land that was important. And these men were the land.

He stopped at one cooking fire to accept a cup of strong coffee. The old man who gave it to him shook his hand and smiled at him with grateful eyes. Human beings were the same everywhere, filled with hopes and dreams and ambitions. What were this old man's dreams, his hopes and ambitions? A small piece of land that he could claim for his own, a strong hut that would protect his family, and the freedom to live in peace? He felt a strong kinship with the old man, one farmer who understood another.

It was evident from the activities taking place that the fighters were preparing for a move. Everywhere they were checking their weapons and packing meager belongings. Chip could sense an *esprit de corps* among them. Was it the presence of The Eagle? Or was it the fact that they were at last going home?

Force had told him of a shallow, swift moving stream where a good bath could be taken. He crossed over a steep hill that overlooked the camp and found it, a slither of bright water that caught the rays of the morning sun and breathed a frosty mist. He hurried down the hill and waded in. The water was icy cold.

Suddenly a sensation that he was being watched swept over him, and he instinctively began to wade back toward the creek's bank where his automatic weapon lay. But just at the creek's edge he spied his scrutinizer and was mesmerized by the sight. At the edge of the bank, dressed in battle fatigues and wearing his green beret, stood Keaton.

"Keaton!" he exclaimed, astonished yet at the same time overcome with happiness by Keaton's sudden appearance. "You! Here! How did you find out about Steelhammer and us?"

Then his expression changed from wide-eyed amazement to one of somber realization, and he shook his head. "You knew all about Steelhammer and Pastora. You knew about everything from the first. It was you who put Steelhammer on us. Why? Just tell me why. Is this what you had in mind all along?"

He started to climb out up onto the bank, but Keaton said, "No, Chip. Stay where you are."

The quickness of Keaton's command startled him. "What's wrong?" he asked.

"I cannot stay, but hear me out."

"Can't stay? But we're here because of you. We've risked everything we have to honor the covenant and you didn't even come to Georgia." His voice trailed off as he stared into Keaton's eyes. "You talked to the major, didn't you?"

Keaton nodded.

"But why him? Why not us?" Chip took another step. "He didn't know about the covenant. He wasn't part of it."

"Search your heart. Can't you see that you are honoring the covenant by what you do here and by what will take place a few days from now near the end of the earth?"

Chip's mouth dropped open and he felt a strong warmth flowing over his body, a powerful energy that was almost magnetic, and it seemed to emanate from Keaton. "Who are you?"

"Do you not know me?" There was an almost hurt look on Keaton's face.

"Yes. I know you."

"Listen to me, Chip, for we have not much time. Do you remember when long ago Jude talked about good and evil?"

"Yes."

"Do you recall his words that there may be times when evil will triumph?"

"Yes, I remember."

There was something final and almost apologetic about the tone of Keaton's voice. "To understand that evil has a necessary place in the universe is to understand one of the great mysteries of creation."

"I may be able to understand it, but that doesn't mean I have to accept it," Chip responded.

"I understand," Keaton said with a smile.

"Keaton, what are you trying to tell me?" he asked, almost afraid of what Keaton's answer would be.

"Everything touches everything else. Nothing can move without moving the whole."

"Keaton, I don't understand."

"You are trapped in a shallow understanding of the nature of time, bound by measurements that have no relevance to the truth. Time is a circle in which everything revolves. You are here then you are gone, then you are here again."

Keaton stepped down into the water. "You have done well, Chip. Your life has been pleasing in my sight. So do not despair. Evil is of the earth. And like the earth, it is only temporary." He placed himself in front of Chip and reached out and touched his shoulder. "Do not be afraid. I will not abandon you, for you are a man of my own heart."

Chip put his hand on top of Keaton's. "But evil?"

"In the scheme of nature, it is sometimes necessary for evil to win."

"I trust what you say."

"Now, one last request."

"Yes?"

"Tell no one of my visit."

"Will I ever see you again?"

"Yes, Chip. Soon. Very soon."

Chapter 47

The ground around the idling Eagle was colored green and red, illuminated by the chopper's navigation lights. In the pitch dark, it was an unnatural sight. Looking out his window, Jake saw small bands of green and red colored fighters standing rigidly in the wildly blowing grass as the big blades of The Eagle began to flex, seemingly mesmerized by the huge aircraft. He gave David a thumbs-up and pulled pitch. Hats flew away and several of the fighters were blown to the ground as The Eagle lifted off and hovered for a moment so Jake could check the torque pressure. Then he lowered the Eagle's nose in order to gain transactional lift and whirled away into the darkness, leaving in its vacuum a portent of quiet. Once he was airborne, Jake switched off the helicopter's lights and began a power climb. In order to clear Mt. Pico Mogoton they would need to fly to the altitude of eight thousand feet. The big chopper, filled to the maximum and near its weight limit, lumbered upward on a heading that would take them straight for Managua, a flight of only forty minutes.

For many of the fighters seated in the cabin, this was a frightening experience. Most had never even seen a machine such as The Eagle, must less ridden in one. Many of the little men and women's faces were frozen in fear as the helicopter climbed upward, its two powerful turbines whining, at a thirty degree angle of attack. No one dared speak.

When the altimeter read eight thousand feet AGL, Jake reduced the engines' power and began a slow reduction in the angle of attack. Once he reached the desired altitude, he leveled the ship, trimmed up the controls, and reduced the power to seventy-five percent. The night was clear and crisp. Patches of bright, twinkling equatorial stars filled Jake's windshield and there was a soft gray tint to the land below. At their altitude, the air was thinner but colder than down below, which enabled him to steer The Eagle with ease. Because they were flying at night, they would not be bumped around by rising air currents. It was going to be a smooth, clear ride, he thought confidently. As they approached Mt. Pico Mogoton, a large yellow moon began to expose itself on the horizon. Jake knew that in another fifteen minutes it would rise high enough in the night sky to light up the ground below like a huge street lantern.

"The mountain's ahead," Jake said.

David stared hard into the darkness, but his night vision was not as good as Jake's, and he could see nothing. "Where?"

"There," Jake said, pointing to a spot on the windshield.

Slowly, David began to make out the outline of Pico's apex. "Yes, there."

Jake shook his head. "If we went down here, no one would ever find us."

"We're not going down anywhere unless you take us down," David replied confidently.

"That's Ocotal on your right," Jake said, pointing out a sprinkle of lights below.

"Ocotal. The map shows Highway One running from it to Managua," David said, looking at the map spread across his lap. "From here," he said as he ran his finger over the map, "and on into Managua, it's quite hilly."

"Look!" Jake said excitedly. Flowing under them like some iridescent snake was a convoy of scores of trucks extending for some two miles, each with its lights carelessly turned on. "You know, they'd shit if they knew an American aircraft was flying right over them. Must be sending troops up to the front. Guess ole Pastora's taking a toll on their natural resources."

David grinned.

Occasionally, Jake pointed out to David large puffs of dark clouds spraying the earth with night showers, but explained all were too far away to be bothersome to The Eagle. By the time Steelhammer brought Pastora to the cockpit, the moon had risen high enough to cast a yellow pallor over the terrain below, irradiating everything in sight. David graciously let Pastora take his seat and then helped him with the flight helmet. In broken Spanish, Steelhammer pointed out the significant terrain features below, but Pastora remained sadly expressionless, seemingly pondering the significance of returning to his homeland. And though he thanked everyone on board for letting him ride up front, he expressed a desire to return to his troops in the cabin to make sure everything was in order for the raid. Steelhammer seemed to understand and accompanied him.

"He's a cold fish," Jake said after Pastora had left.

Doc puffed absentmindedly on one of his long, black cigars as he gazed at the white shrouded ground below. Hill after hill passed swiftly under The Eagle. The terrain reminded him of the highlands, of his first kill. He had a contended look on his face. Keaton had come and had given him his command. In the dark of their last night at Pastora's base camp, Keaton had called to him, a whisper beckoning along the night wind. He had risen from his mat under The Eagle and followed the sound. It had led him to a crag alongside a hill just north of the camp. There, Keaton had waited.

Keaton's face was darkened with red, black, and green camouflage paint. His body was wrapped in a sniper's dark veil.

"Doccc," Keaton hissed, "are you ready?"

He dropped to his knees. "Yes, sir."

"Do you recognize this?" Keaton held out his hand, his palm open. Inside lay a piece of small folded paper.

Sweat pouring down his face, he nodded in recognition.

"Votive paper. Yesss, votive paper used in prayer. Upon it you will find a name. The name of one whom you will kill."

For a moment, looking at the note, he was hesitant.

"Do not fail me!" Keaton shrieked.

He fell back. "I will not fail."

Keaton stood over him. "Yesss, yesss. You will be successful. We will have our revenge. Now, go. I will see you soon."

His eyes glazed over as he now recalled the conversation. His lips were twisted in a cruel looking contortion. He was happy.

Force left Chip sitting asleep in one of the seats. Chip's nerves were shot, but as soon as the helicopter lifted off, his body took over and now he was gently snoozing. He was easy as he left.

He touched Perez on the shoulder. "Father, you worried?"

"I fear the worst."

Force let out a deep breath. "At least we're not going in. The LZ is about a mile away from the power plant, alongside the lake. All we have to do is provide protection."

"I fear the worst for them," Perez said, turning to the fighters.

As Perez gazed upon the scene in the helicopter, unpleasant memories of his first hot LZ suddenly appeared.

He had accompanied a company of Ninth Division troops on a routine search mission near a town called Long Xuyen. Phantoms had prepped the LZ with five hundred pounders and artillery had sprinkled the wood lines with HE. The first chopper landed without incident. His was the second, and it too got away clean. But the third and fourth choppers began to take murderous machine gun fire from a .51 caliber located in the supposedly clear wood line. Both exploded in great balls of fire, spewing men, arms, and legs across the dry rice paddy. And, oh God, the screams. The screams!

"Father, father," Force said.

"It's all right. I am going to be all right," Perez replied.

David sat impassively in the cabin as Pastora gave final instructions to his troops. Perez whispered a translation in his ear.

"In a few minutes, we will be landing," Pastora explained in a clear, confident voice. "We will be returning to Nicaragua, our home. The people we will be fighting were once your brothers. I know how hard this will be for you, but you must keep in mind it was they who chose the path of darkness, not you. You must also keep in mind that your countrymen will be seeing us for the first time. We must not dishonor ourselves. We must show the people that we are with them. We must strike back quickly and then escape, just like we have practiced. Thanks to the colonel, we will be able to reach our destination very quickly. And thanks to these brothers in arms."

Pastora stopped and waived his hands toward the team. "Now, gird yourselves for battle. And may God be with us."

Jake spotted them far out in the darkness beyond the windscreen: the lights of Managua. He called for Steelhammer to come to the cockpit.

Steelhammer slid into the seat. "Yes, I see. Come to a heading of one ninety and then start your descent."

Pastora touched Steelhammer on the shoulder and he looked up. They exchanged a look of mutual understanding. Pastora raised a clenched fist, then disappeared.

"You should see two or three flashing lights just at the edge of the lake," Steelhammer told Jake, his breath quickening.

Jake nodded and turned to David for reassurance. David, standing behind Steelhammer, gave him a look of confidence by nodding his head toward Steelhammer. Jake slowly twisted back the power lever and drew back on the cyclic stick while at the same time, with agility, pitching the blades to slowly bleed off the airspeed. The big chopper began to slow. In the darkness, they seemed to be suspended in midair. Ahead, the lights of Managua were coming up fast. He scanned the lake below, but the moon glowing off the placid water reflected in his eyes, causing him to wince.

"What is it?" Steelhammer asked.

"Nothing," Jake said testily.

"I don't see anything," David said.

"They're there," Steelhammer shot back.

"They are there," Jake said wryly.

Neither Steelhammer nor David could see anything except darkness, but Jake's eyes were phenomenal. He came about to his left and lined up The Eagle for an approach. "Hold on. This maybe a rough touchdown."

Steelhammer unstrapped himself and got up. He stopped next to David. "I'm going with them."

"Why?" David asked.

"You know why. If they were your men, you'd go."

"What do we do if you don't make it?" David asked.

"You wait for those of us that return and then fly to the coordinates I gave your pilot. The fuel you need will be there by tomorrow."

"What if you're wounded?"

"There won't be any wounded left behind, and there won't be any wounded brought back."

David nodded that he understood.

"One other thing," Steelhammer said, "if I were you, I'd be doing the same thing you're doing. Good luck if I don't make it back, and God be with you." Then he touched Jake. "You're one hell of a pilot, man."

Force felt a familiar feeling of excitement. All around him fighters were loading weapons and checking their gear, preparing for battle. A pretty, dark haired girl asked him in broken English to adjust her web gear's straps. Gingerly, he tightened them, noticing that she was shivering with fear. Afterwards, she gave him a nervous smile. She looked to be not more than fifteen.

After he was satisfied that all was ready, Pastora gave everyone the thumbs-up. Once all the fighters decided they were ready, they returned his thumbs-up.

Jake used the moon's reflection off the lake as a landing light. Skimming just a few feet from the surface of the water, he darted for the red lens flashlights of the men on the ground. As he neared the land, he began his flare. The flashlights waved wildly. Touchdown.

Force popped open the door and let in a whirling wind and the deafening whine of the engines as they were being idled. Without hesitation, the fighters scrambled out of The Eagle and headed off in two neat files toward the blinking lights of the power station in the distance. Jake shut off the engines. David and the others left The Eagle and stood quietly in the wet grass as the gassy heat from the helicopter's engines filled their nostrils. Managua in the distance seemed fast asleep. A hot, humid night cloaked them with a wet stickiness.

"The only way they can come at us is down that road where the fighters are or across the small bridge near the canal on the other side of the chopper," Force said to David after surveying the area. The helicopter had the lake to its back and a canal about a hundred yards away on its left. To its right was a flat field that gave a clear view for almost half a mile. The field was wet and would not support any vehicles.

Force was right. The road through the field and the little bridge over the canal were the only ways they could be attacked. The fighters had picked a damn good spot for The Eagle to land.

"We won't have to worry about the road," David said hesitantly. "The fighters will protect that on their way back. And with the lake at our back, the canal is the only other avenue of approach." Then he thought for a minute. "Chip, you and Doc cross over that bridge and go about a hundred yards deep into the underbrush. Warn us of anything approaching. Stay there until you hear the whine of the engines. Understand?"

"Right, major," Chip said, his M-16 at the ready. Doc nodded and followed Chip into the darkness.

"Just in case, I want you," David said to Force, "and Pratt to go about three hundred yards down the road. When you see the fighters coming back, escort them in. Perez and I will stay here with Jake." Force and Pratt scurried off.

Jake had elected to remain at the controls. He told David it would take five minutes to start up and get airborne. He wanted to be ready.

"Ought to be some shit raised real soon," David said, chambering a round into his weapon.

Perez's mouth was so dry his voice cracked when he spoke. "God, I wish this was over." He weakly looked up into the bright moon-filled night.

There was a quiet. Death's quiet.

After thirty minutes had passed, the lights from the power station suddenly went out. David was the first to notice. "Look," he whispered.

Perez turned just in time to see the upward contrails of an explosion. Then another, and another. "My God," he said out loud. Then came the far off sounds of what sounded like muffled thunder.

"They ought to be coming back in a few minutes," David said breathlessly. As he stood at the ready, his weapon cradled in his arms, his finger inching around the trigger guard, he became acutely aware he was experiencing a resurgence of feelings long dormant, long forgotten. He was again one with his environment. To a real soldier, a battlefield is merely an extension of his own being. A combat leader feels the enemy's presence long before he actually sees him. *See the battlefield. See the damn battlefield.* This is the first dictum of every army school of tactical thought. But what every real soldier knows is that a good soldier doesn't just see the battlefield, he feels it. He could feel the grass, the wet field, the canal, and the warm waters of the lake. He and his surroundings were one and the same. He was pleased with himself.

His mouth fell open as he heard the sharp report of automatic weapons fire – lots of automatic weapons fire. There was one hell of a firefight going on near the power plant.

"David?" Perez asked anxiously.

David held up his hand in the moonlight, silencing Perez. "We've got to go forward and cover them," he heard himself saying.

"No, David, I can't," Perez said.

"It's all right. Just stay here with Jake. Jake needs you here."

David moved down the road at a dead run stopping near Force and Pratt.

"Come on. We're going to cover them," he ordered forcefully.

Force jumped up without protest. Grudgingly, Pratt followed, but only after he had blurted out, "I thought we were just along for the ride! Shit!"

They ran down the road, their hearts beating wildly, their breathing fast and hard. As they neared the edge of the field they could see tracers spiraling upwards and hear the sound of men firing at each other in desperate individual duels.

"Not far now!" Force bellowed excitedly.

The road suddenly narrowed and led into a clump of trees. They slowed to an airborne shuffle. Beyond the tree line, great fires lit up the night sky as the power plant's coal and oil stores erupted. The plant was just beyond the bend up ahead. Unexpectedly, they came upon two bodies lying on the road. One, that of a man, was face down in a pool of blood. The other lay on its back. Force bent over it. It was the young girl he had helped earlier. Her eyes were wide open and held in them the yellow moon.

"She dead?" Pratt asked.

Force quickly stuck his hand inside her blouse between her breasts. No heartbeat. He stood up and snapped his fingers in frustration. They moved on. A few yards farther and they were at the entrance of the power plant. They dropped down and watched. The area around the plant was as light as day. Combatants were everywhere, firing at each other from close range, screaming blood curdling cries of death and joy. It was the attack on Tri Ton all over again.

"We'll stay here until they begin their withdrawal," David shouted.

Chip listened apprehensively to the firefight in the distance. He had positioned himself away from the bridge down a narrow weed-bordered trail. Hunched down in the grass, he waited. Doc was at the bridge's entrance. He felt a heart sickness; an inexplicable feeling of moroseness had come over him and a moment of doubt had crept into his consciousness. Moments of doubt always come to the faithful, Jude used to say. He fingered his selector switch, moving it from automatic to safe to semiautomatic and back to safe again. In his imagination, he could picture a Sandinista patrol coming down the trail. They would not be expecting him to be there. He could get several of them before he had to fall back to Doc's position. He looked over his shoulder. There was something about Doc's demeanor that made him anxious.

David heard a loud, shrill whistle blow. That must be the withdrawal signal, he thought. He was right. In the dancing light, groups of fighters started to form.

"They're coming," Force said.

"Let's stand up," David said. Then he saw Steelhammer's tall figure walking resolutely toward them. "Over here!" he shouted.

Steelhammer seemed surprised by their presence. "What the hell you guys doing here?" He shouted in an agitated tone. But then he saw their faces in the light of the power plant fires. "Never mind. Let's get the hell out of here."

"Looks like a first rate job. I'd say ten thousand kilowatts worth," Pratt said sarcastically.

"You got that right, professor," Steelhammer replied, "and even more than we hoped for." "What do you mean?" David asked.

"We picked us up a commandante. The fucking military commissar for Managua. His bad luck to be in the wrong place at the right time for us. Funny thing is, he and Pastora used to be best friends. Should be quite an interesting conversation between those two."

David, Steelhammer, and the others waited until Pastora had accounted for his personnel. Then Pastora nodded to Steelhammer, and when he did David could see an intense expression of sadness on his face. They ran all the way down the road, the fires from the power plant shimmering in the distance.

As soon as Perez saw them, he gave Jake the all clear to start up the engines.

Chip heard the engines start and headed back toward the bridge. In the darkness, he deftly found his way to the spot where he had left Doc.

"Doc," he shouted.

He heard a splashing noise coming from under the bridge. *What was that?* He looked over the railing of the wooden structure.

"Doc, what are you doing? The helicopter's going to lift off."

Below, he saw Doc standing defiantly on the edge of the steep bank near the water of the shallow canal.

"Chip, better come see this. The major's not fuckin' gonna believe this!" Doc shouted with a laugh.

Chip turned anxiously to the helicopter then back to Doc.

"Shit," he said in exasperation, then jumped over the edge of the railing and down the bank. He faced Doc. "What?"

"Chip, my man," Doc whispered.

"Cut this bullshit, Doc. What is it? For God's sake, we gotta unass this place. The chopper . . ." Then a sixth sense took hold of him. Doc stood before him, his body wet with sweat, a chilling grin twisting his face, and a dull, glassy look in his eyes. He had seen Doc like this before. In Vietnam – just before he carried out a Phoenix hit. This was the look Doc had before a kill. "Doc, get hold of yourself," he said cautiously as he began to slowly raise his weapon.

"The covenant," Doc said through clenched teeth. "I am come to honor the covenant."

"Doc . . ."

But before Chip could react, Doc raised his weapon and fired a clip into him, lifting him up and throwing him back into the canal with a splash.

David whirled around upon hearing the report of automatic weapon fire.

Doc had an orgasm. It was as good an orgasm as he had had in a woman's mouth. He let out a deep breath as he watched Chip's corpse float down the dark canal. He whispered, "*Keaton, are you here? Are you satisfied, Keaton?*"

David and Force rushed to the other side of the whirling helicopter and scanned the area around the bridge. After a moment, Doc ran up to them and David grabbed him by the shirt.

"Chip. Where's Chip?" he screamed.

"A sentry. Hit by a sentry. It happened fast, maje. Fast. He be dead. The sentry be dead too," Doc said in a breathless rush, his eyes boring into David's.

"Where is he?" he managed to say, choked by his emotions.

"Fell in the canal."

Force lunged for Doc, but David restrained him. "You didn't try to get his body?" Force shouted, swinging wildly at Doc.

"Stop it, Bill!" David screamed. "There's no time. There wasn't time."

Force let go and held up his fists to the heavens in rage. "Ohhh, God!" he screamed.

David grabbed Doc by the shoulder and shoved him. "Get in the damn chopper, now."

Then he brought Force up to him face to face. "Bill, Bill, there's no time. They'll be here in minutes. It's time to go." He watched as Force cooled. "There's no time," he said again, but softly. Together they ran to the helicopter.

Jake pulled pitch and sped away into the night leaving an American soldier on the field of honor, as the lights went out all over Managua.

Chapter 48

Vicinity of San Juan del Sur, Nicaragua

Jake wasn't told about Chip until they had landed. For a long time, he just sat in The Eagle's cockpit, mournful and bewildered. Finally Force brought him out and he fell asleep, nestled under the fuselage of his beloved aircraft.

Jake had been the real hero of the operation, and everyone knew it. His flying had been an act of courage and unequaled skill. After he lifted off he had flown straight over Managua, skimming the tops of darkened buildings and houses, led only by the moon and his inboard navigation compass. After five short minutes, he was over the Pacific Ocean where the moon glazed off the surface like some huge spotlight. Then he followed the coastline until he saw the lights of San Juan del Sur and headed inland with Steelhammer navigating. Again, there were red lens flashlights, and he set The Eagle down among them.

The base camp, three miles east of San Juan del Sur, was newer and more primitive than the one at Las Vegas. Women had not yet inhabited it. It was situated in a valley between two rows of steep, misty mountains. Inaccessible by road, the fighters had forged three rough foot trails that coiled up the mountains, one leading to the sea, the other two into the countryside and on to Managua. It was a isolated place, a perfect staging area.

At mid-morning, Steelhammer approached David and the others who were camping outside The Eagle. He could sense there was a dolorous mood among them and tread ever so lightly, for he knew that some of Chip's blood was on his hands. Despite his warrior's heart and mission-oriented nature, he felt heartsick because he had been forced by circumstance to draw these men into a conflict not of their own choosing. "I can't tell you how sorry I am about your friend," he said, standing before them in cammo t-shirt, jungle pants, and boots, a .45 in a holster slung around his waist. He looked somewhat disheveled with his close cut hair spread across his forehead, two days' growth of stubble on his face, and his weary eyes. Tried and tired.

"Wasn't your fault," David replied wearily, rubbing the sleep from his eyes. He was bare chested and wore only a pair of boxer shorts.

"The fuck it wasn't!" Pratt yelled. "Chip died unnecessarily and we all know it. We were all blackmailed into going along on that raid. Blackmailed."

"Shut up, Pratt," Jake hissed from his sleeping cot. "We're all sick of your whining. Chip knew what he was doing. He wasn't like you. He was the kind of man who would have volunteered if he hadn't been asked."

Out of the corner of his eye, Steelhammer spied the look on Doc's face and it struck him as odd. It was a spiteful look, contemptuous and hateful. This man could care less about his fallen friend, he surmised. He shook off the thought. "Your fuel will be here in about two hours. As soon as you take it on, you're free to go."

"Thank ya' massa'" Pratt quipped.

Steelhammer ignored Pratt. "I want to assure you of one thing," he said to David. "Chip's wife will want for nothing. We'll take care of her. I give you my word on that."

"Who is *we*?" he asked, squinting at Steelhammer.

"There are those who support what we are doing in Central America. Private people of substance, not connected with the government. They'll know by tomorrow of Chip's sacrifice."

Force stood up and walked over to Steelhammer. The two of them standing side by side, made a formidable pair. He gave Steelhammer his hand. "You owe us no apologies," he said. "Jake was right. Chip would have wanted to be a part of what you're doing down here. And for what it's worth, I'm proud to have taken part in what happened last night."

Steelhammer shook Force's hand and gave him a smile.

Pratt spit on the earth. "This is fucking incredible. Listen to you two. Damn! Macho men of the earth. Arise, your warlords are here!" He jumped up and continued. "Listen, ole Steelhammer, if that's your name, two days' drive up the Pan American highway are a bunch of materialistic gringos named Americans. Their interests are sex, self-gratification, wealth, and power. Last night while Chip was breathing his last breath, you know what most of them were doing? Going to rock concerts, eating at hundred dollar a person restaurants, and fucking and sucking the shit out of each other. And those who weren't doing that were robbing and killing those who were. You think any of them gives a shit about what happens down here? If ole Dan Rather himself had interrupted their TV watching to tell them the whole damn Nicaraguan Army was headed for El Paso, the only thing they'd be upset about was missing the ending of *Dallas*.

"Face it Steelhammer; you care more about your damn country than they do. Americans don't give a shit about anything any more. They don't give a shit about the rest of the world or who governs it. How could they when they don't even give a shit about who they elect to their own damn government? Hell, Steelhammer, they don't even give a shit about each other. Chip died and no one gives a shit. So let's just forget the glory crap. Let's just let it go for what it was – a fucking savage shootout between warlords of a Central America shithole whose interests are not those of mine or yours, not even freedom's. Power, Steelhammer. Raw power. Chip died because someone lusted for power over somebody else. So, fuck off. Don't cheapen his death by making any more of it than it was."

Perez had just bathed his face and shaved. As he gazed at his crumpled reflection in the mirror of The Eagle's toilet, he was seized by the sudden realization that he had just taken part in murder, albeit against his will. And it sickened him.

How he had changed. Hadn't his whole justification for coming along on this magical mystery tour been a burning intellectual curiosity about the *why* of it? He had hungered to know why sane men would suddenly leave their families, their careers, the safety of neighborhood and place their lives in jeopardy for the sake of a woman they had never met and on the command and assurance of a man they hated? *Why?* Even after learning about the covenant, it still boiled down to their following David. Why would they do that? Was the enigmatic Keaton the explanation? If so, he was just a man, a former army sergeant, someone they had not seen or heard from in years. So why would they risk life and limb for him? Was it that they were simply bored with their lives? No. None of them had been bored enough to commit suicide, not even Jake. *So why? Yes, why?*

As he gazed at his reflection, the answer was no more apparent now than it had been in Richmond Hill when the tangled web of this whole affair had begun to ensnare them. And that was the most disturbing of his thoughts. What was happening defied intelligent explanation; none of it made any sense. They weren't here to satisfy some CIA plot hatched by Keaton. That had become apparent with the advent of Steelhammer. And he knew David had not planned any of this. *So, what was the answer?*

He rubbed his chin and pursed his lips. Keaton? Keaton had to be the answer. He was the one common denominator in this whole affair. It was Keaton who had brought the team together. It was Keaton who had found him and told him to get David to Richmond Hill. But if Keaton had planned this, how could he have known about what would happen to Sunny? All of his assumptions began to vanish, and again he was at the beginning. Which, for him, was the end.

The answer to this mystery appeared to be that there was no answer. There seemed to be no intellectual reason behind any of what happened. *No intellectual reason?* This thought tore at the heart of his very being. His intellect told him there had to be a reason for everything. Everything in the universe was explainable. Scientific truths were sacrosanct.

He hung his head. *So why was he still here?* he asked himself. To be here was to contradict his very existence. He raised his head. He *had* changed. For lurking there in his heart of hearts, he knew there might, there just might be an answer for everything that was happening. But he shook his head. To think even for a moment that what was taking place was . . . He let the thought vanish. Yes, he had changed. But not that way.

Then he laughed out loud. Yes, of course. In the final analysis, man is just an animal. More sophisticated, able to think in the abstract, but still a creature of the jungle whose first instinct is to survive. How had Maslow put it? Man is motivated by a hierarchy of needs, each need being a rung in succession. None could be skipped or glossed over. If a man finds himself unable to move past one rung, he is stuck there, unable to progress until the needs associated with that rung are met. So he, the intellectual, was stuck on the first rung. Maslow had called it the rung of safety. Yes, of course. That was it. He smiled happily into the mirror.

None of this made any sense because he was currently fixated on his need to survive! Everything else in his life had become secondary to that need. As soon as his life was secure again, as soon as the killing stopped, as soon as Sunny was freed, he would come to understand why all of this had taken place. So at this point in time, the *why* of it did not matter. For now, he could stop trying to understand why he was here, why the others were here, and why all of this was happening at all. What was important was to survive, to stay alive and not end up like Chip. Yes, he had changed. But when you are sinking in quicksand, that is not the time to try to figure out how you fell into it in the first place. No, it was time to look for something to hold on to.

"Martin," David said. Perez was startled to see David's face alongside his the mirror. "They're about to interrogate that commandante. I want to hear what he has to say. I need you to translate."

Perez nodded. It was something to hold onto.

Jake and Force were with The Eagle supervising its refueling. They needed to keep busy, and neither had any interest in or had any time for communists. Jake was anxious to leave while there was still plenty of daylight. Since he was without accurate weather reports, flying at night would be dangerous. David had promised him a liftoff as soon as the refueling was finished. Their next refueling stop was Bogota, Columbia. Their flight plan would take them over Costa Rica, where they could do pretty much as they wished. However, once they reached Panamanian airspace they would have to divert south and once again head out over the Pacific Ocean to avoid U. S. manned radar. After one hundred nautical miles, Jake would turn inland and make for Columbian airspace. Since unchartered flights flew in and out of

Bogota at all hours of the day and night, they felt reasonably secure in refueling there. Also, he told them, the oil in both engines would need to be changed and a routine maintenance inspection performed. Bogota was the only airport in the vicinity capable of providing adequate maintenance support.

Pratt had procured some locally made spirits and, despite his previous promise to the others, had drunk himself unconscious. He was now sleeping fitfully beside The Eagle's cabin.

David and Perez made their way to a corner of the base camp where they found Steelhammer, Pastora, and two other fighters standing over their prize. It reminded David of another time long ago.

"You needn't be here," Steelhammer said. "This is none of your concern."

"I know," David replied, staring down at the commandante.

"But you're curious, aren't you?" Steelhammer asked knowingly. "Want to see a real live one, don't you? Well, suit yourself. Just please stay out of it."

"His name is Rafael," Pastora explained through Perez. He and I were once comrades and fought together in the mountains against Somoza. He was with me at the National Assembly raid. He was brave."

"I am still brave, Eden. What do you think has happened to me over the years? Do you suppose I have become soft since the revolution? Ha, ha," Rafael said in flawless English with a voice at once sarcastic and friendly. It was as if he wasn't afraid of what Pastora might do to him. He seemed to know Pastora's limits. And he seemed to be talking as much to Steelhammer, David, and Perez as he was to Pastora.

Rafael noticed David's stare and turned to him. Rafael had long, jet black hair that fell over his eyes and forehead. His face was thin and narrow like an eagle's. A beard and mustache rounded it out. His eyes were dark brown and penetrating. And when he spoke, his words came from a wide mouth exposing two gold front teeth.

"So, Eden, who is this gringo?" Rafael asked in Spanish, squinting his eyes at David and twisting his mouth quizzically.

"Never mind who he is," Pastora said. "I want to ask you about Daniel."

"Eden, Eden, do not insult me. I have nothing to tell. And even if I did, you would already know it. Now, what do you want? You want to kill me? That is easy. Just shoot me, okay? But don't play these silly games. Oh, but yes, you do this for the sake of our newfound gringo comrades. Oh, Eden, it is you who has changed."

David noticed Pastora's eyebrows raise and his face become flushed. Was Rafael getting under his skin? "What's he saying?" he asked Perez.

Then Rafael turned to David. "Hey, gringo, you American?"

"Yes," David answered.

"I lived in America for ten years. Studied at Columbia University. I was a political science major. Do you think it has helped?" Rafael laughed and threw back his head.

It was only then that David noticed that Rafael's hands were bound behind his back with a rope. David didn't answer. His mouth was suddenly dry and his skin felt clammy.

Rafael studied David's face. "Yes, you have been in the jungle before. You are experienced in these matters. I can see it in your eyes. So tell me, gringo, are you a soldier? Are you an American officer?"

Rafael laughed. "You don't have to answer. The answer is written all over your face." Rafael dropped his head for a moment as if he was pondering what he would say next.

"This is who we fight," Steelhammer said absently in a matter-of-fact tone. "Very much like our enemy in Southeast Asia was. So much alike."

"Of course we are alike, gringo! You too do not look like you are stupid," Rafael said harshly. "We are followers of the same creed. You, you westerners, you gringos, call us communists. And when the word comes out of your mouths, it loses its meaning. You see us as the ultimate evil in the world. Therefore, you are dedicated to fighting us to the death. So be it. But how blind you are to the truth. For we are not the ultimate evil. You are. And so, we are dedicated to fighting you to the death."

Rafael turned away from Steelhammer and to Pastora. "Eden," he said almost pleading, "why these gringos? You were once one of us. You of all men truly understand the Yankee. You know what he has done to our people."

"I was never a communist. I was a nationalist, and I thought you were the same," Pastora said.

"But these names – communist, nationalist – what do they mean? Nothing. Names given to us by gringos. You know who we are. We are a part of a greater world. Who will save the world if not us? You think the gringos will save the world? It is the gringos who are destroying it."

"We fought for freedom. We fought for democracy. And what do we have now? Dictatorship! Instead of Somoza, it is the Ortega brothers," Pastora replied through clenched.

"Eden, Eden, look at the world in larger terms than Nicaragua. How long do you think Nicaragua can exist if the world around it is destroyed? How long, huh? Do you think we live in a vacuum? Look around you. The world is on fire. The world is being slowly destroyed. How long do we humans have to live? Fifteen, maybe twenty years? Just look at what so-called freedom and democracy have done for mankind. Do you think the peoples of the world have bettered themselves under the capitalistic system? Look at the poverty. Look at the world as a whole. The poor are everywhere in vast numbers. Vast numbers! Who will feed them, Eden? Will President Reagan feed them? Will General Motors feed them? Who looks after their interests in this cruel world? No one, Eden, and you know it. Their governments only look after themselves.

"This is what our world revolution is all about. It is not to enslave man, but to free him from the worst kind of slavery. Economic slavery. Eden, wake up. An explosion of human beings is about to happen. Unless we can get world population under control, unless we can insure that every man goes to bed without being hungry, unless we can insure every person has a right to a roof over his head, to adequate medical care, a meaningful job, then what do we as human beings have? Do you think democracy has done a good job in providing these needs and rights? You know it hasn't.

"But who will? We will, Eden. But it all begins right here in places like Nicaragua. And also in places like Angola, Pakistan, Cuba, Northern Ireland, Palestine, France, Italy, South Yemen, the Philippines, and Arkansas. But it isn't only poverty and inequality we seek to eliminate. It is the pollutants and polluters who are destroying the earth itself.

Whole species of animals are becoming extinct every year. Our water is slowly becoming undrinkable. And worst of all, our very air is being made unfit to breathe. Even the ozone layer is being depleted because rich capitalists want to increase their wealth at the expense of whole rain forests. Who will stop them, Eden, if not us? Who will stop them? You think the capitalist lying by his pool with his legal whore will?

"And you still want to kill us. You and your gringos still hate us. We who are destined to be the saviors of the world. You label us communists as if we were a disease, a plague. While all the time you perpetuate a system that is slowly destroying the world. And yes, Eden, when we have one-world government there will no longer be the need for nuclear weapons. A universal government of mankind, earthmen, not nations. A world at total peace. No need for armies. A world free to explore its own destiny, even on to the stars. And you and I know that there is only one obstacle to all of this happening, and that is America. That is why we will fight these gringos to the death to achieve these goals."

Pastora swallowed hard. "But . . . Rafael, you forget a man is not truly free until he is able to have a choice."

"The time for choices is over, Eden. The world cannot afford to let men exercise their right to be hedonists at the expense of others."

"But you are a people who do not believe in God. How can you expect to treat men within the parameters of moral conduct if you do not have religion as a guide?" Pastora asked.

"Oh, Eden. How long will you deny what your intellect says to you? Why do you continue to believe in the Easter Bunny and Santa Claus and . . . God?"

"America will not roll over and play dead," David heard himself saying after hearing Perez's halting last translation.

"Don't be naive, gringo. America will never oppose us. At least, not until it is too late. Look at what is happening here in Nicaragua. Your people want no part of a war with us. And why is that? Because we have carefully cultivated your liberal news media to see things from our point of view. And it is they who forge public opinion, gringo. And we mustn't forget your grand movie stars. Oh, yes, we remember Jane Fonda. Year after year, we bring them to Nicaragua and wine and dine them. Daniel does a good job. And why? Because the average, dull-witted, beer guzzling American hangs on their every word. Yes, we have studied well the psychology of your famous personalities. We know of their natural tendency to feel guilty about their wealth, and we give them an opportunity for atonement. And as for your news media, we have played on their natural distrust of government. Plant a few false seeds and the rich fools will grow a forest where there is none. So, Eden, we have done well, no? Ha, ha. Ha.

"And, gringo, we mustn't forget your own Congress. Our supporters in the Senate and the House are many. And they are the biggest jokes of all. But be sure, they will be the first to go. Once a traitor, always a traitor. But most of all, we have the Party on our side. The Party's lust for power has made it our greatest ally. Politicians can always be counted on to put the Party before your country. No, my gringo friend, the Party will tie the hands of your president. It will try to destroy him and, in doing so, it will destroy your country's ability to conduct an effective foreign policy, which is exactly what we want. You were right, gringo. We are like our friends in Vietnam. Look at what happened there. You were not defeated on the battlefield. You were defeated by the Party and by the news media. We have learned well from that history lesson."

In the distance, David heard Jake start the engines of The Eagle. The sound woke him, took him away from the trance-like stare of Rafael's eyes. He turned to Steelhammer and Pastora. It was time to go.

But he couldn't help himself. He turned to Rafael. "You can never defeat us on the battlefield."

"Mexico. Your defeat will come across the border in human waves that you will find impossible to defeat. But you will be there. And I will be there. So, gringo, I will see you soon in the streets of El Paso."

Steelhammer handed David a duffle bag as he started up the ramp to The Eagle. "Shaped charges," he shouted to be heard over the whining of the engines. "Just put them next to what you want to blow up and pull the pin. Thought you might need them."

"Yeah," David replied.

All around the whirling chopper, the band of fighters they had brought from Honduras stood holding their jungle hats and waving.

David waved back. From inside the cockpit, Jake gave them a thumbs-up.

Pastora stepped up from the crowd and shook David's hand. He smiled, and then, without saying a word, he disappeared into the smoke of the base camp.

"What will happen to him?" David asked.

Steelhammer turned away toward the base camp for a moment then back to David. "He'll fight on for awhile. But unless I can convince others to back him, he'll run out of ammo, food, everything. Then he'll be forced to make a choice of being an ex-patriot, or . . ."

"Or what?"

"Going back."

"They'd kill him."

Steelhammer shook his head. "He's still a national hero to the Nicaraguan people. His returning to the Sandinista camp would be a public relations and propaganda coup. No, they'd take him back in an instant. That's why, after a while, he'll release Rafael unharmed."

"What about you?" David asked, with a look of concern.

Steelhammer took notice of the look. "I've got a job to do back in Washington and elsewhere. I'll be all right.'"

"But if anyone ever found out what you're doing here?"

"I'm expendable. Others aren't."

"Well, goodbye, and . . ."

"Listen, major," Steelhammer said holding David by the arm, "she's an American. I understand."

David nodded silently and closed the door. He gave Jake the all clear and The Eagle lifted off and sped away from the jungle canopy toward the end of the earth.

Chapter 49

Bogota, Columbia

The mountains and forests of Costa Rica, a brown slither of land six hundred fifty kilometers long, passed swiftly under The Eagle. From a height of eight thousand feet, Jake could clearly see the Caribbean Ocean outside his window and the Pacific starboard, both gray, hazy lakes that spread across the curved horizon. He checked his instruments. He had been putting a lot of demands on this complicated, easily disturbed machine, but so far she had held her own. What was it God said about eagles?

The beauty unfolding below was lost on David. Darkly, he brooded while the others slept in the rear of the cabin. He had troubling thoughts. There was no proof Doc had anything to do with Chip's death. There was only the persistent circumstantial thoughts that kept gathering in the back of his mind, almost a collective sixth sense.

"That's Golfo Dulce over there on the right," Jake told David as he gently banked The Eagle away from the land. "The Panamanian border is just ten nauticals away. I'll be heading out over the ocean now." The helicopter flew for thirty minutes over the blue-gray water, then Jake switched a navigation radio to the Bogota frequency. Slowly he turned The Eagle until the direction finder and the azimuth indicator pointed to the correct heading. "Next stop, Bogota, Columbia, the cocaine capital of the world," he said over the intercom speaker.

In the back, Doc lit another cigar and let out a big laugh.

But Jake had kept from the others a secret. This flight from San Juan del Sur to Bogota would be almost eight hundred miles. Even by using the external fuel tanks, reducing power to sixty percent, and flying at twenty thousand feet in order to lean the fuel, The Eagle should run out of gas right over the airport. But it was a chance that had to be taken, he reasoned, for with each passing day the hope of reaching Los Estados before Sunny was killed was slowly fading. He pressed on toward the mark. The flight, slow and often bumpy, lasted almost four hours.

From their vantage point high up in the air, Bogota looked like any other large sprawling city. Situated in a valley surrounded by high mountains, it seemed isolated from the rest of the countryside. The air map showed only one major highway leading into and out of the city. Along the sides of the mountains that surrounded Bogota were clusters of slum communities that held the majority of its population, the outcasts of the booming drug trade. Not far from the city were the poppy fields.

Jake obtained permission to land and set The Eagle up for an approach to the airport. He had been right; no questions were asked. He hovered over the tarmac until the ground radio gave him taxi instructions. Slowly he inched his way across the asphalt surface to the fuel pumps as his fuel level indicator light blinked on and off, indicating he was out of fuel. Running on empty. "How's your money holding out?" he asked David.

"Just fill her up," David replied tersely.

Jake did just that then parked the chopper next to a hangar where he could begin his maintenance work right away.

David called everyone together in the cabin. With the exception of Doc, they all had tired, dull looks on their faces. Doc's predator's stare, he noted, was as menacing as ever. He knew that now would be the most difficult time to hold them together. Just after a firefight, after a unit had taken casualties, morale was at its lowest. "We'll stay here in the aircraft. I don't want any of the authorities to become suspicious. Remember, Columbia is crawling with BNDD agents."

"How about food?" Pratt asked.

"We'll send someone out. There should be a café or something near the airport. Bill, tonight you'll go." Force nodded.

"David, what if the authorities should come over here and check our passports? We obviously have none," Perez said.

In reply, David simply held up a wad of money.

"Jake, how long?" David asked.

"Tomorrow at dawn, we're out of here."

"From here, run through the flight plan Jake," David ordered. *Keep your men informed* – one of the principles of leadership, David thought.

"I've made some slight variations based on The Eagle's performance," Jake said. "We'll fly out of here and refuel in Lima, Peru. From there, we have four more refueling stops until we land at Nueva Island, our jumping off point to Los Estados."

"In what country or countries are the refueling points located?" Perez asked, lighting his pipe.

"All in Chile."

"How long a flight to Nueva?" David asked anxiously.

"No more than fifteen hours. About three hours a hop between fuelings."

David turned his head. They were only two days away from Los Estados. *Sunny, my love, hold on.*

Darkness found the men sleeping after a filling meal of beans and rice, bread, and wine that Force had procured from an open air restaurant two blocks away from the airport. Jake had already changed the oil and pulled the normal maintenance inspection with help from Pratt, who seemed to have taken an unusual interest in the workings of The Eagle's two engines. The Eagle was fit for duty. Tomorrow would be good flying. Tonight, he needed to rest.

With the stealth of an alley cat, Doc raised his massive head. All the others appeared to be fast asleep. He looked down at his watch; 0100 hours. Slowly he inched his way up and, taking light steps, made his way out of The Eagle and into the moonlit night. He caught a cab at the airport's entrance and, in halting Spanish, told the driver to take him to a villa on the outskirts of the city. The driver gave him a sharp look but, after eyeing him, quickly turned back around and did as he was told. The drive through a sleepy deserted Bogota was familiar. Dim lights, smoky streets, the occasional bum, a lone unconcerned police car on fake patrol. The place wasn't healthy enough to stay up past midnight. All the real action took place inside the affluent haciendas and villas. Carlos would be surprised to see him. But Doc needed a hit. And he needed it now.

The hacienda, enclosed behind twelve foot high walls made of reinforced concrete covered with plaster and painted a mauve color, was situated high on a hill overlooking the airport's runways. It was a marvelous sight, the airport. Red guide slope and green threshold lights accentuated the long white lines of the runways that were intersected by zig zag corridors of blue taxi lights. It was as if Carlos had his own ornate neon sign right outside his patio. The taxi came to a dusty halt next to two large dark metal doors at the only entrance to the hacienda. The driver tipped his hat after Doc rewarded him handsomely, then drove off leaving Doc standing before the doors, alone and unafraid. He pushed the talk button located on the wall next to the doors. The voice of a woman, silky and sweet, inquired of his intentions. He told her he needed to see Carlos. And he told her who he was. After five minutes, the doors swung open. Two neatly dressed men armed with Uzi machine guns invited him in and, after thoroughly searching him, offered him a seat by a large pool located in the courtyard. He waited by the pool as the moon reflecting off the surface of its placid water provided the courtyard's only source of light.

Presently there appeared before him a thin man, dark and tall. He wore an open white dinner jacket and dark pants. He was barefoot and had strung over his neck several gold chains. His face was clean shaven and narrow. A thin lipped smile came across his face as he came to recognize Doc. His eyes were bright and blue. He smelled of just-had sex. He smelled of the tall woman who stood by his side. Doc was struck by her beauty. She was wearing a long white robe that barely concealed her erect breasts and fell just above her thin, suntanned ankles. Her face was smooth and brown and she had high, almost aristocratic, cheekbones. Her full cherry lips were drawn tight as she gazed down at him with saucer eyes, brown and unrevealing. But he was struck by something else besides her beauty. This woman was not a whore. No, this woman was with Carlos because she wanted to be, not simply because Carlos wished it. *So, Carlos can get fo' himself a woman like her*, he thought. *Maybe there's more to this boy than what goes up his nose.*

"What are you doing here in Columbia, my friend?" Carlos cried, feigning happiness. He raised his arms and he and Doc embraced.

"Business," Doc replied evenly, letting go and stepping back.

Carlos opened a gold case and held it level. On the inside of one flap was a mirror. The inside of the other flap held a transparent plastic pouch. Gently, with a spooned out gold cross that hung from a chain around his neck, he took some of the powdery substance from the pouch and offered it to Doc. He nodded and stepped forward. Bending down, he sniffed the white powder up into his nostrils.

"Now, my friend, what business brings you to Bogota?" Carlos asked laconically in a creamy voice, taking note of Doc's manner of dress. Usually, Doc dressed in a fashion befitting his stature and position. But the Doc who now sat before him wore dirty jeans, a sweatshirt, and jungle boots. And he smelled. Something was wrong. Carlos sniffed the air.

Doc gave the girl a look then turned back to Carlos.

"She can be trusted," Carlos said flatly.

"Personal business. Nothin' but personal business. But I need some snort. Didn't wanna take a chance on customs."

"But of course. Why didn't you say so?" Carlos said then summoned one of his men and told him to bring Doc a small bag of cocaine. After a few minutes, the man returned. "Here, my friend. It's on the house," Carlos said. "Now tell me, how did you arrive? When is your flight out? Maybe I can provide a woman for you if there is time."

"I got here by helicopter. Leave at sunrise."

"But why not stay a while?" Carlos said, smiling.

Doc didn't answer. He just gave Carlos a cold stare.

Carlos stiffened, then threw up his hands. "Enough of this. What are friends for? I am honored you would consider coming to me for your needs. After all, when I come to America I have always done the same to you. So my friend, when shall we do business again?"

"Soon, Carlos. Very soon."

"You will of course allow my driver to return you to your helicopter?

"I insist on it."

0500 hours, David thought groggily, looking at his Rolex. He raised up. Everyone seemed fast asleep. Jake lay on the floor of the cockpit, his sleeping bag wrapped around him. Pratt and Force lay against each other wrapped in blankets. Perez was slumped between two seats covered by a parka. And Doc lay still next to the door in the aisle. He almost hated to wake them, but it was time to go. Then he hesitated. One more hour might help. He fell back asleep.

David knew instantly what it was he felt. He had felt its cold steel before. The gun was placed against the back of his head, and next came strangely pleasant words. They were those of a woman. She spoke firmly, but her voice was silky, almost mellow. "Quietly, gringo. No words. No shouts, or I'll pull this trigger."

David rose up ever so carefully. Within seconds, the helicopter was stormed by armed men brandishing Uzis and AK47s and shouting in English for everyone to rise and put their hands over their heads. *A police raid*, David thought. *Somehow they have discovered us. But why would the police be wearing balaclava head gear covering their faces?* It wasn't the police. He was roughly shoved along with the others toward the rear of the cabin. Ten or twelve men and women held them at bay with weapons drawn at waist level. Jake was dragged out of the cockpit and slammed into a seat. He heard someone ask Jake if he was the pilot, but he didn't hear Jake's answer.

Then the woman who had put the gun to David's head spoke to them. She stood directly in the center of the aisle, her gun held in the air. "We are members of Movimiento 19 de Abril, M-19, you gringos call us. And we are commandeering this aircraft in the name of the people of Columbia."

"You're not taking this helicopter anywhere, bitch," Jake shouted from his seat.

The woman lifted up her balaclava and gave him a sharp look. "We'll see about that. Juan," she shouted.

Instantly, one of the men grabbed Perez and threw him on the floor. Without being told, the man put the barrel of his Uzi at the base of Perez's head.

"David!" Perez shouted.

"No," David shouted, "we're yours."

But the woman and her companions seemed bent on a demonstration of their power and resolve. Jake sensed this at the same time as David. Perez was going to be killed. Just to make a point.

"He's a priest," David said quickly.

The girl shot him a questioning look then muttered something to one of the men standing next to her. "Juan," she said again, "another."

Before Juan could grab Pratt, Jake stood up. "You got a pilot, bitch? Huh? You got a pilot? You kill one of them and you can fly this thing into hell for all I care. What do you think we are? A bunch of fucking tourists? Think again, bitch. We eat whores and queers like you for lunch. So go ahead, bitch. Kill somebody."

The woman stared at Jake and saw the resolve in his eyes. For a moment, there was complete silence as she pondered her next move. Then she ordered Julio to let go of Pratt's shirt sleeve. "Fly this thing and you will live," she said with a trace of reluctance in her voice.

"Where to, bitch?" Jake asked, a sarcastic smile on his face.

"I will tell you in time," she said quietly as she turned to the others and gave them a menacing look.

As her eyes met Doc's, a look of mutual recognition passed between them – a fact that did not go unnoticed by David.

Chapter 50

```
Mitu, Columbia
600 statute miles from the nearest civilization
```

The Vaupes River, a deep, unchartered, swift tributary of the Negro and Amazon Rivers, runs from far inside the rain forest of Brazil, through the town of Mitu, then dead ends nearly two hundred miles from Bogota in the quicksand of some of the densest, most treacherous jungle in the world. This stark fact caught Jake's attention as he scanned his Columbian air map after he was given orders by a swarthy terrorist named Bingo to fly to Mitu. He laughed because, for a moment, he thought Bingo was joking. That is, until Bingo hit him across the face with the butt of his Uzi. Jake picked up the map and, after his eyes had retained their ability to focus, charted a course to Mitu. Mitu was situated on the border between Brazil and Columbia. The nearest road was six hundred miles to the west, making Mitu one of the most isolated spots in the world.

    Civilization should have bypassed Mitu, but late in the nineteenth century Spanish and European jungle traders from Brazil established a trading post along a flat bend in the river in order to barter with the prehistoric jungle Indian tribes for skins, jewels, and heads – a business practice that still flourished. They named the bend Mitu: The Place of Myths.

As Jake whirled The Eagle over the seemingly endless jungle canopy, he had the feeling of traveling back in time for below lay before him what could have been the tropical jungles of Laos or Cambodia. At any moment he expected to see an LZ marked by smoke and some desperate SOG or MAT team waving him in. *Anything for the troops on the ground.* And he had another familiar, disturbing thought: as before, if they went down, no one would ever hear of them again. *Keaton*, he thought, *we're flying on a wing and a prayer.*

David had been singled out by M-19 as the leader of the group. The woman had correctly deduced this after noting the way he was treated by the others, and this seemed to puzzle her. She had at first thought Doc would have been the leader. She was also curious to know what this group of men was doing in Columbia. If not drugs, then what? With Doc, Perez, Pratt, and Force confined under guard in the rear of the cabin, the woman ordered David brought to the front of the cabin near the restrooms.

A guard shoved him into a seat in front of her, and for a moment she simply studied him. The man before her was obviously no soldier of fortune. He had the serious look of a man of character, character that could have been forged only through hard and dangerous experience. He was not CIA. He looked too determined, too natural to danger and adversity. A spy would want to blend in, not stand out. And he was not a drug runner. She had experience with them. This man and those with him were on a mission of some importance. But what? "Who are you?" she asked in a non-threatening manner.

David looked up at her. "You speak excellent English."

"Who are you?" she simply repeated, her voice a monotone.

"Who are you?" David shot back.

"M-19."

"I mean, who are *you?* What is your name?"

"Maria."

"David Elliot."

"And what are you doing in Columbia, David Elliot?"

"Buying aviation fuel." He quickly realized his answer may have appeared unnecessarily sarcastic, so he went on. "I'm sorry," he said apologetically, "but it's the truth. My friends and I stopped in Bogota only to refuel and perform some necessary work on the helicopter."

"If that is so, why did the doctor visit Carlos?"

At that, David eyes lit up.

She was taken aback for a moment. She could see by his reaction that he knew nothing about the doctor's visit. "I see," she said, giving him a questioning look. "How much do you know about your friend the doctor?" she asked politely.

"Not much of late," he replied hesitantly.

"I don't understand."

"We, all of us except for the priest, once soldiered together in Vietnam. Up until a couple of weeks ago, I had not seen any of them for over ten years."

"So, why have you and the doctor come to Columbia?"

He didn't answer her. Instead, he gave her a chagrined look. "Look, Maria, you said Doc visited a man named Carlos. When did this happen and who is Carlos?"

"I ask the questions here, *gringo*," she snapped.

He grimaced. From his studies at the War College he knew about the political philosophy of M-19, as well as other groups in the area. A Marxist-Leninist revolutionary group founded in 1974, it had about two thousand hardcore members and another three or four thousand sympathizers in and outside of Columbia. It specialized in a lucrative form of terror called narcoterrorism, the trading of narcotics for guns and explosives and other operating expenses. M-19 operatives sold drugs directly in the U.S. as well as through middlemen such as Jaime Guilloy Lara, the drug kingpin who was the liaison between M-19 and Cuba. M-19 was the smallest of the three communist terrorist organizations operating in Columbia, but it was the most violent. Yes, they would kill him and the others without any urging whatsoever.

He started to speak, but stopped. *Maybe*, he though confidently, *I might be able to make them think we are allies.* "We are going to fly down to Argentina and set free a political dissident who has been imprisoned by the secret police," he stated, looking her directly in the eyes.

"And why would you do that?" she asked, turning her head slightly and eyeing him wryly.

"Because she's my wife."

He thought he saw her lips betray a faint smile. "Do you really expect me to believe that?" she asked haughtily.

"Maybe not. But it's the truth," he said without emotion.

"You and this small band of mercenaries, which includes a Roman Catholic priest, have flown all the way from America?" She gave the others a turned up, disbelieving look.

"We are not mercenaries," David said.

"And your plan is to attack a prison in Argentina controlled by the Group?'

She knows of the Group! "Yes."

"With a priest?"

"Yes."

"She must be some woman," she said, a trace of unmistakable jealousy in her voice.

He did not reply.

"And you obtained this machine how?"

"Stolen."

She laughed, throwing back her head. "Then you are *banditos* instead of mercenaries."

"No," he said firmly, "we are neither."

"No, gringo. You and your companions, especially that one," she said contemptuously looking at Doc, "are scum. American gringo scum. The same type of macho gringos who have enslaved the peoples of Latin America for centuries."

He was determined to chance a question. "Why are you taking us to this town?"

"We are not taking you anywhere. We are taking this machine, or should I say this machine is taking us, to Mitu where it will be our pleasure to kill a rival group that has been cutting into our business. You, gringo, and your scum are just along for the ride."

"And after Mitu?"

"You will have the pleasure of accompanying us back to Bogota."

He gave her a casual look and slumped back in his seat. "Tell me how you know Doc. What harm can it do?" She would have been much more beautiful than she was, he thought, had she not assumed such an aggressive personality. He tried to imagine how she might appear in an evening dress, but he couldn't hold the thought.

She seemed to ponder the request for a moment. Then she spoke chidingly. "Don't you know, gringo? He is one of the leading narcotics dealers on the west coast of America."

He turned to Doc. *Yes,* he thought, *you led them to us. If anyone makes it out of here alive, it'll be you, won't it?*

As if reading his thoughts, Maria spoke up. "He did not betray you. I was at Carlos's villa when he came sniffing around hoping Carlos would feed his habit. The rest was easy. You and your band of men and this machine came along just at the right time. Helicopters of this size are hardly readily available in South America. I would like to know how you got away with stealing it."

"Maybe I will tell you. Later."

Maria chuckled. "Tell me how many times and where you have stopped since you left the United States?"

"Mexico, Honduras . . ."

"There is much happening there," she said, interrupting him and turning away as if the thought hurt her.

He sensed an opening. He knew he had to get inside her head, because he knew a bullet was waiting for each of them upon their return to Bogota. "Met an interesting man there. His name is Pastora."

As if stung, Maria gasped and swung around toward him with a surprised, shocked look on her face. "Where did you see this man?" she said breathlessly. "Tell me. Where?"

Seeking to expand on this possible opening, he continued. "We fought with him."

"Do not lie to me, or I will kill you right now."

"We flew him into Managua where he executed a raid. Then we flew him back into the jungle. I don't know where."

She seemed both confused and hurt. For a moment he thought he noticed tears welling in her eyes. "Is he all right?" she asked, lot looking at him.

"Yes."

Then, just as unexpectedly as before, she shot him a snarling glare. "He would have never been your comrade! How did you come to be with him?"

He measured her. No, this evil woman lacked any compassion. There was no opening. There never would be one with her. Yes, she knew Pastora. But he doubted Pastora would have benefited much from that experience. "He asked for the pleasure of our company in the same manner as you."

She gave him a cruel smile. "Yes, of course," she said spitefully. "Now go back to your comrades, gringo."

Maria joined Bingo in the cockpit. After putting on the headphones, she spoke to Jake in a forceful voice. "Mitu is an armpit, but it has one tantalizing characteristic: It is isolated. In fact, so isolated that government troops would never dare to conduct a raid there. In Mitu is a place where plants are processed into usable drugs for shipment to American schoolyards." She let the thought stay with Jake for a second. "We will get you one way or the other, gringo. But for now, my men and I are going to destroy this factory because its owners have not agreed to see the world in terms agreeable to us. You will put this machine down in a field located on a cul de sac in the river. About a half mile from that field, through the jungle, is the factory. You will wait until we have destroyed the factory and then you will fly us back to Bogota. *Comprendie?*"

"Look," he said, "we don't have enough fuel to make it back to Bogota."

"There is a usable strip located just outside of Mitu. Aviation fuel is available there. Many Lear jets and other turbo-prop aircraft land in Mitu in order to ply the drug trade."

"Money. You know? *Dinero*. It takes *dinero* to buy fuel."

"This will get you your fuel," she said, holding up her AK-47.

"Shit," Jake said and adjusted his altimeter setting.

"Just in case you have any stupid ideas, we will take Mr. Elliot and that one along," Maria said, pointing to Force.

"I gotcha bitch. I gotcha," Jake said under his breath.

The Doppler instrument on The Eagle began to beep indicating that, based on the data Jake had fed into it, they were only five minutes out of Mitu. "*Cinco minuto, asshole,*" Jake said to Bingo, holding up five fingers.

Bingo gave Jake a half smile, unstrapped himself, and ran with Maria back to the cabin. David watched as Bingo told Maria and her men something before returning to the cockpit. A flurry of activity told him they were near their objective.

Maria bent over David. "You and this one," indicating Force, "are coming with us. This will insure this machine will still be here when we return."

"But why take him?" David asked, referring to Force. "I won't be in the way, but two of us?"

"Shut up, gringo, and get up. Both of you, get up!" Maria shouted, pointing her weapon at them.

David and Force stood up.

David turned to Perez, Pratt, and Doc. In whispered tones they began to talk. "They want you to stay here. But after we're gone, make up your own minds," David said.

"Won't they leave a guard?" Pratt asked.

"They don't have enough men for that," Doc said with authority.

"David, what if you and Bill don't return?" Perez asked nervously.

"You'll know what to do," David said, giving each man a stern look.

Jake banked The Eagle hard to his left after Bingo pointed out the flat cul de sac. He was going to come in fast and low. *Might even scare the bastards*, he thought happily. Bingo gave him a nervous look after he felt his stomach go up into his throat. "Ever been in a hot LZ, motherfucker?" he said, grinning at Bingo. "Naw. You ain't got the balls for it." He took pleasure in seeing the sweat pour down Bingo's face.

Mitu was located eight miles from the earth's equator. As David and Force were rushed off The Eagle, a humid gush of air nearly knocked them down with its furnace-like heat. As Jake shut down the engines he saw the guerrillas disappear into a cavern-like trail that seemed literally cut through the jungle, and with them David and Force. After he had switched everything off, he unstrapped himself from his seat and hurried back to the others who were standing forlornly outside the aircraft.

"Shit," Pratt said in disgust. "We keep getting in deeper and deeper. What if they don't come back?"

"If they don't be back, we get the hell out of here," Doc said between puffs on his cigar.

"You forget, Doc, that I'm the only one who can get us out of here. So you better ask me what we're going to do," Jake announced.

"Listen, all you bastards. We better start plannin' somethin' now.

They gonna kill us all as soon as we get back to Bogota. I know 'em. I know 'em all," Doc said.

The others were quiet. They knew that Doc was right.

"They'll be back. I know they'll be back," Jake said desperately. "I'm going to return to the cockpit and wait there so I can get us up when they get back. The major will figure a way out of this. He will. I know he will."

David and Force were being pushed from behind as the guerrillas moved over the trail at a dead, almost reckless run. David noticed that the jungle on either side of the trail was impassable. It would take a tank to cut a trail through it. He wondered how long it had taken the drug dealers to cut this one. As if the jungle resented the intrusion of the path, it was completely covered with an entwined canopy of heavy branches and thick vines that all but blocked out the burning sun. The air inside the cave-like trail was thick with the putrid smell of rotting jungle. It was suffocating. After about five minutes, Maria halted them. David could see her whispering something into the ear of one of her men.

"Must be close," Force said.

"Wonder how many they're going up against," David said.

Force just shook his head.

"You two shut your mouths," Maria snarled as Bingo grabbed David by the arm and shoved him forward.

Up ahead David could see what appeared to be an opening. The guerrillas saw it too and began to run for it, their guns at the ready. Like swimmers coming up for air, they suddenly shot out of the canopied trail. The air was hot, but invigorating but, before David could catch his breath, Bingo slammed him and Force to the ground as the guerrillas started firing their AK-47s and Uzis in all directions. David raised up from the dirt and watched. The camp they were attacking was nothing more than a series of elongated wood huts with corrugated tin roofs. Inside the huts were various cooking devices with large vats and glass urns. He couldn't make out any detail of the rest of what was inside the huts, but his sense of smell picked up a sweet pungent smelling essence that permeated the grounds. The firing was loud and quick. M-19 and the drug runners were in a pitched gunfight at close range. Screams of agony filled the air as men and women tore into each other with a savagery that sent cold chills up his back.

Maria squatted behind David and Force, but for the moment her interest lay in the actions of her men. She jerked and shook with each burst of fire. At times she seemed ready to plunge into the fray but stood her ground, her weapon still aimed at David and Force, even though her eyes flitted from one duel to another.

Then not more than ten yards from where they were, Bingo's brains were splattered across the matted earth as he caught a burst from some unseen automatic weapon's fire. As he fell to the ground with a horrible, rolling, rag doll-like motion, his mouth flew open and his teeth dug into the dirt. Maria let out a scream as she gazed at Bingo's open-eyed death stare.

Force sensed his chance. With a swift backhanded motion, his fist found Maria's face. With a smack and a flop, she fell over on her back. "Let's go!" he screamed.

David turned to see Maria lying helpless on the ground with Force crouched over her body, her weapon in his hands, and he jumped up quickly. Force headed out in front of him back into the dark cave-like trail, but David stopped. The firing was becoming more sporadic, which meant M-19 was mopping up. As soon as they started the burning, they would notice Maria and come after them. Jake would never be able to get the engine started in time. He put his arm around Maria's waist and dragged her with them into the trail.

Force stopped when he realized David wasn't behind him and waited. He was startled to see him dragging Maria. "Are you crazy?"

"Let's hope they have a certain amount of loyalty to her in case they catch up with us before we can lift off," David said, his voice labored with Maria's weight.

Force thought for a second. "Right."

They headed back down the trail with Force covering their rear. After they had gone about two hundred yards, the firing ceased.

"Oh, shit!" Force said. "At least some of them will be coming after us now."

David grunted. Maria was starting to wake up. "She's coming to," he said, and let her fall at his feet.

Groggily, Maria rose up on one elbow. At first, she was disoriented, confused. Then she realized what had happened and tried to jump up, but David's foot caught her in the solar plexus. With a gasp and a cough, she fell back to the jungle floor.

"Don't try to get up," he said flatly.

She raised her head, her hair falling around her face, a hateful, snarling look on her face. Almost spitting at him she said, "You had better be prepared to shoot me, gringo, because I will go no further." David knew by the determined look on her face that she spoke the truth.

Force stood behind him, an anxious look on his face. "Major, for God's sake." He took David by the arm and looked him in the eyes. "We've got to get the hell out of here!"

David looked down at Maria. "Give me the gun," he ordered Force.

Force hesitated for a second, but David's voice was commanding. "Force!"

Force handed David the Uzi. Slowly, he aimed the barrel of the Uzi at Maria's face. She stared wide-eyed at him for a moment then turned her head away and waited. As he stared down the barrel of the weapon he could hear General Knott's voice. What had he said when he had last seen him? *Duty. It's duty that makes an officer. Duty*, he had said. *If I had done my duty and shot Jude, my whole life would have turned out differently. I . . .would have . . .*

He shoved the Uzi back into Force's arms, gabbed Maria under the arms, and held her up to his face. Only a breath apart, she gazed at him, not comprehending. Then he pushed her away and hit her as hard as he could on the jaw. She fell over spread eagled on the ground. He turned to Force who was gaping down to Maria.

"Hey!" David shouted. "Let's get the hell out of here." Force grinned and followed David down the path.

After another hundred yards, David heard shouts coming from behind them.

"You hear that?" he heard Force shout from behind.

"Yes," he answered, out of breath.

"Stop!" Force shouted.

David stopped and turned around. Force stood about ten feet away from him, his feet spread apart, the Uzi held up at shoulder level. Even in the dim light of the path, David could make out a grim, tightlipped look of fear on Force's face. "What's the matter?" David asked, coming back to him.

"We'll never make it," Force said faintly.

"What?"

"They'll get us before we get off the ground. They're so close we can hear them."

"Well, let's quit wasting time talking about it and get out of here."

"No. One of us has to cover the withdrawal."

"Bill, what are you talking about?"

"You covered us on Nui Ta Bec. It was the only thing you could have done."

"That was . . ."

"I know what has to be done, major. Now go."

"Force!"

"Major, you know what I'm saying is true. Do you want to save your wife or not? If someone doesn't stay behind and give Jake enough time to get airborne, she's dead. She'll die and all of this would have been for naught. Chip's death will mean nothing. Now get moving and get out of here."

"Bill."

"Don't. There's no need."

Tears came to David's eyes as he stared at this huge man for what he knew would be the last time. He hung his head and clenched his fists. Then he screamed and ran toward the waiting helicopter.

Force crouched down next to the ground. He could hear the running footsteps of the men of M-19 approaching.

"Bill."

"Who is it?" Force managed to say, looking from side to side in hopes of finding the source of the voice. The underbrush rustled and parted and a figure emerged from its darkness. In the dim light Force could not make out who it was. Then the figure crawled along the floor of the jungle path and squatted down next to him.

Force was awestruck once he recognized the man. "Keaton! Where did . . . how did you get here? Where?"

"They're safe," Keaton said.

In the distance, Force heard Jake start up the engines of The Eagle.

"Keaton, you can't stay here. Men are coming down this trail. Now. They'll kill you if you stay here."

"But, you are staying?"

"Yes, I must. But you must leave at once."

Keaton turned to Force. Slowly, his features became clearly visible in the dim light. From him emanated an iridescent glow, warm and mellow, and suddenly Force was no longer afraid. Keaton was with him, and because of that he felt whole and secure.

"Are you sure you want to stay here with me?" Force asked mournfully.

Keaton reached out and touched Force's shoulder, and a warm radiating feeling flowed through his body. "Yes," he said. "I am here. We shall meet these men together, these men who are the followers of the *Ruler of the Earth*. But be not afraid. They cannot harm you for you are a man of my own heart. You have served me well on this earth. You chose to be one of my children, to take up a profession that I ordained with my honor. And although the Ruler of Darkness has turned many of your brothers and sisters in uniform to his way because he fears them most, you were not swayed by his temptations and remained a child of mine.

"So, now is the time of peril for you. I say, do not fear, for in a few short moments you will be with me in paradise forever."

In the distance, Force heard Jake lift off just as the first terrorist burst down the trail with his weapon blazing.

Chapter 51

Punta Arenas, Chile

Jake had used money rather than the barrel of a gun to get fuel at the Mitu strip. An Indian gas pumper had chatted in pidgin English about the enormity of The Eagle as he gave the team confused and often frightened looks as explosion after explosion erupted from deep inside the jungle down river. It seemed that the Devil was loose in Columbia. After having to once more patiently explain the flight plan to the team, especially to Pratt, who was beside himself with anxiety over the loss of Force, Jake had lifted off, aimed the nose of The Eagle for Bogota, and set the engines for maximum power.

There had been three refueling stops after their brief turn around in Bogota. The first had been in Lima, Peru where they had snuck in under the haze of dusk, fueled in twenty minutes, and flown off again before any questions could be asked. The second had been in Antofagasta, Chile where they had been inspected by a not too interested military police contingent. After all, the tall captain had explained, Americans were liked by the Pinochet regime. The third had been in the nearly deserted town of Lota, Chile where they had been forced to wait nearly four hours for someone to come to the airport and turn on the pumps. At each stop, David made had sure that no one, most of all Doc, strayed from the aircraft. During the ten hour jaunt they dined once again on C-rations and agreed to find rooms once they landed in Punta Arenas.

They would stay at Punta Arenas until the morning of the thirtieth when they would lift off, fueled, fed, and bathed, for Nueva Island, just two hundred forty miles away.

There they would wait for the sign.

The often bumpy flight down to Punta Arenas had taken them over some of the most breathtaking terrain in the world. The Andes mountain range had flowed majestically under the belly of their aircraft, a thin ribbed beauty lying provocatively next to a blue sea. Alluring, sultry, and dangerous. Quietly, as Jake cruised at an altitude of twenty-seven thousand feet, they had watched a majestic spectacle unfold below: a primeval landscape of volcanoes such as the frozen Cotopaxi with its cone of fire, the highest active volcano in the world; salt lakes trapped between towering mountains such as Illumine, that stands guard over La Pazl; and the eerie El Misti, a snow capped peak that rises out of a desert.

But for David, Perez, and Pratt, most of this beauty had gone unappreciated; their mood was one of sadness and foreboding over the loss of Force. David could sense a questioning of intent and purpose rising among them. No one had said anything, not even the normally verbose and confrontational Pratt, but he could feel what they were thinking, could see it in their eyes. And these feelings were compounded by his now obvious contempt for Doc. Unhappily, he found himself once more doubting the wisdom of Doc's continued presence among them, which amounted to questioning Keaton's judgment. It was a feeling he knew he would have to deal with before it compromised his own judgment, which was all that was keeping him sane.

They had been anchored in Punta Arenas for two days now. The Eagle had been fueled and was waiting at the airport, a towerless, two thousand foot asphalt runway located on the town's shoreline. Punta Arenas flowed along the slope of a hill that ended up being the north shore of the Estrecho de Magallanes, the Straight of Magellan, a thin, narrow troth of water that cut through the southern tip of Chile and Argentina and allowed smaller ships to bypass the treacherous waters of Cape Horn. Punta Arenas had a population of about thirty thousand, mostly fishermen and those whose trades catered to fishermen. From what David had observed, the townspeople were a hearty lot who seemed to mind their own business and were tolerant of Americans who landed great white helicopters at their isolated airport without so much as giving them a rich gringo's reason for their visit.

The weather had changed. A cold Antarctic wind had met them as they had first stepped somewhat shakily from the helicopter. Showing good judgment, they had gone back in and broken out the winter parkas.

After Jake had tended to The Eagle, they had taken three rooms at a boarding house that sat conspicuously on the side of a hill that overlooked the runway and the parked Eagle. David and Perez shared a room, as did Pratt and Jake. Doc, as expected, insisted on having his own room. As no one else wanted to be near him, David acquiesced.

Several good meals from the house proprietors and hot baths had helped their morale somewhat, but David knew what was really needed was frank talk. They gathered in his room on the evening of their second day there. "Tomorrow we leave for Nueva Island," he said. "From there, Los Estados is only a thirty minute flight away."

"David, let us stop for a moment and take stock of our situation," Perez said beseechingly, "which is perhaps dictating that we are less than capable of continuing on with this venture as each day passes."

"For God's sake, major, listen to the priest," Pratt said.

Before David could reply to Perez, Jake spoke up. "Uh, just why are we less than capable?"

"Well, maybe if you'd have gotten out of your flight helmet once in a while you'd have noticed we're now short two men." Pratt said contemptuously.

Jake gave Pratt a fierce look. "You think it's been easy for me," he asked, "to fly all the way down the length of the earth knowing that I've lost two friends along the way?"

"Stop it!" David ordered. "Just for a moment, Pratt, think about why they died."

"All right. Why did they die?" Pratt asked with a smirk, jumping up.

"Sit down, boy," Doc growled.

Doc wants to go ahead. He doesn't seem to question anything at all. But why? David thought.

Pratt meekly sat back down.

"Chip and Force died," David continued, "for something they believed in. No one had to convince them of the correctness of the task they were undertaking."

"Are we, at this late date, debating the correctness of what we are doing, or are we debating our ability to do it?" Jake asked.

"I say both," Pratt said quickly.

Jake then turned to David. "Major, it *can* still be done, can't it?"

"Yes," David replied, smiling at Jake. "Three of us can assault the villas while Perez remains with you and protects the helicopter. There are very few guards on duty at any given time. With the explosive devices Steelhammer gave us, we can blow our way in and free her."

"And we've got to do it all in just fifteen minutes. That's all the fuel we can burn up idling and still make it back here," Jake stated pointedly.

"I say we put it to a vote," Pratt said.

"Ain't no democracies down here, asshole," Doc spit.

"Okay, a vote," David said.

"I say go!" declared Jake.

"Yeah, let's go," Doc said through the cigar between his lips.

Perez gave David a blank stare. "My vote doesn't matter. I'm just along for the ride." David nodded.

"I say no!" Pratt said emphatically.

"You outvoted, queer bait," Doc said laughingly

"You're going to get us all killed, major," Pratt said excitedly, almost whining. "Will that make you happy? Chip and Force, weren't they enough for you? Just how much is that woman down there worth? I've got a wife and two kids. Aren't they worth as much as her? Aren't they? Who'll take care of them if I'm killed? Who? Who?"

Jake stood up. "Now listen, especially you, Pratt. We seem to have forgotten one thing. It may be the major's wife that we came here to save, but it's the covenant we are honoring. Have you forgotten that? Have you forgotten Keaton?"

"Fuck Keaton!" Pratt screamed. "Where is he? I haven't seen his ancient face around here. Let him lead us and maybe I'd feel better about everything. Maybe."

"Damn it, Pratt!" Jake growled, glaring at Pratt. "Keaton will be there. He's never let us down before. When we hit Los Estados, he'll be waiting. So let's stop this bullshit session and get some sleep. Tomorrow, I might be going into a hot LZ."

Doc grinned. *Yeah, you be right*, he thought. *Keaton be there tomorrow. He be there all the way. Cause he told me so while you motherfuckers were asleep!*

That night, David fell into a fitful sleep. In his head, he kept hearing his name being spoken. Several times he awoke, expecting to see Jake standing there, or Pratt. But only Perez's regular snoring met his sudden consciousness. Finally, he went under only to find himself outside. The cold air of the still darkness met him as he left the house. He looked down at his Rolex: 3:00 a.m. Pulling his parka's hood up around his head and tightening the drawstring under his neck, he headed for the shore of the Straight about a mile away. With each quick step, his breath seemed to hang in the cold air for a moment before evaporating. A half moon gave off a glow that illuminated the ground under his feet. On the horizon, the Southern Cross twinkled brilliantly in the dark blue sky. He passed the dormant Eagle. It looked mighty and massive, an old war machine called back to duty. *The people at Sikorsky would be proud if they could see her now*, he thought. He left The Eagle and walked on to the shoreline. The waters of the Straight were calm and silvery at this early hour of the morning. Every once in a while, he could see something rise up out of the dark waters and flip playfully in the air. What it was, he did not know. He looked up at the Cross. All of a sudden he felt alone and afraid.

"David."

Startled, he whirled around. Before him stood the tall figure of a man wearing a dark winter coat that was drawn up over his head. "Who are you?" he asked breathlessly.

"David." The man's voice was melodious and soft.

"Keaton?"

"Yes, yes. It is me, David. But who do you fear? I am your friend."

David took a step in Keaton's direction. "I'm sorry," David said, feeling a little embarrassed. "I just didn't expect to see you so soon. I knew you'd be here. I knew you'd be following our progress."

"Yes. I have been following well your progress. I have been with you at all times."

"Then you know about Chip and Force," David said with sadness in his voice.

"Yes."

David let out a sigh. "Keaton, I'm so glad you're here. I've needed to talk to you more than you can know."

"Then let your emotions come to me. Tell me what troubles you most."

David hung his head. The dispirited feelings he had been fighting back suddenly rushed forward. "God, Keaton, I've been trying so hard to do what is right and honorable. I've lost two of my best men, my best. I lied last night when I told the rest of them I was certain we would be successful, but there are now only two I can really depend on. I don't even know if I have enough men to carry out the rescue."

He turned to Keaton with pleading eyes. "Lead me. Tell me what I must do. Must she die? Must she?"

Keaton threw off his great coat. He seemed to take on a larger appearance, as if David's supplications had somehow strengthened him. "You are full of doubt?"

David fell to his knees. "Yes, I'm afraid so."

"Yes. That I can see. You have fear. You are losing faith."

"Yes."

"Then think of where we are, here in this cold, barren place at the end of the earth. Alone and without hope. You are right about your fears. You will be hunted. Your countrymen will not understand what you have done. They will question your judgment and your motives. They will call you evil. They will call you anti-American. They will wave the Constitution in the air and declare you a threat to its existence. Rich Senators and Congressmen will call for your imprisonment. You will threaten the news media's sense of justice, and they will vilify you. All of these things will happen, just as Chip predicted. So think, David. Organize your thoughts. Weigh your strengths against what lies ahead of you."

David grimaced and shook his head. "What are you telling me to do, Keaton?"

"I . . . I am not telling you anything! But think for a moment. You have lost two men. Look at your strengths. Such a small band of men to attack such a large prison. What are your chances of success?"

"But it was you who told me it could be done."

"Have you considered, David, that she might already be dead? Look how long she has been there. And you, of all people, should know the conditions of her confinement. How long could you last?"

"I know, Keaton, but we have to take the chance."

"Chance has already claimed the lives of two of your good men."

"Why are you telling me these things now? It was by your hand that I had the strength to go forward. It was you who planned everything. You brought these men together, even Perez. You're the one who called the covenant due. Now you come to me when I need you most and tell me that everything is hopeless. Are you telling me to abandon her now?"

Keaton drew back and brought his arm up, covering his face. "No. I cannot tell you to abandon what you have started!" he shrieked.

What is wrong here? David asked himself, startled at Keaton's behavior. *Something is terribly wrong here*, he thought. He stood up and carefully studied the man who stood before him. All at once it hit him. "Who are you?" he asked forcefully.

"Do you not know me David? I am Keaton. Have you lost your sanity? Why do you dare question me?" The figure began to pace frantically back and forth, all the while glaring at David with a bone-chilling stare.

The dream. The dream he had the night Sunny disappeared, David recalled. He drew up and squared off against the dark figure. "You are not Keaton," he forcefully declared.

Standing not more than three yards apart, the two figures faced each other in the still darkness.

"Tell me," David commanded. "Who are you?" Then he began to smell it – a horribly putrid smell of decay and rot that was so rancid it began to choke him. "I know you," he managed to say, holding his hand over his mouth.

"Yesss, you know me," the figure hissed and snarled.

David drew back and began to tremble as the figure changed shape in the darkness. He could not see clearly what was before him, but he could see that it snarled and growled and scratched furiously at the pebbled shore. "Yes, I know you now. And knowing you has given me the strength to fight you," he said. Then, defiantly, he turned his back on the creature and started to walk back to the house.

After David had taken just a few steps, he heard the creature begin to howl. "This world and everything in it is mine," it said, "Mine! I make governments. I am the leader of politicians. I am the power. You silly little man, you think you can fight me? Throughout history men with more power and strength than you have ever possessed have failed to win against me. So why do you think you can succeed where they have failed? Don't you know I am in every heart and in every home? I control the actions of men. So why do you even attempt to fight me, you little man?

"Just come back to me. Be mine again, and I will save this silly woman of yours. I will make you successful. I know you have false hopes that your country will see the so-called righteousness of what you do. But don't be foolish. Who do you think has controlled the destiny of your inept nation for so long? As I have done so many times, I have destroyed it from within. It was I who perverted your form of government. It was I who created the Party man, even the Party itself. It was I who made the Party politician. It was I who created the corporate scum who have polluted the once proud marketplace. It was I who created the wickedness that prevails in your public forum.

"No, David, you will not obtain sanctuary in America unless I deem it because I control America. So come back to me, and I will forge the thoughts of the many politicians whom I have placed over your pretentious nation so that they will welcome you back with open arms. I will make you and your woman heroes and rich beyond your wildest dreams.

"So, come back to me. Just turn around and smile upon me. I can read your heart. Just let me in as you once did. Oh, my lover, why do you now deny me? You were once mine. Why have you turned your face from me? Oh, love me again. Worship me, and the world will be yours. David . . . David, I love you like a son. Be my son."

David could hardly breathe. Sweat poured off his face and he trembled from fright. The call from the creature was so powerful, its promises so alluring and so sweet that some part of him wanted to turn back and go to the creature. Yet he summoned all of his willpower and managed to keep walking, even as the creature let out shrieking howls that chilled him to the bone. More than once he wanted to stop and turn back. Instead, he focused his sight on The Eagle as it sat proudly and defiantly on the tarmac.

"David, you will die. All of you will die. Death awaits you in Los Estados. I will be there. David, come back, my son. Don't leave me. Please don't leave me. Ahhrrraahh . . . Uhh . . . David . . . David . . . Ahhrraah!"

David pushed himself to the surface of the darkness and gasped for breath as he awoke. As he looked at the others sleeping in various contortions around the room, he knew that whatever was going to take place in a few days had nothing to do with him or Sunny. "Ok, Keaton, ok," he said quietly, shaking his head. It was time to get the others up. It was time to go.

Chapter 52

And God said to Joshua: "No man shall be able to stand before you all the days of your life; as I was with Moses, so I will be with you. I will not leave you nor forsake you."

"Only be strong and very courageous."

Joshua 1:5, 7

```
Nueva Island, Chile
126 nautical miles from Los Estados
350 nautical miles from the Falkland Islands
```

Nueva is a rocky pancake of an island lacking any trees or vegetation, save the patches of hearty brown tundra that managed to survive each Antarctic winter. Its rocky banks fall off sharply into the Atlantic Ocean, making it impossible for anyone to approach it from the sea. Five nautical miles from its northeast shore is the Beagle Canal Basin. The Beagle is actually a trench that provides a more southerly deep water passageway for ships wishing to escape the rough waters of the Horn. Ships navigating in the Basin area steered clear of Nueva because of its deep, unpredictable swells that sometimes sack ships into jagged rock formations hidden below the water along the edge of its shore.

Strong winds blowing from a storm off the Cape had swept away a three inch snowfall from an Antarctic storm that had pelted the island only a week before the team landed. The dry, hard landing area had been a blessing. The temperature had averaged ten degrees centigrade during the day and minus ten at night with an added minus wind chill factor.

At the start of the team's second day on Nueva, David stood outside The Eagle looking out past the frozen wasteland. *The storm must end*, he thought. *Time is running out.*

It had taken only a few minutes on Nueva for the team to understand the necessity for immersion heaters. Jake had worried the helicopter might not start if the engines remained cold for too long a time. Starting the engines each hour would have been the normal standard operating procedure to insure a warm engine, but this was impossible because of the fuel situation. Instead, Jake had placed two of the immersion heaters on either side of each engine's housing, filled them with fuel, poured water into them that had been drained from the restroom tank, and lit them. The result was warm engines. The other heater had been placed inside the cabin where it kept the inside of The Eagle warm and cozy.

Once they had landed David and the others had discarded their blue jeans and sweatshirts for their uniforms. For some of the men, it had been the first time they had ever worn camouflage fatigues. Weapons had been cleaned, loaded, and test fired into the frozen wasteland. And meals were prepared over the heater. Hot C-rations were a different animal.

David had instructed Jake to turn on his radio to 128.5 and leave it on so all could monitor any civilian traffic in the area. Jake had given David a questioning look, but had done as he was told. David was his leader, and Jake had spent enough time in the military to know that leaders are not expected to explain the rationality of their orders.

At day two, Pratt told David he needed some fresh air and left The Eagle. David, in turn, told him not to stray too far and told him that if he heard the big blades start to rotate, to make tracks for the helicopter in a hurry or he might be left behind. Pratt replied not to worry, for the last place he would want to be left was on this damn island.

Pratt was well-insulated against the cold. His parka with its fur-lined hood kept out the stinging wind. He wore long underwear underneath his fatigue pants. His boots were insulated with warm socks, and he wore mittens. He stood at the top of a small hill that overlooked the helicopter. On the other side of the hill was a steep cliff that fell down a hundred feet into the sea where rushing waves crashed loudly against the cliff's rocky side, sending huge geysers of foamy water high up into the air. The swift cold wind blew over the hilltop. He shivered and turned away from the helicopter. Carefully, he walked next to the cliff's edge and peered down, his mind numb. Would he soon be fighting for his life? There was definitely no turning back now. He would either have to once again fight like an animal, or die. He clenched his fists and gritted his teeth in anger.

In spite of everything he had made of himself, made of his life, he suddenly realized he was nothing more than an educated dog. He started to ponder how he might possibly get back home without going to jail, but he dismissed the thought. What was it they had taught him in Ranger School? *The only task that's important is the one at hand.* And now the task of survival was at hand. *Why doesn't he give us the order to go? Every day we wait here we risk freezing to death . . .*

Then Pratt stood still as he began to sense that he was not alone. He turned and was shocked to see a man standing not more than ten feet from him. His mind raced for a course of action, but all he could think about was to wonder why he had not brought his gun with him. The man wore a dark great coat with a hood pulled up over his head, dark wool pants, and black boots. He appeared to be studying Pratt as if he were pondering what to say to him. *Go on, you mother*, Pratt thought. *Do something!*

Then the man pulled back his hood, exposing his gray hair and grizzled face.

"You bastard!" Pratt exclaimed. "So you finally have the guts to show your damn face. Well, are you satisfied? Are you happy? Has the damn covenant been honored? Two men are dead, and probably a few more will be in a few hours. My life is in shambles, and maybe so are others'. Has it been worth it, Keaton?"

"Yes, it has been worth it Pratt."

Keaton's voice was dry and calm, even affable. "But why can't you see this even now when the last act of this drama is about to be played?"

"Act? Play?" Pratt asked, astonished. "Men's deaths a play?"

"I thought you were a philosopher. How a man dies can have philosophical meaning, can it not?" Keaton said, giving Pratt a wry, knowing smile.

Pratt was angry, but he calmed himself sufficiently to realize that he was allowing himself to become engaged in a useless argument with someone who was far less educated than he, a thing he had studiously avoided in recent years. "Listen, old man," he said, "you may be seen as a wizard of mystical proportions by those idiots down there, but I know you. I can see through all the patriotism crap. We're just pawns in some pointless, insignificant game that you and your friends in Washington have dreamed up. But give the devil his due. It's a beautiful, well planned game. I don't know what the objectives are. Maybe to embarrass the Gauchos. Maybe to show the flag to the Brits. Or is the major's wife an agent who knows too damn much to be left here, whether dead or alive? But I'll tell you one thing. I'm not going to get myself killed. I'll go in there, but you can bet I'll come out alive. And when I get back to the States, I'm going to spill my guts about what has happened down here. Now, how does that strike you, old man?"

"Why do you deny your feelings, my son?" Keaton asked in a mournful tone.

Keaton glared defiantly at Keaton. "Your *son?* Don't talk to me like that. I'm not the same person you knew in Vietnam."

"Why have you let your intellect blind you to the truth around you, my son?" Keaton held out his hand to Pratt. "I want there to be a bond between us."

"Get away from me, Keaton," Pratt said, taking a step back toward the cliff.

"Long ago, I made a covenant with your people. I have never broken that covenant, and I never will. So why cannot you understand me and see my purpose? You, of all men, should be able to understand what is happening all around us, you who have been blessed with the sight of the mind."

"The covenant," Pratt said hatefully. "Do you think I ever took that illusionary promise seriously? That bunch of pathetic jerks would have promised to give up women forever in exchange for getting out of that place. If I remember correctly, your ass was slightly scared too. So don't come to me now so sanctimonious about a promise made in the heat of fear. Remember Keaton, I know all about you."

"Pratt," Keaton countered, "I know you are afraid."

"You're damned right I'm afraid. Any sane man would be."

"Yes, I know you are afraid now. And I knew you were afraid then. When you betrayed the others."

With those words, Pratt felt as if someone had driven a stake through his heart. His body stiffened with a jerk. His mouth fell open and his face drew tight with shock. Wide eyed, not blinking even as the wind sheared across his face, he stared at Keaton, speechless and mortified.

Keaton reached out and put his hand on Pratt's cheek. "I know how, like every human, you react when you are afraid. You need not hide your actions from me by wrapping them in logic. I knew it was fear that made you tell our enemies everything. The others had the same fear. And I knew it was fear of someone finding out about your moment of weakness that caused you to betray us. But Pratt, I forgave you long ago. Were it not so, I would never have asked you to join the others, for the covenant that I honor with you was not made in Vietnam but on Mt. Sinai with your fathers."

"Who are you?" Pratt asked haltingly, now afraid.

Keaton let his hand fall from Pratt's cheek and took a step back. There was a thoughtful, concerned look on his face as he spoke. "Pratt, I have always respected the ability of man to learn and advance his knowledge. I have never stood in man's way, no matter how far into the darkness they traveled, for there are times that the earth must be dark so that men of light can be made. Now is such a time. A darkness is spreading over the earth. A darkness of evil spread by men of intellect. Men who feel they are right in their own knowledge. Men of learning. Men who have forsaken emotion and feeling. Men who cannot believe in what they cannot hold in the palm of their hand. Men like yourself."

Pratt began to shake, but not out of fear, not from the cold. Slowly, he fell to his knees. Looking up at Keaton he said, with tears in his eyes, "I am not evil."

Keaton smiled down at him. "No, you are not evil."

"Please, who are you?" Pratt asked again.

But Keaton just looked up and turned to the sea, and the winds suddenly died.

"Mankind has always found it very difficult to believe in what it cannot prove. The reason for this is that everything in the universe is logical, even emotion, even the mystical. So man, being an intelligent creature, must fight hard to accept that which cannot be proven. But even that struggle has a purpose for mankind, for it is out of the paradox of logic versus emotion that faith is born. And faith is what makes a man human. Everything happens for a purpose. And everything touches and concerns everything else. The darkness will bring forth light. And that is what everything that has happened so far is about, Pratt. You, David, the others, my servant Sonia, will hopefully be a light others will follow out of the darkness that is spreading over the land."

"Keaton . . ." Pratt said, weeping.

"Now I must go, for it is almost time."

Suddenly, from the other side of the hill Pratt heard the powerful engines of The Eagle start to whine.

He gave Keaton a hopeful look. "Will I see you again?"

Keaton outstretched his arms to Pratt and spoke in a powerful, resonant voice. "That will be up to you, Pratt. For faith begins with the choices one makes."

Chapter 53

For those who honor me, I will honor, and those who despise me shall be lightly esteemed.

I Samuel 2:30

```
May 31, 1982
The United States Ship John F. Kennedy (CV 67)
175 nautical miles southeast of Los Estados
Island

Los Estados Prison
```

For the past forty-eight hours, a winter storm had swept across the path of the aircraft carrier *John F. Kennedy* with gale force winds and resulting fifty foot waves, but by mid-morning had suddenly evaporated once the ship crossed in front of Cape Horn. In its place was an eerie calm. The waters of the South Atlantic were now as placid as a hidden lake and the sky was a clear, crisp Prussian blue. The *Kennedy* was now streaming under nuclear power around the southern coast of Argentina. The Argentines had been pounding British beachhead positions on East Falkland Island for the past two days and fighter bomber activity north of the ship's heading had been heavy. The *Kennedy* was well away from the two hundred mile radius around the Falklands that the British had declared a war zone and, being in international waters, the *Kennedy* feared no interference from Argentina. In ten days she would complete her South American tour, dock at Key West, then head for the Indian Ocean to show the flag to Libya.

As recently promoted Commander Andrew Jackson, naval officer and Commander of Fighting Squadron 32, sat anxiously in the electronic cockpit of his F-18A Hornet, there was a flurry of activity on the four and one-half acre flight deck as crews prepared his and two other Hornets for take off. Without air cover, the *Kennedy* was vulnerable to air attacks. Squadron 32's mission was to perform a routine air cover patrol three hundred miles out from the *Kennedy's* position.

Although the air temperature was fifteen degrees centigrade, Andrew had slid back the jet's canopy and was dangling his right arm outside and puffing on a Black Jack. Occasionally, he lovingly patted the high-stressed skin of the Hornet as if to communicate affection. He flipped up the sun visor of his flight helmet with its orange "T" painted on either side, and returned the thumbs-up signal one of the deck armorers had given him to signify that the installation of his two Sidewinder and two Sparrow air-to-air missiles and the loading of his twin M62 20mm cannons with five hundred forty rounds had been completed. Taking in a deep puff, Andrew blew the smoke out slowly in order to receive every bit of satisfaction from the Black Jack's taste and looked up. *What a marvelous looking day*, he thought. *A damn good day for it.* He looked out past the flight deck across the azure sea. *She's out there, just over the edge of the horizon. Is she still alive? She's been down there a long time. Was David on station?*

Andrew knew that what he was about to attempt to do was next to impossible, but today was the only day the *Kennedy* would be in the waters around Los Estados; tomorrow he would be too far away to help. If David had been delayed, Argentine jets would most certainly shoot him and his helicopter to pieces once the chopper entered the airspace over Los Estados. *Shit*, he thought, letting out a deep breath. It was self-defeating to think of that now. Today he had his part to play, and he was prepared to go the whole nine yards. And his was the easy part – lift off and fly toward Los Estados – just close enough to make the Argentine Air Force chase him away. Instrument and radio failure would be his excuse. No one else knew about David and Sunny. He might get an oral reprimand from the captain, but that would be it. After all, jets stray off course all the time.

And maybe, just maybe by the grace of God, Sunny was still alive. If she was, David would damn sure get her out. And he? Well, he would have paid David back for his lack of friendship when David had needed him the most. And as for Sunny? *Sunny.* He let the thought of her linger in his mind as he put his lomaxed gloved hand inside his pocket and took out a picture. It was a photo of her standing next to the railing of a boardwalk, an ocean breeze blowing through her hair. Her arms were folded safely across her breasts and she was smiling a sad smile, a smile of acceptance. *Well, Sunny, I'm going to help David. And maybe you'll be proud of me.* He secured the picture on the instrument panel.

The *Kennedy* had a crew of over five thousand, and at launch time it seemed that most of them were on the flight deck. Scores of men clambered over the steel surface of the ship performing the varied tasks required to launch aircraft. An aircraft carrier's mission is to send up and bring back jets, so launches took precedence over everything. Each man on deck had a specific mission which, when allied with other men's missions, made it possible to launch jets in one smooth, concerted effort. In addition to the scores of men running to and fro over the deck, there were dozens of multi-million dollar aircraft lined up in a seemingly disorganized manner along the edges of the flight deck. F-14A Tomcat fighters lined the starboard side of the ship. On the opposite side where Andrew sat, was his newly formed squadron of F-18A Hornets. Sprinkled in between were several A-6 Intruder aircraft -- EA-6Bs, with their electronic jamming and countermeasure gear on board; and the 6E, that had been converted into an airborne refueling platform. Parked just past the ship's bridge toward the stern were the *Kennedy's* E-2C Hawkeye early warning radar planes with their saucer like radar domes; the newer jet-powered S-3A Viking anti-submarine aircraft; and the carrier's SH-3D rescue helicopters.

It was an incredibly crowded flight deck that, to the casual onlooker, might have seemed like a mass of confusion. In reality, everything that happened on deck was tightly controlled by the Air Boss who was located in a tower just above the ship's bridge on its starboard side. No one took off or landed without his approval. The other officer who had command status, and in some instances when a danger to aircraft was present had authority to override the orders of the Boss, was the deck officer who controlled the actions of the catapult crew and gave permission for planes to land. The actions of the crews who armed, fueled, and hooked the planes up to catapults were as well orchestrated as a ballet, but far more dangerous. An aircraft carrier was one of the most dangerous places in the world, which was why Andrew loved being there.

The Boss radioed Andrew and his wingmen, telling them to engine up. He watched for a clear sign from the deck officer who was identified by his distinctive red stocking cap. He got the sign, in the form of an upward pumping motion of the deck officer's arm, indicating that his rear exhaust area was clear of personnel. Reluctantly, he stubbed the Black Jack out in the palm of his gloved hand and put the butt in his pocket. It was time to go to work.

He turned on the fuel pump, flipped up the generator switches to his right engine, put the fuel to it, and hit the igniter switch. The Hornet's panel instruments told him that everything on the aircraft was performing correctly. Inside his flight helmet, he could hear the sound of the engine humming. He turned on the left engine. The deck officer got a "go" signal from the deck crew whose responsibility it was to supervise starts. Andrew's jet was purring righteously. When the deck officer radioed for him to line up the Hornet for a hook on the catapult launcher, he gently steered the jet onto the clearly marked hook up bay with deft movements of the rudder pedals. While holding his jet to a halt with the foot brakes, he went over the rest of the Hornet's checklist. When he had finished, he put the checklist back into the Hornet's log book and put the log book back in its rack.

With steam rising from the deck's exhaust portals, the area around the catapult resembled some prehistoric tar pit. In the final quiet moments before violent action, Andrew made a radio check with his wingmen and the Air Boss who, after the deck officer indicated his jet was ready, would give him the warning that he was about to be fired off the deck a distance of two hundred feet in two seconds, reaching a flight speed of one hundred sixty miles per hour. Then he waited.

On the opposite side of the deck, one of his wingmen was waiting for a launch on the catapult. Andrew gave him a critical look. The young aviator gave him a salute and Andrew nodded. As soon as he cleared the carrier, Andrew's second wingmen would be hooked up and fired off in his direction.

After the deck officer gave Andrew the engines run-up signal, he pushed the accelerator handle forward to full power and the jet strained against the grasp of the catapult's hooks. He readied his fingers on the afterburner switch. As soon as the deck officer dropped his arm, he would flip the switch, let go of the brakes, and wait for the jet to clear the deck. The wing flaps were already set to a full deflection for maximum lift capacity. He pushed the joystick forward, lowering the horizontal stabilizer in the rear of the jet which would keep the tail of the plane near the catapult. Once he cleared the deck, he would have to reverse this by leveling the stick then pulling back on it hard in order to gain altitude. He would have to do all of this in one and a half seconds.

Andrew looked to the deck officer and saluted him, indicating he was ready. The radio warning came through his helmet. The deck officer held up his arm. Andrew waited. The arm dropped and swoosh! Instantly, he flipped on his afterburners, causing him to be flattened against his ejection seat, reversed his stick altitude, giving him maneuver control over the Hornet, switched on the landing gear retractor lever, and banked the Hornet into a steep climbing turn to the west. All less than two seconds. The Hornet was the most advanced fighter in the world. Andrew felt its power and its confidence in the palms of his hands, in the soles of his feat, and in the seat of his pants. As the jet sped through the crisp air, he began to assume the jet's power. He was the Hornet. The Hornet was Andrew.

Behind him his first wingman, just slung away from the *Kennedy*, flew toward him at full throttle. Out of the corner of his right eye, he caught a glimpse of the wingman catching up to him then banked the Hornet again, turning 180 degrees so that he could fly over the Kennedy. That would allow his second wingman, who was just now taking off, time to catch up.

He turned off the afterburners and withdrew the flaps. After he had overflown the *Kennedy*, he made a gentle bank out to sea. His second wingman lined up on his left wing. Now, with protection on either side, he began to climb to twenty thousand feet heading into the midmorning sun. He reached twenty thousand feet in fifty-seven seconds and leveled off, reducing his cruising speed to three hundred fifty knots. Looking left and right, he saw that his wingmen had their attention properly focused on his aircraft.

It was Dozier on his right and Pence on his left, both ensigns, both looking for adventure. *Well, today,* Andrew thought deviously, *might be their day.*

Andrew switched one of his navigation FM radios to 128.5. Fifty miles out from the *Kennedy*, he banked the plane to a heading that would take him on a collision course with the Argentinean Air Force. Los Estados was only fifteen minutes away.

He hit the send button the 128.5 radio. "Freedom One, over," he radioed.

Only a crackling silence.

"Freedom One, Old Hickory One, over."

Silence.

"Freedom One, Old . . ."

"Old Hickory, this is Freedom One!"

"I'll be damned!" Andrew shouted in the confines of his Plexiglas bubble. He hit the button again. "You made it."

"Yes. What's your position?" David's voice could not conceal his excitement, even from over a hundred miles away.

"I'm on schedule. Should arrive over the target area in about fifteen minutes. You ready to lift off?"

"Roger. We'll start turning the blades now."

"Keep on this frequency. I want us to be able to keep up with each other's situation."

"Roger."

Pratt came tearing down the slope of the hill as David stood in the door of The Eagle watching him anxiously as the helicopter's huge blades began to pick up speed. The hot immersion heaters had been discarded and lay simmering on the tundra. As he watched Pratt's return, he had the feeling of being on a distant planet. One day, other visitors would land here and find the immersion heaters. Junk left on the moon.

Pratt ran up the ramp and fell breathlessly into a seat as David slammed shut the door and sealed it. Pratt said nothing as he reached over and grabbed his M-16; he just crammed a clip into it and chambered a round.

"That was close," David said, walking past Pratt and giving Jake the thumbs-up for takeoff.

Again, Pratt did not reply.

Perez noticed he had a distant look on Pratt's face, as if his mind was focused on some image far away. He reached over and touched him on the arm. "Are you all right?"

Slowly Pratt turned and faced Perez. "Uh huh. I know what I'm doing now," he said with a half smile.

Jake pulled pitch, hovered and, after gaining transactional lift, lowered the helicopter's nose and flew out over the shore of Nueva. Once he had cleared the island, he headed off at full throttle for Los Estados, skimming over the ocean at a height of only fifty feet.

"Who was that on the radio?" he asked, turning toward David.

"A friend," David replied flatly without looking at him.

"Is that what we were waiting for?"

"Yes, now fly."

David jerked off the head set and left the cockpit. In the cabin he and the others checked their weapons and other equipment and went over the plan of action once more.

"Martin?" David asked, pointing to his own throat with a questioning look. But Perez did not answer. Instead, he turned his face away. Prior to their taking off from the island, he had made up his mind that if he were caught he would stand a better chance of surviving with the Argentineans if they viewed him as a priest rather than a mercenary. Then they fell silent, each man contemplating what he was about to do.

Andrew had known that at any minute he would be receiving a call from the *Kennedy* questioning his heading. He only hoped his wingmen would have sense enough to back off. Now came the time for games.

"Old Hickory, Blue Center, over," came the expected call.

But he did not answer. Instead, he feigned not hearing. A radio malfunction in a new aircraft. The call came once again. Then he noticed the wingman on his right move forward as if to attract his attention.

When Andrew gave him a reprimanding look, the wingman touched his hand to his helmet. When Andrew gave him a fake questioning look, the wingman touched his helmet once more. Andrew just shook his head as the *Kennedy* radioed him again.

"Blue Center, the Bulldozer, ah, my leader seems to be having radio trouble. Say again last transmission," the wingman radioed.

"Roger, Bulldozer. Understand Old Hickory unable to read this station. Message follows: You are on an improper heading. I repeat, an improper heading. Come to a heading of 95 degrees immediately. I repeat, come to a heading of 95 degrees immediately."

"Roger, Center. I'll try to intercept the leader."

Intercept, Andrew thought laughingly, *intercept my ass*.

The wingman shot in front of Andrew and rolled over to another heading. He watched as the jet fell quietly away from him. Seeing this, the wingman on his right started a slow barrel roll around him. Andrew knew it was time to up the anti. He would be over Argentine airspace in eight minutes. If he was an Argentinean radar controller in Los Estados, he'd be telling the duty officer they were under attack by now. *If I can hold on to this charade for another few minutes, they'll be up and we can let 'em chase us for a while,* he thought as he hit the afterburner switch and shot out ahead of the rolling wingmen.

The operations center of the *Kennedy* was a super quiet room filled with radar and radios and a large Plexiglas situation board from which every aircraft within a five hundred mile radius of the carrier was plotted. As soon as the air controller tracking Andrew's flight realized that a real world problem existed with one of the planes, he notified the bridge.

The duty officer took the message and notified the captain, who was sitting relaxed in his command chair overlooking the entire length of his ship. "Have them radio Jackson again," he ordered calmly.

The order was repeated to the controller, who tried again, but this time the wingman informed him of Andrew's burn.

"What?" questioned the captain.

"He's fast approaching Argentinean airspace, sir," the exec said, a look of exasperation on his face.

"Oh, my God."

Sergeant Pablo Gonzalez had been tracking the movement of the three unidentified aircraft for the past ten minutes. As they neared the airfield, he became more nervous and decided to awaken the night duty officer who had just gone to bed. The sleepy captain now stood beside him, his eyes fixed on the three blips fast approaching their position not believing what he was seeing.

"Do we know their nationality?"

"No, Señor. All I know is they're not ours."

The captain held in his hand a telex he had received only two days ago warning that the *USS Kennedy* would be sailing past the southern coastline. "They could be American."

"Not English?"

"It's a bit far north for their Harriers. Unless – where did you pick them up?"

"About one hundred ten miles southwest."

"British Harriers could have refueled in the air farther out, dropped down low, and then come up from the surface to mass for an attack."

The radar operator gave the duty officer a startled look.

As he saw one of the jets begin to speed up, the duty officer said, "Mother of God! We're under attack. Alert the Grupo to scramble at once!"

The pilots of Grupo 3, Fuerza Aerea Argentina, were lounging comfortably in the Grupo's day room, a room heated by a large rock fireplace. On top of the fireplace's mantle were several coffee cups that had been turned facing the wall. Each cup had once belonged to a pilot who had lost his life over the Malvinas. Adorning the walls of the hardwood floored room were pictures depicting their heroes: the British Royal Air Force in various combat scenes from the Battle of Britain. Two black Labradors lay subserviently near the closed bar. The pilots wore their loose fitting, single piece flight uniforms so that they would be ready to fly on a moment's notice. Each pilot also wore a scarf tied carelessly around his neck; no scarf was the same. They were mostly young men, even their leaders. Thoughtfully, they sipped strong, rich coffee as they read the morning's news dispatches. Most had already had breakfast.

The red alert phone that sat conspicuously near the bar began to ring. Its shrill sound startled the pilots and they turned in its direction as an officer with swept back, jet black hair and a full, dark mustache quietly picked up the receiver.

This man was Colonel Alberto Colombo, the group's commander. His face became ashen as he received the order from the base commander. He put the receiver down and turned to the pilots. "Gentlemen, we are about to be attacked by unidentified aircraft. Everyone is to man his aircraft at once and form a defensive box over the airfield."

The pilots dropped everything and ran to the aircraft that were parked on the flight line. Ahead of them, the ground crews had already warmed the engines of their Dassault Mirage III jet fighters. Each jet was fully armed with 30mm cannons and three Matra air-to-air missiles. The Grupo normally had thirty-six aircraft but, because of losses over San Carlos and Goose Green, they were down to only fifteen.

Colonel Colombo strapped himself into his ejection seat and, after slipping on his flight helmet, cleared the aircraft and started down the taxiway. If he was going to die today, he wanted it to be in the air, not sitting on the damn runway.

Behind him, jet after jet followed.

Andrew watched his radar screen with intense interest. If the Argentines were true to the form they had displayed during the last two weeks, they would be on him any minute now. His plan was that as soon as he saw them approach, he would bank away over the Atlantic and hope they gave chase. If they broke off the chase before David needed them to, he would have to make another pass at the island, but he would cross that bridge when and if he had to.

He looked left and right. No wingmen. Ahead, he saw the island. *Sunny, I'm here*, he thought. And sure enough, there they were, little specks of aircraft rising off the runway and heading at afterburner speed in his direction.

Seeing what was coming at him, he came to a shocking realization. Intelligence had said the Argentines were flying the slower Super Entendard. Instead, fast approaching him were Mirage IIIs that were capable to speeds over Mach 2. Even though the Hornet could fly at Mac 3, this was going to be a little closer for comfort than he had anticipated. They must be going crazy back on the ship, he thought.

Andrew radioed David. "Freedom One, Old Hickory. Over."

Jake hit the button. "Who are you?"

Andrew didn't reply for a moment. This guy doesn't know who I am, he thought. "Put Major Elliot on now," he ordered.

Jake banged his helmet with his fist. "Major," he turned toward the cabin and shouted. David hurriedly slid into the copilot's seat.

"Go ahead," he radioed.

"I'm right on top of the island. The Argentines have scrambled everything they have. What's your position?"

"We're three minutes out. I can see the coastline up ahead," David radioed back after looking over the instrument panel.

Jake grabbed his arm. "What's happening? Who was that, Major?"

"Does it really matter now?" he said, giving Jake an apologetic look.

Jake didn't reply. He just bit his lip and turned his attention to the task at hand, which was the rapidly approaching island.

Andrew banked hard to his left and dove down toward the island. *Yes, there you are.* He could see the whirling blades of The Eagle. From his vantage point it looked like a slow flying insect. He pulled back on the joystick to execute a straight up climbing maneuver in order to draw the Argentines away from David. As he kicked in the afterburners, the Hornet lurched forward, straight up toward the dark blue space covering the earth.

Colonel Colombo had reached a battle altitude of twenty thousand feet. As he searched the sky for the intruders, he looked up to see what appeared to be a rocket shooting for the heavens. "Jesus!" he said through his radio. He had taken off so fast that he had left both his wingmen behind. Nevertheless, he switched on the jet's afterburner and headed for the aircraft above him.

When Andrew reached forty-five thousand feet, he inverted the Hornet. As he soared across the sky upside down at one thousand miles per hour, he surveyed the action below. With his eagle's eyes, he could see the Argentines forming into three groups of about four planes each. In a proper tactical posture, they spread out and were forming a defensive box around the air base. When he saw Colombo's shooting star, he yelled, "Shit!" and, with a flick of the wrist, flipped over and shot down toward the earth.

Colombo's Mirage just missed Andrew's Hornet as they passed each other at terrifying speeds. Colombo gasped as the blue and white flash filled his windshield then, with a roar, fall behind him. He instantly rolled over and started down after Andrew with a shot of afterburner for good luck.

Andrew twisted and turned as he pushed the throttle full forward. He knew the Argentine pilot was dead on him. *This guy is good*, he thought. But then, they were all good. Pretty soon, British pilots would be hanging pictures of the Argentinean Air Force and Navy on the walls of their lounges.

Colonel Colombo radioed what he knew no one at either the Los Estados airbase or in Buenos Aires would believe. "Grupo 3, the aircraft I am chasing is an American Hornet type naval plane. She is evading me at this time. Am in pursuit."

Major Phillipe Baigorri, commander of Squadron 2 of Grupo 3, heard Colonel Colombo's radio call, but couldn't believe what he was hearing. "Americanos?"

He radioed his three wingmen what they were leaving the zone and heading to Colombo's aid. Afterburners blazing, the four jets shot off toward their commander's last known position.'

Andrew was getting nervous. He had not intended to engage the Argentines, just cause them to remain airborne and divert their attention. Of course, the Argentine pilot chasing him wasn't aware of his true intent. This guy was going to shoot him down if he had the chance.

Then he heard Pence's voice come over the radio. "Hang in there, Commander, we're about to slice through this gaggle that's attacking you."

The nose of The Eagle crossed over the shore of Los Estados just as Colonel Colombo closed with Andrew. David was not aware of what was happening in the sky above him. His attention and the attention of the others was focused on the three buildings coming up fast to their front. His heart was pounding. He had tired to imagine how he would feel once he arrived here, but nothing is ever as it seems it will be when you actually get there.

"Okay, Jake, it's all yours. I'm going back and lead the others in.

Father Perez will be just outside the door. As soon as I have her and I give you the thumbs-up sign, we get the hell out of here and head for Punta Arenas," David said as he left the cockpit.

He grabbed his weapon and handed three explosive charges to Pratt and three to Doc, keeping three for himself.

Turning to Perez, he said, "Martin, you must cover the chopper. You must. Don't let anyone get near it." David had a demanding look on his face.

Perez nodded his head. "I'll . . . try."

Then David turned to Doc and Pratt. "We'll hit the second building first. Shoot anyone who gets in the way and blow the doors. We find her, we free her, then we get back to the chopper. Understand?"

Doc and Pratt nodded. Pratt had a wild eyed, desperate look on his face, while Doc serenely puffed on a cigar as if he was going on a turkey shoot.

Jake moved The Eagle over the tundra at a height of only a few feet and headed straight for the center of the buildings. He thought he saw a pack of wolves scatter as The Eagle flew over them. The ground around the buildings was barren and flat. There was no snow. It had evidently been blown away by the dry winds from the Horn. And there was no sign of life anywhere. It was an eerie sight. He flared The Eagle to a landing.

A red light on his panel told him that David had already opened the door.

Captain Alvarez had just finished admonishing one of the guards at Internment Two. These matters were always delicate because of the high strung temperament of his specially selected men, but the guard had been raping female prisoners, and such things had to be stopped for efficiency's sake.

And there was another reason. The war in the Malvinas was not going well. While the Air Force and the Navy had done a heroic job of sinking British ships, the Army had failed miserably and was giving up everywhere. The *junta* were bracing themselves for the worst. Because of these developments, the Group had been ordered to cut back on arrests. Internment Two had only seven live prisoners, and one of them was dying, and Internment One was empty. Consequently, the morale of his men was down. So scolding had to be done ever so tactfully.

To show his oneness with his men, after the dressing down Alvarez had stayed with them at Internment Two to take coffee. That afternoon, a helicopter would fly in from the mainland and take him back to Buenos Aires. He was gingerly sipping coffee when he was startled by The Eagle's enormous noise as it flared to a landing just outside the building, but he thought nothing of it, assuming it must be his helicopter come early. The war had put schedules in disarray all over the country. For instance, he had been told informally that Grupo 3 over at the air base would be stood down because it had suffered severe casualties, yet only moments earlier he had heard them take off and they were still over the island conducting maneuvers. Evidently, they were going to be sent in against the British once more. But such were the fortunes of war.

He smiled at his men. "Make some more coffee for the pilots of the helicopter," he ordered. One of the guards smiled and bowed.

Andrew knew that the Matra air-to-air missile was not as accurate as his Sparrows and Sidewinders. Still, he was going to get a very hot surprise if he didn't shake loose the aircraft that was on his tail. His other concern was his two wingmen who were about to take on the other Mirages that were heading in his direction. The time for the ruse was over. He flipped his radio selection switch. "Penceman and Bulldozer, this is Old Hickory. What is your position?"

"Old Hickory, Blue Center has been trying to reach you. We are way out of our AO," answered ensign Pence in an excited voice.

No shit, Andrew thought.

"Bogeys are trailing you at your six o'clock position," Pence continued.

Right behind me!

"We are catching up with them in their six o'clock, but their ground radar should let them know about us any second now. Expect them to break off and engage us."

"Negative. I repeat, negative. You are to break off engagement and head back to Blue Center," Andrew ordered, knowing that the *Kennedy* would be monitoring his transmissions.

Then the *Kennedy* radioed Andrew. "Old Hickory, Blue Center."

"Old Hickory."

"What's your situation?"

"I've had radio and navigation problems. I seem to have wandered into Argentine air space and caused them to react. Evidently they thought we were going to attack them. Right now I have a bogey on my tail, but I think I can shake him."

Then another voice came over the air. It was a deep voice that held unmistakable concern. "Old Hickory, this is Blue One." It was the captain of the *Kennedy*. "Break off and return to home at once. Acknowledge."

"Acknowledged," Andrew replied. Now all he needed was the cooperation of the Argentines. At least David was on the ground.

"Old Hickory." It was Blue Center again. "AWACs indicate approximately one-five bogeys in and around your location. Present heading of bogeys seems to be in your direction." Andrew knew the *Kennedy* was receiving radar images from the now airborne Hawkeyes. They were watching the whole show on their scopes.

"Breaking off," he heard Pence radio.

Good boys, he thought.

Colonel Colombo had now closed to within one mile of the twisting and looping Hornet. He switched on his arming system. Now, he thought, and fired a missile. The bright red flames and exhaust of the missile flew past his cockpit and sped off after the American jet.

Beep, beep, beep, went an indicator in Andrew's cockpit. A damn missile! He pulled back in the seat and his pressure suit started to expand. The Gs were so heavy he felt himself blacking out. *No, not now*, he thought. As he started to lose consciousness, he thought he heard Pence radio Dozier that he had seen a missile fired at him, but he couldn't be sure. He let the Hornet travel upward for about three seconds, then pulled back again and nosed the Hornet over in a dive for the sea. Out of the corner of his eye, he saw the missile shoot past him. He let out a sigh of relief and began to regain his senses.

Colombo flipped the Mirage over and fell to the earth in a Split-S to catch the American. What puzzled Colombo about this American was that he was not attacking back. He seemed to be only evading him. *But why?*

Ground radar had warned Major Baigorri of the approach of the other two American aircraft. Slyly, he had decided to wait until they were on top of them until he gave orders to split up and attack. Then ground control had told him the Americans had broken off contract and were heading away from Los Estados. Ground control was now warning him the Americans had turned around and were coming after them at full afterburner. Enough was enough. Baigorri gave his flight the high sign and screamed into his helmet's microphone the battle cry of the Argentinean Air Force, which had been respectfully borrowed from the RAF, "Talley ho!"

Like a bomb burst, the Mirages split apart and headed toward the oncoming Americans at supersonic speed. In the war room of the *Kennedy*, the radar operators, systems analysts, and the ship's senior officers watched the drama unfolding over Los Estados with horrified expressions.

As David, Pratt, and Doc leaped from The Eagle, the air overhead seemed to explode with the sounds of a dozen or more jet fighters breaking the sound barrier. It caused them all to duck.

"What tha fuck?" Doc hollered.

Then David realized what was going on. "Let's go!" he yelled.

Perez jumped from the ramp and crouched down next to The Eagle's empennage, his M-16 chambered and on semiautomatic. As he watched David and the others charge Internment Two, he felt a strange calm overtake him. It was almost a feeling of euphoria. He swallowed hard and focused his attention on the other buildings.

David and Pratt charged up to Internment Two and slammed themselves against opposite sides of the door. David tried the handle. Locked. Quickly, he took a shaped charge out of his parka's pocket and stuck it against the door handle. He gave Pratt an "okay" sign then pulled the string. They both rolled away from the door and crouched against the wall. The door exploded with an orange flash and a bang. David was stunned for a moment and shook his head. Pratt let out a laugh, and they charged in.

A guard who had been sitting at the desk just inside the door lay moaning on the floor. Pieces of the door had peppered his chest and face. David spied the key rack, but there were so many keys and they had only a few minutes to find her. He reached down and drew the injured guard up to him, bringing the guard's face close to his. "The American. What cell? *Comprenende?*"

The guard painfully shook his head, no.

"*Americano?*" David yelled again.

"Look out!" Pratt yelled as two guards came running out of the library. Seeing David, the guards started to fire their pistols, but Pratt cut them down with two automatic bursts.

David pulled out his Webley and stuck its barrel in the guard's mouth. "*Americano,*" he said, his mouth twisted in anger.

The guard's eyes opened wide. "*Numero trienta.*"

David pulled the barrel away and the guard pointed to the key on the rack. David put his hand on the key he thought the guard had pointed to and the guard nodded his head, yes, then fell back.

"Let's go," David said, taking the key from the rack. But suddenly he stopped and turned to Pratt. "Where's Doc?" he asked.

Pratt gave him a puzzled look. "He was with us at the door, wasn't he?"

"I don't remember," David responded.

"It doesn't matter, Major. We don't have time to look for him," Pratt replied.

David knew Pratt was right. He snapped his fingers and they headed for the stairs.

After the explosion, Captain Alvarez had sought shelter under the table in the library. He could hear the machine gun fire outside its door. He thought about calling to the guards, but knew from the silence that they had been killed. His body shivered with fear. He could not believe what was happening. An attack. An attack by the British. But why? Then a thought came to him. No, that could not be. Such a thing was a tactical impossibility. What was it she had said? *He is coming.* Could they be Americans? It just wasn't possible.

Slowly he drew his Beretta. He was wet from his own sweat and his mouth was so dry from fright he could not swallow. He looked at his hand and saw it was trembling. He tried to stop it, but couldn't. Then he felt a sudden sick feeling in the pit of his stomach, and his bowels felt like mush. *So this was the feeling he had caused in so many others*, he realized. And then he thought, *I don't want to die.* His mind raced for a way out. *No, I don't want to die.* He crawled along the floor and began to whimper like a baby.

Ensign Pence fired a burst from his Hornet's cannon into the mass of Argentine fighters as they cris-crossed his path and went into a high barrel roll in order to end up behind one of the Mirages that had flown over him. The Mirage was in a high G turn. He rotated the Hornet and, sure enough, just like they had taught him at Mirimar, he found himself coming out of the roll with the Mirage squarely in his gunsight. He fired a Sidewinder. The little rocket separated from his wing tip and shot out after the Mirage. As Pence watched, he was awestruck by the sight of the missile tracking the Mirage and then hitting it. The Mirage exploded in a silent blur of orange flame. He pulled the oxygen mask away from his face and searched the sky for a parachute, but there was none. For reasons he could not explain, he felt a sadness because of the Argentine pilot's death. Only now did he understand what his instructors had told him; air-to-air combat is a deadly form of hard work. He put on his mask and headed down on the deck where his radar told him two other Mirages had teamed up.

"Great shot," Dozier radioed, as he streaked across the sky trailing a Mirage. His Hornet's TV camera picked up and automatically focused on a Mirage. It was like watching television on an eight hundred mile an hour roller coaster. The Mirage pilot must have sensed he was being followed, or one of his fellow pilots had radioed him, because he started a series of split Ss, high G escape turns, and hammer heads, all in a desperate attempt to shake Dozier off his tail. But Dozier clung to him like glue, twisting and turning, throttling up, and kicking in bursts of his afterburners. The Mirage pilot simply could not get away from the Hornet. But Dozier was inexperienced. Dog fights were never individual duels. A pilot always had to take into consideration that he could be the hound and the fox simultaneously.

Major Baigorri couldn't believe what he was seeing. The American was tunnel-visioned, fixated on another aircraft. Swiftly he lined up his Mirage for a missile firing. As he carefully maneuvered his Mirage, the American jet became larger and larger in his gunsight. "Now, gringo," Baigorri said as he fired his missile, then veered away to escape the blast. Looking over his shoulder, he caught sight of Dozier's Hornet exploding into a thousand white hot pieces of metal.

On board the *Kennedy*, the captain sat stone faced, watching helplessly as Dozier was blown out of the sky.

"It's thirteen to two," his air officer said pointedly.

The captain looked up at the air officer with a look of finality on his face. His men were being killed. "Launch one of the squadrons and have them proceed supersonic to Jackson's aide. These are my orders and my orders alone."

The air officer saluted and left the war room at a brisk pace. He would be the first pilot off deck. The stunned officers and men in the war room fell silent as the captain slumped back into his elevated chair.

As Perez crouched next to the idling Eagle, he saw four guards come running out of one of the buildings and head for David's location. The guards hadn't noticed him yet. In a moment of decision, he lifted his rifle, took aim, and shot all of them down with several automatic bursts.

He stood for a moment, shocked at what he had just done, then threw down his rifle and ran to where David was, leaving The Eagle unguarded. As he ran toward Internment Two, he was knocked down from the shockwaves of three explosions that came from another of the buildings. Picking himself up, he saw that the other building was in flames. He thought he saw Doc running from the burning building, but he was so dazed he couldn't be sure.

David and Pratt exchanged confused looks as they heard the explosions from the adjacent building. "Doc," Pratt said, shaking his head.

David nodded that he understood, then picked up his weapon and climbed the stairs. Cautiously, he inched his way down the hall until he found the cell where the guard had said Sunny was being held. Quickly, he stuck the key in the door lock and turned it. Pratt stood breathless at his side. But after he had unlocked the door, he stopped.

"Major, what the hell are you waiting for?" Pratt yelled.

"I'm afraid to see what she looks like. I don't know what I'll do if she's . . . if she's dead."

"Just open the damn door!" Pratt screamed.

He took a deep breath and pushed open the door and slowly stepped inside. Pratt stood guard at the door's entrance. When he saw her, he could barely move. She lay huddled against the wall. Her head was cradled in her arms, and she had not moved when he entered. Overhead, the loud roar of jets was deafening, but she seemed not to take notice of them.

Slowly, he knelt down beside her and smoothed back the matted hair from her face. He touched her neck. "She's alive, Pratt," he shouted with joy.

Pratt grinned and clenched his fist.

He dropped his rifle and lifted Sunny in his arms. She was so light, nothing but skin and bones. A rage erupted in him and he wanted to kill whoever it was that had done this to her. "Oh . . . God!" he screamed with his teeth clenched, looking up.

Then he felt Sunny's thin fingers touch his lips and he looked down. She was staring at him in wonderment. Her eyes were sunken and dark, her lips thin and blue, but in that look, he understood. She was alive and she was his. Then she managed to do something she had not been able to do in a long time. She smiled.

"Let's go," he said. Then he kissed her.

He followed Pratt out of the door.

As they passed a cell, he heard a feeble voice calling to him and stopped. He recognized the voice.

"Pratt, stop."

Pratt halted and turned.

"We need to blow this cell. Someone I know is in there."

"What?"

"Just blow it, will you?"

Pratt placed a shaped charge on the door of the cell and, after setting it, pulled back against the wall. David yelled for the cell's occupants to get back, then shielded Sunny from the blast. After the explosion and when the dust had settled, he motioned for Pratt to go in and stood in the doorway as Pratt entered.

There, lying on a mattress in the center of the room, was Rita. She was holding Jorge's head in her lap. She had a blank look on her face. Dully, she looked up at Pratt, then David. After a moment, she seemed to recognize David and began to sob. "He's going to die," she managed to say.

"No, he's not," Pratt said, lifting them both up and under his arms. "Now Major, can we get the hell out of here?" he asked David sarcastically.

"After you, warrior," David replied.

Supporting Jorge and Rita, Pratt struggled down the stairs ahead of David and Sunny. To his surprise, he saw Perez standing in the doorway. As he passed, he gave Perez a questioning look. *Why aren't you guarding the chopper?* But Perez was walking around and around like a wild man, shaking his head and mumbling something to himself. Pratt just shook his head and continued on toward the helicopter.

Sunny began to convulse, so David stopped before he got to the stairs, laid her down, and turned her over on her stomach. She coughed and spit, but her stomach had nothing in it. He picked her up again and continued toward the stairs. But as he neared the stairs, Alvarez darted out in front of them. He had been hiding in the empty cell next to the stairwell. The blast from the shaped charge had frightened him to the point that he had soiled himself. He seemed startled to see David. He had obviously thought Pratt was the last man.

David started to go for Alvarez but realized he had left his weapon in Sunny's cell and, with Sunny in his arms, he couldn't get to his Webley. Hearing a noise from the first floor, he looked down and was startled to see Perez in the building. Even more startling was the fact that Perez was carrying no weapon. *Where was Perez's weapon?* Alvarez stared wild eyed at David then looked down at Perez. A quick smile of surprise came across his tear streaked face when he realized that neither of the men was armed.

Sunny's cheek was next to David's. She opened her eyes and looked at him. She could tell by the look on his face that something was frighteningly wrong. Then she turned and saw Alvarez pointing his Beretta at them. David heard her gasp and saw the look of terror on her face. Seeing the fear this man evoked in her, David knew instantly this man had been her tormenter, and a look of pure hate came across his face. He snarled and Alvarez's smile quickly vanished as he realized the man who stood before him was this woman's husband. *He is coming.*

David screamed, lowered his head, and charged into Alvarez.

Startled, he pulled the trigger of his Beretta, but the bullet went high. David's head hit him just under the chin with such force that he was lifted up and over the railing that protected the hallway. Perez watched in horror as Alvarez tumbled over the railing and, screaming with his arms swinging wildly in the air, fell to the floor.

David came running down the stairs, but Perez did not seem to notice him. Instead, he was staring down at Alvarez who was slowly writhing in a pool of blood. Even when David came up to him with Sunny in his arms, he scarcely glanced at her. He only looked relieved and gave her a quick touch of his hand.

Then he bent down over Alvarez. Alvarez had noticed Perez's turned around collar and had reached up to him with a bloody hand and spoke in a faint, choking voice. "Father."

"Martin," David said anxiously, "let's get out of here for God's sake."

But Perez dropped down on his knees and looked up at David. "You go. You have what you came for, so go quickly."

"Don't be stupid. We're not leaving here without you," David said.

Then he looked down upon Perez's face and saw in it a look of contentment and wonder. And, yes, happiness, unmistakable happiness. The same happiness he had felt that stormy night in Georgia when Keaton had given him a new life and let him walk in the light of men once more. He reached down and grasped Perez's hand. Then smiling, he let it fall and hurried with Sunny held tightly in his arms toward the door.

Father Martin Perez then bent down over evil and offered himself as a bridge to God's grace.

Sergeant Gonzalez stared in horror at his radar screen. One hundred miles out and closing fast were almost a dozen radar blips. The Americans were attacking in force. He radioed this information to Colonel Colombo and Major Baigorri.

"How many?" Baigorri asked in disbelief.

Gonzalez repeated his transmission, adding that the estimated time of arrival of the Americans was five minutes. Baigorri did not reply. Inside the cockpit of his Mirage, surrounded by the cold quiet, he took out a gold crucifix and clutched it tightly in the palm of his hand. This day, he knew, he would meet God.

After Pratt had secured Jorge and Rita in their seats, he gave Jake a slap on the helmet and exited the helicopter. Now, crouching next the chopper and with the ground around him blowing wildly as the big blades roared overhead, he realized David and Perez would need cover. But where were they? He considered going back to the building, but before he could decide he saw David running in his direction with Sunny in his arms. But no priest.

Then from one of the burning buildings came automatic weapons fire. The dirt around David began to kick up and churn as the sniper started to pace him. Pratt leveled his M-16 and sprayed a thirty round clip into the top floor of the building when he saw the smoke from the sniper's gun barrel and the firing stopped. David had almost made it to the helicopter when there was another report of gunfire, this time from the last building. And it was heavy. Pratt slammed another clip into his weapon and fired into the building, but the firing continued. Bullets kicked up dirt all around the helicopter and he heard the dull metallic thud of rounds striking the helicopter's skin. If the Argentines hit the fuel tanks, he and everyone else were goners.

"Hurry!" Pratt screamed, firing off another covering blast.

As David neared the machine, Pratt yelled, "Where's the priest?"

"He won't be coming with us. Help me."

David stumbled up to Pratt. With Pratt's help, he climbed the ramp, covering Sunny's body with his own as murderous machine gun fire from Internment Three racked the retractable stairs and then trickled along the length of The Eagle, reaching the cockpit.

"Where's Doc?" Pratt screamed.

David searched the cabin and looked out across the flat windswept ground. "Don't know, but we've got to go!"

Jake felt a searing pain inside his left shoulder blade and cried out in pain. He could feel a white hot piece of metal burning inside him. He turned and looked. There was a neat hole in the window where the bullet had entered. His left sleeve was turning red as blood ebbed from his wound. He turned when he felt David's hand pop him on the helmet, his face twisted in agony. "Is she safe?" he gasped.

"Yes. Now let's get the hell out of here."

Then he noticed that Jake had been wounded. "What?"

"I'm all right," Jake said, seeing the look of concern on David's face. "Go back to the others. I just hope whatever is taking place above us is of no concern."

"We have a guardian angel," David said, patting Jake's helmet. He then headed back to the cabin.

"Any sign of Doc?" he asked Pratt. Pratt shook his head no.

Despite the pain in his shoulder, Jake pulled the switch and deftly lifted The Eagle off the ground. Fire was pouring at them from the ground as he lowered the nose of the helicopter and gained transactional lift. He could feel the helicopter take hit after hit as he flew off past the burning command building. But they had made it. They were heading for freedom. When he noticed that the Door Closed light was still burning, he stretched around and saw that the door was still open and the stairs extended. Evidently the door had been too shot up to close. It wouldn't affect the flight characteristics of the aircraft; it would just be a very cold ride for everyone but, from the happy looks on their faces, he didn't think they would mind. He turned back to the task at hand. Punta Arenas was still a ways off.

Andrew heard Pence send a radio transmission to the *Kennedy's* approaching aircraft telling them of his position. Like a good wingman, Pence had been desperately trying to come to Andrew's aid, but each time he got close, he was jumped by a Mirage and ended up in a desperate dog fight. But this day, Ensign Pence had already shot down five Argentine aircraft, which made him the first American Ace since the Vietnam War.

And in a few short minutes, a squadron of F-18s from his ship would be on station and engaging the Argentines. A shooting war was about to be fought between Argentina and America, and Andrew had started it. He felt a twinge of guilt. But then, as he banked the Hornet and headed down to the ocean, the feeling of guilt left him and in its place came pride. Sunny was an American. He was an American. Pence was an American. The American government had known one of its citizens was in peril and had chosen to do nothing about it. That kind of action could be expected from bureaucrats who needed to protect their careers and from rich politicians who betrayed their country on a daily basis and called it politics. But he and Pence were American warriors, patriots of the highest order. An American had been down there, alone, afraid, and deserted. It had been his duty to come to her rescue, and not because he loved her. That's what separated Americans from everyone else in the world.

"Old Hickory, Freedom One." The radio call he had been waiting for. He switched the radio selector switch.

"Go ahead, Freedom One."

"She's alive and free and we're off to Chile now. Good luck to you, whoever you are."

It wasn't David's voice and, from the sound of the pilot's voice, he was in pain. Whatever had happened down there on Los Estados had not been pleasant. "Godspeed," Andrew said, then switched off the radio.

Andrew knew that he was pitted against a great pilot, and the only way he was going to be able to shake him was by enlisting the aid of the Hornet. The Hornet's top speed was Mac 3, or about two thousand four hundred miles per hour. The Mirage was capable of speeds of about one thousand eight hundred miles per hour, but only above the height of thirty-one thousand feet. So he decided to fly close to the surface of the ocean and hit the afterburners. He would simply fly away from his pursuer.

Colonel Colombo followed Andrew down to the surface of the ocean, then noticed that the American was on a direct heading for Los Estados. Colombo radioed his position and the American's heading to the Los Estados base. The base controller immediately ordered two of the Mirages not engaged with Pence to break off and provide protection to the airfield.

As Andrew slowly applied power to full throttle, the Hornet began to increase its airspeed dramatically. The ocean under him started to blur. He watched his instruments, and when he had reached a speed of one thousand four hundred miles per hour, he kicked in the afterburners. The Hornet lunged forward and shot across the ocean.

Colonel Colombo watched helplessly as the American jet sped forward at a terrific speed and disappeared from his view. He had never seen a plane fly so fast so quickly. He radioed ahead to his two Mirage pilots who were circling the base on a protective sweep.

At two thousand one hundred miles per hour, the world as Andrew had known it simply no longer existed. At this speed, sound was far behind him. A vortex of twisted light emanated from his aircraft causing a blur to envelope the plane. He could not see clearly outside. All he could do was hold on and not move a muscle. But it had worked. His pursuer was now well behind him.

Then he saw Los Estados coming up to his front, and realized what he had done. David had just lifted off and now here he was, and with him would follow Argentine jets. It must have appeared to ground controllers on Los Estados that he was attacking the airfield. He turned off the afterburner and reduced throttle and the world outside started to slow down. But at the speed he had been flying, he was already over the island. Below he could see the fires from burning buildings, and about a mile away, he saw the slow moving helicopter. Then he saw something else. Two Mirages had noticed the helicopter and had peeled off in its direction. He had inadvertently led them right to David. He shot off after the two Mirages.

Colonel Colombo heard the report about an attack on the state prison and the radio transmissions from his two pilots that they were pursuing a helicopter that had just taken off from there. The pilots were requesting instructions from the tower concerning the helicopter and the tower and the ground controllers were vacillating. "Shoot down the helicopter," he ordered. His pilots radioed back their acknowledgment.

Andrew knew that unless he engaged the two Mirages before they got too near the helicopter, his own heat seeking missiles might accidentally shoot it down. He locked himself on to the Mirages and armed both his two Sparrow and his two Sidewinder missiles. At three miles, he fired them all; there was no room for error. The four missiles zoomed out in front of the Hornet in the direction of the two French-made jet fighters that were fast closing in on The Eagle.

Colonel Colombo watched from five miles away as the American fired all his missiles at the pilots who were following the helicopter. He tried to warn his men. "Missiles! Take evasive action. Missiles!" he yelled. But Colombo's transmissions were lost in the frantic calls of the other pilots of Grupo 3 who were now becoming engaged in mortal combat with the aviators of the *Kennedy* on the high plain of honor over Los Estados Island. One of Andrew's missiles missed and crashed into the sea, but the other three hit home. The Mirages exploded in balls of fire; their pilots never knew what hit them.

Colombo hit his afterburner and shot down after Andrew. Closing in at two miles, he fired a missile. Andrew pulled up and performed an aileron roll over the burning Mirages, a salute. Inverted, he saw Colonel Colombo's missile speeding at him. He immediately executed an inverted dive and started for the earth. The missile with its stubby wings couldn't make the turn and sped harmlessly out to sea.

Colombo bit his lip and dove after Andrew. Andrew pulled up just before hitting the ground and shot straight upward. Hitting his afterburners, Colombo followed, and when he had aligned himself directly behind the American, he fired his last missile and then flipped over and rolled back upright. The American would have to work hard to escape the last missile. While he was preoccupied with staying alive, Colombo would go after the helicopter and shoot it down.

Andrew heard the beep, beep, beep of his missile warning indicator. He instantly realized his aircraft was in the worst possible flight altitude it could be in to outmaneuver a missile. *Think, think*, he told himself. *Yes*. He turned off his engines. After losing all of its power, the jet was merely sailing through the air like a very heavy glider. The Hornet began to slowly fall, then tumble. Having lost its heat source, the Matra missile flew past his cockpit toward the sun. Now, all he had to do was get the engines started again while he was in a tumbling position.

Colombo turned the Mirage from one side to the other, hoping to get a glimpse of the American aircraft exploding, but he could see nothing. Leveling, he searched the ground below for the helicopter. The island looked deserted. No helicopter. Then he caught a glimpse of a whirling white insect over the ocean past the island and headed in the helicopter's direction.

Andrew breathed a sign of relief as the big Pratt and Whitneys kicked in. *Well now, boy*, he thought, *it's just you and me in a duel with guns*. He picked up the Mirage on his radar scope, kicked in the afterburners, and shot out after the Argentine.

Colonel Colombo had positioned his Mirage about a mile from

the helicopter and was closing in for the kill. He switched his arming system from missiles to guns. It had been a long time since he had fired his cannon. He adjusted his red lens gunsight. Then he saw red and white balls of fire passing across his nose and realized the American was attacking him from off his right wing. He executed a split-S, diving to the deck as fast as he could.

But Andrew had anticipated the Mirage's move and went into a high loop that would roll him right out of the Mirage's tail. He went up and over the earth, falling away and then filling his windshield. And at the bottom of the roll, there was the Mirage. He read his ammunition gauge. He had three hundred cannon rounds left, enough for four or five bursts. Once the Mirage was positioned square in his HUD, he fired. The red flamed rounds seemed to envelope the Mirage, but nothing. He fired again. The Mirage rolled over and peeled way. He fired again, but he was empty. He drew back on the stick. He was out of missiles and he was out of cannon rounds. He looked off to his right. The helicopter was still on course, speeding away to the mainland of Chile.

Instinct told Colonel Colombo that the American was out of ammunition, but just in case, he did not attack the Hornet. Instead, he found the helicopter and made a dash for it. If the American was still armed, he would try to intercept him. If not, then this deadly business would be over shortly. He aimed the Mirage for a course for the helicopter. Once again, he had the helicopter in his sights. He fingered the cannon firing button on his joystick. But suddenly, right off his right wing was the American jet. Colombo was shocked. The American was flying in formation with him, the American's wing only a foot from his.

Andrew flipped up his sun visor and pulled off his oxygen mask. Then he reached inside his flight suit pocket and took out the Black Jack stub. Turning to the Argentine Mirage, he put the cigar in his mouth, lit it with his Zippo, and gave the pilot a scowling look.

He mocks me, Colonel Colombo thought angrily as he watched the American glaring at him. But he suddenly realized that, no, the American wasn't mocking him; he was daring him. The American was daring him to try to shoot down the helicopter. He swallowed hard.

As he puffed on his Black Jack, Andrew carefully watched the

Argentine pilot's head. Colombo turned his gaze from the American and back to his gunsight. When he saw the Argentine pilot turn back to take aim at The Eagle, he used the last weapon he had at his disposal. He flipped his Hornet into a left bank.

The occupants of The Eagle had not been not parties to the violent battle that had taken place high above them. Their view of the cold world of Los Estados had been limited to the fierce gun battle on the ground, the roaring of The Eagle's engines, and the rushing of the cold air past the open door. And while they could hear the constant cracks of sonic booms made by the Mirages and the Hornets as they full throttled at tremendous speed toward and away from each other, their heroism had been too high and too far away from the limited sight of David and the others to comprehend and admire.

David shielded Sunny from the cold blasting air that buffeted in and out of The Eagle. Next to him, Jorge lay limp in Rita's arms, still alive yet uncomprehending. Pratt knelt down holding onto a seat arm as The Eagle, passing through crosswinds from the sea, was shaken left to right, up and down.

For the first time since the attack, David let himself relax. He took a deep breath as he gazed down at Sunny's dirty face. He had done it. They had done it. Now came the next step.

"That was sure some show, maje," came a voice rising above the noise of the wind.

Startled to hear Doc's voice, David and Pratt turned to see him standing at the rear of the cabin, the door to the storage area open behind him. Doc's voice was sinister, but even more sinister was the automatic pistol that he had aimed at them.

"Are you aiming that gun at us?" David asked, feigning incredulity.

"You're very smart, boy," Doc said hatefully. "That her? She don't look like much."

David didn't answer.

"You put that gun down and move over across the aisle," Doc told Pratt.

Pratt laid his gun down carefully and stood next to the row of seats across from David. Doc moved up and stood in front of the door.

He looked out the door and then down at David. "It be a long way down."

David gave Pratt a look of desperation as Doc lifted his Beretta. Doc turned to Pratt as if to warn him not to move. Then Sunny raised up and, seeing Doc aiming the gun at Pratt, screamed. At the sound, Doc swung around toward David and pulled the trigger. But the bullet zipped past David and flew out the window next to his head. As soon as Doc fired at David, Pratt lunged for him and caught him at the waist. Together they fell out the open door and into the sea below.

And in the cockpit a man of God's own heart kept The Eagle on a true course toward the mark.

About the Author

Phillip Davidson is an attorney who lives in Nashville, Tennessee. He is a former infantry Captain who commanded a group of Cambodian and Vietnamese Kit Carson Scouts on a night ambush team in the Mekong Delta. He is currently at work on a second novel.